Her new husban… as if she were a fas…g, maddening mix of temptress and puritan.

"We're dancing around some things," Warren said. "And we need to settle it. I just want to have an honest conversation with you."

"Me, too," she said. "I didn't know what to say after leading you on, so it seemed easier to stay away from you."

His brows lifted but he schooled his expression quickly. "You didn't lead me on. I went too far and you have every right to call a halt to something that was making you uncomfortable."

That was so much the opposite of what she'd expected him to say that she blinked.

"But I asked you to kiss me." And oh God, had she wanted him to.

"I don't care if you asked me to strip you naked and put my tongue between your legs. You're allowed to say stop at any time. I will always honor that, Tilda."

She could barely tell him to stop at all.

* * *

Contract Bride

CONTRACT BRIDE

BY

KAT CANTRELL

First Published in Great Britain 2018
By Mills & Boon, an imprint of HarperCollins*Publishers*
1 London Bridge Street, London, SE1 9GF

ISBN: 978-0-263-93587-5

51-0118

MIX
Paper from responsible sources
FSC™ C007454

This book is produced from independently certified FSC™ paper to ensure responsible forest management.

For more information visit: www.harpercollins.co.uk/green

Printed and bound in Spain
by CPI, Barcelona

USA TODAY bestselling author **Kat Cantrell** read her first Mills & Boon novel in third grade and has been scribbling in notebooks since she learned to spell. She's a Harlequin So You Think You Can Write winner and a Romance Writers of America Golden Heart® Award finalist. Kat, her husband and their two boys live in north Texas.

One

Women must have some kind of manual they passed around to each other, opened to the section labeled "How to Dump a Man."

If so, it would explain why for a record fourth time in a row, Warren Garinger had received the same text message: You're the world's worst workaholic. I hope you and your company will be very happy together.

He didn't think the women meant it as a compliment. Nor did they understand what it took to run a billion-dollar conglomerate. The Garinger family bottled and sold nearly half the world's pick-me-ups. You couldn't escape the logo for Flying Squirrel, the number one energy drink, no matter where you looked.

Women did not appreciate the effort that had gone into that kind of success.

Tilda popped her head into his office. "Got a minute?"

Except that one. He nodded instantly.

Tilda Barrett was the one woman he always had time for. Partly because he liked her Australian accent more than he should. "Sure. Come on in."

But mostly Warren liked Tilda because, as his marketing consultant, she'd exceeded his expectations. And that was saying something. His expectations were always sky-high, for himself and for everyone in his orbit. Flying Squirrel wasn't performing as well in the Australian market as he'd like, and Tilda was changing that. Slowly but surely.

"I saw the numbers on the new campaign. They're promising," he said, as Tilda strode into his bright corner office overlooking downtown Raleigh. Of course, he rarely glanced out the window unless he needed to gauge the weather in advance of a sporting event Flying Squirrel had sponsored.

Today was no exception. Tilda commanded his attention easily, both because of her professional role and because of the one she played in his head. Yeah, he'd had a fantasy or two starring Tilda Barrett, and he refused to be ashamed that he'd noticed she was very feminine beneath her buttoned-up exterior.

Not one strand of swept-up hair dared escape her severe hairstyle and, not for the first time, he wondered what would happen if it did. Most likely, her sheer will would tame it back into submission. She was the most hard-core professional woman he'd ever met. They got on famously.

"The numbers could be better," she countered. Nothing ever satisfied her save absolute domination, and the fact that she was on his team made him downright gleeful.

Tilda took the straight-backed chair to the right of his desk, as was her custom when they had briefings. The company's main competitor, Down Under Thunder, owned the Australian market, and Tilda's strategic expertise filled a gap in Warren's roster that he'd been thus far unable to bridge any other way.

"But that's not why I'm here," she said—and hesitated.

Tilda never hesitated.

Something was up. The dynamic between them had shifted. Normally they worked so well together that he scarcely had to speak before she'd already read his thoughts, and vice versa. But he couldn't get a bead on her blank face.

Warren leaned forward to steeple his hands on the desk that had nothing more on it than his laptop and cell phone. Paperwork was for other people to handle, a hallmark of the CEO philosophy that had allowed him to focus on ideas and game plans instead of minutiae. Thomas had taken to the role of chief operating officer like a duck to water, and Warren had never questioned letting his younger brother assume the reins of daily control while Warren got to have all the fun in the corner office.

"Please speak freely," Warren said, a little concerned he'd had to clarify that when Tilda had spent hours in his company during this project. Normally, he preferred people respect the distance and reserve he deliberately injected into all of his professional relationships. But he hadn't insisted on being so formal with her. There'd been no reason to. Tilda had always struck him as the female version of himself—dedicated, professional and, above all, never overtly familiar.

In this moment, however, things felt different, and he didn't like it.

"Right-o. The thing is, I'm not sure how free I am to speak about this issue," she began cautiously, her accent rolling through him accompanied by inappropriate heat, especially given the gravity of her expression. "At this point, all I can say is that I'm being pulled from this project."

"What?" Warren shot half out of his seat before catching himself. He sat back in his chair with deliberate care. "You cannot be pulled from this project. The contract I have with your firm is for a full year and we've barely covered a quarter of that."

She nodded once. "The contract doesn't specify that I will be the consultant for the full year, and unfortunately, there's an issue with my visa that they've chosen not to address. I'm being chucked back to Australia and they'll provide you with an American replacement."

Outrageous. Warren clamped down against the flow of obscene words on the tip of his tongue. He'd hired the best consulting firm on the planet precisely so that "issues" with visas did not impede his progress. "That's a breach of contract. I need an Australian expert who has been immersed in the culture for the whole of her life, not an American who's read some things on the internet."

"I'm afraid I can't speak to the specifics," she intoned, as if the entire project wasn't now in complete jeopardy. "My superiors seem to believe replacing me is well within their contractual rights. I do apologize for the short notice."

Warren ran a hand through his hair as he contemplated contingencies that didn't exist. This project needed Tilda. Period. "How short?"

"I'm to wrap up with you today and be on a plane by Friday."

"Friday? As in the day after tomorrow?"

This was a disaster. And only in being presented with a looming deadline could Warren admit that *he* needed Tilda, as well. He couldn't work with another consultant who didn't get his style the way she did. He could be gruff, short and to the point, and she took it all with grace.

Plus, he liked listening to her talk. Sometimes, when they worked through dinner, she relaxed enough to laugh and he could indulge in a very harmless fantasy about what her chestnut hair might look like when it was down around her shoulders. He'd undone enough hairstyles in his day to know that hers likely hit her midback and would be shiny and smooth under his fingers.

Warren was as adept with a well-shaped fantasy as he was with running Flying Squirrel.

Harmless fantasies fueled a man who was still at the office during the hours other men might indulge in all things female. Harmless fantasies worked for him on so many levels because he'd never act on them. Tilda's expertise on this project was too important to add her to the list of women who would eventually gift him with an unoriginal text message.

Tilda folded her hands together in that no-nonsense way he'd always secretly appreciated. Her slender fingers locked in place with strength of purpose. No stray movements, as if she never accidentally got into an uncomfortable position worth correcting. Lack of mistakes was as much a part of her personality as her incredible efficiency.

"Yes, this Friday," she said. "I have about four hours to get my things in order. My replacement should be here in the morning to pick up where I left off."

"That's not happening." As if Tilda could be replaced. It was ridiculous to assume even for a moment that this was a done deal. "Who do I need to speak with at your firm about this? If nothing else, I'll sponsor your visa."

Surely that was doable. Tilda gave him the name and number of her superior and strode from the room to update the project plan in the event his call didn't go as planned.

It didn't. The contact at the consulting firm cited a mix-up in renewing Tilda's visa and then informed Warren that Tilda had to leave the country before her immigration papers expired on Saturday, or she wouldn't be permitted to return once the renewal had been sorted out. He cited several clauses in immigration law that the firm couldn't in good conscience violate, which was entirely too much legal jargon for one o'clock in the afternoon.

Warren ended the call and immediately consulted an immigration lawyer. What was the point of having a lot of money if you couldn't spend it where you needed to most? Two hours later, he was out of time and out of options. Save one. A green-card marriage.

The lawyer cautioned Warren about the dangers of fake marriages for residency but allowed that the immigration department was overrun with work, so likely wouldn't be examining things too closely.

Warren was just desperate enough to pitch the option to Tilda. Odds were good she'd say no so fast his head would spin. But he had to try.

She had an all-business persona that lent itself to an in-name-only relationship. She'd definitely welcome the continued distance and reserve he would insist upon. He didn't do deep dives beneath the surface. Not anymore. He worked like a fiend for a reason—his relationship skills left a lot to be desired. The more he worked, the easier it was to forget he'd been responsible for his college roommate's death.

Marriage was the last thing he should be contemplating. Not given the pact he'd made after Marcus died; Warren had sworn to never fall in love. Jonas and Hendrix, who'd also been friends with Marcus, had vowed, too, but they'd broken the pact by falling for their wives. Warren refused to dishonor Marcus's memory that way.

But surely, with a woman as professional as Tilda, if she said yes, he'd have no problem keeping their relationship one hundred percent business. A green-card marriage was the only solution he could pull together before it was too late.

He had to try this last-ditch alternative. Down Under Thunder had a large piece of Warren's pie and he wanted to crush the competition. Tilda was his magic bullet. He would convince her to stay, no matter what it took.

When Warren called Tilda back into his office later that day, she had to do a serious gut check to see if she'd gotten the wild swing of emotions under control. Thank God she hadn't *actually* burst into tears in Warren's office earlier.

That would have been highly unprofessional. Tilda relied on the aloof front she'd erected to prevent anyone from getting too close. Displaying the slightest vulnerability felt squicky.

Of course, it wasn't any more professional to have a minibreakdown in her own office, either. Telling herself that hadn't stopped the panic that had welled up right after her boss, Craig, had called to drop the news. Not only was her visa expiring, the firm had decided against getting it renewed. Too difficult a climate right now, too expensive, he'd said. Sorry about the mix-up, but she could have a job in Australia, no problem.

Except there was a problem…named Bryan McDermott, her ex-boyfriend who was evil personified, a man with police force clearance, friends in all the right places and zero conscience. He didn't technically have the powers of God, but he sure put on a good enough show to make her believe he did. That's why she'd left Melbourne. Why she could never go back.

This time, he might make good on his threat to kill her with his bare hands if he caught her with another man, never mind that they'd been broken up for over a year.

Okay, not doing so hot on getting her emotions under control. Warren was waiting on her to reappear in his office. There was no way he'd sorted out the procedure for renewing her visa in a couple of hours, though if anyone could do the impossible, it was Warren Garinger. He took no prisoners, left no stone unturned and put whip-wielding oxen drivers to shame in the motivation department. In other words, he was every inch the chief executive officer the plaque on his door claimed him to be.

She might have a little crush on him. Who could blame her? He was gorgeous, never hit on her and could buy and sell a man like Bryan before lunch. She was pretty sure Warren could clock her ex and easily be the one to walk away from the fight with nary a scratch.

What was wrong with her, that the ability of a man to cause bodily harm to another man turned her on?

Deep breath.

She stuck her head into his office. “You rang?”

Warren waved her in, clicking his laptop shut the moment she crossed the threshold. That was one quality that set him apart. He never multitasked, except in his head. His brain worked in fascinating ways she could scarcely comprehend, describing the big picture as easily as he did the details many people overlooked.

She was going to miss him more than she’d let herself admit.

“Sit, please,” Warren said. “We have much to discuss.”

As was his custom, Warren stayed behind his desk, keeping them separated by glass and wood. He never breached that space between them, never let his gaze stray to her nondescript suit, which displayed none of her assets by design.

That was another of his qualities she admired. Other men never seemed to understand that familiarity wasn’t easy for her. That she didn’t want a man anywhere close to her, not after Bryan. He’d been so successful at sucking away her confidence that the first time he’d smacked her across the face, he’d somehow spun it as being her fault.

The worst part wasn’t having abuse in her past. The

worst part was when she woke up at 2:00 a.m. in a cold sweat because a small part of her might believe it *was* her fault Bryan had hit her. And she couldn't exorcise that small part, no matter what she did.

She squared the tablet computer in her hands. "I've taken copious notes for my successor—"

"Not necessary." Warren waved that off. "You're not going anywhere."

The wildest bloom of hope sprouted in her chest before she could stomp it flat. "You got Craig to agree to fix their screwup?"

Warren could sell hay to a farmer. Getting Tilda's boss to admit he'd made a mistake had probably been child's play.

But Warren waved that off, too. "No, of course not. You were right. Your boss is an ass who can't be trusted with a box of animal crackers, let alone my campaign to expand in Australia. So I fired him and threatened to sic my lawyers on him if he so much as breathed the phrase *cancellation clause*."

"Oh." She'd have paid good money to be a fly on the wall during that conversation. "So, I'm at a loss on what to say next. Dare I hope you found a way to get my visa renewed in two days?"

If by some miracle he had, she wouldn't have to go back to Melbourne. She could stay here and work, burying herself in this job that had come to mean so much to her—

"Not exactly."

Of course not. Warren wasn't here to make all of her dreams come true, especially not the ones where she imagined him riding to her rescue like a modern-day knight in a shining Tom Ford suit.

Deflated, she fought to keep her face blank. Wouldn't do to communicate an iota of her emotional state. That was how men got the ammunition they needed to hurt you. "Please elaborate."

Warren leaned into his steepled hands, a move he made often, which she'd come to recognize as his game stance. It meant he was ready to get serious.

"I spoke to an immigration lawyer. He assures me the best option here is to immediately file for an extension and renewal. But, as you may be aware, that can take months and you would have to travel to the nearest consulate to get the renewal, which would be either Canada or Mexico, depending on your preference, but that means—"

"I would be out of status when I went." The reality of the legal ramifications swamped her and her shoulders slumped. Ruthlessly, she straightened them. "They wouldn't let me back in the country if the extension wasn't in place yet."

"You see the problem, then." Warren nodded once. "The project would be on hold again and you'd be stuck in whichever country you traveled to. It might as well be Australia, at that point. The key is that you can't be out of status when you go to the consulate."

She felt like Warren was leading her somewhere, but she couldn't for the life of her figure out where.

"Then I would have to go before Saturday, and the renewal paperwork isn't even filed yet." Thanks to her employer's snafu, she would be in a lot of trouble if she stayed long enough to let her paperwork expire. "That would be a wasted trip."

As he'd said, she might as well go back to Australia. Maybe she could sweet-talk the firm into assigning her a job in Queensland instead of Victoria. Brisbane might be far enough away to escape Bryan's insidious reach. Of course, if he had friends on the police force there, her precautions wouldn't matter. He'd set up surveillance on her phone and house, like he had last time, and she'd have no recourse because he was too slippery to get caught.

She shuddered. The problem was that she didn't *want* to go back to Australia. She felt safe here. Valued. As if her contributions mattered for the first time since she'd escaped a relationship where she constantly was made to feel *less than*. This job had saved her and giving it up was unfathomable.

But what other choice did she have? Warren wasn't presenting any alternatives that justified his hope-inducing opening comment that she wasn't going anywhere.

"Yes. Completely wasted. *If* you were out of status." His gaze locked onto hers. "The lawyer suggested the easiest way to ensure you're not out of status at that indeterminate point is if you already had a green card."

"Green cards are even harder to get than visa renewals," she blurted out. The rules were inconsistently applied, pending which way the immigration office interpreted them. And Warren was talking about a green card, the Holy Grail for someone in her circumstances. "I would never be able to file for a green card so quickly."

Warren held up a finger. "There's one way. If you marry a US citizen. It would be easy enough for us to go to the courthouse Friday morning and get this taken care of. The marriage would be in name only, of course. Our professional relationship would continue as is."

The sound in her ears increased to a dull roar as she processed his meaning. He was offering to *marry* her in the most unromantic proposal she could have imagined. They'd be lawfully wed with no hope of any sort of physical relationship. Warren would be her husband, yet never even try to touch her.

Something was definitely wrong with her, because it sounded so perfect she feared the tears pricking the backs of her eyelids might actually fall.

But she'd fallen prey to the illusion of perfection in the past. The only way to ensure there were no repeats was to spell out every possible contingency she could think of.

"We'd be married in name only. That means no intimacy," she said briskly. "None. Forgive me if I find it hard to believe a man of your stature would accept such a thing."

At that, Warren actually smiled, a tilting of his lips that lanced her through the stomach as sharply as if he'd actually touched her.

"That sounds vaguely like it should be a compliment. Don't worry about me. I can handle a few months of no intimacy."

The way he caressed the term with his American accent did not settle the swirl still heating her core after being treated to his smile. One minute into their business discussion about resolving the issue with her visa her body had already betrayed her. She cleared her throat. "And when my visa is renewed, we will dissolve the marriage."

He nodded. "An annulment. My lawyers will take

care of everything. I've already laid out the pertinent points to them in an email. I just need your agreement before I hit Send."

This was moving far too fast. She could feel the threads of control slipping from her fingers. If she married Warren, he could easily change his mind about the no-intimacy clause. They'd be legally married and she hadn't a clue what kind of recourse she might have if he decided they would consummate the marriage whether she liked it or not.

If he knew she wore racy lingerie beneath her staid suits, would he change his mind?

She shook off those thoughts. Warren wasn't offering this solution so he could take advantage of her. They'd worked together late into the night many times, long after the last of his employees had gone home. He'd never been anything but the soul of propriety, which was why she loved this job. He listened to her, valued her opinion. Otherwise, he wouldn't have gone to these lengths to keep her on the project.

That alone went a long way. Her knees might be weak at the thought of putting herself at his mercy. But she was also continuing in a positive environment that was good for her battered psyche.

There wasn't really a choice. She could never accept her employer's mistake and take the offered job in Melbourne. She'd have to agree to become Warren's bride by contract.

The thought unleashed a shiver she couldn't control. They'd be living together. Wouldn't they? How could they convince the authorities they were married unless she moved into his house? But that would make it so much harder to keep her normally vivacious personality under wraps, lest she accidentally give Warren the impression she welcomed his advances.

The complications rose up in her throat like a big black rock, cutting off her air.

"Tell me what you're thinking, Tilda." Warren's quiet voice cut through her angst easily. "Do you want to keep this job or go back to Australia? If it's the former, let's work through this from the top and mitigate all of the potential landmines."

As frequently as they'd been on the same wavelength over the course of this project, it shouldn't be such a shock that he'd picked up on her reservations. Could he see the panic, too? Surely not.

She'd tried hard to hide what was really going on beneath the surface for the entire length of their acquaintance, adopting the granite-hard professionalism that she'd been convinced no one could crack.

Warren Garinger managed to crack it without breaking a sweat. Likely without even realizing it. This was her opportunity to retake control.

"All right." *Deep breath.* "I want to keep this job."

That meant she had to take the issue of her visa seriously and consider his offer. *Marriage.* It was a dizzying proposition, rife with pitfalls, both legal and personal.

But still viable, nonetheless.

"Good. I want you to keep it. What else concerns you about this plan?"

Oh, God, *everything* about this plan concerned her. One hurdle at a time. "No issues with your wife working for you?"

"None. This is a family company through and through. Thomas's wife is head of accounting and all of the shareholders are named Garinger." Warren flashed her another brief smile. "If you like, I would be happy to give you a block of shares as a wedding present."

She swallowed as the black rock grew in her throat. The gesture had probably been an act of good faith, but no one had ever offered to make her a part of a family with such decisiveness. It felt…nice. She got to belong for no other reason than because Warren said so. She nodded, since speaking wasn't possible.

"What else?" he prodded gently. "I have a master suite at my house that connects to a smaller bedroom via the bathroom. The door locks from the other side. You may have that one or one on the first floor if you like. My staff is paid well to exercise discretion, so we don't need to worry about them tattling to the immigration bureau that the marriage is fake. Of course, we will need to put on some appearances as if we're happily married."

"I'm not sure I can do that." She cut in before thinking better of it. How could she explain that she didn't think she could let a man touch her without jumping out of her skin? She didn't have to. Warren didn't miss a beat.

"I don't mean with public displays of affection." His smile turned wry. "No one who knows me would be shocked if I never touched my wife in public. What would be shocking is if I put my cell phone down long enough to do so."

That did it. Her lungs loosened, allowing her to breathe. Finally. Sweet air rushed into her system and she went a little lightheaded from relief. She found herself matching his smile without fully realizing he'd affected her enough for that. "I see your point. They would probably call the authorities much faster if you showered me with attention. Perhaps we'll let them think of us as having an affair of the mind."

They shared a moment of understanding that grew sharper the longer they stared at each other. The man was brilliant, sexy without being in your face about it and respectful of her boundaries. How much closer could they become if she lowered a few?

Warren cleared his throat first and looked away. "What I meant was that you might have to accompany me to family functions so as not to raise eyebrows. The last thing we need is immigration questioning whether we married strictly for the green card. The attorney I consulted said they do investigate red flags."

She nodded. "I got you."

"Also, you should know that I'm not warm and fuzzy in a relationship. Acting like I'm in love is frankly outside my skill set. I wouldn't know what that looks like, nor do I intend to learn."

"That's fine with me." Perfect, actually. She didn't know what love looked like, either, and trying to fake it would only bring up issues she'd rather leave in the dark. Boundaries were her friends. Always. "In that case, I accept your proposal."

"Great. I'll have some papers for you to sign tomorrow, a standard prenuptial agreement and the marriage license application. We'll go to the justice of the peace on Friday, as mentioned, and then it will be done."

Warren reached out a hand and she clasped it. A handshake to seal the deal. Should have been innocuous enough and seemed appropriate under the circumstances.

But the moment their flesh connected, a jolt of electricity shot up her arm and her awareness of him as a man settled deep inside. Not just a man. One who would be her husband.

Her little crush might be wholly inadvisable, but as Warren held her hand, she didn't for a moment believe she had the will to stop finding him inconveniently and enormously attractive.

Two

Jonas Kim and Hendrix Harris met Warren at the courthouse on Friday. Predictably, his best friends since college didn't miss the opportunity to give him a hard time about his impending marriage. Warren had fully expected it after the equally hard time he'd given both of them when they'd gotten married.

The difference here was that Warren wasn't breaking the pact the three of them had made their senior year at Duke University. Jonas and Hendrix had. They'd broken the pact seven ways to Sunday and without shame, no less. After Marcus had committed suicide over his irreparably broken heart, the three surviving friends had shaken hands and vowed to never fall in love.

Warren would stick to that until the day he died. His friends might have found ways to excuse their faithlessness to themselves, but Warren was still working on forgiving them for putting their hearts at risk in their own marriages.

"Well, well, well." Jonas crossed his arms and gave Warren a once-over that held a wealth of meaning as his two friends cleared the metal detector at the entrance to the Wake County Courthouse in downtown Raleigh. "I do believe this is what eating crow looks like. Don't you agree, Hendrix?"

"I do." His other friend shot Warren a grin that sharpened his already ridiculous cheekbones. "It also looks like I should have put money on whether Warren would eventually get that mouth full of feathers when I had a chance."

"Ha, ha. It's not like that," Warren growled.

It wasn't. His marriage did not compare to his friends' situations; both of them had married women they already had relationships with. Jonas had married his friend Viv to avoid an arranged marriage with a stranger, and Hendrix had married Roz to end a scandal caused by risqué photographs of the two of them. They'd both sworn they weren't going to cross any lines, but it had only been a matter of time before things started getting mushy.

Mushy was not even remotely in the realm of possibility for Warren.

"What's it like, then?" Jonas asked. "Tell us how it's even possible that you're getting married after being so high and mighty about it when me and Hendrix came to you with our plans."

"I'm marrying Tilda because I can't trash Down Under Thunder without her. This is a Hail Mary designed to keep her in the country. No other reason. End of story."

"Oh, so she's a hag you would never look at twice on the street. I get it," Jonas said with a smart-ass nod.

Hendrix shook his head. "That's just sad, if so."

"Shut up. She's not a hag. Tilda is gorgeous." The headache brewing between Warren's eyes stabbed a little harder as his friends gave each other knowing glances laden with a side of I told you so. "This marriage is strictly business. I would never be anything less than professional with an employee."

"Except you are," Jonas countered. "You're moving her into your house tomorrow. Trust me when I say that leads to all sorts of things you might swear on your mother's life you would never contemplate, but it happens, man. First you're having a drink together after work and next thing you know, you're giving your in-name-only bride diamonds and orgasms in the foyer."

"Or in the linen closet at your wedding reception," Hendrix threw in helpfully with a gleam in his eye. He and his new wife had pulled just such a disappearing at the social event of the season.

"There are no linen closets here," Warren pointed out unnecessarily, not that he had to explain himself to his friends. But he was going to anyway, because they needed to be clear that he was the lone holdout in their pact.

Marcus's suicide was not something Warren had ever taken lightly, and neither was the vow he'd made to honor his roommate's death. Love had stolen a young man's life. Warren would never let that be his fate. "I've never done anything more than shake Tilda's hand as a form of sealing our arrangement. She's working on my project, not working her way into my bed. This is not about my sex life. Period."

"We'll see about that." Hendrix jerked his chin over Warren's shoulder. "Would that lovely lady be your intended bride? She looks like your type."

Warren turned to see Tilda striding toward him, her sensible heels clacking on the marble floor of the courthouse, hair swept up in the no-nonsense bun he'd dreamed about again last night and a serene expression on her face that didn't change when she caught his gaze.

Good. She'd been edgy in his office the other day and he'd half expected her to back out at some point. After all, he hadn't really had to sell her on the idea of a marriage to keep her in the country. It had been remarkably easy to talk her into it, and for some reason, he'd become convinced that she'd change her mind after she had a chance to think about it. Marriage was a big thing to some women and maybe she'd dreamed of falling in love with a capital L.

But she was here. His shoulders relaxed a bit, releasing tension he'd been carrying since Wednesday. This was going to work. Down Under Thunder was toast. And if he had the opportunity to develop a few more harmless fantasies starring his wife, no one had to know.

Tilda halted in front of him smelling fresh and citrusy. Funny, he'd never noticed her scent before and his imagination galloped toward the conclusion that she'd wanted to do something special for the occasion.

"We have a conference call at one o'clock with Wheatner and Ross," she said by way of greeting.

A timely reminder. That's why she was worth every dime of her paycheck. But he couldn't seem to stop looking at the thin strand of hair that fell from her forehead down across her temple.

It wasn't more than a millimeter wide, but it followed the line of her face to hit just under her jaw, and he had the strongest urge to slide it along his fingertips as he tucked it behind her ear. What madness was this, that she'd missed that miniscule bit of hair when she'd gotten dressed this morning?

New perfume. Defiant hair. Was it possible she was affected by the gravity of what they were about to do? Because he was. He'd lain awake last night, unable to close his eyes as he thought about the realities of having Tilda under his roof, how he'd see her in the morning before they left for work, have a cup of coffee together, even. Maybe he'd give her a ride. It only made sense that they'd go to the office together since they were coming from the same place. They could talk about things and—

Jonas might have a point about the inherent lack of professionalism that would come with having an easily accessible woman in his house. Too late now. He'd have to bank on the fact that he and Tilda had already discussed the necessary lack of intimacy.

Warren cleared his throat. "Then we should get on with it."

She nodded with a slight smile. "It helps when we're on the same wavelength."

They always were. They were cut from the same cloth, which was what made her so easy to work with. Conversely, it also made it easier to imagine slipping in deeper with her, loosening her up, finding ways to make her laugh more. They'd be good together, if he ever did find himself unable to resist crossing that line.

No.

There would be no line crossing. The project was

too important to take those kinds of risks. His vows were too important. He gestured to Jonas and Hendrix as he doled out the introductions.

"Mr. Kim." Tilda shook Jonas's hand briskly. "I worked on the campaign for your hybrid printer during the global rollout two years ago."

Jonas's brows lifted as he nodded. "That was a great product launch for Kim Electronics. I didn't realize you were on that team. It was very impressive."

Crossing his arms, Warren tried not to smile too smugly, failed—and then decided there was no shame in letting it be known that he only hired the best. Which shouldn't be a surprise to anyone.

Hendrix slid right into the space Jonas had vacated, charm in full force as he shook Tilda's hand for about fifteen beats too long, which *wasn't* a surprise to anyone. The man would probably flirt with a nun, given the chance. Regardless, Warren did not like the way Tilda smiled back, never mind that Hendrix was happily married to a woman who could command a cover spot on a men's magazine.

"We have a marriage to conduct," Warren reminded everyone briskly before he had to punch his friend for taking liberties with his wife-to-be.

Employee. Wife was secondary. Which shouldn't be such a difficult thing to remember.

The strand of hair across her temple settled into place, drawing his gaze again. He couldn't take his mind off it, even as they navigated the courthouse maze to find the justice of the peace who performed marriages.

They stood in line waiting for their turn, an oddity in and of itself. Warren had never given much thought to what should constitute a proper wedding ceremony, especially since he'd started the week with zero expectations of ending it married. Not to mention the fact that his marriage had strict business connotations. But these other couples in line surely had more romantic reasons for tying the knot. In fact, they were probably all in love, as evidenced by their goo-goo eyes and the way they held hands as they waited. A courthouse seemed like an inauspicious start to a marriage that was supposed to be till death did them part.

He shrugged it off. Who was he to judge? It wasn't like he knew the proper ingredients for a happy marriage, if such a thing even existed. Divorce rates would indicate otherwise. So maybe Warren and Tilda were the only couple in the Wake County courthouse today who had the right idea when it came to wedded bliss: no emotional component, a carefully worded prenuptial agreement, a date on the calendar for follow-ups with proper government agencies so the annulment could be filed and mutual agreement to part ways in the future. No surprises.

Tilda engaged him in a short conversation about the campaign she'd been working through. He fell into the rhythm of their work relationship easily, despite the weirdness of doing it while waiting for the justice's inner chamber doors to open. They'd enter single and emerge married.

It wouldn't change things between them. Would it?

All of these other couples surely had some expectations of things changing or they wouldn't do it. They'd just stay an unmarried couple until the day they died, but instead, they'd done exactly what Warren and Tilda had. Applied for a marriage license and come down to the courthouse on an otherwise unremarkable Friday to enter into a legal contract that said they could file their taxes differently. Why? Because they'd fallen prey to some nebulous feeling they labeled *love*?

"Warren."

He blinked. Tilda was watching him with a puzzled expression on her face, clearly because she'd asked him something that he'd completely ignored. God, what was wrong with him? "Sorry, I was distracted."

Why couldn't he just talk to Tilda about the project and stop thinking about marriage with a capital M, as if it was a bigger deal than it really was? Like he'd told his friends—business only. Nothing to see here.

Wedded bliss wasn't a thing. And if it was, Warren Garinger didn't deserve it. Marcus's death was his fault and a lifetime of happiness with a woman wasn't the proper atonement for his crimes.

Flying Squirrel was Warren's focus, the only thing he could realistically manage. For a reason. A company didn't have deep emotional scars. A company didn't waste away while you looked on helplessly, unable to figure out how to stop the pain. A company didn't choose to end its pain with an overdose after you thoughtlessly said, "Get over it, Marcus."

That was the real reason Warren would never break the pact. It was his due punishment to be alone the rest of his life.

The county clerk gestured Tilda and Warren into the justice's chamber. Her pulse fell off a cliff, skipping beats randomly as her stomach churned. The effort she'd made to talk shop with Warren, strictly to calm her nerves while they'd waited in the hall, had evaporated, if it had even done any good at all.

They were really doing this. What if they got caught in a green-card marriage? Was it like the movies, with instant deportation? She'd be forced back to Melbourne, and after Warren's unceremonious threat to Craig and the firm she'd worked for over the last eight years, she had no illusions that a job waited for her. She'd be lucky to get a reference. Which mattered not at all if Bryan figured out she'd returned. Finding a job would be the least of her concerns.

Warren had stipulated several contingencies in their agreement that meant she'd be well compensated in the event the marriage didn't resolve her residency issues. But that wasn't the point. She didn't want money; she wanted to feel safe and she wanted to do this project with Warren, in that order. This job gave her a sense of purpose that she'd never fully had before. When she'd worked on other projects, she'd never been the lead. The Flying Squirrel campaign was her baby, one hundred percent, especially now that she'd cut ties with Craig.

That went a long way toward getting her pulse under control. She had this. The wedding ceremony wasn't a big deal. A formality. Warren wasn't flipping out. He shot her a small smile that she returned because the last thing she wanted was for him to clue in that she wasn't handling this as professionally as she'd like.

But then, marrying her boss hadn't really been in the job description. Maybe she was allowed to have minor cracks in the hard outer shell she'd built around herself with severe hairstyles and monochrome suits that hung on her figure like potato sacks.

She just had to make sure any potential cracks didn't reveal things underneath that she wasn't ready to share, like the fact that she *hated* monochrome suits. The lacy red underwear and bra set she'd chosen in honor of her wedding day was for her and her only.

The ceremony began and she somehow managed not to flinch as Warren took her hand with a solemnity she hadn't expected. Fortunately, the exchange of words was short. Simple. She relaxed. Until the justice said, "You may kiss the bride."

At which point her pulse jackhammered back up into the red. They weren't really going to do that part, were they? But Warren was already leaning toward her, his fingers firm against hers, and she automatically turned her face to accept his lips.

The brush of them came far too fast. Sensation sparked across her mouth and she flinched like she always did when something happened near her face that she wasn't expecting. Not because the feeling of his lips was unwelcome. Kissing Warren was nothing like kissing Bryan. Or any other man, for that matter, not that she had a lot of experiences to compare it to. He wasn't demanding or obtrusive. Just…nice. Gentle. And then gone.

That brief burst of heat faded. Good. It was over. Back to normal. But she couldn't look at Warren as they left the courthouse.

She'd walked over from the Flying Squirrel building on Blount Street, but Warren insisted on taking her back via his limo, citing a need to go over some notes for the meeting with Wheatner and Ross. He said goodbye to his friends and then she and Warren were swallowed by leather and luxury as they settled into his limo.

"So," Warren said brightly. "That went well."

"Yes. Quite well."

God, everything was weird. This was supposed to be where they relaxed back into the dynamic they'd had from day one, where it was all business—the way they both liked it. But as she turned to him, a little desperate to find that easiness, her knee grazed his. The awareness of their proximity shot through her and she couldn't stop staring at his mouth as a wholly inappropriate lick of desire flamed through her core.

Where had *that* come from?

Well, she knew where. Warren had kissed her. So what? It shouldn't be such a big deal. She shouldn't be making it a big deal. But the part she couldn't figure out was *why*? There was no law that said they'd be any less married if they skipped the kiss. Had he done it strictly for show or because he'd been curious what it would be like?

She'd had absolutely zero curiosity. None. Not an iota. Or, at least, none that she'd admit to, and now that it was out there, she couldn't stop thinking about what he'd kiss like behind closed doors.

Ugh. She had to get back into her professional head space already.

"Um, so the senior partners themselves are attending the meeting today," she threw out, mortified to note her voice had taken on a husky quality. "We should press them on the social media presence they've presented. I don't like the ratio of ad placements between the various platforms."

Warren didn't seem to notice her vocal quirks and nodded. "I was thinking that, as well. Tell me what you'd do instead."

Tilda reeled off the changes she'd prepared and then memorized last night at midnight after she'd given up on sleep. The familiarity of talking numbers with the man who was now her legally wedded husband somehow soothed her to the point where her tone evened out.

Until she realized Warren's gaze had strayed to the side of her face. She faltered. "What?"

"Oh, nothing." His gaze snapped back to dead center. And then drifted again. "It's just that you have this loose strand of hair—here, let me."

Her hand flew up defensively at the same moment he reached out to brush her cheek and their hands collided. Oh, God. She'd batted his hand away from her face. Now he'd know she was a freak about people touching her.

Everything shifted back into awkward again as they said "Sorry" simultaneously, and there was no way she could ignore how her skin tingled where he'd touched her. The errant strand of hair he'd made her so very aware of lay across the spot, sensitizing it.

"I'll fix it when we get back to the office," she murmured, at a loss for why her stupid hair had generated such interest that he couldn't keep his focus where it belonged—on her stats.

"Don't fix it," he said instantly. "I like it."

Not what she'd expected him to say.

Heat prickled over her face and not all of it was in her cheeks. Unlike what would have been a becoming blush on anyone else, her whole face got red when she was embarrassed. Like now.

He liked her hair.

It was the most personal comment he'd ever made and she turned it over in her mind, examining it from all angles.

"Oh," Warren continued. "I forgot that Jonas and Hendrix asked if we could join them for dinner. To celebrate. It'll be low-key, just them and their wives. Is that okay?"

She nodded, though she'd rather have said no. But refusing would have felt petty when clearly he meant they were supposed to be celebrating their wedding. Social events were a part of the deal, whether she wanted to avoid opportunities for more weirdness or not.

Get a grip, she scolded herself. The weirdness was all on her. Warren wasn't Bryan and she had to stop cringing as if her new husband was going to morph into someone completely different after lulling her into a false sense of security. Not all men did that.

She hoped.

For the remainder of the afternoon, she forced a smile and slayed the meeting with Wheatner and Ross, earning approving nods from Warren, which shouldn't have meant as much as it did. He'd always approved of her work. That's why she was still in the US and not on a plane at this moment, as she'd fully expected to be when she walked into his office on Wednesday to explain the issue with her visa.

Now she was married, complete with a gold ring on her finger that contained nine emerald-cut diamonds sunk into the band. It was exactly the right ring for her, low-key, not at all flashy. How had Warren known what she would like? Luck? She would have been fine with a plain band from a vending machine. This one had weight. She curled her hand into a fist but she could still feel it on her finger.

Warren herded her back into his car at the end of the day to take her to the restaurant where his friends were waiting for them. He'd made it very clear that they wouldn't have to do any sort of acting like a lovey-dovey couple in public, but she still had a fair amount of trepidation about whether she'd get along with his friends' wives. She knew how things among men worked, and she didn't want to fail this important test of fitting into his world for however long she would be required to do so.

"Is it okay to go straight there?" Warren asked politely as they settled into his car for the second time that day. "If you want to go home first to freshen up, that's fine."

"No, thank you." What would she do, shellac the errant lock of hair to her head that Warren had already said not to fix? Not a chance. And she didn't own any suits that weren't dove gray or brown, nor would she ever change into something like jeans and a T-shirt to meet his friends, so she was as ready as she ever would be. "I appreciate the offer."

He dove into a very long summary of the day's progress, which was fairly typical of how they usually parted for the night. But today they weren't parting. Would it ever *not* be weird to realize they were a couple now?

At the restaurant on Glenwood Avenue, Warren's friends had already arrived, crowding into a round booth with a table in the center that was probably meant for six people but seemed quite cozy given that she'd only met Jonas Kim and Hendrix Harris for the first time earlier today.

The two women at the table slid out from the booth to meet her. Tilda shook the hand of Rosalind Harris, Hendrix's wife, a gorgeous dark-haired woman who could have come straight from a catwalk in Paris. Her friendly smile put Tilda at ease, a rare feat that she appreciated. Viv Kim, Jonas's wife, immediately pulled Tilda into a hug, her bubbly personality matching her name perfectly.

"I'm thrilled to meet you," Viv said and nodded at Rosalind. "We've heard absolutely nothing about you, and when our husbands keep their mouths shut about something, we're instantly curious."

Rosalind scooted a little closer and plunked her martini glass down on the table.

"Tell us everything," Rosalind insisted, leaning in with the scent of something expensive and vaguely sensual wafting from her. "How long do you think you'll have to be married before your immigration issues will be resolved? Are you going to stay in the country even after you annul the marriage?"

"Um..." Tilda's butt hit the table as she backed up, and she briefly considered sliding under it. Warren had apparently told his friends the truth about their marriage, so obviously she could trust them, but still. These were things better left out of polite conversation. You could never be too careful.

Salvation came in the form of her husband, who scowled at the two women, clearly having overheard despite his involvement in his own conversation with

Jonas and Hendrix. "We didn't agree to dinner so you could gang up on my wife."

For some reason, that brought a smile she couldn't quite contain. In one short sentence, Warren had turned them into a unit. They were *together*, an integrated front. She was his new wife just as much as he was her new husband, and it apparently came with benefits she hadn't anticipated. But liked. Very much.

Rosalind scowled back, clearly not cowed in the least. "You have to know that we're curious."

"Darling." Hendrix held out his hand to his wife. "Your curiosity is one of my favorite qualities. Come over here and be curious about the advantages of a round booth when you're sitting next to your husband."

An intense smile that held a wealth of meaning bloomed on Rosalind's face. She clasped his outstretched hand, allowing him to draw her into the booth and over to his side, where he slung an arm around her. He murmured something in her ear and she laughed, snuggling against him with such ease that Tilda got a lump in her throat while watching them. They were so clearly in love, so obviously the kind of lovers that trusted each other implicitly.

The white-hot spurt of emotion in her chest was nothing but pure jealousy. Naming it didn't make it any more acceptable or understandable. Where had that come from? Longing for that kind of intimacy with a man had gotten her into trouble with Bryan, leading her into dangerous water before she fully realized she'd left the shore behind. Tilda swallowed as she tore her gaze from the two.

"Don't mind them," Warren said with a note of disgust in his voice. “They embarrass the rest of us, too. They have no boundaries in polite company.”

“That’s so not true,” Hendrix countered with a smirk, scarcely lifting his gaze from his wife’s luminous face. “We’ve turned over a new leaf. No more public nakedness.”

That broke some of the tension, and Jonas slid into the booth with his wife, which left Warren and Tilda. He sat next to Hendrix, leaving Tilda at the edge. Which suited her fantastically. She liked nothing less than being trapped, and luck of the draw meant she wouldn’t have to be.

Across from her, Viv settled in close to her husband. Viv and Jonas might not have sensual vibes shooting from them the way the other couple did, but it was clear they were newly married and still in the throes of the honeymoon phase.

Happiness in marriage wasn’t a goal of Tilda’s. Burying herself in her job was. That was all she could handle at the moment, all she would allow herself to hope for. Intimacy wasn’t on the table in her marriage, by design, and that was a good thing. After all, she couldn’t trust herself any more than she could trust a man.

Warren had left a solid foot of space between his thigh and Tilda’s. Appropriately so. He would never slide his arm around her and nestle her close, turning his head to murmur something wickedly naughty or achingly sweet into her ear.

And it shouldn’t have taken the rest of the evening for her to convince herself she didn’t want that.

Three

The moving company Warren had hired arrived at his house with Tilda's things around midafternoon on Saturday, meager as they were. She'd apparently not brought very much with her from Australia, just a few paperback books with well-worn covers, several boxes of clothes and shoes, and a set of china teacups.

He was curious about both the teacups and the books. But asking felt like a line they shouldn't cross. Too personal or something. If she wanted to explain, she would. Didn't stop him from thinking it was a strange state of things that he didn't feel comfortable getting personal with his wife.

The lack of boxes meant she didn't need any help unpacking and he had no good reason to be skulking about in his bedroom as she settled into her room on the other side of the connecting door in his bathroom.

He couldn't find a thing to occupy his attention, an unusual phenomenon when he normally spent Saturdays touring the Flying Squirrel warehouses with Thomas.

But his brother was on vacation with his wife—somewhere without cell phone reception, apparently, as he'd not answered his phone in several days. That was unfathomable. Who wanted to be someplace without cell phone reception?

If Warren had been occupied with work—like he should have been—then he wouldn't have heard Tilda rustling around in the bathroom. Nor would he have wandered through the door to appease his sudden interest in what she was doing. She glanced up sharply as he joined her in the cavernous room.

Immediately, she took up all the space and then tried to occupy his, too, sliding under his skin with her presence. He'd been in a small room with her before, lots of times. But not at his house, a stone's throw from the shower where he'd indulged in many, many fantasies starring the woman he'd married.

The problem wasn't the married part. It was the kiss part. He probably shouldn't have done that.

Or, more to the point, he should have done it right. Then he wouldn't be thinking about what it would be like to kiss Tilda properly. He couldn't take his eyes off her mouth. That short, utilitarian peck yesterday had been ill-advised, obviously. But the officiant had said to kiss the bride. Warren hadn't seen any reason not to. It was a custom. He wouldn't have felt married without it, a twist that he hadn't anticipated. So he went with it.

But it hadn't been worth the price of admission if he was going to be constantly on edge around Tilda now.

Constantly thinking about whether it would change their working dynamic if he kissed her as thoroughly as he suddenly burned to.

He cleared his throat. "Settling in all right?"

She nodded. "You have a lovely home."

Which she never would have seen, even one time, if they hadn't gotten married. "It's yours, too, for now. I have to admit, I was a little surprised you picked the adjoining bedroom. It would have been okay to take the one on the first floor."

But she was already shaking her head. There were no loose strands in her hairstyle today. He'd somehow expected that she'd adopt a more casual look on a Saturday, but Tilda had shown up in yet another dove-gray suit that looked practical and professional. But it also generated a fair amount of nosy interest in her habits. Even he wore jeans and T-shirts on Saturday, despite the assurance that he would put in an eight-hour day in the pursuit of all things Flying Squirrel before the sun set. Did she ever relax enough to enjoy a day off?

Well, that didn't matter. What the hell was wrong with him? He didn't take days off, either. Why would having a woman in his house change his ninety-hour workweek? And certainly finding himself in possession of a wife didn't mean they should take a day off together like he'd been half imagining.

"I know you said the staff is very discreet," she said and nodded to the open door behind her that gave him only a glimpse of the room beyond. "But taking this bedroom seemed like less of a problem. Less obvious that we're not, um…sleeping together."

Well, now, that was an interesting blush spreading over Tilda's cheeks, and he didn't miss the opportunity to enjoy it. He crossed his arms and leaned a hip against the nondescript marble vanity, which suddenly seemed a lot more remarkable now that it had several feminine accoutrements strewn across it.

"Yes, that was why I suggested it," he drawled.

But now he was thinking of the reasons it was less obvious they weren't sleeping together—because of the accessibility factor. This was an older home, designed in the style of a hundred years ago when women had their own chambers but understood the expectations of producing heirs. These women needed discreet ways to travel between their bedrooms and their husbands', and vice versa, without disturbing staff members.

He'd never even so much as imagined a woman using that adjoining chamber. And now he couldn't unimagine how easy it would be to steal into Tilda's bed in the middle of the night. She wouldn't be wearing a suit, that was for sure. What *did* she wear to bed? In all of his fantasies, she was naked.

And that was absolutely not the right image to slam into his mind during a conversation with his in-name-only wife while stuck in a netherworld between two beds that were not going to see any action of the sensual variety. A man with his imagination should be putting it to better use dreaming up new ways to sell energy drinks, not undressing his buttoned-up employee with his eyes.

"Did you want to go over the project plan?" she asked, very carefully not looking at him as she pulled open an empty drawer to place her hairbrush inside.

"In a little while. After you're settled. And only if

you want to. I don't expect you to work weekends just because we're together."

The drawer slammed shut, the sound echoing from the mostly bare walls, and she flinched. "Sorry, I'm not used to your house yet. Even the drawer mechanisms are higher end than what I'm accustomed to. Takes hardly any force at all to close."

He eyed her, not liking the way the vibe between them had gotten more stilted. They'd been easy with each other for so long. He yearned to get that back.

"No problem. I don't expect you to automatically know how everything in the house operates. You take some time to get acclimated and we'll have dinner together later. In fact, no work for you today. I insist."

Dinner. That sounded nice. An opportunity to keep things casual, learn some things about each other. Get used to being married and find their way back to the easiness that had marked their working relationship.

But instead of taking the hint and nodding enthusiastically, she froze. The vibe between them grew icicles and he scouted around for the reason she'd suddenly gotten so tense.

"Dinner?" she repeated. "Will it be like a…date?"

Mayday. Obviously she didn't want the icicles between them to melt, and if her tone was any indication, the idea of a date was not welcome.

That needled him. Was he so terrible a companion that she couldn't even fathom having a dinner that wasn't about business? Lots of women enjoyed his company…right up until they realized his cell phone was an extension of his arm.

This conversation was going south in a hurry.

"No, of course it's not a date." Dates came with connotations that he didn't know how to deal with, either. All of his dates consisted of interruptions due to work emergencies and the occasional late-night booty call that left him feeling increasingly lonely. "Would it be so bad if I did mean it that way?"

Wow, he needed to shut his trap, like, yesterday.

"I, um…don't…know."

She looked so miserable that he had to take pity on her. Clearly she didn't know how to respond to that, and technically, he was her boss more than he was her husband.

"It's just dinner," he practically growled. "I want to eat with you. Let's not attach any more meaning to it than that."

She nodded, her eyes a little wide.

There was a reason he didn't have more practice at this. *The pact.* And, frankly, drawing out his wife for the express purpose of getting to know her wasn't a good plan. Where could this possibly go? Granted, she already knew he was a workaholic, so that realization wasn't likely to stall things out before they got started. But in order for that to matter, they'd have to have some type of relationship beyond business.

Now was probably not the right time to figure out that that sounded really great.

Tilda spent about an hour rearranging her clothes in the closet of her new bedroom. If *closet* was even the appropriate term when the thing in question was the size of the entire corporate apartment she'd been living in for the last two months as she worked on the Flying Squirrel campaign. She'd expected to stay in that tiny apartment for the entire year. Funny how things worked out.

Not so funny were the second thoughts she'd been plagued with about selecting the bedroom near Warren's. The reasons she'd given him were sound. The effect of his proximity was not.

Sure, she'd had an academic understanding that the rooms connected via the enormous bathroom. There was an ocean of wide marble tile between the two doors, locks on either side and then a lot of carpet. They never had to see each other except perhaps in passing—she'd presumed.

That hadn't worked out. He'd just wandered in while she was putting away her things, perfectly fine having a chat in the bathroom. Why hadn't she taken the bedroom downstairs? Well, she knew that one. Because she'd had a moment of panic at the idea of being adrift in this huge house. Warren was the only person she knew in this place, the only person who had given her a measure of comfort in the whole of the United States. She shouldn't have to second-guess choosing the bedroom that meant she'd be closer to him. If she liked the fact that he was convenient, no one had to know. Nor would she ever act on that convenience. He was her boss and she owed him a debt of gratitude for keeping her out of Australia.

Plus, he'd backed off in a hurry when she'd tried to put parameters around this nebulous thing he'd called "dinner." Of course, it was crystal clear now that he hadn't defined it as a *date* in any way, shape or form.

Which was good. She was telling herself it was good, even as she tried to figure out what you wore to dinner with your husband who wasn't really a husband. One of her serviceable dove-gray suits felt too… officey, despite the fact that she'd been wearing one all day. Jeans and a T-shirt, like what she wore to the grocery store, seemed too casual. But then, Warren had mentioned they'd be dining at the house, so maybe casual wasn't off base.

In the end, she couldn't do it. She picked the brown suit and hid a peacock-blue silk bra with corded straps and a matching thong under it. Defiantly. It was her favorite set, bought with her first paycheck from the Flying Squirrel campaign. She'd waltzed right into that high-end lingerie store in downtown Raleigh and bought the classiest, most beautiful fabrics in the place. The clerk had folded her purchase into silver tissue paper, then tucked her lingerie into a foil bag the size of a paperback. Nothing she'd bought needed a bigger package, since both scraps were tiny and revealing.

Not that she'd ever reveal any of it to anyone. Her little secret. A kick in the teeth to Bryan's memory, who had never wanted her to wear anything remotely flashy or skimpy. She didn't dress that way on the outside, but that barrier of boring clothing was for her own peace of mind. Better to avoid attention than to seek it.

Dinner was exactly as advertised. At home, low-key and not a date. Warren wore the same T-shirt and jeans he'd had on earlier, but of course he looked like a dream in anything. She so rarely saw him in something besides a suit that she took time to enjoy the way his shoulders filled out the soft cotton, graceful biceps emerging below the cuffs.

Wordlessly, he pulled out a chair at the twelve-seat dining room table off the foyer.

"Do you entertain a lot?" she inquired politely, since she felt like she had to say something, and *hee-bie-jeebies, are you a good-looking man* didn't seem appropriate.

"Never. This was my mother's idea. Apparently it's the done thing to have a room big enough for a basketball team to dine in."

She smiled at the joke and slid into the chair he offered, careful not to brush him as she sat. But as he helped her push in the chair, it caught on an uneven slat in the hardwood floor and his fingers grazed her shoulders.

The coil of heat low in her belly surprised her with its intensity. The man had barely touched her. What was wrong with her that she had to fight the instinct to lean back against his hands in wordless invitation?

But his heat vanished from behind her as quickly as he'd established his presence. Taking a seat to her left, he eased into his own chair and turned his focus to her.

"Are you unpacked yet? Need any help?" he inquired.

She shook her head. "No, thank you. You've already been so generous with your staff and in allowing me time to get settled. We should really go over the project plan again, now that we've got Wheatner and Ro—"

"No work." Warren broke off as his housekeeper came in with plates of white fish and green beans, serving dinner with precise efficiency. Once he'd nodded his thanks, she disappeared. "We're just eating dinner tonight. As a couple. Not as coworkers."

"But we're not a couple," she countered, wondering how she was supposed to eat with such a thing thrown down between them. And wondering whether that note of panic had sounded as squeaky to him as it did to her. "We agreed. In name only."

A couple. She'd never been part of a couple, or rather, a *normal* one. She turned the term over in her head, trying not to attach any significance to it. Her dating life had been nothing remarkable. She'd longed for the kind of relationship that seemed to come so easily to everyone around her, but nothing had ever clicked for her. Until Bryan, whom she'd met at her university roommate's wedding.

In retrospect, they'd clicked far too easily, largely owing to her desperation to finally have the kind of companionship and intimacy she'd craved.

And over the last year, she'd proven that she could live without either. Being one half of a couple wasn't her goal any longer.

Warren didn't pick up his fork, despite having just laid down the law about the activity they were pursuing. "We did agree to in name only. But I'd like to get to know you. We're going to have some interview rounds for your green card. It would be beneficial if we didn't stumble through basic things like the names of our siblings or where you were born."

"I'm an only child and I was born in Melbourne. Your brother is Thomas. I was thinking that after Wheatner and Ross come back with the revised promotional—"

"Tilda."

Warren's voice snaked through the low light of the dining room to seep through her chest with jagged teeth, freezing her vocal chords.

"Is it that difficult to put work aside for an hour?" He cocked his head. "No judgment on this side of the table, if so. I'm the last person to cast the first stone when it comes to being all about the work. But it's Saturday night and I want to have a nice dinner with my wife, not with a project manager."

He wanted to *what*? "I'm only your project manager. The rest is strictly for show. In order to keep me in the country."

Wasn't it? Something unnamable gripped her shoulders, tightening them as she contemplated the gorgeous face of the man she'd married, who didn't seem all that boss-like as he nodded his agreement.

"Yes. And no. It strikes me as ironic that we're so similar. Here we are, married, and we can barely have dinner together without resorting to work. Maybe it's an opportunity to practice relaxing. For both of us. I like that we're on the same wavelength about nearly everything. It facilitates a good working relationship. I don't want the fact that we now live together to interfere with how we work together, and it feels like there's a potential for that if we can't eliminate the weirdness."

Oh, God, she was going to botch this whole thing up. He could feel her hesitancy, the way she tensed up the moment he looked at her with the slightest bit of warmth. And he was calling her on it. How was she supposed to stop being a freak about a man getting personal with her? "Seems to me like the best way to eliminate the weirdness is to talk about work."

Yes. Work. The one place she felt one hundred percent safe.

He flashed her a smile. "Which is what I'd rather do. I'm asking you to humor me, as this is a difficulty of mine as well."

How could she say no to *that*? He was asking her for help with his own social clumsiness, which she'd never have called a failing in a million years. "I like that you're so business focused. There's a certain confidence required to be the CEO and you carry it well."

It was far sexier than it should be. She'd never admit it out loud, but she could certainly visualize how those skills might extend to the bedroom. She could pretend she might drop a few hints about the nature of her undergarments, just to see where that led.

Now that she was thinking about them, the tiny scraps chafed the intimate places they covered, teasing up a fair amount of unexpected heat. She couldn't seem to ignore the fact that she was wearing the most daring lingerie she owned while having dinner with her husband.

What would he say if he knew?

The bubble of awareness grew until she could hardly stand it.

His gaze caught hers, burning with a strange intensity, as if he'd guessed the direction of her thoughts. "I like that you think that."

What was this conversation they were having? Normally, Warren had the concept of distance down to a science. That was why they worked so well together.

This had nothing to do with feeling pressured and everything to do with the sudden chemistry between her and Warren that she had no idea how to handle. Okay, she had *ideas*. So many ideas…

"But," he continued. "I was being serious about the interviews. No time like the present to get more comfortable about being a couple. Soon enough, we'll have to do it for real in front of government officials."

That popped her bubble in a hurry. She'd been lulled into a false sense of security where she could ignore the marriage part of this marriage and still get her green card. He was right. It simply wasn't going to be that easy. And utilitarian tasks she could handle.

"I like books," she offered warily. "Cozy mysteries."

"I don't think I know what that means." Finally, he picked up his fork, starting to eat as if this really was a casual dinner between a married couple with no expectations. "Tell me."

She launched into a rundown of the difference between cozy mysteries and detective stories. This was an innocuous enough subject that she didn't feel uncomfortable. But she was going to have to figure out how to be a little more open with him or they could be in trouble with her green card. How much trouble, she didn't want to find out.

He asked her a few questions, guiding the conversation well enough that she'd taken the last bite of her green beans without realizing she'd cleaned her plate. Huh. Somewhere along the way, he'd gotten her to relax. Good. She could do this. Being married to Warren wasn't any different than being his employee, and they'd navigated dinner without a lot of hoopla.

"Have a glass of wine with me," he said without preamble as the housekeeper picked up their dishes. Her gaze flew to his and he shrugged with a solid smile. "I have a beautiful terrace overlooking the garden and I never use it. Sit with me and let's continue the conversation."

She shouldn't say no. Not when a lot rode on playing the part of a wife. And maybe, in the grand scheme of things, it was okay to stop being such a sook and admit she didn't want to say no.

And not all of her reasons had to do with green cards.

Four

The terrace was one of Warren's favorite parts of the house. He'd bought this historic home in an exclusive Raleigh neighborhood for many reasons, mostly having to do with boring concepts like asset management, resale value and tax write-offs, but he'd made the decision to sign on the dotted line the moment he'd stepped through the double French doors.

Wrought iron curlicued through the railing like an endless black vine, affording an unobstructed view of the half-acre garden that the groundskeeper kept thriving through some alchemy that baffled Warren. Dollar signs, he understood. Living things, not so much.

Tilda would be one such example. She had turned into a quiet mouse the moment she crossed the threshold of the terrace. She'd been off-kilter all night. He'd been trying to change the dynamic, move them past boss and employee for God knew what reason. She clearly wasn't on board. Gingerly, she took a seat on one of the wicker chairs with bright orange cushions. The thing swallowed her; it was big enough to seat an elephant or two cozy lovers, which they definitely were not.

Which didn't necessarily mean he couldn't slide into the chair next to her and see if he could coax a little more cheer out of the woman he'd married. Funny, he'd never even noticed the size of that chair. Perhaps because he seldom came out here. A shame.

And now that was all he could think about. Giant chair. Pretty woman. Beautiful view. Lots to enjoy.

He cleared his throat and extended the wine bottle dangling from his fingers. "Red okay?"

She nodded, relaxing not an iota as she shifted in the chair. He had the distinct impression she would have agreed in exactly the same manner if he'd casually suggested paint thinner as their after-dinner drink.

It was nearly painful how thick the tension had grown, and that was not going to work come Monday morning when they'd spend hours in each other's company doing the job she'd married him for. That was his excuse and he was sticking to it. Though the miniscule bit of intel he'd gleaned during dinner had only whetted his appetite to draw out this puzzle of a woman from her workaholic shell and see what made her tick.

There was a part of him that wondered if he'd figure out what made *him* tick in the process. The point wasn't lost on him that there were two uncomfortable people on the terrace, neither of whom had a lot of practice at putting work aside. Why couldn't they practice with each other? The fact that they needed to *get* comfortable—for more than one reason—was just a bonus.

He uncorked the wine that his housekeeper had already opened and then poured it, handing Tilda the glass of deep red wine by the stem—deliberately. Their fingers brushed and he wasn't a bit ashamed to enjoy the blush that worked across her cheeks. The setting sun threw all kinds of interesting shadows across the terrace and the atmosphere was far more romantic than he'd fully anticipated. Seriously, he'd just hoped to spend a little more time with Tilda before it was back to all business, but this had turned out better than he could have dreamed.

And he'd done a lot of that. Fantasies were harmless. The problems cropped up when he couldn't figure out how to engage the real woman, especially since he didn't have the possibility of dropping them both into one of his sensually charged imaginary scenes.

Bad thing to be thinking about. And still be thinking about. His lower half had gotten uncomfortably tight in half a second, and she was going to clue in that his groin was stirring if he didn't reel it back.

Not that there was anything wrong with a healthy attraction between two people. They just happened to be the two worst people on the planet to indulge in any kind of attraction, healthy or otherwise. They needed to be relaxed around each other, not hot and heavy. Though he was markedly better at the kind of conversations that he had with her in his head, the imaginary ones where all the words were sexy and led to both of them getting naked very fast.

Get a grip with a capital G right now.

Instead of taking one of the smaller chairs near the railing, he pulled over the footstool that went with Tilda's chair and perched on it, sipping his wine as he contemplated her.

"Tell me more about your life in Melbourne."

Her eyes widened. "Why?"

Yeah, practice definitely needed, stat. Along with an icebreaker, more wine and maybe a nice fire at the Flying Squirrel warehouse that would allow him to escape, because of course it would take hours to untangle.

He bit back a sigh. "Tilda, we're married. We work together. The green-card people will think it's weird that I know nothing about you, your childhood, your hopes, dreams. That's what people who get married talk about as they're falling in love."

Didn't they? He'd never talked about stuff like this with women. Hence the reason he was failing at it. Quite handily, too.

"Right-o." She shut her eyes for a blink and then glugged about a third of her wine in one shot. "I'm not very good at this, either. I don't date."

That was an interesting admission. "Really? Not at all? It seems unlikely that you don't get asked out. You're an attractive woman."

Something bright flared in her eyes and then vanished. "It might not have escaped your notice that I work a lot. Means I don't have much time for dating."

"You might have noticed that's something we have in common." The smile he flashed her was immediately returned and that was so encouraging that his widened involuntarily. "This is good for both of us. Indulge me in something. Relax," he told her as she raised her brows in question. "It's just me, and I solemnly swear not to tattle to the boss that we didn't spend the evening talking about spreadsheets."

That actually got a laugh out of her and it warmed something inside to hear. Because it meant she was taking his point seriously. That he might not be so bad at this, after all. Emboldened, he sipped his own wine and nudged her knee with his. "Melbourne?"

To her credit, she didn't edge away from the physical contact, and he gladly took it as a small victory.

"I lived there with my parents, attended Victoria University on a full academic scholarship."

"That's impressive."

She shrugged that off. "We weren't wealthy by any stretch. If I wanted a degree, that was the only way."

"You went to work for Craig right out of college?"

Nodding, she sipped more wine and the conversation ground to a halt. Okay. They were stuck together and he owed it to her to keep her eyes from glazing over.

"Come on." He stood and held out his hand without thinking better of it.

But then he didn't pull it back to his side. They could touch each other. It wasn't a rule that they couldn't. In fact, he'd say it was expected that a husband and wife touch each other, both in public and at home. How else would they get comfortable with it?

She eyed his hand. "Are we going somewhere?"

"Yes, to the railing so I can show you the garden. The personal conversation was too forced and people can get to know each other by means outside of the third degree."

That got her vote of confidence. She slipped her hand into his and let him help her from the gargantuan chair. Now that she'd done so, he couldn't help but notice that her hand was small and feminine in his. She was so capable and focused. He forgot occasionally that she couldn't, in fact, walk on water, and if she had vulnerabilities, she didn't advertise them.

He liked the reminder that she had softness hidden away, so he didn't release her hand. Instead, he guided her to the edge of the terrace and stood with her at the railing, as promised, wedging in close.

She didn't comment on his proximity, just stared over the circular rows of flowers that radiated outward from the center of the garden like a pinwheel. The sun was in the last throes of setting and the landscape lighting had clicked on sometime back, illuminating the grounds. The brightness was a security measure, but he pretended it was an extension of the romantic atmosphere. Everything in his life felt utilitarian all at once, and he wasn't in the mood to continue in the same vein with his wife.

"This is a very unusual garden," she remarked, pointedly not looking at their joined hands. But she didn't pull away. "Do you spend a lot of time in it?"

He couldn't help but smile, both at the hilariousness of the question and the fact that she'd fallen into personal conversation in a snap, exactly as he'd hoped. "My groundskeeper occasionally consults me on things like whether I'd like to change out the annuals, but no. For the most part, it's just magic that I enjoy occasionally when I remember that it's here."

"If this was my house, I'd be out on this terrace all the time."

And that was as telling a comment as any. "You are aware of the fact that you live here, yes?"

She smiled. "Not permanently. And, yes, I don't seem capable of forgetting the fact that I now live here. With you."

The landscape lighting did her no favors when it came to hiding the blush that sprang up, spreading across her cheeks and into her hairline. It was as becoming as it was intriguing. She clearly didn't like to discuss personal matters, but he couldn't quite put his finger on whether it was because she didn't like to give up details or because she worried that she'd say the wrong thing.

"Yes, that's an important part of the equation. We live here together. Have you not ever lived with a man before?"

She shook her head and, lo and behold, one rebel strand of hair escaped her severe hairstyle, floating down to graze her cheek. And of course that made him wonder why she always shellacked her hair into place when there was at least part of it that didn't want to conform to its mistress's will.

The hank of hair caught his gaze and he couldn't stop thinking about what her hair might look like down. Better yet, what it might look like with his fingers shoved through it.

And that was the tipping point. He wanted to touch.

He reached out to sweep the strand from her cheek. But she jerked backward before his fingers connected, moving out of reach. Her hand slipped from his and the softening vibe between them shattered.

"I'm sorry," he muttered, though he wasn't quite

sure what he was apologizing for. "You had this piece of hair—"

"No, I'm sorry," she cut in, more color rushing into her face. "That was uncalled for."

"It's fine. We're not at the place where we can act like a couple yet. We only got married yesterday."

"But we are married."

She looked so miserable that he almost reached out again, but he caught himself this time. She didn't want him touching her. That much was obvious. "Yes. Are you regretting that?"

"No!" A horrified expression replaced the embarrassment of a moment ago. "I'm just... I told you I don't date, and you surprised me. Not that you can't—I mean, I'm not *that* much of a... Sorry. I'm rambling."

Shutting her eyes, she waited about four beats, as if collecting herself, and then opened them. He gave her that time because he was busy reading her nonverbal signals. Her arms had stolen around her midsection defensively, though he couldn't imagine a scenario in which she'd have to be defensive. Was she afraid of him? Or did she object to him personally in some way?

His first instinct was to blaze through this problem, the way he would any challenge that came across his desk.

But this was not a thorny personnel problem with Flying Squirrel or an accounting discrepancy that someone needed to explain. It was Tilda. He respected her. He'd *married* her. Warren forced his shoulders to relax and bit back the first phrase that had sprung to his lips, which sounded a lot like what he'd said to Marcus. *Get over it.*

Whatever had been going on with Marcus prior to

his suicide was not something he could just get over, no matter how logical a solution that had seemed to Warren at the time. What he'd really meant was *move on*. Forget about it. Focus on something else. Whatever worked.

Marcus had needed compassion, not directives. Warren had missed that. He couldn't make that mistake again, which was why he limited his personal interactions as much as possible. Distance was his friend for a lot of reasons. But he needed Tilda for his project. And maybe to assuage the sudden protective instinct that had sprung up out of nowhere. Tilda was his wife and it was not okay that she was so skittish around him. He had to figure out how to change things between them—without his CEO hat on—or his project would go down in flames.

The terrace had been a bad idea.

Or rather, the terrace was fine. It was Tilda who was the problem. What had she been thinking when she'd agreed to a glass of wine and getting cozy with Warren? Well, that was no mystery. She'd assumed he'd never breach that physical distance between them, that the natural reserve he'd always exhibited would be her saving grace. Big mistake.

The hand-holding had been one thing. That, he'd allowed her to ease into, which was precisely what she hadn't known she'd need. Though it had been entirely unwitting on his part, she suspected. But then he'd lifted his hand toward her face. She hadn't been fully prepared for it and now he was looking at her with a mixture of hesitancy and concern. Because he thought she was slightly crazy, no doubt.

Who flinched just because a man's hand had come toward her face?

Only the victim of previous abuse. And unless she wanted to start explaining that to him—which she'd rather not do—she had to pull it together. A woman who could handle a project the size of Flying Squirrel did not flinch. For any reason.

"I'm sorry," she repeated a little more strongly. "It's a difficult transition from employee to wife."

His expression softened. "I'm not making it any easier, either."

"You absolutely are." Oh, God, now he thought that he was the problem. None of this was his fault. "You've been nothing but kind to me. Extremely patient."

"Really?" he asked with a wry quirk of his lips. "Because from my side of the table, it seemed like I was rushing you."

This was a disaster. She'd thoroughly enjoyed the idea of Warren showing her his garden. It was sweet. Low-key. Exactly the kind of thing she'd have loved if it had been the tail end of a real date. For a moment, she'd let herself pretend that was what was happening. That he'd closed the distance between them because he'd correctly perceived that she needed to practice touching. There wasn't anything threatening about it, yet her instincts had triggered automatically.

That was not who she wanted to be. Not around Warren. Rationally, she knew she could trust him. They'd been acquainted for two months. He'd been more than fair in their agreement. What more incentive did she need to use this opportunity to get over her fear?

"You're not rushing me," she said. "This is important. We have to work together and we have to convince people that we're married for reasons that have nothing to do with green cards. If anything, we're taking it too slow."

Surprise filtered through Warren's expression. "Would you like another glass of wine, then?"

"Yes," she told him decisively and held out her glass. "Let's start over. Tell me a funny story from your childhood."

That was the kind of thing that seemed like a good segue. Finally, she felt a little more in control and her lungs expanded as Warren filled her glass, then his, with the remainder of the wine. This, she could do. If she knew what to expect, could guide the conversation, then she'd be okay.

Warren obliged, recounting a time when his brother had let Warren cut his hair. By the time he got to the part where their mother had caught Warren with the shears and tufts of Thomas's hair under his bed, her smile was genuine. He let one of his own bloom and it did funny things to her stomach. Or perhaps that was the wine.

"It sounds like you were a mischievous little boy," she said.

"No," he corrected with a laugh. "I was always in charge. If I wanted to do something, I did it. That's how I ended up as the CEO. It was the only job I was interested in."

"I didn't think work talk was allowed," she teased and bumped him with her elbow. See, she could initiate contact without freaking out.

"That's not work talk. It's personal. I like getting what I want."

The way he was watching her lent an undertone to the statement that made her shiver. In a good way. It was a little decadent and a lot delicious. What would happen if she stopped being such a weirdo about her boundaries and let her professional veneer drop away? Warren wouldn't fire her. He certainly wasn't going to hurt her.

She was still in control. Which meant she got to guide where things went next.

"Curious," she murmured. "What were you going to do with my hair?"

His gaze shifted to the strand that was still grazing her cheekbone. That errant lock had set them off on the wrong track earlier. Maybe now it could get them on an entirely different track. One that would get them over this hump that caused them to be so cautious with each other.

"Tuck it back," he said simply. "I should have just mentioned it."

The floodlights from the garden played over them as they stood at the railing. A few stars had started to twinkle in the sky but she couldn't seem to take her eyes off his face. They were in the middle of a vibrant city, but here on this terrace, they were insulated from everything else—bad, good or otherwise—and it was easy to pretend they were the only two people in the world.

"You commented on that in the car. After the wedding. Is it bothering you?"

"Yes," he admitted, surprising her. "You're normally so perfectly put together. It's like this little piece of you is begging to be free of the confines you've imposed. It's extremely distracting."

That was a fair assessment of her entire personality. Intrigued that he'd picked up on that, she decided to press it. "I thought you liked it. Remember? You told me not to fix it last time."

"It's distracting because it makes me wonder what you look like with your hair down," he responded huskily.

Somehow, they'd drifted a little closer together. He'd picked up on the shifting vibe and had angled his body toward her. Not too close, because he wasn't an idiot. Her minor freak-out earlier had cost them a degree of ease she wanted to recapture.

"Wearing my hair up is professional," she informed him. "Since we've banned all work talk, maybe that should go, as well."

Before she lost her nerve, she reached up and pulled the clip loose from the twist at the back of her head. As she tucked it in her pocket, her hair cascaded down her back, with a bit of volume for once because it had dried in the chignon.

Warren made a noise low in his chest and it sounded far hungrier than she would have supposed would be appropriate for a simple thing like taking down her hair. She shook it out, her scalp crying in relief. Releasing her hairstyle was one of the highlights of her day, usually, and doing it in front of Warren added a measure of intimacy that she hadn't expected. It was like he was watching her undress at the end of the night, and a hum of expectation started up in her core.

It had been a very long time since a man had looked at her with an edge. The way Warren was looking at her now.

"As your boss, I must insist you continue to wear your hair up at the office." With that odd pronouncement, he plucked her wineglass from her hand and set it, along with his own, on a table behind him then returned to her side. "As your husband, I hereby ban that twisted-up hairstyle from crossing the threshold."

"What are you saying, that the moment I enter the house I should take my hair down?"

"Or I'll do it for you." The temperature of the sultry evening rose a few degrees as Warren's gaze played over her face. "You should really never wear it up. But, selfishly, I want to keep this secret all to myself."

The heat that prickled across her cheeks then should have spread clear down to her neck, but she'd been the one to introduce this new dynamic. Boldly. It was getting a far bigger response than she'd expected. Were they practicing for a green-card interview or was this something else?

More important, what did she want it to be?

"It's not really a secret," she said inanely.

The real secret was beneath her clothes and she couldn't stop imagining what might happen if he'd made a random comment about how distracting her suit was. His expression might heat with something entirely different if she started shedding clothes. The scraps of lingerie left almost nothing of her body covered. And that's why they were hidden.

She had very little practice at flirting and even less practice at taking control in intimate situations—or, at least, not successfully. Bryan had chipped away at her confidence every time he called her those horrible names whenever she was aggressive. Professionally, she knew her strengths, could easily pivot between situations with confidence. This was way out of her depth and she had to stay in control or panic would overwhelm her.

"Oh, yes, it's a huge secret," he countered, his voice low. "With your hair down, you transform from an attractive professional woman into a complete temptress."

That thrilled through her to the core, easily eclipsing the panic. No one had ever said anything like that to her before. "What could I tempt you into doing?"

"Anything."

The moment stretched out to the point of snapping, but still he didn't shift his gaze from her. Boldly, she stared back, hardly recognizing herself in this scenario. A man had invited her to his private terrace and plied her with wine, setting the scene for a seduction that she was actively participating in.

And yet, he was holding back. She could feel it. He didn't want to step over her boundaries, a detail she appreciated far more than he could ever know. They'd mapped out an in-name-only marriage that had seemed simple on the surface. That was before she'd known all this heat would spring up between them. Before she'd known she'd want to see where things might lead.

This was her seduction to move forward. Warren wasn't Bryan. Logically, she knew this was different. He'd flat out said she could do the tempting and he'd follow her into whatever she laid out. It was heady and powerful, and she couldn't stop marveling at the amazing qualities of the man she'd married.

"Warren," she murmured. "I mean this in all sincerity. You're the most patient man I've ever met. Too patient. I feel a distinct need to have my hair tucked back."

His expression slipped, falling into a category more easily defined as carnal. It was delicious as he slowly reached out to slide one hand through the loose strands at her nape, and then she had a whole different problem as his touch electrified her skin, zinging through her core with heat that weakened her knees.

He picked up on that, too, easing his other hand to her waist and pulling her into his body. It was slow and sensuous and exactly what she needed in order to acclimate before things ratcheted up a notch higher.

And that happened quickly. Before she realized it, his arm had stolen around her, engulfing her in an embrace that aligned their bodies. He was hard in all the right places and all those places were teasing hers, particularly the ones covered by shockingly small scraps of silk. The fabric toyed with her breasts in combination with the rub of his body and it was the most turned-on she'd been in a very long while.

Without taking his gaze off her face, he brushed her hair back behind her ear, his thumb lingering far longer than the simple act required. It turned into a caress and her breath caught as she read the intention in his eyes. He wanted to kiss her. But wouldn't unless she gave him the all clear.

"Is this part of the green-card interview?" she asked breathlessly as her lungs caught up with the rest of her body, clueing in that something momentous was going on here.

"No. This is because your hair is driving me mad," he murmured, shoving his hand deeper into the recesses of the mass, his touch sensitizing the back of her head beyond anything she'd ever imagined. "If you like, I can tell the immigration department that."

"That's okay. We'll count it as part of the secret."

And now she and Warren had secrets. That, more than anything, solidified them as a couple. The smile her comment put on his face rushed through her with heat, enlivening her blood.

"As secrets go, I like this one."

"It's pretty tame," she countered with a small wrinkle of her nose. "Perhaps we should add a few more. Just to keep the authenticity factor."

His brows lifted. "I can't find anything wrong with that. Though now I'm insanely curious what might count as a non-tame secret in your world."

"You should kiss me, then, and find out."

To his credit, he didn't blink, just leaned down and laid his lips on hers in a cautious kiss that had none of the heat she'd envisioned when she'd made such a bold statement. Her fault. He was still feeling her out, exhibiting incredible patience that nearly made her weep with gratitude. And that was the sole reason she could twist her fingers into the soft material of his T-shirt and yank.

Their bodies slammed together and, instantly, the kiss intensified. Warren groaned, his fingers nipping into her neck as he angled her head, his tongue sliding into her mouth. The first demanding lick of it between her lips electrified her and she opened automatically, drawing him in, welcoming his mastery over her man-starved senses. But she wasn't capable of letting him have complete control and switched the angle herself, dragging him along as she deepened the contact, sliding her hands up his back to acquaint her fingertips with the spread of muscles.

That galvanized him, her enthusiasm seeming to act as permission for Warren to let go. He spun her, backing her against the railing and shoving a hard thigh between her legs to rub at the tight, sensitized spot that was already enflamed. Heat erupted in her core, shamelessly flinging her into a miasma of sensuality.

His hands roved up and down her body as he kissed her and the railing bit into her back. His erection, so prominently pressing against her pelvis, awoke something primal inside her and her back arched, raising her breasts higher against his torso. He took that as invitation, sliding a hand beneath her suit jacket and blouse to cup her bare waist.

The shock of his fingertips against her flesh tore something open inside, and all of the things she tried to keep under wraps spilled out. Desire, longing, carnal needs—they all welled up, drenching her with a flood of damp heat, engulfing her so fast that in that moment, if he'd stripped her, she would have demanded he take her right there on the terrace, hands gripping the railing as he drilled into her from behind.

That was enough to jolt her into pulling away. The kiss ended abruptly. Warren took one look at her face and stepped back, running a hand through his hair with something akin to confusion. Of course he didn't know what to think—she'd been into it and then she wasn't.

"Did I overstep?" he asked cautiously.

Her lips stung as she stared at him. How was she supposed to explain that she'd forgotten for a moment that she couldn't do normal? She was wanton and shameless, and when she let a man find out how truly wicked she could be, he changed, morphing into something monstrous.

She shook her head. “I’m sorry.”

And then she fled before he could ask any questions, or God forbid, kiss her again.

Five

Warren prowled around his bedroom until one in the morning, far longer than he should have before giving up the idea of sleep. Stalking to his study, he logged on to his PC and pretended he had the capacity to focus on Flying Squirrel, when in reality, every bit of his mind was on the woman he'd married.

She was, hands down, the hottest kisser he'd ever met.

Who could have seen that coming? Not him. And he'd imagined her in every dirty scenario his liberal imagination could spin up. But he'd never expected her to *actually* give his fantasies a run for their money.

Ms. Straitlaced Suits knew her way around some tongue action. It was killing him that he'd used that as an excuse to take it up about twelve notches, only to be shut down. And he couldn't quite work out why. She'd been like molten lava in his hands and then *poof.*

Turned into an ice cube instantly. It was almost fascinating how quickly she'd shut herself back behind her reserve, or it would have been if it had happened to someone else.

As it stood, he was the one it had happened to and he was not happy about it. Especially given that he'd seen genuine distress in the depths of her gaze when she backed away from him. There was something going on with her that he was just not getting, and she wasn't planning to be forthcoming about it, either.

Clearly he was going to have to figure it out on his own.

Because he couldn't help himself, he did a quick search on Tilda Barrett and found several mentions of her in relation to campaigns she'd done for her former employers, including the one she'd done for Kim Electronics. Huh. There she was, looking much the same in a staid suit, standing next to a man the picture identified as Craig Von, the same ass who had screwed up Tilda's visa.

Obviously she'd been wearing boring suits since puberty. In his head, she wore red dresses with plunging necklines. After kissing her on the terrace, he was of the opinion that the red dress fit her better. She didn't seem to be of the same mind, nor did she give the impression she had any intention of showing off her hot kissing skills again—not with him, anyway.

His mood went from bad to worse when he couldn't find anything online about Tilda that told him who she was. They'd had two stilted personal conversations and one wet dream of a kiss. And all that had done was whet his appetite to get under those suits and see what else Tilda was hiding.

The next morning, he didn't see Tilda at all. As far as he knew, she'd never left her room. Avoiding him? That was crap. Except, he didn't own her, and as long as she showed up for work on Monday, he had little call to barge into her room demanding to know what was so horrible about kissing him that she felt compelled to turn herself into a prisoner in his home.

Well, clearly the kissing part was the problem. *Oops. Married a man I'm not attracted to and now we're stuck together until I get my visa.*

By midday, he'd started to grow concerned when she still hadn't emerged. What, she wasn't going to eat? He tracked down his housekeeper and learned that Tilda had asked to have meals delivered to her room. Mollified that she at least wasn't going to starve herself on his account, he removed his presence from the house so she could have some peace.

The warehouse staff was not pleased to see him on a Sunday, and without the buffer of Thomas, they got the full brunt of Warren. Usually he visited the distribution center with the chief operating officer because, technically, this part of the business fell under Thomas's umbrella. His brother genuinely liked the people who worked for him and he did a great job managing the daily ins and outs of the minutiae required to get pick-me-ups into the hands of customers. But Thomas reported to Warren, so the staff also technically reported to him. Much to their chagrin. And Thomas was on vacation.

The warehouse manager, a solid Midwesterner named Bob Page, scurried along behind him as Warren barked out questions. "Have you made the changes to the inventory locator software?"

Page nodded. “Last week.”

The man wasn’t scurrying fast enough; he barely kept pace with Warren as they rounded the corner to the main section of the warehouse where the rows and rows of canned drinks sat waiting to be loaded onto eighteen-wheelers. “Thomas gave you schematics on the new layout of the pallets. Done?”

“Almost.”

“Doesn’t count. By the end of the day.” Surely there was something else he could tear apart. “How are contract negotiations going with Chuahan?”

“I…haven’t been updated,” Page admitted.

What he meant was, he hadn’t bothered to ask anyone in Legal about the incredibly important contracts Flying Squirrel had with their main equipment manufacturer. If they didn’t have pallet loaders, forklifts and other various machinery in top shape, distribution would grind to a halt. “Get updated.”

“It’s Sunday,” the beleaguered man pointed out. “Legal isn’t in the office.”

“We are. They should be, too.” Though odds were good no one else working on a Sunday was doing it for the same reason Warren was—to avoid putting undue pressure on the woman he’d married who regretted kissing him on the terrace last night.

Though she had asked him to. That’s what was sticking in his craw as he blasted through a few more areas of the distribution center. By the time he left the warehouse, there was little that had escaped his fine-tooth comb and he’d endeared himself to no one.

Fine. People weren’t his forte and he’d definitely earned his reputation for being remote with the staff.

If they didn't like it, they could find someplace else to work.

When he got home at seven, the house had an empty quality that he'd never noticed before. It was filled with staff, but they usually stayed invisible, as he preferred. But there was a distinct lack of Tilda.

What the hell was wrong with him? She'd only moved in the day before and already he found himself looking for her, wondering why she wasn't using the solarium to read a book or lounging around the pool.

He ate dinner alone and answered emails on his phone. Same as he did most nights and had for a very long time. It was teeth-numbingly boring all at once.

Was it so bad to be thinking that companionship could be a benefit of having a wife under his roof? Sure, there was the utilitarian purpose. He'd already filed the forms required to petition for a green card for his alien family member, a phrase that still made him smile, and now they were just playing the waiting game until it was approved. Then she'd file for her green card. But, in the meantime, they both lived here, and he was insanely curious about the woman he'd married. Also, he was perhaps still a little crushed about the way she'd backed off last night.

Surely he could do better. Take it a little slower. If she'd just make an appearance.

Nada. At nine o'clock, he was back in his bedroom staring at his Louis Moinet Magistralis. After all, what good was it to have such a precise, gorgeous wristwatch if it wasn't to mark each painful second of the day as it crawled by?

As he stormed through the bathroom door to shower, he found his wife. Tilda whirled. All the blood drained from his head as the sight of her in sheer white lace axed through his gut. Instructions spurted through his consciousness. *Abort. Huge mistake. Get out.* He couldn't move.

Tilda snatched a robe from the counter and slung it over her shoulders, fumbling with the belt, and that's when he slammed his lids closed. Didn't help. The vision of her killer body decked out in *sheer white lace* had been seared into his mind.

And it wasn't the virginal kind, either. The cups of the bra had scarcely covered her nipples, which mattered hardly at all since the lace had been mostly transparent, begging for a man's tongue to taste her through it. Little scraps of lace V'd down between her thighs, held in place by three silken cords over each hip and, yeah, he'd had *plenty* of time to note it was a thong. He'd gotten only a glimpse of one bare butt cheek, but it was enough to know that she had a high, rounded rear that would fit into the hollow of his groin perfectly as he ground into her from behind.

His whole body strained to do exactly that, and he was so hard he couldn't drag enough oxygen into his lungs.

"Sorry," he mumbled, eyes still closed as he felt around for the vanity.

He gripped the marble with one hand, mostly to keep himself off the floor, because his knees were in very real danger of collapsing beneath him. All the blood that should be feeding his muscles was currently coiled up in his groin, poised to strike. Hell, maybe he should just let his knees hit the floor, but it was a toss-up whether he'd end up groveling for forgiveness or begging for her to slide that robe off so he could worship that lingerie set the way it deserved.

"What are you doing?" Tilda squeaked out. "You shouldn't be in here."

"I know. I'm sorry," he muttered again. "The door wasn't locked," he protested weakly. Stupid. That's what he should have led with. *I'm sorry. By the way, what the hell kind of lingerie is that for a woman who wears boring gray suits every day?*

Better question—*who are you wearing it for?*

"I thought I did lock it," Tilda shot back. "You have these fancy tumblers that don't click when they're turned so I thought it had engaged. We've both learned otherwise."

Her accent had deepened with her distress and that was not helping matters because, God, was it sexy. Coupled with the secrets he'd learned about her—*hot kisser* being first and foremost in his mind right after *hot lingerie wearer*—he was about to come apart.

"Are you...covered?" he rasped, terrified that if the answer was no, he'd cop another peek. He squeezed his eyes shut so hard that sparks exploded against the dark of his eyelids. "I'm not sure I can edge out of here blind."

"You can open your eyes."

He did. She'd burrowed so far down into the robe that her face was half covered by the lapels, and somehow she'd managed to get her hair mostly swept up into her trademark twist, but bits of it were falling down into her face, which was nearly as hot as when her hair was down.

Frankly, it wouldn't matter if she cut armholes in a

potato sack and wore a bird's nest as a hat. Everything about her was a turn-on now.

"So, the problem is that I can't unring this bell," he muttered and, no, he should not have spoken aloud. He should have been exiting stage left and ordering diamond earrings that doubled as an apology to his wife. Instead, he was standing there staring at her like an imbecile.

"Sorry?"

Warren shook his head and was a half second from spinning on his heel to flee the torture chamber his bathroom had become when he had a flashback to last night. Tilda had been the one doing the fleeing then—*after* asking him to kiss her. As a result, he'd spent the day in a crappy mood, and there was too much unsaid.

His wife was a fascinating, maddening mix of temptress and puritan, and he wanted to know which one was the real Tilda Barrett.

"We're dancing around some things, you and I. And we need to settle them." Her eyes went wide and, again, there was the flash of distress that he'd noted last night. His pulse stuttered. "Please. I just want to have an honest conversation with you, but not like this. Get dressed and meet me in the solarium."

Then he left.

Tilda spent a solid ten minutes after Warren vacated the bathroom getting her lungs working again. He'd been so close and she'd been so aware of how little she had on under the robe—and so very aware that he *knew*.

Her panic was only matched by the level of wanton heat that the whole scene had generated. If only she could just stop being such a freak long enough to have a simple physical reaction to a gorgeous man who kissed like a dream, life would be a lot easier. And better. But it wasn't like she could snap her fingers and change or she would have stuck around on that terrace last night instead of scrabbling away as fast as her scaredy-cat legs could carry her.

And now Warren wanted to have a little chat, did he? Because he'd figured out that she wasn't being on the square about her demure suits, most likely. He expected her to answer for her deception. Now what was she going to do? If he was angry enough, he'd fire her for being a liar and send her back to Melbourne, wouldn't he?

Nothing to be done about it now. The cat was out of the bag and, by God, she was wholly sick of sticking her natural personality under wraps. He'd said he wanted a candid conversation; maybe it was time to take him at his word, whether he knew what he was asking for or not.

As such, there was no way she was putting on a suit to talk about why she wore atrocious suits. Tilda slipped into a pair of jeans and a T-shirt, one of two sets she owned, tried not to think too hard about what a horrifically bad idea it was to have kept on the lacy white bra and panties under her clothes, then strode to the solarium before she lost her nerve.

Too late. The second she spied Warren sitting in one of the wicker chairs, staring out over the pool through the glass walls, everything inside started quivering. He held her life in his hands and she'd thoroughly messed up, first by kissing him and second by not figuring out the locks to the bathroom better.

When a competent woman had secrets, she didn't screw up. This was all on her and she needed to fix it.

Her bare feet squeaked on the hardwood floor and Warren's gaze flicked to her, darkening with something she could only misinterpret if she'd arrived in the solarium blindfolded. Maybe not even then. The awareness that had permeated the bathroom had followed them to the solarium, not at all lessened by the fact that she'd traded her easily untied robe for jeans and a T-shirt.

"I didn't know you owned any clothes that aren't brown or gray," he commented, his voice deep with a color that had only recently become a thing.

She liked it when he let her see that she affected him. It bolstered her confidence in a way nothing else could have in that moment. "Surprise."

"Yeah, there's a lot of that going around," he said wryly. "Which is why I shouldn't be so shocked that you actually showed up after avoiding me all day and then receiving an unwelcome guest in a place that should have been sacred."

There was a half second when she considered lying, or at least downplaying what he'd already guessed, but in the spirit of the evening's apparent theme, she surprised herself by nodding. "Me, too. I didn't know what to say after leading you on, so it seemed easier to stay away from you."

His brows lifted but he schooled his expression quickly. "You didn't lead me on. I went too far with that kiss and you have every right to call a halt to something that was making you uncomfortable."

That was so much the opposite of what she'd expected him to say that she blinked.

"But I asked you to kiss me." And oh, God, had she wanted him to.

"I don't care if you asked me to strip you naked and put my tongue between your legs. You're allowed to say stop at any time. I will always honor that."

Her eyelids fluttered shut as she internalized the absurdity of a notion like asking him to *stop* if he was between her legs pleasuring her with that wicked tongue. Uncomfortable and achy all over again, she sank into one of the seats and crossed her arms in hopes that he couldn't, in fact, see how hard and pointy her nipples were through the sheer bra and thin T-shirt.

"Thank you for that," she said and, yes, she meant for both the carnal image he'd put into her head and his promise. What else was she supposed to say at this point? Might as well get this crucifixion over with. "You wanted to talk."

"How are you?" he asked out of the blue, instead diving right into a litany of her sins. His open gaze roved over her face and held nothing of the censure she'd been expecting. "I...missed you today."

"You, um...what?" Her heart tumbled over itself in an effort to beat and swoon at the same time. Except she shouldn't be swooning over pretty, bewildering words.

"Honest conversation," he reminded her somewhat ruefully, which was also unexpected. "I wasn't kidding about being straight with you."

Yeah, apparently not. "I was under the impression the honesty you were after was mine."

"Why would you think that?"

His brows scrunched together in confusion and it was a testament to her utter befuddlement that she was watching his nuances so carefully. This was where things would take an ugly turn, when she wasn't paying attention. When she let her guard down. Which was why she needed to stay in control of the conversation and not let it get away from her into subjects better left out of the mix.

"Because you ordered me to appear straight away after you saw my underwear. You must feel deceived."

"That's..." He shook his head. Hard. "No, I didn't order you. I said please. It was a request. I'm screwing this up."

That's when he did the most surprising thing of all. He knelt by her chair and took one of her hands into his, holding it against his thigh gently as his dark gaze latched onto hers, thoroughly capturing her. It should have been easy to break away if she wanted to. But she didn't want to, all at once. The sheer beauty of so much masculinity at her feet, particularly when the most commanding man she'd ever met was encased inside, overwhelmed her.

Speechless, she stared at him as he swept her into his orbit without moving at all.

"Tilda, the honesty that needs to be happening is on my side. The marriage was one hundred percent conceived with the intent of keeping you in the country. I want you to believe that. But I was...attracted to you before that."

He paused to let that bombshell sink in, and when it had reached optimal depth, that's when he detonated it.

"Now that I've kissed you," he continued, his voice dropping a few smoky degrees, "and seen exactly what I'm missing out on under your clothes, I'm afraid I can't go back to thinking of you as only an employee. It's impossible. I'm sorry."

"You're, um…what? Did you just apologize?"

She was the one who should be apologizing, and he hadn't even gotten to the part where it was disingenuous of her to pretend to be a staid matronly type while hiding centerfold wantonness underneath. Bryan had made it clear how men felt about a woman who wanted to express her sexuality. At odd times, in her head, she still heard the names he'd called her.

"I did. And I'll do it as many more times as I need to in order to get you comfortable with the idea that I can't unsee you in that lingerie you were wearing earlier. If I'm being completely honest, which is the goal here, I don't want to forget. You're an amazingly beautiful woman," he murmured, and his grip on her hand tightened. "I can't help the fact that I want to kiss you again, but I totally understand that you don't feel quite the same way about it. I'm telling you it's okay. I'll back off."

Speechless—again—she worked her throat, somehow managing to swallow several times in a row, a minor miracle since her mouth had turned into a desert. What a patient, saintly man she'd married, speaking of deceptions. He'd sold himself as remote, a banger of a professional. A CEO who brooked no nonsense—look how quickly he'd dispatched Craig and solved her problem in one shot.

This sweetness she had no idea what to do with. Other than return a bit of the honesty that seemed to be what he was looking for.

"Warren, I—" Wow, this was not the conversation she'd prepped for, and when she wasn't in her element, the words weren't so forthcoming. The fact that he wasn't pressing her about her suits was throwing her off. "Trust me when I say my hesitation is not you, it's me."

"That's what they all say," he said with a bit of a smile that coaxed one from her, as well. "It's fine if you're not attracted to me in return. This is supposed to be a green-card marriage and I will keep it that way despite my earlier statements."

"Not attra—" She choked on that so hard that she coughed, sputtering around the rest of the syllables until her throat cleared. "That's patently ridiculous. Please, sit in your chair."

She couldn't think with him crouched at her feet like Romeo come to court her. Romance wasn't a part of her world, nor could it be, no matter how much she yearned to have that between her and Warren.

It wasn't happening. And he needed to understand why.

When he'd taken his seat, she dragged air into her lungs and watched him as she launched into the short version of how she'd met Bryan. To his credit, he listened without interrupting or asking what in the blazes any of this had to do with him.

She'd get there. "Our relationship was fantastic, at first. He showered me with gifts and compliments. I was so in love. After two months of dating, he asked me to move in with him because he couldn't stand the thought of being apart. It was too soon, but I walked into that willingly."

That was the part she couldn't forgive herself for. She'd had reservations but swept them aside for the romance of a man being so caught up in her that he couldn't live without her.

The changes had been small, at first. He'd murmured that he loved her so much that a thing like passwords shouldn't come between them and given her his. Of course she'd reciprocated, and then at odd times her phone wasn't where she'd left it. Once she'd gone into her laptop's browser history to find the website where she'd seen a pair of shoes she'd liked and noted several visits to her favorite links that had occurred the day before, when she'd been out to lunch with her mother.

Bryan had been checking up on her, she explained to Warren, and when she confronted him about it, he got angry. Demanded to know what she was accusing him of and then got upset that she didn't trust him. That was the beginning of the downward spiral that had gotten uglier, but she'd gone along because he always turned it back on her.

"Everything that happened was my fault in some way," she said quietly. "Even when he hit me."

And that was when her voice broke. She'd gotten through most of it pretty well, reciting the facts by rote as if they'd happened to someone else, and in some ways, they had. She wasn't that naive anymore, nor did she trust so easily. She was taking steps to become a permanent resident of the United States. If she could, she'd give up every bit of her Australian blood and embrace the safety she'd found here.

"He hit you?" Warren's voice had gone tight. "On purpose?"

She nodded and told him the unvarnished truth. "It was in a fit of rage because he'd found out that I went to a party for work that I hadn't told him about. I shouldn't have gone, but Craig strongly encouraged me to make nice with the senior partners if I wanted to get better assignments."

"You should have called the police is what you should have done." Warren's hands had clenched into his lap but he uncurled them and gripped the armrests of his wicker chair. "Please tell me he's in jail."

"No." That would have been too poetic. "Bryan is a police officer. Who would have come to arrest him? His cronies? He bragged to me once that he could have his record completely expunged if I so much as made a single complaint to the police force. I moved out of the house we shared after the second time he hit me and hid out at my mother's house. That's when he got really bad. He was so angry, he used detective grade equipment to stalk me. Threatened me. Followed me around and scared my mother."

"No wonder you're so skittish sometimes," Warren muttered. "I owe you a whole lot more apologies, then. I'm sorry if I pressured you in any way. Please don't take what I told you earlier as any sort of demand on you. I need you at Flying Squirrel. If you quit, the campaign will never be the same."

Why in the world would she quit the best job that she'd ever had? "I have no intention of quitting. This is my explanation for why I bolted from the terrace. Why I avoided you all day. I don't do normal interactions with men very well. This is my apology."

"Tilda..." He shut his eyes and sighed. "This is a lot for me to process."

"I know." This marriage of convenience had been so perfect for someone like her who needed to fade into the background. If only she hadn't asked Warren to kiss her, she might have kept up the facade. "I'm sorry if I've disappointed you or led you on or gave you false hope. I'm kind of a mess, so keeping things professional is best."

It was better this way. She'd confessed her shame and it was oddly cathartic. Oddly as if she'd gained a confidante in Warren. He'd go back to treating her with the same reserve he'd exhibited thus far, never barge in on her in the bathroom again and she'd continue to feel safe and in control.

His eyes flew open and the calm, detached CEO had fully vanished. Her breath caught. He was nothing less than fierce and magnificent as he stood, towering over her.

"I'm not disappointed," he said. "I'm a lot of things right now, but that's not one of them. Until I sort out the rest, you bet we're keeping things professional, because if nothing else, we've always worked well together. Nothing that's happened this weekend changes that."

Six

Warren wasn't a jogger. There was something so inane about running for the sake of running. It made so much more sense to have a destination if you were going to tax your body in that manner.

But after learning that he had a desire to murder another human being in cold blood—someone he'd never met and who currently resided half a world away in Australia—running was the only thing that had the slightest chance of keeping him sane. Otherwise, he might get on a plane and make good on the need to see Tilda's ex so Warren could explain a few things to the man. With his fists.

The farther he ran from his house, the easier it was to keep his hands off Tilda, too, which wasn't so much of a given after her incredibly brave recitation of the horrors that she'd left behind in Australia. His first instinct had been to reach for her, to engulf her in his embrace. As a shield, first and foremost. She'd needed protection from her ex and hadn't found it. He was more than willing to step up where the authorities had failed.

First thing tomorrow, he'd hire a fleet of private detectives to find the bastard who had struck Tilda and then Warren would make his life a living hell.

In the meantime, the Australia campaign required his undivided attention and he had about as much chance of working platonically with Tilda as he did of sprouting leaves and bark. But he was going to try because he'd told her he would. They'd both needed space while he spent the night calming down.

The next morning had dawned well before he was ready. He'd subsisted on four hours of sleep before, many times, but never after having erotic dreams starring his wife wearing white lace, a smile and nothing else. He awoke with his body on fire and his mind filled with dirty images that he had no shot at eliminating from his consciousness, not considering he'd be closeted in a small space with Tilda for a good long while.

Of course, the fates had a field day with his beleaguered senses. Tilda emerged from her bedroom at the same time he came from his and they met in the hall.

"I thought we could ride together," she said with a small smile that was but a shadow of the one she'd worn in his dream. It didn't seem to matter to his already primed body. "If that's okay."

"Sure," he croaked. "We're going to the same place."

A total and complete lie. She was going to Flying Squirrel. He was going insane. As she slid into his limo and perched on the seat next to him, he got a whiff of something fruity, but he couldn't put a name to what she smelled like. Because it couldn't be something simple like apple or cherry. Whatever it was had coupled with her natural scent to become wholly exotic and slightly spicy. Delicious. He had the wildest urge to unbutton her blouse and bury his nose in her cleavage on a mission to discover the source of the fragrance.

While he was there, he could satisfy his burning curiosity for what she had hidden under the suit today. They never had circled back around to that after she'd thrown him totally off track with the story about her ex.

Today was a new day. Plenty of opportunity to nose around, so to speak.

The torturous car ride mercifully ended a few minutes before eight when Warren's driver dropped them off near the entrance to Flying Squirrel. Warren's father had built the corporate office complex about fifteen years ago and then left his sons in charge when he retired. Invisible hands kept the grounds meticulously groomed, and a cheerful fountain gurgled in the central pool in the middle of a courtyard area shadowed by a large arch spanning the entrance. Typically, Warren didn't register much of it because he always had his phone out as he swept through the courtyard, but it seemed rude to be face down in his email with Tilda by his side, so the phone stayed in his pocket.

He should keep his phone in his pocket more often. A quiet sense of pride sneaked over him as he soaked in the landscape of the company he ran with his brother. This was his legacy, the continuation of the drinks his father had started making in his mother's kitchen during the seventies. That's why Warren worked as much as he did. He truly loved what he was doing here, contributing to the vision on his way to global domination.

Tilda was a big part of that. For now. Eventually the campaign to smear Down Under Thunder off the map would be successful and his need for Tilda's marketing expertise and project management skills would be at an end. Then what? She no longer worked for Craig. She'd have a green card, so she could stay in the US if she wanted to, but that didn't necessarily mean she'd choose to stay in Raleigh or even continue her association with Warren once their marriage was dissolved. They'd have no reason to see each other again.

Unsettled Warren shrugged that off, nodding to the people who worked for him as he and Tilda navigated the building to the executive office suite on the top floor.

"Get some coffee and meet me in my office," he told her brusquely, and she scurried to do as requested.

God, did he always sound like that? He'd never really paid attention to how he talked to his staff other than to notice whether they did as he'd directed. It was his job to run the company, not to make friends, and the more distance he employed, the easier it was to avoid complications that came with his drive to run other people's lives in much the same way he did Flying Squirrel.

That's what ultimately had happened with Marcus.

But Tilda wasn't a run-of-the-mill employee. She never had been. And when he'd admitted that he'd been attracted to her prior to the marriage, he was also acknowledging it to himself. Her response? *I'm skittish because the man in my past is an ass.*

When she bustled into his office with coffee in one hand and her tablet in the other, she wore her game face and what he'd noted earlier was the world's ugliest suit. He had the strangest urge to take her shopping. She was his wife. Wasn't it normal to want to buy her pretty dresses? She'd look spectacular in green. One of those soft fabrics that draped at the hip, a wrap-around maybe, with a neckline that crossed over her breasts into an X that marked the spot Warren could not stop obsessing over.

"I was thinking we should start with the Wheatner and Ross proposal," she said and took her typical seat on the other side of his desk.

Too far away. That was not where he wanted her, but somehow he didn't think she'd appreciate the suggestion to hop up on his desk so he could get to work stripping her out of that horrific suit. It was criminal that she hid such an amazing body behind the boxiest, most unattractive outfit imaginable.

"That's a great place to start," he told her as he rose from his seat and rounded the glass desk to sit in the matching chair next to hers.

Her slightly widened eyes tracked his progress as he settled in. "What are you doing? You always sit behind your desk."

"The view is better from here."

As he let his gaze trail down her legs, the only part of her she hadn't hidden, her cheeks pinked up. "You can't say things like that. We're at the office. We agreed to keep things professional between us."

"I agreed to no such thing. We work together. Ergo, our relationship is defined as professional by default. But that's not the extent of it and you know it. I can't unsee you in that white lace." He pointed to his temple. "It's all right here."

"It shouldn't be," she countered under her breath and shot a glance at the shut door, like the lingerie police might burst in at any moment to arrest her for daring to wear something racy under her utilitarian suit.

All at once, it dawned on him, and *wow*—he wasn't normally that slow. The only excuse he had for not realizing the source of her ups and downs was that she'd fried his brain from second one. "You like wearing things that show off your body. But he didn't like it at all, did he?"

That son of a bitch.

Fiercely, she shook her head and she might as well have had *denial* stamped all over her. "My style is my own and I'll thank you to stop questioning me about it."

"Come on, Tilda. I thought we agreed to be honest last night. I was honest with you and I thought you were reciprocating. But you only told me half the story, didn't you?" Guilt crowded into her gaze and he pounced on it. "That's why you were worried I felt deceived. Because you're lying to everyone. Every day."

"It's not lying," she whispered.

He bit back a curse, feeling as if his heart had been wrenched out of his chest to land somewhere on the floor, still beating.

Her ass of an ex had done a number on her, obviously. She'd flinched when Warren raised his hand, hid her sexuality beneath a layer of boring and then plainly told him not to bother with her because she was messed up.

To hell with that.

"Tilda, I'm sorry," he murmured, but it wasn't enough.

Last night, he'd let the conversation go because he'd genuinely feared he might put his fist through the wall since he couldn't unleash it on Tilda's ex. But she needed something else from him.

So he did what he should have done yesterday. He stood, set the computer tablet in her hands aside and pulled her into his embrace. For a half second, she hesitated, her body vibrating with a million unspoken emotions, and then, holy God...she melted into him, conforming to his contours as if she'd been fashioned from a mold with his exact dimensions.

"I'm sorry," he murmured, not even sure why he felt compelled to repeat what had become a common phrase between them, but he wanted her to know he *was* sorry—for Bryan's behavior and his own. "I don't mean to keep upsetting you."

What else would be the result of a cross-examination? He knew how to get results, not how to comfort. Look what had happened when he tried to comfort Marcus. He'd truly hated to see Marcus in so much pain, had truly wanted to help. But he'd ultimately failed.

"You're not the problem," she said, her voice muffled against his lapel because she hadn't bothered to move her face from where she'd snuggled into his shoulder, which felt a lot nicer than it should. "I am. I tried to tell you that."

"Stop. Your ex is the problem. And I'm not him."

Her amazing, sexy body unpeeled from his. "You think I don't know that?"

She stared at him, composed and blank faced. It was nearly miraculous how she morphed so easily back into the formal woman he'd first met a few months ago when she'd started on this project. Obviously she'd had a lot of practice at hiding behind her reserve.

That made two of them. And this was not one of those times when he could retreat.

"No. You don't know that. Maybe rationally, you can repeat it to yourself. But it's not sticking where it counts."

"Now you're an expert on me?"

He cocked his head. "That wasn't a denial."

"I'm here to do a job, Warren. Can we just focus on that and forget about the personal side of things?" The desperation in her tone hurt nearly as much as the tears.

He nodded, but not because he agreed that the conversation was over. His problem in a nutshell: he was as much of a liar as she was. He didn't maintain distance with people because he liked being that way. It was how he protected himself from failure.

Yes, he was pushing her. Because she was free to be as sexy as she liked around him and he'd treat it like the gift that it was. She needed to *feel* sexy and have a bone-deep understanding that it was okay to be as demonstrative with it as she wished. She needed to know that she was desired, but at the same time, that she could kiss a man and back off without retaliation. Bottom line, she needed Warren to undo all the damage the bastard had done to her.

He'd failed Marcus, but he couldn't fail Tilda. She was his wife. Not in all the ways that counted, but that didn't seem to matter to his bleeding heart, which was still somewhere on the ground.

Tilda was his do-over.

Warren had shut up about her sexy underwear, thank God, but the overwhelming vibe of awareness in the room never faded. By lunchtime, Tilda was a wreck.

This was so far from the professional veneer she'd worked hard to maintain. What had possessed her to spill all her secrets to Warren? She could have left it alone, appeared before him last night in the solarium with some made-up explanation about her lingerie set and gone on. But no. She'd had to blab about Bryan and give Warren enough ammunition to figure out that her ex had stripped away her confidence when it came to her interactions with men.

Easier to not engage. Which she'd tried to do by avoiding him, only for him to yank her back into his presence with a flick of his wrist. She should hate how dictatorial he was about everything, but of course, she didn't. Apparently all he had to do to fix that was hug her in what should have been an awkward show of comfort and support.

Not awkward. A total turn-on. Warren was an authoritative man with a kind streak who was keeping her away from Melbourne. Her little crush on him had exploded into something she had no idea what to do with.

Warren, on the other hand, had plenty of ideas.

"Let's go to lunch," he announced at ten till noon.

"We're in the middle of crunching these numbers from Wheatner and Ross's revised proposal," she reminded him—unnecessarily, since they'd been doing it for hours. But hey—at least her voice hadn't squeaked.

The very last thing she wanted to do was go somewhere with Warren. The less he clued in that she was a quivering mass of nerves and emotion, and had been ever since he'd touched her, the better.

"They're crunched. We both knew the revisions were on target the moment we looked at them. Now we've both appeased our obsessive tendency to overanalyze and we can move on. The only thing that makes me hungrier than overanalyzing is being obsessive. Indulge me."

Against her will, she had to smile at his perfect assessment of why they'd spent an entire morning buried in a proposal she'd known by nine o'clock that they'd accept. "Fine. You pick."

Dumb, ridiculous idea. She should be spending her lunch hour getting herself under control, not having lunch with her boss in the middle of downtown Raleigh where everyone would see them.

Clearly she needed to redefine her parameters, because the moment they left the building, Warren ceased to be her boss. He held doors for her, helped her into the limo and settled into the creamy leather so close to her that it would have been awkward if he didn't sling his arm around her, so, of course, that was exactly what he did.

She braced for more discussion about stuff she'd rather not talk about, but it never came. Warren sat in the car with her as if they always cruised around town in a pseudo embrace as he pointed out various landmarks like her own personal tour guide. In all the weeks she'd been in Raleigh, she'd never once done any sightseeing. There'd never been time—one of the symptoms of being a workaholic.

When she actually relaxed, she noticed that Warren's body was warm and she didn't hate the little hum in her core that seemed her constant companion lately. How could she help it? He seemed to know by some kind of osmosis exactly what she needed and when she needed it most. It was unsettling. And wonderful.

When the car rolled to a stop—at home—she glanced at him. "I thought we were having lunch."

"We are." He pulled her from the car by the hand, but instead of guiding her inside, he took the stone walkway leading around through a wrought-iron gate and they emerged in the circular garden she'd seen from the terrace Saturday night.

Her breath caught.

Warren had obviously called ahead. A lavish picnic had been painstakingly spread out in the center of the blooms in the grassy section of the garden. "What is all this?"

"A circus," he shot back wryly. "What does it look like?"

It looked like the perfect place for Warren to pick up where he'd left off this morning, poking into things that he shouldn't while hiding her away from prying eyes. It was far more brilliant and devious than taking her to a restaurant, where they couldn't have any sort of frank conversation. Instead, he'd gone for romance. Seduction.

"It looks like a man who's playing dirty."

His eyebrows lifted. "Then my work here is done. Come. Have a glass of champagne."

At lunch? On a Monday? Baffled, she watched the CEO of a multibillion-dollar corporation pull a bottle from a bed of ice and pop the cork. He handed her a glass flute that had been blown into the shape of a delicate tulip, the stalk of the flower forming the stem.

When in Rome. She sipped the champagne because she had a feeling she'd need it. Warren clinked his glass to hers, watching her over the rim as he drank his own. And then, when her attention was fully occupied, he reached up and pulled the clip from her hair.

As it fell out of the twist and down around her shoulders, he stuck the clip in his pocket. "I'll put it back later. Still my secret."

"Warren," she squawked and choked on the word as she registered the rising electricity arcing between them.

"Shh. I'm only looking at you."

She should protest. Or something. But they were hidden from the street, encased in their own private sanctuary. Her hair brushed her nape and it was incredibly freeing. What was the harm in letting her scalp breathe for a while?

When Warren led her to the heavy canvas spread across the grass, she found out.

Instead of focusing on drinking his champagne, he took off his shoes and reclined on the ground, gesturing for her to join him. She followed his example and stretched out. It took less than a second for his gaze to grow heavy with dark, delicious intent.

"I love your hair," he murmured. He didn't move, but she felt his voice curling through her midsection like a dense fog. "It's such a rich color, and with that slight wave, it looks like it's alive."

"It's just hair." But there was no harm in being secretly pleased with the compliment.

"I beg to differ. 'Just hair' wouldn't do this." Before she could protest, he pressed her hand to his chest. His heartbeat galloped along at a breakneck pace, and if she didn't know better, she'd think he was as swept up in the romance of this garden lunch date as she was.

"Maybe you should lay off the caffeine," she advised. "You always drink at least two test items from the research lab every morning."

"Tilda. Don't be dense." His thumb stroked down her palm as he set aside first his champagne flute, then hers. "My out-of-control pulse is not because I had an energy drink. It's all you. You're so sexy, I can't process it sometimes."

Heat prickled through her cheeks, flooding along her hairline. Might as well sport a big neon sign that announced he'd flustered her. "Not in this outfit."

"In that outfit," he corrected and trailed a fingertip along the buttons of her tailored shirt. "Because I know what's under it. Secrets. Here, let me show you." When she started to pull away, he clamped down on her palm, holding it in place against his thundering heart. "Stay with me. Trust me. I'm just going to show you how sexy you are."

That statement was so intriguing that she didn't move. Couldn't. He fingered the top button of her shirt and slipped it free, then slid to the next one. She couldn't breathe as the intensity of the moment pushed down on her chest while his touch simultaneously lit up her center.

It was a horrible, magnificent paradox. She'd long given up feeling safe enough to be with a man again, but Warren had patiently sorted through all her barriers. Still was. But she was still half turned-on and half anxious.

The next button popped from its slot and he peeled back her blouse into a V that revealed the slightest bit of cleavage. His hum of approval vibrated against her palm and it loosened something inside her.

Without a word, he leaned over and replaced his fingers with his mouth, kissing the slice of breast he'd uncovered but going no farther than the line he'd created with her blouse. She let her fingertips nip into his chest, registering his heartbeats as a barometer of his excitement—it was nearly as good as having a mindreading device. How great a concept was *that*?

It got even better as he mouthed his way up the column of her throat and wandered along her jawline. If she moved her head a fraction, they'd be kissing. The anticipation coiled through her belly, releasing as he settled his lips at the corner of her mouth in a light, exploratory nibble that rushed through her center.

One taste wouldn't kill anyone.

She turned her head to catch him just right. The kiss brewed for a half second before becoming a reality, mouths aligned and so very hot. She moaned as his hands slid down her back, and he rolled her half beneath him. The kiss turned carnal and heavy in a flash as his leg notched between hers, riding against her skirt, which he quickly gathered up at her thigh, exposing more of her secrets than she'd expected for a Monday afternoon.

But his thigh was so delicious against her burning core as he chafed it, feeding the flames as he shifted even further, covering her with a full-body press. He was big and firm, and the feel of him should be thrilling through her. But it wasn't. Instead, it was too much.

She gasped for air as her throat closed and she couldn't speak to save her life. Her nerves frayed, sending her into a panic attack. She pushed at him weakly, knowing she had absolutely no chance of moving him unless he chose to remove himself.

Warren froze and pulled back, his gaze roving over her face. He swore and sat up, running a hand through his hair.

"I got carried away again," he mumbled, his eyes shut. "I have no excuse for not checking in with you sooner. Please forgive me."

God, this was a never-ending nightmare of a merry-go-round that she desperately wanted to exit.

"No, Warren." She crawled to him and pulled his jaw into her hands to force him to look at her. "Don't apologize. I'm the one botching this."

She couldn't stand that he thought this was in any way his fault. Couldn't stand that she had no idea how to fix the way her insides got too tight when she felt threatened. Why did she feel threatened? Who knew? It was a mystery to her; otherwise, she'd figure out how to shut it off for good.

"Do we need a...code word or something?" he asked cautiously. "Or have I already ruined things so much that you're through with all of this?"

"Nothing is ruined. You're so incredibly patient with me and I feel like a sook. But facts are facts, and I've got some issues. You shouldn't pin any hopes on this marriage becoming anything more than a way to keep me in America."

The lovely vibe between them dissolved and vanished like so much smoke from a chimney. Great. Leave it to her to be the one ruining things with her angst and back-and-forth, as if she couldn't make up her mind whether to be hot or cold. It wasn't fair to him.

Slowly, he reached out, his gaze on his fingers as he rebuttoned her shirt to the very top.

"Who said I had any hopes for our marriage? What's happening between us has nothing to do with that and everything to do with giving you a safe environment to express your sexuality. You're so much the opposite of who you pretend to be. If you get to a place where you feel free to be yourself while you're with me, then that's all I could hope for."

Oh. She blinked, but the seriousness in his expression didn't fade. He wasn't suffering from the effects of an unrequited love, which was a relief. Or, at least, it would be a relief as soon as she convinced herself of it, which was practically the same thing.

She obviously couldn't handle a relationship right now and he'd realized that. Because he was paying better attention to her emotional landmines than she was.

But that didn't stop the twist of disappointment that he wasn't falling at her feet, spouting poetry about his poor broken heart that could only be healed by her love. Silly. She didn't want that. It was just that she'd thought the surprise picnic meant something that it didn't. So it wasn't quite the romantic gesture that she'd believed, but it was, in fact, something better. A safe place. Not a magic fixer-upper love potion that wouldn't have worked anyway.

She was still the one with the biggest stake in working through her problems, and he'd given her permission to skip the guilt if she failed because Warren wasn't emotionally invested.

"I'm having a very nice time at lunch," she told Warren solemnly, which made him smile, so she considered the outing a victory all the way around.

Despite the slight hollow feeling in her stomach where the warmth of Warren had been a few moments ago.

Seven

The way things had gone down at the picnic bothered Warren for two solid days. The date had ended on exactly the right note, with zero pressure on either of them. Tilda had learned that she could be and act however she wanted around him. Wear sexy lingerie. Let her hair down. What else could he have expected out of the afternoon?

He had some work to do in the pay-attention-to-her-subtle-cues department, but mostly he'd passed the test of proving he could back off when she needed him to. He had a feeling he'd be proving that one over and over again, but that was okay. It had to be. Tilda needed slow. It wasn't the end of the world.

So, why was he still on edge?

Maybe because he wasn't sure what the next step was. He was flying a little blind here, especially given that his usual go-to mode was distance. *Out of his element* didn't begin to describe it. Where he normally buried himself in work to cope with feeling ineffective on the people side of things, the source of his frustration was front and center in his professional life—by design.

Everything was tied together, and the more time he spent with Tilda, the more she dazzled him. She assassinated items on the project's to-do list like an Australian ninja, shining at whatever task she picked up. Sometimes it was dizzying when she really got going, but that's why he'd fought for her to stay.

He needed her. Or rather, Flying Squirrel needed her. But they were slowly becoming one and the same. And, near the end of the week, he started to question whether it hadn't always been that way.

On Friday, she emerged from her bedroom with chunky strands of hair falling to her temples on each side. Deliberately. He smiled and met her in the hall, as had become their habit. One he would never have said would become so entrenched in his routine so fast. But he enjoyed riding to work with her and then riding home again afterward as they recapped the day. So far, they'd eaten dinner together every night, too.

"That might be the sexiest hairstyle I've seen on you yet," he murmured, then he indulged himself by first holding his hand up as a notice that he was about to touch her, and then doing it, sliding a finger along her jaw to turn her face to the side as he evaluated. "I like it when you experiment with ways to drive me mad."

"Is that what I'm doing?" she volleyed back saucily. “Then you probably don’t want to know what color my underwear is.”

He groaned, which only made her laugh. She’d been experimenting with her flirting, too, and—not for the first time—it had taken a naughtier bent, which he fully deserved for creating this monster. “You’re so wrong. I absolutely want to know.”

She leaned into his touch, another jerky step forward in this dance. His reward for learning that he had to tread carefully with her.

“Ice-blue silk.”

“My favorite,” he murmured, his gaze tight on her as they stared at each other.

If she’d been any other woman, he’d have segued this serendipitous moment into a kiss, but he’d blown it twice now by getting too frisky too fast. And, of course, ice blue could be any number of shades, and he’d be hard-pressed to not slip a few buttons free as he kissed her so he could see this color for himself. Which was probably a bad idea.

This was a delicate balance of push and pull, and when she stepped back, letting his hand drop from her face, he knew he’d made the right call. Biting back his disappointment, he let her go ahead of him down the stairs and spent the day imagining the hell out of Tilda spread out on his desk in her ice-blue bra and panties.

To say that the day ended up a waste of time on his part was an understatement. Tilda did all the work while his brain stayed stuck in her cleavage. Which he could not actually see.

Clinical insanity might be a blessing at this point.

Things did not improve at dinner as Tilda launched

into a discussion about a study she'd read in a trade publication about energy drinks and their positive effects on college students' ability to concentrate. Animated, Tilda talked with her hands, and every time she gestured, the collar of her shirt wrinkled an iota. His gaze strayed to it over and over, but like all his other frustrations, nothing good popped out.

Interrupting the one-sided conversation, which she seemed not to notice he'd yet to participate in, he put his fork down. "Tilda."

She paused midstream, mouth open. "I'm talking too much."

"You're not talking enough," he corrected. "About the right subjects. Why did you tell me about the color of your underwear earlier? Just so we can be clear. Was it strictly to drive me over the edge or were you inviting me to see it? Because I don't want to upset you, but I don't want to miss a signal, either."

She blinked and blinked again. "I…didn't have an agenda."

"The hell you didn't."

He reeled back his temper, which, rationally, he knew was only due to old-fashioned sexual frustration. But naming the source didn't ease it any. Only a good long session between his wife's thighs would take care of that, and at this point, he wasn't particular about the nature of the activity, only that he was about to bust something inside if they didn't move past this nebulous in-between place where they'd gotten stuck.

"Warren, I—" She rubbed at her temples. "I don't know either. I like flirting with you. I think about letting you see my underwear all the time."

"Really?" That piqued his interest in a big way. "Like you wish I'd burst in on you as you're undressing again? Because that can be arranged."

He'd clear his schedule for a week straight. All he needed was a green light.

That got a small smile. "Maybe not that. But I need...something to move the needle. I don't know what."

So she was feeling a little stuck, too. That was news, and as headlines went, he was a fan of this one. It meant she was equally frustrated. Neither was she telling him to back off. More like, "come and get me." But that hadn't worked so well for them before, which put them right back where they started—dancing around each other.

It was killing him.

And not just because he genuinely cared about getting Tilda to a better place. She was slowly coming out of her uptight shell, and the woman who was emerging could tie a man in knots.

One who would let a woman do that to him, of course. Not Warren.

"Tell me what happens. In your fantasy where I see your underwear," he prompted.

A guard snapped over her expression and Warren nearly cursed, but he kept his mouth shut because they had to do something different. Also, he was wildly curious about what she'd say.

"I wouldn't call it a fantasy—"

"I would." And he was definitely an expert at them. "If you're thinking about it, some scenario came to mind. Where are we? What's happening? Don't pull punches with me. I'm not judge and jury in the trial of Tilda's imagination. I'm just the poor guy you're teasing."

A tinge of pink swept along her skin and he really shouldn't be so pleased to see it, but odds were high the images in her head were very, very naughty given the sheer volume of color in her face, and he desperately wanted to hear what she fantasized about.

"Tell me, Tilda," he murmured, dinner completely forgotten. "You're safe with me."

"I think about coming to your room. With my robe on," she said, her voice growing steadier as she spun out the scene. "You're on the bed. Watching me. And I take off the robe, then climb—"

"Whoa. You're going way too fast." He held up a hand, thrilled his muscles still worked as the erotic images spilled through his own mind's eye. "Give me a moment to catch up."

"What, are you fantasizing about that now?" she whispered, glancing around as if someone might overhear them in the cavernous dining room that could fit a basketball team or the erection she'd given him, but not both. No way.

Holy crap. How hot was the thought of her climbing *anything* while wearing skimpy lingerie? Very.

"You bet." He hummed a little in his throat as he let that last bit play out in his imagination as she climbed *him* and straddled him with her thighs wide—wait. *She* comes to his room, *she* takes off the robe, *she* climbs onto the bed, *she's on top.*

It was all so bafflingly simple. How the hell could he have missed that she needed to be in control?

The only excuse he had was that all the blood in

his body pooled in his lap anytime he was around Tilda lately.

"Here's what we're going to do," he growled, so incredibly peeved with himself at having wasted all this time that he couldn't find the wherewithal to be civil. "You go to your room, put on the most daring thing you own under your robe and come find me. I'll be the one on the bed."

Oh, God. She was really doing this.

But not in this outfit. Tilda stripped off the black lace mesh bralette that left little to the imagination and the thong that left absolutely nothing to the imagination. It was too…dirty, or something.

Sunshine yellow satin bra and panties. Total antithesis of black naughtiness. She posed in front of the full-length mirror that comprised half a wall in the walk-in closet. Nope. Too…yellow.

Tilda changed her outfit five more times, only to end up back in the rose-colored baby doll with matching thong that she'd first selected and then discarded in favor of the black outfit. It was the only thing she owned that she'd ever imagined wearing for a man. It wasn't the slightest bit utilitarian, like a bra and panties. Those she wore every day, could reasonably argue that she was wearing them for herself.

But this outfit…the baby doll bisected her breasts, revealing a healthy slice that almost—but didn't quite—let her nipples peek over the edge. The thong dipped so low that it looked like she was naked under the flirty, floaty fabric of the top. There was no way a man could see her in this and not know she'd worn it for him.

Which was why she wasn't doing this.

What was she thinking? She *worked* with Warren. Getting this personal was a very bad idea.

Stripping off the baby doll, she threw it in the drawer and leaned on it so she couldn't open it again. She couldn't follow through. It was too big a thing, with too many pitfalls.

Except… Warren was also her husband. Not in the traditional sense, but they had a relationship beyond work. She liked him. Was attracted to him. There was nothing wrong with that. And she shouldn't have to spend so much time justifying it to herself, either.

Also, he wasn't asking her to do something hard. Just giving her the opportunity to play out her fantasy. If she didn't feel comfortable doing anything other than dropping her robe and letting him look at her, he'd be fine with that. If she asked him to have drinks on the terrace while she wore the robe and never took it off, that's exactly what would happen.

But none of that was what she *wanted.* What she wanted was to explore the things she felt when Warren looked at her like she was his next meal. *All* the things. She wanted *sex* in all its glory, with more orgasms than she could count, a man who could keep up and free rein to do whatever she wished without fear of being called names.

Maybe that's what *would* happen. She pulled the drawer open. Shut it.

Maybe that's not what would happen. Maybe Warren would be shocked by the positions she'd envisioned them in, horrified by the filth coming out of her mouth, or at best, dismayed that she wasn't the straitlaced woman she'd presented herself as.

Excuses. He already knew she was a big liar. Had called her on it. She pulled open the drawer so hard it came free from the runners and landed on the carpet. Lingerie spilled over the edge in an explosion of colorful silk and lace. As metaphors went, that one was a little too perfect. The drawer couldn't contain her secrets any better than she could.

Her phone vibrated. Warren had texted her a message: Just checking in.

He knew she was waffling. Of course he did. The man missed no tricks.

Warren: If you're not ready for this, it's okay. Remember, you're in control of everything that happens.

A sharp tug in her core filled her with something powerful. She could be in control. Warren was telling her so.

How much control? Would he do things that she asked him to?

Warren: You call the shots.

Yes was apparently the answer. It was like the man had gained the ability to read her mind in the span of an hour. Intrigued against her will, she scooped up the puddle of rose silk and slipped it over her head before she could chicken out again. She had a written guarantee that she could let this evening play out precisely the way she directed. Warren would never go back on his word. She trusted him, and that alone was huge enough to warrant forgetting about everything else for a few hours.

The robe skimmed over her bare skin as she slipped it on and belted it. The fabric was nothing special as she hadn't bought it with the intent of using it in a seduction scene. Oh, God. Was that what she was walking into?

It was if she wanted it to be. She was in charge. The tug in her core transformed into long liquid strings that yanked pieces of her free that she hadn't realized were so deeply buried.

She was really doing this.

Instead of going to Warren's room through the hallway, she ducked into the bathroom. The hallway was where she met him in the mornings to go to work. The bathroom connection between their rooms was more secret. She liked that they had secrets. Liked that they had an easy way to keep their personal and professional lives separate. It was almost poetic.

When she opened the door to Warren's bedroom, she had to pause a moment to fully appreciate the scene he'd set up for her. He was, indeed, lying on the bed, wearing nothing but a pair of boxer briefs that hugged his hips. Wow. So he was just going to be lying there mostly naked, then. As visual gifts went, that one took the cake. He was a beautifully built man, not that she'd expected anything less, but reality brought her up short with a sense of wonder.

"I see you dressed for the occasion," she said wryly to cover the fact that her pulse had just tripled.

"Why beat around the bush?" he asked with smile that did not help her pulse. At all. "Figured it was easier."

Oddly, it was perfect. She was more dressed than he was, and she suspected that the imbalance wasn't an accident. Hot did not begin to describe it. And he'd single-handedly eliminated whatever nervous tension might have sprung up.

But just the nervous tension. The rest of the tension was purely sexual as the atmosphere grew more charged the longer she drank in the nearly naked form reclining on the bed. It was nothing like the fantasy she'd had. In those, he'd always been a little shadowy because she didn't really know what he looked like under his power suits.

Now she was worried that she wouldn't be able to think of him clothed. He was sublime—still powerful, but in a much different way than he was at the office. Mouthwatering, even, strong, muscular.

He could do whatever he wanted to her and she could do nothing to stop him. Her pulse sped up and it had not been slow in the first place. Rationally, she knew she wasn't in danger, but still…

"I'm not moving from the bed unless you tell me to," he advised her. "Think of me as a marionette, if you like. Pull my strings and I do as you command."

His voice rang with the same authority it always had, creating the strangest paradox. Only Warren could pull off maintaining his masculinity while simultaneously telling her she controlled him. The liquid threads of her desire elongated as she traversed the ocean of carpet toward the bed.

"Then I want you to stay there. I'm going to take this robe off," she told him. "And when I do, I want to see how much you like what's underneath."

If it went the way she hoped, she could gauge his reactions. He couldn't surprise her.

"I'm fairly certain that was going to happen anyway." He jerked his chin at his lower half. "Goes with the territory of wearing something that has no shot of disguising how much you turn me on."

That was such a delicious point that she couldn't resist testing it out. Slowly, she untied the robe but didn't open it. Instead, she slipped off one shoulder, and then the other, holding the robe closed as she let the fabric ride her breasts.

"That's a gorgeous color on you," he said huskily as he noted the straps of her outfit. "I can't wait to see the rest of it."

She let the robe fall, unveiling the baby doll all at once. The noise he made in his throat warmed her, and he sat up but made no move to leave the bed, as promised. His gaze hungrily drifted over her, catching at all the right places as he drank in the details. His shorts gained a prominent bulge, the outline of which drew her gaze.

"This is more difficult than I thought." His voice had gone thin and hoarse. "I want to touch you so badly."

But he wasn't going to. Unless she gave him permission. His expression burned with longing—a desire he was denying himself because he'd told her he would. The control was so heady that a smile bloomed, and it was wicked.

"It so happens that I want you to touch me."

His gaze zeroed in on hers, hot, hungry, edgy. But he didn't so much as flex a muscle in her direction, exercising extreme patience and mastery of himself. She couldn't help but appreciate both.

"Give me more parameters, Tilda. Here? There? Touch you how?"

All of the above. She was still in control and he was proving it to her moment by moment. The last of her anxiety dissolved and she waltzed to the bed, pushing him back onto the mattress. She crawled up the length of his body and straddled him, settling against that bulge until it nested into her core exactly the way she wanted it.

"Put your hands on my breasts," she instructed, and when he reached up, her insides went slick with need. But not panic. There was a huge difference. Of course he could easily flip their positions, but she trusted he wasn't going to do that.

The first firm contact of his palms on the underside of her breasts felt better than anything she'd imagined. Then his thumbs flicked across her taut nipples, tugging her core so hard that she gasped. "More."

He stroked again and then reversed the position of his hands, sliding his thumbs under the fabric to touch her bare skin. "What else would you like, Tilda? My mouth?"

She nodded because speaking didn't seem to work too well as he leaned up to flick his tongue across her covered nipple, wetting the silk.

"Pull down the fabric," she murmured, and cool air kissed her aching breasts a moment later. "Suck on me."

His lips closed around one nipple and the swirl of his tongue lit her up inside. Fortunately, she had the perfect hard length to grind against, and he was right there, circling his hips to create greater friction at her core. She fell into the fire, eyes closed, sensation exploding through her body.

This was nothing like she'd expected. Having a man do exactly as she directed was far more thrilling than she would have guessed.

Warren switched to the other breast without being told, laving at her flesh so expertly that she couldn't argue that she hadn't wanted it. She did. She wanted it all. Gasping out his name, she tangled her fingers in his hair, arching her back to give him better access. His teeth scraped across her nipple so exquisitely that she felt it all the way to her toes.

Wrapping her legs around him, she urged him closer with her heels, wishing she'd had the foresight to skip the underwear. But wasn't that the benefit of having a man at her full command?

"Strip me," she told him and couldn't find a shred of embarrassment at how easily she fell into this role.

He didn't hesitate. In one second, the baby doll top hit the floor and then he eased her back onto the mattress between his legs. He watched her as he hooked the waistband of her thong and pulled it free from one leg, then the other.

"Please tell me the next thing you want me to do is spend a lot of time pleasuring you," he said, and the look on his face…pure heat and carnal intent. "Because I can't see you like this without wanting to taste you."

"Yes. That. I want that."

"I need to move you. Is that okay?"

She nodded and he slid his hands under her buttocks to maneuver her to the edge of the bed. Then he dropped to the floor on his knees between her legs, kissing her quivering thighs. Why she couldn't control the shakes, she didn't know.

"Shh. Relax," he murmured. "I'm just going to touch you."

He did exactly and only that, running his hands up her legs to her stomach. But he never tried to hold her down, never made any quick movements. It was costing him, though. She could see the restraint in the lines around his eyes. He was holding back *for her*. The effort he'd undertaken, the patience, the sheer magnitude of what he'd done—continued to do—overwhelmed her.

After an eternity of bliss that nearly made her weep, he spread her legs, opening her up. "Stop me if I do anything that bothers you."

He waited until she nodded again. And then his tongue circled her fevered center and she could do nothing but mewl. The harder he licked, the better it got, until her body was bucking against his mouth, silently begging for more. He gave it to her, somehow sensing that she didn't have the words. It was too big, too amazing, too much, too little. His fingers stroked her in places she didn't know were erogenous zones, and his tongue hit spots over and over that made her body sing.

Frenzied and feeling like her skin was going to incinerate, she babbled something but had no clue what she'd told him to do. Whatever it was must have done the trick, though, because he lapped harder and twisted his fingers through her center, splitting her apart. The orgasm tensed her whole body and she came in a rush of a release, crying out his name.

So *that's* what all the fuss was about.

He let her come down, backing off immediately to lie next to her on the bed, not touching her at all. She stared at him, her chest heaving, and wished she had something to give him. A medal. A plaque maybe.

"I've never had an orgasm that way before," she said, instead of the gush of things in her heart that sounded mushy and blubbery and not at all the kind of thing a woman said to a man she'd married for a green card.

His brows raised. "Seems like you're a natural at it, then."

She laughed. "That was all you."

"I had good instructions."

Yes. She had a knack for it. Who knew? "Am I still calling the shots?"

"Of course. If you're done, you say so and get up and leave. Or stay here and sleep in my bed, and I'll go someplace else. This is your fantasy."

None of this added up and she was insanely curious about the million-dollar question that she should have asked a long time ago. "Why? Why on earth would you do all of this?"

"What, let a gorgeous, sexy woman do a strip tease for me and then indulge myself in the extreme pleasure of watching her in the throes of an orgasm I gave her? Yeah, that is a mystery. I must be crazy to have signed up for that."

"Stop. You did it for me, not you."

"That's the secret, Tilda. It was good for both of us."

More secrets, and that one was her favorite so far. The distance between them was too much, and she inched closer, linking their hands together, which was nice. "But you're still…you know. Not done."

"Oh, no. Far from it. I can go for hours and hours still, but as discussed, this is your show to run. I'm just here for the party favors."

"Then I'm not done, either. But here's the thing." She hesitated, because how was she supposed to tell him that, while she appreciated having ultimate control, she was nowhere near experienced enough to know how to please him? And she wanted to. So much. He deserved to be treated like a king. "Can we be co-hosts of this party?"

Eight

Cohosts. The phrase shouldn't make him smile, not when everything inside ached with so much unrequited need that Warren couldn't stand to be in his own skin. Her thumb stroked over his knuckles and he'd never have said that would be a turn-on, but pretty much anything Tilda did got him hotter than July, so it shouldn't have been such a shock.

"You're going to have to help me out with what that means," he said when he thought he could speak. "Cohosts might have a totally different connotation in Australia than it does here."

"I'm doing okay," she murmured. "With you. Here. Naked. It's good. You don't have to be so…careful with me. This should be about you, too, not just me."

Understanding filtered through the sexual haze that had saturated his brain. "You mean, you're okay with it if I do some things that you didn't verbalize. That I have permission to be creative."

She nodded and something bright filled his chest. He'd done what he'd set out to do—get her comfortable with him. How fantastic. And brave. There'd been no guarantee that they'd ever get to this point, no matter what he did, and even less of a guarantee that she'd tell him so.

All at once, his throat closed as he internalized the magnitude of the gift Tilda had just handed him. Instead of telling her, it seemed appropriate to show her. It worked out well that he wanted to dive back into her, anyway, and talking wasn't high on his list of bedroom activities.

Warren took a moment to shed his briefs and Tilda watched him, her eyes bright, rewarding that decision with a sound low in her throat.

"I don't know why you ever get dressed," she muttered. "It's almost sinful to cover all that up."

The grin spreading across his face might have been a little sloppy. "I take it I meet with your approval."

"And then some. I used to think I liked you in suits. Now I'm wondering what I was thinking."

"You were thinking we had a professional relationship?" That was a dumb thing to bring up. The last thing either of them needed were reminders that they still had to work together tomorrow. But on the flip side, they did work together, so maybe it was okay to be real about the situation. "That doesn't have anything to do with what's happened here at home. We can keep them separate, right?"

"No. Absolutely not."

His heart ground to a painful halt for a half second until she continued.

"I like it when you use your boardroom voice. It's sexy."

He had to laugh at that. "You mean my boss voice?"

She wasn't the first woman to express a similar sentiment. But she was definitely the first one who had needed to be in full control.

Once again, he was flying blind. The only thing he could do was pay attention to her cues. Easier said than done. But he was doing okay so far tonight. Much better than he'd expected when he'd suggested the idea of her coming to his room in her robe.

He wouldn't apologize for the bone-deep desire to erase *prim* and *proper* from Tilda's vocabulary.

"Maybe talking isn't the right approach to take here," he murmured. Distance was the only way he could guarantee no one would get hurt, and all the conversation wasn't helping.

He rolled closer and resettled her into his arms. She came willingly and all her gorgeous skin snugged next to his. The heat dialed up a notch, not that it had cooled all that much in the first place.

Naked Tilda eclipsed all his fantasies and he still couldn't quite believe she was here, in his arms. The sexy lingerie had been nothing more than a precursor to the main event, and he was not sad that she'd asked him to remove it. Catching her mouth in his, he dropped them both into a kiss that quickly grew intense.

His first inclination was to touch more of her, but even though she'd said she was okay with creativity, he'd prefer some guidelines.

He lifted his mouth and murmured, "Did I mention how thoroughly hot it was when you told me the things you wanted me to do to you?"

She shook her head. "It was a turn-on for me, too. Surprisingly."

"You've never—" He bit that back. Of course she'd never had a man clue in that she'd needed that or they wouldn't be here right now. She'd needed him to pull it out of her, just like she'd needed him to come up with the idea of playing out her fantasies.

What else did she need that he hadn't discovered yet? His curiosity exploded.

"We're not finished letting you explore that," he advised her and shut up in favor of kissing her.

Her sweet mouth opened under his and he groaned. So trusting. It was beautiful how responsive she was after almost no time. Tentatively, he set himself into exploration mode, swirling his tongue forward, but she met him halfway, thrusting into his mouth with no fear. She arched against him and he had to check his urge to roll her under him in order to increase the contact.

So he rolled her on top of him. Her thighs fell between his and her stomach ground against his erection, which was so good, his brain melted. No downside to this position that he could find. From this angle, the kiss got deeper still, and as a bonus, his hands were free to thread through her hair. The silkiness flowed over his fingers and he felt it in his blood. He couldn't help circling his hips against her, automatically seeking more.

She moaned and shifted, igniting him with friction,

and there was little chance he was going to be able to hold off much longer if she kept that up.

"Tilda, I need to be inside you. Is that—"

"It's okay. I want that, too."

There was literally no way to misinterpret that, so he went for broke and sheathed himself with a condom in what had to be the land speed record. She'd barely moved enough for his hands to have room to work, which meant a lot of touching of hot, wet parts. In an instant, she sank down on him, drawing him into the most bliss-filled joining imaginable—and he'd imagined this moment a *lot*.

It was far better than anything he'd conjured up in his suddenly feeble fantasies. She felt amazing, tight and, best of all, *enthusiastic* as she rolled her hips to find a rhythm she liked. This position had just shot to the top of his list. He groaned as she took him deeper, and let the sensations break over him.

"That's it, sweetheart," he murmured. "You work me exactly the way you want."

She blinked down at him, registering his words. Slowly, she changed the angle, experimenting with a new speed as her hair fell into her face in the sexiest of manes, and he nearly went blind as heat exploded through his midsection.

"You're so gorgeous," he told her, almost before realizing he'd spoken. What was going on with him tonight? Tilda had turned him into a talker in bed. Insanity. Only people who were intimate with each other talked, because it meant they had stuff to talk about. This was just sex, solely designed to give her some confidence.

"You think so?" she asked, but it wasn't the coy

question of a woman fishing for compliments. She was almost…shy. Asking for confirmation, even.

"Oh, yes." He nudged his hips higher, doing some angle changing of his own to see what spots he could hit to get that expression of bliss on her face that he'd only glimpsed earlier. "When your hair is down around your face, you're ethereal. Amazing. I love you being on top. The view from here is like staring into the face of heaven."

Geez, next he'd be spouting poetry. But he couldn't take it back, not when a smile bloomed on her face that was every bit the opposite of the angel he'd just likened her to.

"I like it, too. The view is pretty good from here for me, as well." She put her hands on his chest and used him for leverage to increase her speed yet again, her eyelids drifting to half-mast as she gasped out his name.

When Tilda was in control of her pleasure, it was breathtaking. He wanted more and ground his thumb into her center. That was the magic button, apparently, because she threw her head back and rode him faster, hollowing him out with her sexy moans. After he'd spent what felt like an eternity clawing back his own release through sheer will, she finally closed around him with a strong pulsing ripple.

He let go with a cry, emptying himself in a release that eclipsed anything he'd ever known.

Tilda collapsed to his chest and his arms locked around her automatically. To keep her in place. That was his story, but in reality, he was holding on—because if he didn't, he feared he'd float away in a haze of bliss.

And he didn't miss the fact that she let him. She was amazing, putting herself out there despite her fears and blazing through to a brilliant finish.

She murmured nonsense phrases against his skin, or rather, his brain was too mushy to interpret something so complex as language, not when she'd just rearranged every one of his molecules into something different. Something he didn't fully understand yet.

But he did know one thing. He'd lied to her earlier.

What was happening between them had everything to do with their marriage because they'd just consummated it. Brilliantly, no less. And he wasn't done.

He cultivated distance to keep people from being hurt by his tendencies to be blunt and abrupt, but even that was a shield against his genuine desire to help when someone was hurting.

He'd dropped all his careful barriers to get Tilda to this point, which he didn't regret, but it was going to be hell to put them back together.

But necessary.

That feeling in his chest? It was happiness. And he didn't deserve that.

When Tilda woke up, there were arms around her and she had a moment of panic. She half pulled away and turned, but it was dark. She couldn't see, and the panic escalated, pounding through her veins. The arms were holding her down. Forcing her to do something she didn't want to.

Then it came to her in a flood. *Warren*. He'd taken her to bed last night and she'd fallen asleep with him. His face floated through her consciousness, so precious, and it centered her.

She was okay. She was in Warren's bed. He was holding her because he was extending their intimacy, not trying to keep her someplace she didn't want to be. That didn't seem to matter to her pulse. Snuggling back against his chest was a lot harder than she'd have guessed. What was wrong with her? If nothing else, Warren had always been about safety.

Lying in the dark, she stared at the ceiling she couldn't see and tried to get her automatic reactions back under control.

"Hey." Warren's soft voice whispered across her shoulder. "You okay?"

She nodded. A lie. He was so wonderful, and this was all about her being damaged beyond repair. But she couldn't breathe. The air wasn't getting into her lungs somehow and dizziness overwhelmed her.

"Do you need to go back to your own room?" he asked.

Yes. That was exactly what she needed. Nearly sobbing with gratitude, she took the out and rolled to kiss his forehead. Then she snatched her robe and fled.

Back in her own room, she snapped on the light and threw on a pair of flannel pajamas, crawling into the bed she'd been sleeping in for the last week, ever since she and Warren had gotten married. It hadn't taken too long to end up in his bed, though. She'd moved way too fast, caught up in the fantasy he'd pushed her to enact. Okay, he hadn't had to push her very hard.

She couldn't deny that she'd wanted to be with him. He hadn't forced her in any way. Quite the opposite. If any tactic would have worked to get her out of the dungeon Bryan had put her in, letting her have at least the illusion of control was it. She wasn't at all fooled, though. Warren could just as easily flip and start controlling all aspects of her life if he so chose. They were married, after all.

The light stayed on. It burned into her retinas as sleep evaded her. She'd screwed up by taking things with Warren so far. She was his employee and she needed to start acting like one. This job was all she had, and she'd started out intending to dazzle him with her skills. Instead, she'd let herself be seduced by things that weren't available to her, like happiness and fulfillment.

Bryan had stolen that dream from her. Sex was one thing, and she didn't even handle that very well. But anything else was completely off the table.

In the morning, she took a long shower and washed away all thoughts of the man who had so expertly made love to her the night before. Then she dressed in the dullest suit she owned and set up shop in the library, which was adjacent to Warren's study. Last Saturday had been wasted on moving and getting settled. Today she had a long agenda of things to accomplish that wouldn't get done if she sat around and daydreamed about the reasons her muscles ached so badly.

The reason popped his head into the library a little before eight o'clock. "Good morning."

Warren's long, delicious gaze wouldn't let hers go, or maybe that was her fault because he was so gorgeous and so dressed and she shouldn't be thinking about beckoning him into the library so she could strip him out of the jeans and T-shirt he'd donned in deference to the weekend.

"Good morning," she squeaked and cleared her

throat. "We have a lot to do before Monday. I've got meetings scheduled with the major entertainment venues—"

"Have you had breakfast?" he cut in. "Work will be there later. Come have some pancakes with me."

"I, um…no, I haven't." Pancakes were her favorite. She had to spend all day in his company, anyway. Might as well get pancakes out of the deal while she tried to figure out how their dynamic had changed.

Because it had. The fact that he hadn't readily jumped into her work discussion told that tale. He'd been hot to have these meetings for weeks because Down Under Thunder had deals with all the music festivals and such. Warren and Tilda had been planning to upend his competition's foothold with the concert crowd.

"The dining room is too formal," Warren announced and led her out to the terrace where more invisible hands had set up a white bistro table inlaid with shiny bits of glass that caught the morning sunlight.

Charmed against her will, she let him pull out one of the chairs for her and settled into it. Then there was nothing left to do but focus all of her attention on the man across from her.

"The meetings will be a great first step toward choking off Down Under Thunder," she said in a rush, mostly to keep her mind centered on the important things instead of letting her gaze wander across his broad shoulders.

She might have used them as a handhold more than once last night, and for some odd reason, she could not stop wondering if she'd left nail marks in his skin. Heat climbed through her core as she recalled the exact position, his body under hers, joined so very intimately. She'd ridden him with abandon. It had been glorious.

"Sure that's what you want to talk about this morning?" he asked lightly as the cook served plates with stacks of fluffy pancakes, a platter of bacon and syrup warmed in a small white urn, then vanished. "There's not something else on your mind?"

The heat in her core intensified as she stared at him. What was she supposed to say to that?

Yes, you rocked my world and I want you again right now?

Because that would be both true and a horrible idea.

She ate pancakes, instead. They melted in her mouth too fast to be a good diversion from the conversation because he just kept watching her as he forked up his own bits of fluffy goodness.

"Nothing is more important to me than getting this project completed," she said firmly, because she had to say something. And then she shook her head. "I mean, not that I'm in a rush to be finished. I want to do a good job and it's very important that each detail—"

"Tilda." Warren reached out and laced his fingers with hers, no hesitation, which told her that he was already far more comfortable with her than she was with him. "You'll ace this project, no doubt. We're having breakfast on the terrace on Saturday after we took our relationship someplace unexpected. If you don't want to talk about what happened last night, fine. Pick another subject. But not work."

Agape, she stared at him. "Work is all there is between us."

"No." His fingers tightened, and his thumb found a sensitive spot on her hand to caress. "Not when you can't even sleep in the same bed with me all night long, it's not. We have an impending interview with the green-card people and the subject of sleeping arrangements may come up. Wouldn't it be better to be prepared for that?"

Something with a dark edge flared through her stomach and she didn't like the direction of the conversation. "What are you saying?"

He let her hand go and ran his fingers through his hair as he sat back in his chair. "I thought…it's just that last night was amazing. Wasn't it?"

Remembering last night, her heart went a little bonkers, flipping over on itself in time with a bird's chirp in the garden below. "It was. So amazing. So unexpected." But she'd made a resolution while lying in bed unable to sleep, and she would stick to it. "I don't want to talk about last night. It was a onetime thing, a fantasy. We're not a couple. We work together. The marriage part of our relationship is incidental."

A heavy block of something landed on her chest and she couldn't breathe.

Was that all there was for her for the rest of her life? The inability to sleep with a man and barely the ability to have sex with one? What about later, when she didn't have someone as patient and kind as Warren? Who would care enough to tease out her fantasies, pay enough attention to her to know that she would like being on top when she didn't even know that about herself?

It was too much. She couldn't do this intimate breakfast on Warren's terrace the morning after they'd slept together.

Of course, fleeing to her room didn't help. She was

still completely out of sorts. Warren seemed to understand that she needed space and left her alone.

For about fifteen minutes.

The knock on the door had his authoritative ring to it. The housekeeper had a much lighter touch, and besides, what had Tilda expected, that he'd let his project suffer because she was being difficult about having slept with him?

"Tilda," he called through the door. "Talk to me. Please."

And say what? Not talking was much easier and avoidance was her current coping mechanism. She'd sneaked away from Bryan when he'd been on an assignment, she'd left Melbourne the first opportunity Craig had given her and she continually shoved Warren into a box called "work" so she could pretend none of the other stuff was happening.

But that didn't make it right to run.

She opened the door and his beautiful, masculine presence immediately swelled into the room, filling up places she'd only begun to realize were empty. "I'm sorry. I tend to run away from anything that scares me."

"That's part of the problem, Tilda." His voice betrayed none of his emotions. But his eyes told a different, far more interesting story. "I don't want to be one of the things that scares you."

Mute, she stared up at him as a wealth of emotions surfaced in his gaze that she'd have missed if she'd never opened the door. This was difficult for him. She was causing him distress. And maybe some pain? The whole time, she'd had a sort of academic understanding that he was being patient and kind, but had never really acknowledged the cost. She'd seen evidence of it last night. How quickly she'd forgotten the effort he'd made to treat her so well. Selfishly, she'd assumed any cost was physical, but there was a very real possibility that he was paying for it emotionally, as well.

That brought her up short.

"Come in." She held the door open wide and stepped back. Did he understand that such a gesture cost her, as well?

Instead of crossing to the bed or lounging against the door frame, he leaned forward and kissed her on the forehead. "Thank you."

Seemed like the answer was yes—he did understand that certain things didn't come easily to her. This was the part where she had to get over herself and start paying attention to what he needed. "What did you want to talk about?"

That's when he took a seat. Not on the bed but in the lone chair situated in the corner near the reading lamp. Crossing his legs at the ankle, he looked at the ceiling and blew out a breath. "I hated that you couldn't sleep with me last night. I… God, this is hard."

"What, Warren?" She moved across the carpet and knelt by his side. "You can tell me."

"Can I?" He flashed her a brief smile. "While we're discussing the things that you run away from, we should have a chat about my problems in the relationship department. I'm not very good at telling a woman how I feel, apparently."

How he felt? As in *feelings*? As in, what? He was *falling* for her?

Her mouth worked but no sound came out. This was a disaster. He couldn't fall for her. That's when everything had shattered with Bryan, the moment he started talking about how much she meant to him; that's when his controlling tendencies showed up.

But at the same time…oh, how she longed for a bit of normality, where she could tell Warren she was falling for him, too.

"Let's start with the basics," she said shakily. "Is this a conversation about how you've got expectations now about our personal life?"

"What? No! Absolutely not. I…" Warren swallowed and there was the longest pause. "I should tell you about Marcus."

Instead of confessing something she was not ready to hear, Warren spun a tragic story about his college roommate and how the poor guy had gotten a fatal case of broken heart. Somewhere along the way, their fingers intertwined and she listened while holding his hand, though she couldn't have said who reached for whom or which of them needed the comfort more. He had awfulness in his past, and she had a lump in her throat by the time he wrapped it up.

"He died, and I swore I'd never go out that way," he said, his gaze dark with memories and pain. "Love isn't in the cards for me and it's been shockingly easy to avoid that, given that I'm usually accused of being married to Flying Squirrel."

That was…not what she'd expected to hear. But, oddly, it was exactly what she'd needed to hear. It loosened the tight clutch of emotion inside her. "Yet here you are. Married to me."

"By default. It's not supposed to matter."

"But it does." Their gazes caught and the very air shifted as the hugeness of the moment blossomed.

He nodded once without hesitation. "It does. Because I can't go back to just working together, but neither can I promise you anything. I hate that we're at this place—"

"But that's okay," she said in a rush, almost laughing with relief. "I don't want promises. I want to feel like there's no pressure. Like we're going to be okay no matter what. Working together isn't affected, the green card isn't in jeopardy and we can just float along wherever the whims of the moment take us. I'm totally fine with that."

She was. It was freeing in a way. She could have secret feelings and he didn't expect her to share them. Once again, he had some kind of sixth sense about what worked for her and it was awesome in every sense of the word.

"But you left last night," he said quietly. "I convinced myself it was because you were sorry that we'd taken that step."

Her heart fell open and she had to clamp it shut.

There was the emotion she'd seen when she first opened the door. She'd fled from his bed last night, then refused to talk to him about it. Of course he'd misinterpreted her angst.

"Not sorry." She shook her head so hard that several strands fell out of her bun. That thing needed to go. Reaching up, she pulled out the pins and let her hair rain down. "See how far I've come already? This is not something I would do with just anyone. Our secret."

His smile grew a wicked edge. "That's not something I want you to do with anyone else."

Feeling bold, she hiked up her skirt and crawled astride his lap, settling on it with surprising ease, given the hard length jutting into her core. “That’s all it takes to get you hot? Me taking my hair down?”

His hands clamped down on her waist, holding her in place, but it was thrilling. Because he wanted her with simple, uncomplicated desire. It was in his gaze, the heat of his expression. This, she understood. He was always so careful with her, so gentle.

“All it takes is you walking into a room,” he muttered and flexed his hips in a little friction dance that nearly set her on fire. “And I’m wholly unprepared to have a sexy woman in my lap.”

“Feels like you’ve got all the right equipment to me.” She wiggled, pushing him deeper into the thin barrier of her panties. He felt so good, and she loved that they could be honest with each other about what was going on inside, whether it was desire or pain.

In response, he stood, boosted her up with both hands on her bare buttocks and strode toward the bathroom. She wrapped her legs around him and went to work exploring his neck with her mouth, nibbling on anything she came across. Warren tasted delicious, like heat in flesh form.

The cool marble of the vanity stung her thighs as he set her on it and, giving her a quick kiss, he rifled through a drawer until he came up with condoms. Holding them up to show her, he then tossed them on the counter and stepped back between her legs.

“Where were we?” he murmured.

“I was playing out another fantasy of mine,” she informed him, saucily. Warren did bring out her vixen side with shocking ease. “Where you come into the bathroom and take me apart.”

His mouth curved. “I have that fantasy, too. Let’s see how they compare.”

Slowly, he raised his fingers to the buttons on her blouse and undid the top one. Then he moved on to the next one, watching her with careful, heated intent.

“Not even close. Try this.” She grabbed both sides of her blouse and ripped them apart, revealing the white lace bra she’d been wearing the other night. “Not slow this time. Fast.”

His mouth was already on hers, sucking her into him as he kissed her. Their tongues clashed, writhing together in search of more sensation. His hands were everywhere, in her hair, shrugging off her jacket and ruined shirt, sliding along her thigh as he fingered aside her panties.

White lightning forked through her center as he thumbed her. She gasped and let her head fall back, thrusting her breasts against his chest. He bent and took one nipple into his mouth through her bra.

“Now,” she commanded hoarsely. “Don’t make me wait.”

He complied instantly, dropping his pants and shouldering off his shirt. She circled her hips, desperate for him to hurry. An eternity later, he was back in place, pushing aside her panties instead of removing them, and the urgency of it thrilled her. There was nothing slow or easy about the way he pushed into her. It was all raw need and power, and she reveled in it because she’d asked for it.

He groaned as she took him. She urged him on with her heels, hands at his waist as he powered her to a dense, heavy release that broke over her without warning. He drew it out with hard, fast thrusts that built on the sensation until she was gasping and sobbing nonsense. His own release triggered and he held her tight to his chest as he came.

That was her favorite part. He was so dominant everywhere but in her arms; with her, he let himself be vulnerable, pulling back a little to catch her in a long sweet kiss as their torsos heaved with the expulsion of passion.

She kept waiting for him to be something other than perfect, but it hadn't happened. He liked it when she was wanton, liked her sexy underwear, liked her. It was…everything.

"Warren," she murmured against his mouth. "I want to sleep with you."

"Tilda." She felt his lips curve up against hers. "It's ten o'clock in the morning. Hold that thought and we'll pick it up again in about twelve hours. Now, about those meetings next week…"

Nine

That night, after thoroughly pleasuring himself on the sound of Tilda's moans, Warren finally let her go to sleep sometime after midnight. But he couldn't do the same. What if she had a nightmare? Or needed a drink of water? He had to be alert and ready to handle whatever happened.

He didn't want her to leave this time.

Nothing happened. She slept through the night or, at least, that was what he assumed was the case. He'd fallen asleep, after all, only to wake with her watching him, one arm under her head and a smile that could mean a thousand things stretching across her beautiful face.

"Good morning," she said simply.

And he couldn't help but reach for her. She came willingly, eagerly snuggling against his body, and she felt so good that he couldn't do anything but wrap his arms around her. What had started out as a bone-deep need to kiss her melted into something else entirely.

She was still here. In his bed. The enormity of it soaked through his body and he tried really hard to push it away, but he couldn't help the tenderness that filled that moment. They should be celebrating the fact that she'd taken huge steps to overcome difficult emotional landmines. Instead, he was fighting the realization that he'd been missing out on this kind of intimacy for the whole of his life.

He liked her in his bed. He shouldn't. But there was no going back now. The baby steps they'd been taking in deference to her triggers had worked on him, too, but for a far different reason. She'd slowly seeped into his consciousness until he didn't know if he'd be able to untangle her from his arms, let alone from his insides.

Thank God they had already decided on a divorce. Once she got her green card, everything would go back to normal. She could move out and he could...what? Go back to being lonely?

That was crap. He had Flying Squirrel. He didn't need anything else to make his life perfect.

But as they finally dragged themselves from the bed and crossed the finish line by having breakfast together, he couldn't sell that lie, even to himself. Before Tilda, his life had been something, all right—empty. What else could he call it when the word to describe how it felt now was *full*?

Fine. He could roll with it for the time being.

They didn't work at all on Sunday in favor of spending the day together. She'd posed it as a way to practice for the green-card interview but the conversations always veered into something that no one from the immigration department would ever ask because the content was X-rated, at best. It seemed they'd both had a lot of fantasies to work through, which lasted the whole of the week, as it turned out. So far, taking her from behind on his desk in the CEO's office at Flying Squirrel was his favorite with a capital F.

The campaign for increasing Flying Squirrel's market share in Australia was going well. He got some numbers from Thomas on Friday that pleased him so much, he immediately invited Tilda to a lavish dinner in celebration. For some reason, the impending dinner put her in a strange mood. She vanished to her office, a rarity, and stayed there for a couple of hours.

Were they still not at a place where she could tell him honestly what was going on with her?

And then she appeared at four o'clock. And knocked. Which she hadn't done in quite some time.

He did not like the idea that their relationship had seemed to regress. Nor the fact that backing off now was likely a good idea, pending how long the approval took on his petition for her green card application. They might have weeks, but they probably had less.

He didn't want to think about it. So he told her tersely, "You don't have to knock."

"Can I come in?" she asked tentatively.

He sighed. His tone had put her on edge. Because he was an idiot. "Of course."

Tilda's hair was coming loose from her bun-like thing and he was pretty sure his fingers had been the cause. Probably from the stolen kiss in the stairwell that he'd initiated as they'd come back from a meeting with the board earlier today. How had they gotten to the point where she was cautious with him all over again in a matter of hours?

"I have a problem," she said and hesitated, stopping just inside the door. Usually she beelined for the seat near his desk. "I didn't want to bring it up, but I feel like I should."

Bracing, he sat back in his chair. "I'm listening."

"I don't want to wear a suit to dinner. But I don't have anything else to wear."

The laugh of relief that bubbled up made him downright giddy. *That's* what had her tied up in knots? "That's not a problem."

She scowled. "It is to me. You of all people should understand."

Screw the distance between them. He skirted the desk and shut the door behind her so they could speak privately, then he leaned on it with his arms crossed. "I do understand. That's why I know it's not a problem. You wear those suits so you can pretend you're a proper consultant to the rest of the world because that makes you feel safe. On the flip side, the kind of clothes you want to wear make you uncomfortable, so you shy away from them. You're stuck in the middle. How am I doing so far?"

Since her mouth had been agape pretty much the whole time he'd been talking, the question was largely rhetorical.

"I pay attention," he told her. "Because I care."

The phrase had come out of his mouth before he could catch it. But the truth settled into his chest, fitting into the nooks and crannies far better than he would have expected. He did care. There was nothing wrong with that. It wasn't the same thing as love, and besides, he already had his out predefined. There was no forever kind of happiness on his horizon with Tilda, nor did he want that.

Or rather, he didn't deserve it.

Which wasn't the same thing at all. He swallowed the bitter taste in his mouth.

"Since you're so smart, what am I supposed to do about that?" she asked him, hands on her hips.

He shrugged. "Easy. You let me take you shopping. The only caveat is that you have to wear whatever I pick out."

"You'd do that?" Now she just sounded suspicious, like he made a habit of offering to take women shopping for nefarious reasons.

"Make no mistake. I'm picking out what you wear under it, too. None of this is for you. It's all for me."

When her shoulders relaxed, that's when he risked reaching out to pull her into his arms. She melted against him and it was every bit the sweet victory he'd hoped for.

"Okay," she murmured into his jacket. "You win. But only because I can't wait to see what you have in mind."

That made two of them. He'd never shopped for a woman before, unless you counted birthday presents for his mom, and that was so not applicable here that it wasn't funny. But he could not deny that he'd longed to dress her in outfits of his choosing.

"That's a secret I can't share yet. Soon."

He kissed her temple as the last of the tension between them dissolved. Funny how often he found himself doing something that had its basis in comfort or affection. Before Tilda, he would have said a kiss led to sex a hundred percent of the time; otherwise, why bother?

But he liked providing Tilda with comfort and affection. And if it helped her, great.

But as he wrapped up work for the day, his mind was squarely on the question of whether it was helping her—or him.

There was no good answer for that.

He led his wife out to the limo that would whisk them to the exclusive shopping center he'd learned about from Hendrix's wife, Roz, and pushed all his questions to the background. Tilda needed a dress.

Actually, the dress needed Tilda.

On the hanger, lifeless. On the woman? A work of art.

Warren could not take his eyes off his wife as she emerged from the dressing room in the teal midlength dress with sleeves to her elbows. It was both elegant and stylish, showing nothing but a bit of leg, which left the eye of the beholder to notice only Tilda's radiance.

"I like it," she said softly, and he nodded because he didn't trust his voice to work. "I'm going to wear it out."

Warren handed the beaming clerk his credit card without looking because he didn't want to miss a moment of Tilda in that dress. "Don't put your hair up."

"I wasn't going to. Thank you." She settled a hand on his arm and her warmth bled all the way through his suit jacket. "For the dress. And coming with me."

"The pleasure is all mine." Understatement.

Warren took Tilda to the priciest restaurant in Raleigh. Not because he cared about being seen, though there was plenty of that going on. More than one diner had shot a sidelong glance at their table, and there was a discreet photographer making rounds who probably worked for a society column. Since it was all good for Tilda's green card, he didn't mind.

What he did mind was how difficult it was to sit across from his wife in a public place knowing what she had on under the teal dress. Yeah, he'd followed through on that, selecting a matching silk bra and thong. There was nothing daring about the lingerie, either. All in all, the whole ensemble was relatively respectable.

What was driving him nuts was how Tilda had blossomed the moment she'd stepped into the room wearing it. She owned her beauty, her confidence. Wore both fiercely, as if daring anyone to try and take them from her. He'd never been more proud of another person in his life and the lump in his throat could not be washed away with any amount of wine.

In the end, he might as well have taken Tilda to McDonald's for all the attention he'd paid to the food. He honestly couldn't have said what he'd ordered or what color the wine had been that they'd drunk, though he was relatively certain he'd noted the bottle had cost him five hundred dollars when he glanced at the bill.

In the car, he scooted Tilda close to him and murmured all the wicked things he planned to do to her when they got home. She suggested a few of her own, which only intensified the heat that had sprung up the moment she'd walked out of that dressing room. Or, if he was being honest, he'd been hot for her since this morning, when he'd woken up next to her after a night of holding hands while they slept.

When they spilled through the front door, laughing over a joke Tilda had made, he almost swept her up in his arms so he could carry her upstairs. It would be the fastest route to getting her out of that amazing teal concoction so he could lick the gooey center of his treat.

But an envelope on the sideboard caught his eye. That was where the housekeeper put ultraimportant items she'd deemed worthy of his immediate attention, and a sixth sense told him he should heed the recommendation. Clasping Tilda's hand so she couldn't escape, he led her across the foyer. Exactly as he'd hoped, the return address was the immigration bureau.

"Fantastic," he said. "This should be the approval of my petition."

The response had been pretty fast in the grand scheme of things. He picked up the envelope and tore it open, scanning the first line. The envelope fluttered to the floor from his suddenly nerveless fingers as he reread the words over and over.

"Warren. What is it?" Tilda asked, concern crowding her eyebrows together.

"Denied," he said flatly and handed her the paper. "They've had an influx of applicants due to the immigration uncertainties going on right now, and they're not approving any new petitions for the next six months until some of the new regulations can be ironed out."

"What?" All the blood drained from Tilda's face. "What does that mean?"

She had to leave.

"We got married for no reason." Lightheaded all at once, he rubbed at his temples. "With all the illegal immigration talk in the news lately, it never occurred to me that the department would be in such flux."

Denied. His petition had been denied.

Tilda couldn't apply for a green card at this point. They hadn't even gotten that far. None of this mattered, not talking over a glass of wine, not the budding confidence Tilda had gained, not the way she looked at him sometimes, as if he was a hero.

"I don't understand," Tilda whispered as her eyes scanned the page. "We're married. What if I was pregnant? That wouldn't make a difference to them? We'd still be split up?"

"What?" Dumbfounded, he pushed the paper away and grabbed Tilda's hand, his gaze tight on hers as he filtered through her expression seeking more information. "Are you pregnant? You can't know that already. Can you?"

The very foundation of the earth started to spin as he internalized the vast and unforeseen complications that had just been dropped in their laps, if so. The sense of awe and wonder had no place in his gut when there were too many other things to worry about.

Pregnant. Tilda could even now be pregnant with his child and—

"No!" She shook her head. "I'm saying *what if.* God, could you imagine?"

Yeah, he could, and that was part of the problem. All of this was a problem. He shouldn't be this devastated. What were they going to do? They'd only just started discovering all the wonders of their relationship. She'd held his hand all night long—more than once. It was a huge stride and it was so sweet.

"I'm sorry, Warren," she said quietly. "I know how important this project is to you."

Project?

He stared at her for a full minute before it registered that she was apologizing because the petition denial meant the project was in jeopardy. The fact that he hadn't even considered the project swirled through his gut.

He was in trouble. Big time.

For the first time in his life, the vow he'd taken in college felt extremely precarious. Panic swirled through his gut and he couldn't even lie to himself that it was due to the imminent danger of breaking the pact—it was all because he *could not lose her.*

"Yes. That's true." He squeezed his eyes shut, but the project didn't magically become the most important part of this equation. That was not a good thing. "We can do it remotely. It'll be fine."

It would not be fine. It would be horrific. He couldn't touch her through a screen. Tilda would be thousands of miles away where he couldn't kiss her whenever he felt like it. She wouldn't be in his bed. Worst of all, she wouldn't be the author of his stolen moments of happiness. The ones he didn't deserve but had come to want. Fiercely.

"Fine? Are you serious?" She stared at him, a shadow dropping over her expression. "I can't go back to Australia. What can we do to fight this?"

"Nothing." His voice sounded hollow, even to his own ears. "We shouldn't fight it. There's no reason you can't work with the Australian contacts there and the American ones via video calls. People do it all the time."

The faster she left, the better. The sooner he could get her out of the nooks and crannies of his soul, which shouldn't be such a hard task to contemplate…

But it was.

All the more reason to get her gone. This was all on him. He'd pushed her into his bed, never realizing how deep things would ultimately go.

He'd lost sight of her importance to Flying Squirrel. Distance could give that back to him. Maybe this petition denial was a blessing in disguise. Her leaving was the only thing that would work.

"I'm not *people*, Warren," she choked out and he glanced at her, finally pulling himself out of his own head long enough to note that the panic going on wasn't all on his side. Her face was still white and her hands were trembling. "Bryan is in Australia."

Oh, God. He hadn't even considered how terrifying it must be for her to contemplate the idea of facing her ex again. "You're so much stronger now than you used to be. Surely the time we've spent together helped?"

She shook her head, her mouth a firm line. "I can't. I cannot go back to Australia."

So all the strides they'd made—that he'd made with her, denying his own needs and desires until she was ready—none of that mattered.

Of course it didn't. He had no business letting his bleeding heart run this show. "I'm not sure what choice we have."

"That's it?" Baffled, she glanced up at him, her eyes wide and rapidly filling with tears. "You can't call someone, or fly me to Canada or England? Surely there's someplace in the world we can go—"

"*We* can't, Tilda." Before she could spin more fairy

tales that could never come true, he had to cut her off. He was the CEO. Flying Squirrel was his life. "If you want to go someplace that's not Australia, we can look into it. But I can't come with you. You know I have to stay here."

And in that moment, a part of him knew he'd have given it all up for her. Which was why this *could not* be happening.

It was an impossible quandary. He wanted things to be the way they had been, where there were no choices and he'd been forced into this bit of wonderful for reasons beyond his control.

"So, all of this is over?" she whispered. "You're done with me now that your project has taken a hit?"

"All of what is over? Our marriage, definitely. That's all there ever was. Now there's no need for it. What else are you looking for?"

The distance in his voice was perfect. Exactly what he wanted. It matched the numbness and vast empty spaces inside that he'd only recently realized were Tilda shaped.

"I...don't know." She crumpled the paper in her hands and held it tight in her fist. "Some indication that you haven't just been leading me down a path to nowhere. You've been so kind and I thought... Well, it doesn't matter now, does it?"

"You thought what? That I might have feelings for you?" He clamped down on the truth before he blurted out things that wouldn't be good for anyone in this situation and shook his head. "I told you about Marcus. What did you think was going to happen, knowing I took a vow?"

Certainly not that he would fall in love with his wife. If he couldn't have predicted that, how could she?

She nodded. "I get it. Everything is a means to an end for Flying Squirrel. The people involved are just incidental."

And with that, she turned and walked upstairs without a backward glance.

Somehow, Tilda was not shocked that Warren followed her to her bedroom.

"This conversation is not over," he told her as he stood at the door, his arms crossed over his incredibly hard heart.

She had to pack. Blearily, she tried to think about where she'd put her suitcases in the cavernous room, but her brain was as frozen as the rest of her. "What else is there to say?"

"What are you going to do? Let me help you figure it out."

"Because I'm your employee? Or your wife?"

What did it matter? She already knew the answer. He was Warren Garinger, CEO of Flying Squirrel. Despite the fact that he'd told her he cared, anything she'd let herself believe—including that—was a lie.

"You're both," he argued. "That was the deal from the beginning. I couldn't have one without the other."

"Right. If my visa hadn't been messed up, the wife part wouldn't have happened." She'd have missed all the gloriousness of being with Warren: his patience, his selflessness. The terrace. This dress.

Falling for him.

"And I wouldn't have you as my wife unless you'd been my employee first."

He came into the room, treading across the carpet slowly, as he'd done from the first. Even now, he was still patiently working through her triggers, as if he *cared.*

Why would he tell her that he paid attention because he cared and then send her back to Melbourne where the worst nightmare imaginable awaited her?

"Tell me what you're thinking," he prompted again. "You don't have to do this alone."

"Don't I?" She surprised them both by laughing bitterly. "What are you offering me this time?"

Halting well shy of touching her, he took her measure. "To help. I'll put you up in an apartment anywhere you like. Name the country. You can go there as if you're on vacation, and the moment you have to leave due to any immigration issues, you can go someplace else."

If she couldn't stay here—and the letter was frighteningly clear on the fact that she couldn't—it didn't matter where she went. Because Warren wouldn't be there. It was an inescapable fact that he'd become her whole world. Of course, the job was important, too, and yesterday, she'd have said it was more important than anything. But in light of the hole in her gut due to these new circumstances, to say so would be skirting the truth.

She was in love with him. Against her will. If only she hadn't come to him with her need for a new dress, he wouldn't have told her he cared and opened up hopes in her heart that had no place there. She'd been fighting her feelings just fine until that had happened.

"So, I'd be living out of a suitcase at the whims of the country's immigration laws." That sounded like the opposite of what she wanted. Anything that wasn't staying in Raleigh with Warren sounded like hell. "I can't think about this now. I just want to go to bed."

And then, tomorrow, she'd have to leave the US. It wasn't like she had a lot of time to comply with the immigration bureau. Thanks to Warren's petition, they knew who she was, where she lived and who she worked for. And when her visa had expired, which was weeks ago.

"I need to know that you're going to be safe." Warren surged forward to grip both of her arms. The automatic recoil she couldn't control threw a heavy wrench into the works. Instantly, he dropped his hands with a curse. "God, Tilda, I'm sorry. I don't know why I did that."

"It's okay," she whispered and rubbed at her arms where he'd grabbed her, not because it hurt but because it wasn't okay. She wasn't okay.

How many more clues did she need that they'd never work? Inside, where it counted, she didn't trust anyone, obviously. The scars went too deep.

Even if he'd professed his undying love, it wasn't fair to saddle him with a wife who couldn't stop herself from jumping when her husband did something as simple as reach out to express his concern. Leaving suddenly felt like her salvation, not the end of their relationship, as she'd been painting it.

There was nothing to end. There'd have to have been a real relationship between them in order for there to be anything to kill.

"I'll go back to Melbourne," she said dully as her heart sheared neatly in half. "I have family there. I can work remotely until the project is complete, as you've specified. You'll send the divorce papers via courier when you have them drawn up?"

"Are you sure that's best? What about your ex?"

"I'll get over it. I'm nothing if not professional. You'll get your market share in Australia, as promised, so don't worry about the project."

She couldn't let him know that she was breaking down inside. That's when it was the worst. When a man got the information he could use to really hurt you.

His expression didn't change, but the distance between them increased exponentially. The very atmosphere grew icicles as he stared at her. "That's great. I do want to get my money's worth."

Ironic how she'd fallen for two very different men. One clung to her like a cocklebur and the other couldn't hold on to anything outside of his bottom line.

Something must be wrong with her that she couldn't find a man in the middle, who understood that she stood firmly in the middle, too—one foot in each camp between proper and provocative.

Warren had been that man for a far-too-brief blip in time.

No. That had been an illusion. Good thing. She couldn't imagine the conversation if her residency status had gone differently.

Because, in the end, if he'd asked her to stay married after she got her green card, she wouldn't have refused.

Ten

Get over it.

The phrase haunted Warren. Had haunted him for a decade. But it had been fresh on his mind all day, courtesy of Tilda, who was on her way to the airport in his limo.

Without him.

Because he couldn't get his head on straight.

Tilda needed something bigger than he was capable of giving her. Obviously. After everything that he'd done and tried and bled all over, she still flinched when he forgot to be careful with her. And clearly he'd forgotten. His ham-handed qualities had been proven over and over.

Still. He could have gone to the airport with her, if for no other reason than to say goodbye. Right? They had a professional relationship that would extend for the next nine months or so. They'd be speaking by conference call on Tuesday, if not sooner, pending whether her connecting flight from LAX was delayed.

The reason why he didn't accompany her had to do with the burn in his chest, the one that made it impossible to explain he couldn't stand the thought of watching her fly out of his life. He couldn't go with her. He couldn't keep her here. It was a merry-go-round nightmare that had no exit.

How the hell had he gotten here? His nice, simple green-card marriage had exploded in his face, and he couldn't even turn to his friends for comfort because they would laugh. The word *sanctimonious* would likely come up. "I told you so" would be thrown around more than once.

The house echoed with emptiness. Or was that his heart? Both. Neither.

The staff hadn't gone anywhere and there were no fewer than five people within shouting distance. But, as always, they were invisible, keeping their distance because that's what he'd always preferred. His heart had no business feeling anything other than guilt for the sin of bleeding all over Marcus and then Tilda.

Loneliness was his due, and he'd been combating that for eons. Of course, that had been easier when he didn't have a basis for comparison. The ghost of Tilda was everywhere. In his bed, in the bathroom, at the dining table. Behind his eyelids when he closed his eyes. Thankfully, he wasn't in the habit of frequenting the terrace, so he didn't have to see it or the garden below ever again if he didn't want to.

That was a good plan. Just avoid everything that reminded him of how he'd screwed up and gotten in way too deep with the woman he'd married.

So deep that it had actually wrenched his soul from his gut when she'd flinched last night. Just as well. He didn't need it anyway. Souls were for people who didn't have a friend's suicide on their conscience.

That's why it was better for Tilda to go. He wasn't good for her. In fact, he'd let her go for her own safety, because he *did* care.

If he repeated that a thousand more times, it might sink in, too.

Morose and sick of himself, Warren barricaded the door of the study and drowned himself in work. That lasted about an hour. He'd gotten so good at delegating as he focused on the Australia project over the last three months that he had little to do. Blasphemy. There was always something for the CEO to do. He captained the whole ship, for crying out loud.

Digging into some of Thomas's reports put him in slightly better spirits. There were discrepancies in the inventory numbers. Grateful for the distraction, he fired off an email for an explanation and moved on to the next report. Five minutes later, an email popped into his inbox. Thomas's reply: I'm aware. That's why the discrepancy is explained in the quarterly report I sent out three days ago.

Warren rolled his eyes. Fine. He dug around until he found the report in the wrong folder on his desktop, read it and had to agree that the explanation seemed reasonable enough. What was the world coming to, that his brother had a better handle on the operations of the business than he did?

That was a question better left unanswered. And now he was thinking about Tilda all over again.

His phone dinged and greedily he snatched it up,

hoping for a text from Tilda that her flight had been canceled or the airport had been destroyed in a tornado. Australia had fallen off the map. Anything that meant she wouldn't be getting on a plane and going to the other side of the globe.

Jonas: Roz and Viv are doing a girl's thing tonight. They want to pick up Tilda. Okay?

He groaned. Excellent timing. Now what was he supposed to do, tell them everything?

Warren: Tilda is.

What? Sick? Busy. *Tilda is busy.* But, instead, the word gone appeared on the screen and he hit Send in the millisecond before he realized his Freudian mistake. He groaned. No point in recalling it now.

Jones: We'll be there in fifteen minutes.

They made it in ten. When Warren swung the door open after waving off the housekeeper, Jonas and Hendrix both stood on his doorstep.

Jonas held up a six-pack of longnecks. "Figured we'd come fortified. The girls went somewhere that I have absolutely no desire to hear about later, so you're stuck with us until maybe Monday."

Rolling his eyes, Hendrix barged into the house without being asked. "Such a liar. They went to a spa that shows romantic movies while they're doing nails and some such. Viv will talk about Hugh Grant when she gets home and you'll listen to every word."

"That's frighteningly true," Jonas agreed with a nod and followed Hendrix, pulling out a beer to hand to Warren, who was still standing at the door with his hand on the knob.

"Please. Come in," Warren told both interlopers sarcastically. "I insist."

"The Tilda story is a doozy," Hendrix said to Jonas in a loud whisper that deaf people in Timbuktu heard. "I told you to get two six-packs."

"I have my own alcohol." Warren shut the door because the smart-ass duo was already in the house. "Is there any chance you're going to shut up and let me sulk in peace?"

"None," Jonas and Hendrix chorused. "We can do this in the foyer or you can let us spread out in the game room. The Devils are playing."

Basketball sounded like as good a distraction as anything. Warren took the lone leather chair that reclined, leaving Yin and Yang to lounge on his couch as they jabbered about their fantasy basketball brackets.

Beer flowed, and in the middle of his second one, Warren started to relax. The name Tilda hadn't come up yet and he appreciated his friends' glaring omission of it more than he could possibly say.

They'd come right over, no questions asked, to keep him company without fully understanding why he'd needed it. Which was a trick and a half considering that *he* hadn't even known he needed them.

They were his friends through thick and thin. Even when the thickness was his own skull.

"Tilda's green card was denied," Warren muttered.

Jonas and Hendrix both glanced away from the second-half tip-off in progress on the screen, their attention firmly on him instead of the game.

"That's rough, man," Hendrix said sympathetically. "Did they say why?"

Warren nodded and threw out the legalese from the letter. "She left this morning. She'll work remotely until the project is done, and in the meantime, I don't know. Maybe I can fly down there occasionally to attend some in-person meetings. Not really sure there's a point in that, though."

His friends glanced at each other, their expressions laden with meaningful eyebrow gymnastics.

Jonas held up his beer in a pseudo toast. "You're a rock. A total inspiration. You escaped that marriage without falling in love and I have to say, I'm impressed. I'm fifty bucks poorer, but eh. Easy come, easy go."

"You bet on me?" Warren tried to get up enough energy to be mad, but pretending he wasn't thinking about Tilda was exhausting.

"Of course," Hendrix threw in. "We had a pool. Roz won. She said you'd never unbend long enough to see that Tilda is as perfect for you as if we'd ordered her from a catalog. Me, I was, like, no way it could fall apart. If she's perfect for you, she'd figure out how to pull that CEO stick out of your butt long enough for you to get there."

The circular logic made his head hurt. Especially given that he'd always thought the same thing. Tilda was a female version of himself, save one aspect—she deserved happiness. He didn't. "Get there? Where is 'there'?"

"If we have to tell you, you're hopeless." Hendrix sipped his beer and high-fived Jonas as the Devils scored a three-pointer.

They let Warren stew in his own juices for an agonizing five minutes until he muttered, "I don't have a CEO stick in my butt."

"Figure of speech," Jonas answered pleasantly, without looking at him. "And we were wrong to bet on Tilda, obviously. Sorry about the lack of faith in your ability to stick to the pact."

Was it going to feel like a hot iron poker had stabbed him in the gut every time someone mentioned her name? How was he going to manage working with her for the long term? "We can stop talking about this any time now."

"You brought it up," Hendrix reminded him. Also without looking at him, because the game was apparently tight enough to keep their attention riveted on the screen.

Geez. His friends were something else. They were supposed to notice that he was quietly coming apart and, like, care or something. "Because I figured you wanted to know, or you wouldn't be here. Your sympathetic ear leaves a lot to be desired."

As if he'd flipped a switch, Jonas swiveled on the couch, completely turning away from the TV, and Hendrix went so far as to turn it off. They both gazed at him expectantly.

That was way too much attention. His chest started to hurt.

"We were waiting for you to admit there was sympathy needed," Jonas allowed, his dark eyes warm with compassion. "You do too have a stick. You're way too proud of yourself for sticking to that ridiculous pact. I'm guessing that's why Tilda is on a plane and you're not on it with her."

"The pact is not ridiculous," Warren countered and couldn't even celebrate the fact that his temper had started simmering. It just meant that he wasn't numb, after all, and frankly, he'd prefer to continue not feeling. "Just because the two of you broke it and figured out how to justify your faithlessness to yourselves doesn't make—"

"Hey," Jonas cut in quietly. "I get that you're upset Tilda's gone. But we were not faithless to the pact. Maybe the letter of it, but not the spirit. You're missing the point. We're still here, still friends after a terrible tragedy."

"I'm not upset." They didn't even have the grace to accept that lie.

"We haven't forgotten Marcus," Hendrix added, setting his beer down on the coffee table and leaning back into the couch cushions with a contemplative expression. "I like to think that what I have with Roz is a fitting tribute to his memory. I never would have married her if I'd thought there was a chance I'd fall in love, and yet, it grew between us, anyway. Without the pact, I would still be alone and I'd have missed out on the best thing that ever happened to me."

"The key is that you have to understand when to admit defeat." Jonas jerked his head toward the door. "After the woman you've fallen in love with gets on a plane to go to the other side of the world is too late."

"I'm not in—"

Too late. It was too late. He couldn't even finish that sentence because the falsehood wouldn't form. Warren's head started to spin in time with his heart.

The pact was irrevocably broken.

He had fallen in love with Tilda. That's why all of this hurt so much.

"It's okay," Jonas said with every bit of the sympathy Warren had railed at him for not providing. "Give it a minute. You put up a good fight."

"The problem isn't that I can't admit I broke the

pact." Wearily, Warren let his head fall back against the chair. Not a problem. But not easy, either. "It's that I kept the pact for a reason."

"We all did." This from Hendrix. "I didn't want to lose our friendship. It's important to me. So I used it as an excuse to avoid what I was feeling. Jonas had his reasons, too. You're sticking to it because you can't imagine loving something more than work, I imagine."

At that, Warren's head came off the back of the chair and he glared at Hendrix. "Really? You think that's the reason? Because Flying Squirrel is more important to me than Tilda?"

Hendrix shrugged. "Seems like as good an explanation as any."

"Except it's not true. I kept the pact because it's my fault Marcus died." Something broke inside as he verbalized the thought that he'd kept quiet for a decade. He'd never uttered those words out loud.

Sitting up straight, Jonas rubbed at his temples. "Warren, Marcus committed suicide. Unless you put him up to it, it's not your fault."

"I..." *Yes.* It was his fault. What could he say to explain this decade-old crime? "I don't mean I killed him. I mean, I thought he was going to snap out of it. I believed that firmly. So I started talking to him. Looking up bits in psychology books I found in the Duke library. At one point, I read that you should pay attention to the depressed person's cues and counter the messages they're giving themselves."

You were supposed to do it nonverbally. Like the way Tilda startled easily. No big mystery how to handle that—you moved slowly and always showed your hands so she got the message that you weren't a threat.

It had worked more often than it hadn't. It was only when he'd let his temper get the best of him that he screwed up.

Like he had with Marcus.

So, frustrated with the lack of progress, he'd blurted out "Get over it," totally convinced that Marcus could have moved on from his broken heart if he'd just tried. Instead, his roommate had swallowed a bunch of pills while Warren had been at a party. Stumbling over his roommate's lifeless body just inside the door of their condo had sobered him up quickly.

Jonas heaved off the couch and sat on the arm of Warren's chair, breaching the invisible shield that had always been in place, even between friends. It should have been weird. Warren had always maintained that distance. When they went to a bar with bench seats at the table, Jonas and Hendrix shared and Warren sat by himself. As he should. Marcus had been his roommate and the empty seat next to him served as a constant reminder.

But it was nice, to have his remaining friends here at a time when difficult memories were his constant companions.

"Will it surprise you to learn that I talked to him, too?" Jonas asked. "I called his mom twice. There were a lot of people concerned about him, and all of us did what we thought was best. But in the end, the blame has to lie with Marcus. He made that decision, not you."

Intellectually, Warren knew that. But his gut was where things didn't feel right. "How can I go on and be happy when Marcus doesn't get that opportunity? It's not fair."

Hendrix sat forward on the edge of the couch. "What, like you have to punish yourself for the rest of your life for someone else's choices? Trust me when I say you'll end up miserable if you do that. You deserve to have whatever relationships you're willing to work for in life. It's that simple. This is about you, not Marcus."

Warren shook his head. "I'm not good with people. I screwed up with Tilda. She left because I can't be what she needs."

"I thought she left because of her immigration status," Hendrix said blithely. "Do tell."

Walked into that one. "I fell for her, okay? Happy now? Is that what you wanted to hear?"

Jonas made a noise in his throat. "Yeah, but only because you needed to hear it, too. You let her walk away because you're scared to be happy, not because you're not good with people. That's an excuse that won't fly here. You don't have to be good with people. Just Tilda. Are you good with her?"

So good.

And he'd let her go.

It was killing him slowly and would only get worse. "Doesn't matter. She only cares about the project. That was the last thing she said to me. Send me the divorce papers and don't worry about your market share."

"Yeah, I'm sure you jumped right on that and told her that market share meant nothing to you," Hendrix said sarcastically. "What a complete and utter shock that any woman who's spent more than five minutes in your company could possibly be confused about your feelings for her versus Flying Squirrel."

"You don't have to be an ass about it," Warren muttered.

The point wasn't lost on him. Tilda's parting words had been a far more painful variation of *Why don't you marry your company?* Every woman in his life had butted up against his workaholic tendencies. Tilda didn't have any special shield against it just because she was as enthusiastic about work as he was.

"Seems like that's the only way to get through your thick skull," Hendrix said. "And while we're on the subject, here's what you're going to do. Get on a plane, go to Australia and tell Tilda you're in love with her. If she says it back, then you can spend the rest of your life figuring out how to feel like you deserve it. If you don't get on a plane, you'll spend the rest of your life regretting that you didn't. It's really not that hard."

"I can't do that." Oh, he wanted to. His heart rate tripled as he envisioned doing exactly that. But he couldn't. What if he forgot about her triggers and grabbed her again? He might destroy her the same way he had… Marcus.

No. That wasn't his fault. Greedily, he clung to that absolution from his friends.

Except it wasn't sticking. He'd messed up with Tilda, too. Clearly, he wasn't good at this kind of thing.

Groaning, he put his head into his hands. Either he believed the things his friends were telling him or he didn't. Getting past this was as much his decision as it had been Marcus's to take his own life, and all at once, Warren didn't want to take on the responsibility for other peoples' choices. Just his own.

And he was choosing happiness.

No, he hadn't bothered to try with Tilda. He'd just

sent her back to Australia to protect himself from further screwups. But what if they could work through her triggers? If she even wanted that. How would he know her mind unless he talked to her? It didn't have to be hard. Like Hendrix had said.

He'd made a mistake in letting her go. The biggest one of his life. And that was a turning point, as well, considering that, for the longest time, he'd have said failing Marcus was his biggest mistake. No longer. He could fix *this* mistake.

"You guys need to leave," he said to them both as he stood, nearly toppling Jonas from his perch on the armrest. "I have a very long flight ahead of me."

Melbourne welcomed Tilda in much the same manner as it had seen her off—with little fanfare. Of course, she'd sneaked away to the US without telling anyone but her mum and had landed at Tullamarine upon her return as quietly as possible.

No point in stirring the pot. She had enough on her plate, what with nursing a bruised heart and a job that she still had to do alongside a man she was trying to forget. Adding Bryan McDermott into the mix would not make things any better. But if he stayed true to form, he'd find out she was home soon enough.

Oddly, she was too numb to remember what it felt like to be so fearful of him. As the taxi drove down her mum's quiet street, the only thing she could focus on was how much she did not want to be in Melbourne, but for far different reasons than the ones she'd expected.

She missed Warren. She'd fallen in love with his house, his smile, the way he held her hand as they slept because he'd somehow figured out she didn't like waking up with his arm across her chest. But she liked being connected to him and he'd known that, as well. Somehow.

Too bad his sixth sense hadn't extended beyond that. He obviously had no clue she'd fallen for him, and how she'd hidden it, she had no idea. But she'd pulled that off brilliantly, hadn't she? He didn't have to contend with a mess of a wife much longer.

Mum was waiting for her at the door, blubbering about how thin Tilda was, the pastiness of her complexion and a multitude of other sins that needed to be fixed right away, apparently.

"I'm fine, Mum." Tilda dropped her bag in the entryway of the small clapboard house at the end of a neat row of similar houses. "I'm tired. I need to sleep."

She had no idea what time it was or when she next had to be on the phone with Warren. Or how in the world she'd handle that when the time came. Melbourne wasn't nearly far enough away to dull the ache that just thinking about him caused.

Falling into the bed located in the small guest bedroom, Tilda let her eyes drift shut, craving the oblivion. When she came to, it was midafternoon and Mum was nowhere to be found. The note on the dining room table said she'd gone to the market and would be back soon.

A knock came at the front door. For a half second, she hesitated—Warren's staff opened the door, not the lady of the house. But she wasn't the lady of any house anymore, and Warren was thousands of miles away. Blearily, Tilda crossed the small living room to answer it.

"Forget your key, Mum?" Tilda asked with a small smile as she swung open the door.

All the blood drained from her head. *Bryan.* Standing on her mother's doorstep as if he had all the right in the world to be there. Struggling to breathe, she gulped air and tried to get her legs to move. Her arms. Something. *Slam the door*, her brain screamed. *Shut it. Right now.*

"Nice to see you, Tilda," he said in that menacing voice she heard in her nightmares.

No! He couldn't be here. Not so soon. How had he learned she was back so quickly? This was ten times worse than she'd ever imagined. He must have people at the airport. Or listening devices on her mother's phone.

"I can't say the same."

Good. Okay. She could talk. She could breathe.

If she slammed the door in his face, would he break it down? She had to think. Distract him. Call someone.

"I've been waiting for you to come back," he said. "We have unfinished business."

That put her back up. What was unfinished? He'd stripped her of everything, and only because she'd wanted her confidence back had she gone in search of it. Warren had given her that and so much more. He'd given her purpose. Meaning. The freedom to be herself.

Actually, Bryan was right. They did have unfinished business. "So, you've come to apologize?"

He blinked. "I'm here to collect what's mine."

"A black eye? That's the only thing that you'll leave here with."

Had that really just come out of her mouth? A quiet

sense of pride joined the sick fuzzies in her stomach, nearly settling it at the same time.

Confidence. She knew what it felt like now and this was it. Bryan wasn't stealing it from her again.

"Are you threatening me?" Bryan asked as if he couldn't quite believe it. "If you so much as touch me, I'll have you arrested. You know I can make your life miserable."

She crossed her arms and leaned on the doorjamb, letting a small smile play about her mouth. "So, you're saying you'd be willing to testify in a court of law that a woman half your size clocked you?"

That sounded like fun. She might even do it just to see if he'd actually follow through with calling his buddies to do his dirty work.

He blinked again. "No. That's not what I'm saying."

"Too bad. I'd love to see the looks on the faces of the guys on your squad when you tell them you let a girl punch you and wouldn't they please run over to arrest her."

Bryan took a step back and it was every bit a retreat, whether he realized it or not. "You wouldn't punch me."

"Won't I?" She swept him with a scorn-filled glance, seeing him for the coward he was. The power of it roared through her, sweeping away cobwebs she'd long grown accustomed to. "I've been in America, as I'm sure your sources informed you. I learned a lot of things about how to protect myself. I wouldn't be too sure what I would and wouldn't do, if I were you."

And it wasn't even a total lie. She had learned a lot about how to pick up her pieces. No matter what, Warren had renewed her faith in herself. And given her the ability to talk down to her former abuser, apparently.

It was not her fault he'd hit her. Not her fault he'd been jealous and possessive.

And she was not taking his crap ever again.

"This is not over," he warned as he stepped back once again. "We're not over. You're mine and—"

She slammed the door and locked it. Sure, he could probably bust through the wood frame easily, but she didn't think he would. She'd stood up to him with stellar results, the likes of which even she couldn't believe.

Warren had given her back her life in more ways than one.

"Tilda," Bryan called through the door. "I—"

"Go away, you piece of garbage. I have my phone in my hand and I will call the authorities to have you picked up for trespassing." It wasn't an idle threat. Surely there would be someone on the Victoria police force who wasn't in Bryan's pocket and would be willing to uphold the law. She'd keep dialing until she found that person.

It went quiet outside and she peeked through the curtain to see Bryan slinking back to the gutter he'd come from. The victory was a little hollow but it was still a victory.

She ate dinner with her mum and didn't think about Bryan at all. Until the next day, when he knocked on the door again while her mother was getting her hair done.

Marching to the entrance, she flung open the door. "You can't be here." As she met the gaze of the man on her mother's doorstep, her knees went weak.

Warren. Not Bryan. So not Bryan she couldn't even process it.

"I know." Warren held up his beautiful hands as if to ward her off, and why wouldn't he? She'd practically attacked him before even getting the door open. "I should have called. I'm sorry."

"No. It's fine. I thought you were…someone else." But on that note…she slid a once-over all the way down his body, drinking in his wrinkled slacks and the shirtsleeves rolled to the elbows. "Why are you here? You're really here, right? This is not a figment of my overactive imagination?"

The caution eased from his face as he smiled. "Really here. I flew all night on Roz's father's private jet."

Her mouth might have been hanging open. "Why?"

"Because that was the fastest way to get to Australia. And you," he said simply, and everything else in the world melted away as she stared at him.

Her heart threw itself out of her chest and latched onto him greedily, lapping up every bit of his nearness.

"You told me to get on a plane," she reminded him and pushed back the sudden desire to jump into his arms. Their horrible parting still sat in her stomach like a rock. "Only for you to follow me? You're not making any sense."

Clearly flustered, he ran his fingers through his hair, and that's when she noticed he didn't have his cell phone in either hand. Her well-trained eye didn't locate it in either of his front pockets, either, which meant it must be charging in the long limo behind him. That or the apocalypse were the only two things she could think of that would pry his phone out of his hand.

"Only because I'm exhausted and all I can think

about is how much I want to kiss you," he said, and his small smile shouldn't have warmed her as much as it did.

"Oh, I get it," she said before he could say some more things that would make her forget how hopeless it was to think they could be together. "You came to Melbourne for a few days to micromanage the project. The idea of me handling all of it here at ground zero without you in the middle must have really freaked you out. Nice that you can combine your first love with a little side action, courtesy of your project manager."

"Please, Tilda." Warren shook his head, his eyes warm with some emotion she couldn't fathom. "Listen to me. I shouldn't have started with kissing. I haven't slept because I spent the entire flight working out the details for Thomas to take over as CEO."

"You…what?" Her brain was having trouble processing, obviously. "Does CEO stand for something other than what I think it does? Chief Energy Officer?"

He rubbed at his temple as if she was giving him a headache. "It means I gave him the reins. I walked away from Flying Squirrel. There's no Down Under Thunder project anymore. Well, I mean, I guess Thomas can pick it up if he wants—"

Her lungs seized, and she tried to inhale and exhale at the same time, then choked on it. Coughing, she held up a finger to Warren who had a tinge of panic coloring his expression.

"Hold on," she wheezed. "I swear it sounded like you just said you walked away from your company."

"That is what I said. Tilda…" Warren held up a hand, fingers spread, and then dropped it. "I forget that I don't have the right to touch you anymore. It's automatic now to broadcast every move I make when I'm around you, but my muscles didn't get the message that I screwed up and let you go."

She felt his words in her bones. "I don't understand anything you're telling me right now. You gave Thomas the company and got on a plane to Australia to manage a project that doesn't exist anymore?"

"I got on a plane to follow the woman I love."

And that simple phrase changed everything, including the will to stay so far away from him.

"I think you better come in." She opened the door wider, but as he crossed the threshold, she planted herself in his path so neatly that he almost bowled her over. The only way to keep them both off the ground was for him to throw his arms around her, which—not so coincidentally—was what she'd been going for.

"Price of admission," she told him, and his grip tightened, hefting her closer until she fit into the grooves of his body like a second skin. Perfect.

God, he felt so good. Solid, warm, everything she'd been missing, and here he was, in her arms. She shouldn't be so free with her affections, not when he'd ended everything so easily with scarcely a goodbye wave. But he'd followed her, and that counted for a lot.

"I had a whole apology planned out," he said, his voice rough with emotion. "But I'm having a hard time remembering it."

"This is pretty good as apologies go."

That's when he pulled back to catch her gaze in his and she nearly growled in frustration as his heat left her.

"No. It's not. I was stupid to let you go. I should

have told you that I was falling in love with you the moment I realized it."

That was even better than an apology. "Say it again."

"I love you, Tilda Garinger. Assuming you're okay with taking my name and making this a real marriage. I know we have so many things to work through. I haven't been as understanding about your triggers as I could be. If you'll forgive me, I'll spend the rest of my life standing by your side as we work through whatever we need to. I won't abandon you to deal with this alone. I promise."

"You didn't," she protested weakly, still stuck back on *a real marriage*. "You were always patient with me. More than I deserved."

She hadn't wanted to burden him with her problems. But only by coming home could she have dealt with the last remnants of her nightmares. And she had. The blackness inside had lifted, leaving her wide open to accept the things he was telling her.

"You deserve whatever you need to get to a place where we can be together," he told her fiercely. "I'm all in. We can live wherever you feel the most comfortable. Greece, Italy, Canada. You pick. I'm at your complete mercy."

It dawned on her that, once again, he was giving her complete control over their future, and that broke the last of her barriers. "I don't care. As long as I'm with you, we'll make it work."

That's when he kissed her. Fiercely. Possessively. And she loved the idea of being claimed by a man like Warren.

Happily-ever-after was in her reach this time.

Epilogue

In the end, Tilda couldn't pick just one place to live. When Warren handed her the world, she took it. And he had never been happier that he'd gotten on that plane in search of a permanent do-over.

For two people who couldn't have properly spelled *vacation* a month ago, Tilda and Warren were making up for lost time. The word *work* was never uttered. By either of them. He'd sent Roz's father's plane back to Raleigh and bought his own so they'd never run out of options for travel as they tried to figure out what country they wanted as their permanent residence. Since he'd left his cell phone on the nightstand at his empty house in the States, there was nothing to distract him from doing the thing he'd come to enjoy the most: buying his wife clothes.

The city of Milan as a whole appreciated Warren's

money. He'd spent more of it on custom-made Italian lingerie, dresses and shoes for Tilda than he had on the entire Down Under Thunder campaign. Which was fitting, in his mind. She was worth far more than any success Flying Squirrel had to offer.

As they had dinner on the private terrace of the four-story villa Warren had rented in the center of Piazza Giulio Cesare, an exclusive area of Milan, he couldn't help but take a moment to drink in the sight of her beautiful face. Tilda had twisted her hair up into one of her loose chignons, which she only did with the express intent of having him undo it later.

He always undid it later. And sometimes he couldn't wait. Like tonight. He needed to touch all that hair. Dinner would still be there after.

Automatically, he fanned his fingers to be sure she saw him reaching for her, then pulled the clip free. She shook her head with a smile, letting hair rain down her back.

"It's one of those nights, is it?" she asked—rhetorically, as she'd already slid out of her chair on her way to his.

Boldly, she climbed into his lap, dinner apparently forgotten on both sides. She settled into her favorite position—on top—and framed his face with her hands to hold him still while she kissed him. He let her. There was nothing that turned him on more than when his wife took control of her pleasure.

The house phone rang, enough of a rarity that it distracted him from the warm, sexy woman burrowing through his clothes to get their skins touching as fast as possible. Normally, he'd ignore everything but Tilda, but he'd been expecting a call.

Standing easily with Tilda in his arms, he carried her into the house to set her on the back of the couch, her legs still wrapped around his waist as he answered the phone that was sitting on the end table. As he'd hoped, it was his private detective calling, and he listened to the man with half an ear as Tilda got very intrigued by this new position he'd unwittingly found for her.

Warren barely had two brain cells left to rub together when she started unbuckling his pants, stroking him through his underwear. Finally, he got the chatty detective off the phone and let his wife's busy hands finish the job she'd started, namely to drive him insane.

Quickly, she got him good and primed, and within moments, they were both moaning their way through a spectacular finish against the back of the couch. As he crested in a glorious climax, he pulled her into his arms and held on. She returned the favor, keeping him on earth with her solid, amazing presence alone.

"Let me take you to bed," he told her hoarsely, and she nodded, but once he got her there, all he could do was look at her, touching her face reverently as he worshipped her with his gaze. "I love you."

"I love you, too," she returned sweetly. "Sorry I made you get off the phone."

"You should be. I barely got the information I needed in order to give you the good news."

"I like good news. Tell me."

"McDermott is in jail." Finally. All of his efforts to get the case against her ex buttoned up had worked. Warren could give her closure to that nightmare, once and for all.

Her brows shot up. "I hope he finds a very nice boyfriend in prison. One who treats him as well as he treated me. And I'll thank you to never mention that filth to me again."

He smiled. His wife's strength was amazing, and her confidence was one of her sexiest qualities. "Done. Now that you're free from that terror, what would you like to do next?"

"Sweetheart, I was already free." Tilda kissed him gently and she poured so much emotion into it that the backs of his eyelids pricked. "I wouldn't have agreed to a real marriage with that still hanging over us. I never want the past to overshadow the present. Or our future."

And that was the best endorsement of love with a capital L that Warren had ever heard.

* * * * *

Don't miss the first two IN NAME ONLY *books,*
Jonas's story:

BEST FRIEND BRIDE

and Hendrix's story:

ONE NIGHT STAND BRIDE

And for more of Kat Cantrell's sexy,
emotional style,
pick up these other titles!

THE THINGS SHE SAYS
MARRIAGE WITH BENEFITS
PREGNANT BY MORNING

Available now from Mills & Boon Desire!

“Was that to make the engagement seem more real?” Ellie asked.

The question came out as a whisper. She regretted it a second later, sure that he would use it as an excuse to switch back to the cool, in-control Derrick she’d met that first night.

He smiled down at her. “Do you think there are cameras in here?”

“I meant were you trying to get me accustomed to kissing you.”

“I kissed you because I wanted to kiss you.” He skimmed his thumb over her lower lip. “For the record, fake engagement or not, I don’t want you to kiss me unless you want to.”

“We seem to be stepping into dangerous territory.”

“Agreed.” He cupped her cheek and his fingers slipped into her hair. The simple touch, so light, felt so good…and so scary.

This was fake. This was about saving her brother and restoring Derrick’s reputation.

That was all it could be.

* * *

Pregnant by the CEO
is part of The Jameson Heirs series—
They’ll do anything to save the
family business—even fall in love!

PREGNANT BY THE CEO

BY
HELENKAY DIMON

First Published in Great Britain 2018
By Mills & Boon, an imprint of HarperCollins*Publishers*
1 London Bridge Street, London, SE1 9GF

ISBN: 978-0-263-93587-5

51-0118

MIX
Paper from
responsible sources
FSC™ C007454

This book is produced from independently certified FSC™ paper to ensure responsible forest management.

For more information visit: www.harpercollins.co.uk/green

Printed and bound in Spain
by CPI, Barcelona

HelenKay Dimon is a divorce lawyer turned full-time author. Her bestselling and award-winning books have been showcased in numerous publications, including the *Washington Post* and *Cosmopolitan*. She is an RT Reviewers' Choice Award winner and has been a finalist for the Romance Writers of America's RITA® Award multiple times. This is her first Mills & Boon Desire novel.

One

The DC Insider: *Rumor has it Washington, DC's most eligible and notoriously difficult bachelor—the man named the* Insider*'s Hottest Ticket in Town for three years running—might finally be off the market. All that talk about bad security and bad management? Could be a disgruntled baby brother getting even with his sister's new beau. When asked about a supposed secret girlfriend and her meddlesome brother, hotshot businessman Derrick Jameson would only say, "Ellie Gold is lovely." Sounds like an admission to us. Stay tuned.*

Ellie Gold had never punched anyone before, but she vowed to end that lifelong streak right now.

Wearing the only cocktail dress she owned, simple and black, with a matching black lace overlay, and spiky heels that made her arches ache, she stepped into the private dining room on the top floor of the historic Hay-Adams Hotel named, interestingly enough, the Top of the Hay.

For a second the anger choking her brain cleared. Her breath hitched as her gaze wandered around the sparkling space with the fancy chandeliers and cream-colored walls. Only the business people milling around with death grips on their drinks, all looking awkward and out of place in their navy suits, threatened to ruin the fairy-tale moment.

French doors lined the outer walls and vaulted skylights soared above her. She stretched up on tiptoe to peek around more than one set of shoulders to the stunning view of the White House below.

Her balance faltered and she might have landed headfirst in a nearby tray of champagne glasses but fingers wrapped around her elbow and steadied her. She glanced up to say thank-you and saw a face...*his* face.

Derrick Jameson, the oldest son of a vast empire that included everything from commercial real estate in Washington, DC, to a prize-winning horse farm in the Virginia countryside. The guy who excelled at making her life miserable.

Just seeing him made her forget how to spell. She wasn't all that sure she could recite the alphabet if pressed, either. She wanted to blame the fury flowing through her, but even she had to admit that might not be the real reason for her hottie-induced speech lapse.

She'd researched Derrick before tonight, reading online in stories that droned on about his money and dating life. But seeing him up close? No one had prepared her for that.

The black hair and striking light brown eyes. She'd read about his family background and picked up on the subtle hint of Japanese heritage passed on from his maternal grandmother. The firm chin. Those shoulders.

The features combined into a potent package of tall, dark and delicious. He gave off a confident vibe. In control and assessing. But his unspoken determination to destroy her reputation and rip her family apart marred her appreciation of his pretty face.

"Ms. Gold." He nodded and threw in a little smile for a group of people walking past him. "I didn't expect to see you at a business function."

Her voice came back to her in a rush. So did the rage swirling in her gut. "Interesting tactic."

"Excuse me?"

"That charming thing you're doing?" She leaned in closer and dropped her voice to a whisper, ignoring how good he smelled. "I'm not buying it."

He continued to hold her arm. Not in a tight grip. No, his thumb brushed back and forth over her bare skin in a gentle caress, as if trying to soothe her. The guy seemed oblivious to the fact that he was the one causing her stress. Well, him and everyone and everything else in her life.

He might not know it but she hovered right on the edge and his decisions kept shoving her closer to the abyss. Her baby brother, Noah, was in a strange emotional downward spiral, all thanks to Derrick and his claims about Noah stealing from him.

She'd practically raised Noah after their parents died in a car crash. He wasn't easy, but he wasn't a thief. Her brother had been argumentative and frustrated back then, much more so than other kids. She'd dragged him to a specialist, who diagnosed him with oppositional defiant disorder, something she'd never even heard of before that moment.

She'd scraped together the money for the therapies not covered by insurance. But even now, at times of stress or when he felt cornered, the flashes of anger would come back and he'd buck authority. Something about Derrick had Noah's negative behavior kicking to the surface again.

The worst part was that Noah didn't even see it. She did. She'd watched him make bad choices as a kid, tried to help him to the point where she'd sacrificed her personal life to spend all of her extra time with him. The idea that his issues were resurging now, at twenty, deflated her.

She'd deal with that later. Right now she needed to handle Derrick.

"This is serious." Serious enough for her to track him down through a series of calls to his office.

"Is it?" Amusement filled his voice as he handed her his glass of champagne.

She couldn't think of anything more annoying than that welcoming lilt to his voice. The whole fake-charming scene threw her off. She didn't realize he had shifted and moved them toward the elevators until she looked around the room and saw the space between them and the rest of the party.

She didn't know if this was a rich guy's way of escorting her out of the building or something else. Either way, she was not ready to be dismissed. There was too much at stake for her to give up now. "Mr. Jameson, I—"

"Derrick."

She'd investigated Derrick's business when her baby brother got a job there seven months ago. At first, Noah had talked about Derrick in a nonstop cycle of hero worship. His enthusiasm had rubbed off on her. She'd clicked on every photo of him. Let her mind wander, tried to imagine what it might be like to see that shockingly handsome face close up.

Now she knew.

She worked in human resources up until six weeks ago. She hadn't reached management level yet. The Jameson family was the equivalent of DC royalty. She didn't move in their world. She also possessed a general distrust of people who rolled around in that kind of money. But Noah had been impressed. And, up until that point in his life, almost *nothing* had impressed her brilliant but moody brother.

In theory, Derrick was more mature and reasonable than her brother. But thanks to this gossip site silliness she wasn't totally convinced that was true.

"The *DC Insider* posted a note about us." The comment rolled out of her mouth as if it made any sense. She still couldn't believe she had to confront him about this.

For a second Derrick stared at her, not saying a word, then he nodded. "I know."

Words backed up in her brain until she finally pushed them out. "What kind of response is that?"

"My name is in the social column because I allowed it to be there."

Good grief. "Are you kidding?"

He frowned at her. "No."

"I'm thinking people have let you get away with nonsense for far too long." When he started to pipe in, she talked right over him. "I mean, really. Do you know how condescending you sound?"

This time he studied her. She could feel him assessing and reordering his strategy as they talked.

"I called you *lovely* in that *Insider* quote, if that helps," he said.

It took a second for her brain to catch up again. She silently blamed all the people in suits standing around, staring at them and whispering, but she worried his smooth tone might be the *real* issue with her concentration. "It doesn't, and that's not the point."

"Should I have used a different word?"

His focus on vocabulary made her head pound. She shifted until she put her back to most of the room. Maybe not seeing the gawkers would help. "Stop talking."

He made a sound that came close to a growl. "People don't usually speak to me that way."

"Which is probably part of the problem here." She'd never worked in a classroom but her mother had. Ellie called up that disappointed-fifth-grade-teacher tone without even trying. "Okay, so you're admitting you planted the article?"

"Of course."

The champagne sloshed over the side of her glass. "The one about me?"

Because that was the point. She came there to pry the

truth out of him about the planted story, maybe put him on the defensive. He ruined her plans by admitting to spreading the gossip, like it was no big deal.

He slipped the flute out of her fingers and put it on the small table behind him. "Technically, the story is about me."

She inhaled, trying to bring some air into her lungs and refresh her brain cells. She refused to get lost in his words or have a "him" versus "them" fight because she had the very clear sense confusing wordplay was one of the ways he won arguments. "Okay, why do it?"

"To change the public conversation from your brother's false allegations while I figure out what he did with the money that is now missing from my business accounts." Derrick answered without blinking, following their conversation with ease as it bounced around.

She decided to ignore the money part for now. "But you named me as your…well, I guess as the woman you're dating?"

"That's right."

She had no idea what to think about that nonchalant response. "We don't even know each other. Why would you think that's okay?"

"My *business* is the most important thing to me."

She didn't try to hide her wince at his sudden stern tone. "My *brother* is the most important thing to me."

"Wrong answer, Ellie."

Was he really making a tsking sound? "What is wrong with you?"

"I have two brothers, both adults," Derrick explained with all the emotion of someone reading a recipe. "They take care of themselves. I take care of me and the business."

"That's cold…bloodless."

He actually smiled. "Is it possible you're the one with the confused priorities?"

She swallowed a gasp, along with a bit of her anger and possibly some of her dignity. The whole conversation was ridiculous but she could not tear herself away from him… not yet.

"Let me get this straight. A perpetual bachelor and notorious ladies' man who is being trolled on the internet by my little brother in his antibusiness videos is giving me advice on interpersonal relationships?" She wanted to sigh, throw things. "Listen, Mr. Jameson."

"It's still Derrick."

The way he stayed calm made her temper spike even more. The heat rose inside her and flooded her cheeks with every controlled word he uttered. She refused to believe the sudden need for a fan had anything to do with his perfect face or that sexy smile. Not that she found either all that appealing. "Do not mention my name to anyone ever again."

"Now, Ellie." His eyes narrowed. "You don't think that's maybe—just a little—extreme."

Apparently she was not the only one familiar with the teacher tone. He threw it out there and nailed her with it. As if she needed another reason to dislike him. "Leave my brother alone."

"When your brother comes clean and then backs off those videos, I will."

"You're a grown-up."

"So is he." Derrick leaned in close enough for his warm breath to brush her cheek. "My suggestion to you is that you start treating him like one."

"I'm not kidding around."

His eyes traveled over her face, lingering on her mouth. "I can see that."

She fought off the tremor moving through her. "Leave me out of your games."

Before he could say anything else or touch her again, she

slipped around him and through the crowd of people heading toward them. Kept going until she got on the elevator and watched the doors close on his smiling face. Getting her breathing to return to normal and the image of his face to disappear from her mind took longer.

An hour later Ellie poured a glass of red wine as she kicked off her stupid heels. Thanks to a bout of storming and muttering, she'd wasted most of her energy and hadn't made it to her apartment. She needed to vent and that meant taking the Metro to her best friend's condo instead.

Vanessa McAllister's one-bedroom place was small but cozy. Light bounced off the bright yellow walls. During the day, the sun beamed in from the large window at the far end of the living room.

A steady beat of background conversation came from the television. Ellie had no idea what show was on and didn't care. Vanessa didn't appear to, either.

Of course, very little ruffled her. Between her navy career father and her French mother, Vanessa had been all over the world. She spoke a ridiculous number of languages that served her well in her job at the museum.

Ellie trusted Vanessa with any secret. They'd met in college and had been best friends ever since. They supported and cheered for each other. And right now, Vanessa was frowning.

She sat on the stool at her kitchen's breakfast bar. She sipped from her almost-empty glass of red wine as she scowled at the laptop screen in front of her. "Tell me again what happened at that fancy cocktail party."

The somewhat distant tone. That wasn't good.

Ellie was almost afraid to answer. She did, anyway. "I met Derrick Jameson and told him to back off."

The explanation sounded good. So strong. Just what Ellie wanted to be. After years of racing around, trying to keep every ball in the air and failing most of the time, Ellie wanted to be in control of her life and not running behind it, trying to catch up.

Vanessa tapped on the keyboard. "Uh-huh."

Yeah, not good. "What does that response mean?"

"Did you happen to see a photographer while you were there?" Vanessa sat straighter and waved her hand in the air. "Forget it. I'll just go ahead and read it to you before you explode."

Ellie dropped the paper napkin she was twisting in her fingers. "Wait, read what?"

"The latest from that *Insider* site."

"No." Ellie's stomach fell. She could have sworn it hit the floor.

"'Derrick Jameson and Ellie Gold made an official appearance together at the swanky Hay-Adams Hotel tonight. No word on whether they got a room, but they did leave the business party one right after the other, making more than one partygoer wonder if Derrick sprang for the presidential suite…'"

Silence screamed through the room. Ellie could feel it hammering in her head as it rumbled through her.

"Okay." Vanessa cleared her throat. "So, that happened."

"It did *not* happen." Ellie reached over and turned the laptop to face her. "We argued. We fought."

She started tapping random keys. Anything to make that now familiar *Insider* website disappear.

"Wait, go back. There's a photo." Vanessa swatted Ellie's hand away then leaned in and pointed at the screen. "Why does it look like you're hanging on his arm?"

As if Ellie could deny it. The evidence, even though it didn't show the whole story, was right there. Her pressing against him, looking up at him. Anyone seeing this would believe they were having an intimate chat.

"That's not… I was just…" The words clogged her throat in the rush to get them out. "I'm going to kill him."

Vanessa winced. "You can't think that he—"

"Of course he planted this. I'm his PR plan." And he wasn't even trying to hide it. He'd been very clear. She just hadn't realized he'd turned it on full-time.

Vanessa made a humming sound. "He really is cute."

"Don't."

"But clearly a gigantic ass." Vanessa's voice sounded harsher that time.

"Better." But still not good enough. Ellie wanted to forget all about his smug face.

"Hating him doesn't fix the Noah situation," Vanessa said, being far too reasonable for the moment.

"Or help with my income issue or get my life under control. Yeah, I know."

Vanessa's shoulders fell as she sighed. "I can give you money, or move in here with me and don't pay rent for a few months. Give yourself a financial break."

"I can't."

"You can." Vanessa made a grumbling sound as she said something under her breath that wasn't quite clear. "I'm thinking about stuffing twenties into your purse while you're not looking."

With that, Ellie felt some of the Derrick-related anger drain away. She reached over and gave her friend's arm a quick squeeze. "You're awesome and I love you, but this is bigger than a short-term money problem. It's like everything is spinning and I can't make it stop." Even now her life choices ran through her head as she questioned each one. "I still can't believe I got fired for something that wasn't my fault."

"So, take it back." Vanessa grabbed the bottle and refilled her glass. "Control, I mean. Start with one thing. You take a small piece, conquer that and then move on."

The advice rolled around in Ellie's head until it took hold. She knew exactly which battle to wage first. "Right. Derrick Jameson."

"Um, no. I was thinking more like you could get a temp job and rebuild." Vanessa topped off Ellie's glass. "A guy like Jameson is not easily managed. Forget him. Handle what *you* need first."

The suggestion made sense but Ellie couldn't survive that way. She'd spent so much of her life fixing things. First, for her father, who had one pipe dream after another, and her mother, who had fought to keep them together as a family. Then for her brother. She didn't have the energy left to tackle straightening out her life, but she would. Later. Once she'd dealt with Derrick and Noah was back on track. "I have to handle these other pieces first."

Vanessa shook her head. "Ellie, you can't fix everything."

"I can fix this. If Derrick Jameson wants a battle, he's going to get one."

Two

The DC Insider: *The hottest romance in town just got more interesting. Ever wonder what happens when the lady in question calls our office to insist there is no romance? Well, we call the gentlemen for his comment. And Derrick Jameson did not disappoint. The usually demanding businessman chuckled and said, "You should listen to Ellie. I enjoy acquiescing to her." These two are never dull.*

She'd been summoned.

The call came at a little after nine the next morning. Ellie debated ignoring it. She wasn't exactly the type to jump when a man ordered, but then Derrick was no ordinary man. He seemed to enjoy ticking her off.

Yet there she was, two hours later, walking along a long hallway on the fifteenth floor of the Jameson Industries' office building. Pristine white walls surrounded her as her heels clicked against the polished hardwood floors. People moved in and out and around cubicle walls. They carried stacks of papers and shuffled with a sense of urgency.

She missed the energy of a busy office. Insurance underwriting wasn't the most exciting topic but she'd worked in human resources, slowly taking on more responsibility.

She loved coming into a pile of files waiting on her desk each morning and solving problems.

Everything went fine until the big boss took an overactive interest in her. She'd done everything she'd been trained to do. Documented his behavior. She'd known how hard it was to report that sort of thing up the chain of command without becoming the subject of gossip. Before her boss made his move she'd set up a system to handle the concerns. Then she got fired before she could implement it.

The attorney she contacted about the firing but could barely afford said she had a good case. But her former boss had the resources to drag the thing out and exhaust her.

She tried not to think about that as two men headed straight for her. She slipped to the side, banging into the wall and knocking the corner of a painting. One that likely cost more than her car. After that, one more turn and she moved into a quieter part of the floor. No one scurried here.

Sleek furniture made of unblemished leather with shiny chrome accents filled the open reception area. That, and a desk covered with piles of files, was all that stood between her and a set of closed double doors. Those and the guy next to her. She couldn't remember her escort's name, wasn't even sure he'd offered it.

Before she could ask, he reached out and knocked on the door to the right in front of them. One brisk thwack then he opened it. Even gestured for her to step inside in front of him.

No, thank you.

Her legs refused to move, anyway. The threshold seemed innocent enough, but the man on the other side was not. Every inch of this place screamed money. Something she'd never had enough of and worked liked crazy to stockpile in case her life hit a bump...just as it had. More like a Himalayan mountain, but still.

She couldn't see Derrick at the moment, but she did have an unrestricted view of his desk. The thing had to be eight feet long. Formidable, like the man who sat at it.

She refused to go one step further. Decided to call out instead. "What do you want?"

"Come inside," the faceless voice said from some hidden corner of the office.

She noted the deep and commanding tone. Yeah, this was going to be a quick meeting.

"I'm fine here," she said.

The security guy put his hand over his mouth to cover what sounded like a fake cough. He hesitated a second before saying anything. "You really should obey him."

Apparently she'd gotten off the elevator and stepped back a century. "Did you use the word *obey*?"

"Don't fight with Jackson. It's me you want," Derrick said, still without making an appearance.

She glanced at the man looming next to her. He stood well over six feet with brown hair and a lean athletic build. Attractive in a liked-to-run-along-the-Potomac sort of way, he looked far too amused by what was happening. "Is Jackson your first name or last?"

Before he could answer, Derrick stepped out of the room off to the side of his office and into the doorway. Hovered right in front of her. He nodded as a small smile played on the corner of his mouth. "Ellie, it's good to see you again."

The warmth in his eyes. That tone. A strange dizziness slammed into her when he got close. No way was she being reeled in by that charm thing he seemed to have flicked on. Nope, she knew better.

She managed a nod. "Mr. Jameson."

"Come inside. Despite our argument last night, we have a lot to discuss." He swept a hand toward the inside of his oversize corner office.

The very real sense she was out of her league slammed into her. "What would you do if I said no?"

He frowned. "Why would you?"

"You have this guy following me around the hallways… no offense." She winced as she glanced at Jackson before looking at Derrick again. "Then there's the part where you ordered me to come here. Today. Right now."

"Ten minutes ago."

"What?"

"I *asked* you to meet with me ten minutes ago. I assumed you being late was some sort of power play. Unless you have a problem with tardiness. If so, we'll need to work on that."

She glanced at Jackson again. "Is he serious?"

Jackson nodded. "Almost always."

"Ellie." That's it. Derrick just said her name then turned and walked across the room, stopping next to his desk.

"Your manners need some work." She didn't bother mumbling as she followed him. If he wasn't going to be subtle, neither was she.

"So I've been told."

"Then there's the very real sense you're setting me up." Not so much a sense as a fact. If he planted one rumor, he could plant many. And that seemed to be his intent.

"How so?" He had the nerve to look confused.

She refused to believe he was that clueless.

"I complain about a story on the internet about us and suddenly there's a photo of us up there, complete with a new quote from you." An annoying quote. One that didn't say anything yet managed to say a lot. "I called them and denied that we were together and you…actually, I don't know what you were doing when you talked to the *Insider*."

"I was being a gentleman."

She took a few steps. Hovering there in his office gave her confidence. "You mean the I-don't-kiss-and-tell thing?

Oh, please. You were toying with them because it amused you."

"Admittedly, I'm not often at a loss for words, but I'm not sure what to say to that comment."

"You could admit you set me up to be featured on the *Insider*. Again." The sound of a cough and rustling had her turning around.

Jackson stood there with his attention focused on Derrick. "Do you need anything from me, sir?"

"No, but it would be wise to stay close by in the hall in case Ms. Gold brought a weapon."

She had forgotten poor Jackson was still there. Hearing the door click behind her as he left, she tried not to fidget. Now it was the two of them temporarily trapped in a room bigger than her entire apartment.

Rather than retreat, she stepped forward. Followed Derrick's trail until she stood on the opposite side of his desk and watched him slip into his chair. "As if I could have gotten anything through the two rounds of security."

He leaned back. "I find myself a bit more careful these days."

"These days?"

"Since your brother stole from me then turned around a few days later and tried to throw the scent off him by taking public shots at me." Derrick motioned toward the chair next to her.

"So, that's it. The rumors, the photos, the fake social news suggesting we're together." She dumped her purse on the seat but remained on her feet. "You're coming after me to get even. This is some sort of weird revenge."

Derrick nodded. "A fascinating theory."

That really was the only explanation. Even though money had always been tight, Noah wasn't the type to steal.

"I see the dramatic streak runs in the family." Derrick's exhale filled the room. "Lucky me."

Right. I'm the dramatic one. "Says the guy who has a private butler and an office set off from everyone else."

"Security."

Everything inside her froze. "Excuse me?"

"Jackson is my head of security."

She relaxed but not much. Something told her she needed to be on her toes with this guy. He might talk smooth and look like he stepped out of her hottest fantasy, but that didn't change the facts. He was a ruthless jackass. "Do that many people want to kill you?"

"My family has significant business interests. That sort of thing tends to attract trouble."

She'd never been called that before. "Are you referring to me as the trouble?"

He shrugged. "Let's hope not."

She'd taken about all of the put-her-on-the-defensive moves that she could stand. It was time to get to the point so she could run out of there. "Mr. Jame—"

"I believe I asked you to call me Derrick."

That's what she called him in her head… "Do you think that's wise?"

"I'm afraid you've lost me."

"You and my brother are locked in some sort of public pissing match. You're threatening him with lawyers. He's making you look bad on the internet, which has bled over to traditional media." She put her palms on his desk and leaned in. "What I'm saying is that fake rumors or not, we're on opposite sides of this battle."

His gaze skimmed over her. "We don't have to be."

He hadn't moved but the heated words swept over her in a caress that had her shaking her head and standing straight again. She not only needed to be careful with Derrick, she needed body armor.

She blocked out every other thought and concentrated

on the guy she'd come to think of as cold-blooded. "Has anyone ever pointed out your cryptic way of speaking?"

"Then let me be clear." Derrick balanced his elbows on the edge of his desk and leaned in toward her. "Your brother took money out of my business accounts and is going to go to jail unless I step in and save him."

"No, that's not—"

Derrick held up a finger. "There's nothing to debate. That's a fact." He let his hand fall again. "But I am willing to help him."

She could almost feel a trap closing over her head. The need to bolt overtook her but she forced her legs to stay still. "Why?"

"Most people would ask how."

She refused to be taken off guard by double-talk. "I'm not like everyone else."

"I'm starting to see that." Derrick watched her for a second. His gaze moved over her face in the silence. After a visible inhale, he began again, his voice louder and more firm. "I will help your brother but he has to do something for me."

"You don't like that he's making you look like a complete jerk, maybe even a bit incompetent." She got that.

Derrick fired Noah eight weeks ago, exactly two weeks before she lost her job. Noah's videos started out as a way to let off steam. Then he gained followers. A lot of them. He even managed to make money off his internet work, but she had no idea how.

He'd become a symbol for the "little man" fighting against the corporate machine. As his following grew, so did his stories about Derrick and the company.

Blame it on Noah's baby face or his sarcasm, but media and online sites had picked up the battle. Then Derrick's lawyers had made contact...and so had the prosecutor's office about the missing funds.

And now Derrick had the *Insider* and its gossip network working for him.

"I have shareholders and business associates," Derrick said.

"So, this is about money."

Derrick's frown deepened. "Isn't everything?"

Not an unexpected answer, but still… "It worries me that you don't know how scary that question is."

"I'm proposing a quid pro quo. I make your brother's legal issues disappear. He shuts down his site and I assist him in finding other more profitable and appropriate ways to channel his technology experience."

That sounded somewhat reasonable, which scared her. "That's the entire deal you're offering?"

"No."

She beat back a wave of disappointment. She'd taken care of her brilliant brother for so long. Tried to keep him occupied and out of trouble. The idea of having someone else handle that job sounded really good to her at the moment. With her life in shambles and the need to find a new job nipping at her, she loved the idea of having one less stress to deal with.

"I haven't told you what I get out of this," Derrick said.

Her heart sank. She held in a groan before it could escape her lips. "You did. He stops running the site."

It might sound easy but it wasn't. Noah didn't have anything else right now except for his anger at Derrick and the attention from his videos. It was the "thing" that kept Noah going. It also provided him with more attention and praise than he'd ever gotten.

"The damage is done. He's lied and caused me what could be irreparable damage," Derrick said.

His words pounded her but she kept her shoulders up and her back straight. "That sounds like a legal term."

"Because it is."

That meant more fighting. More lawyer fees on top of the ones for her employment attorney. "I thought you were worried about the lost money."

"There are bigger issues here."

She couldn't imagine money being a side concern. "Noah is a kid."

"Noah is twenty and a genius." When she opened her mouth to respond, Derrick talked right over her. "You are twenty-nine, which means you're old enough to know he's looking at criminal charges and civil repercussions for the money, which I'm willing to overlook right now."

"I'm going to pretend I know what that means and jump ahead. What is your part of the quid pro quo? Because you don't strike me as a guy who does things to be nice." That wasn't quite true. He'd hired Noah and ignored his lack of a degree and questionable people skills. But he'd also had security escort Noah out of the building months later. Now that she knew how that felt, she had even more sympathy for her brother. "What do you want?"

"You."

A weird, high-pitched ringing filled her ears. She shook her head but it refused to die down. "What?"

"The carefully placed stories about us have been aimed at diffusing some of your brother's damage."

"In other words, you're using me to somehow make yourself look better."

He shrugged. "That's not the way I'd put it."

"Of course not, since you're clearly clueless about women."

That had him sitting straighter. "Excuse me?"

Bull's-eye. The idea that she'd found the one thing sure to grab his attention—questioning his success with women—filled her with relief. "You're letting people believe we're together and—"

"Dating. People are starting to believe we're dating

and that your brother doesn't like it and is trying to break us up by launching false charges against me." Derrick looked far too pleased with himself. "Which was exactly my plan."

"That's ridiculous." She could think of a lot of other words to describe it but kept the conversation G-rated.

"I thought so, too, when the PR team suggested it, but I guess the public does like a good love story."

A scream rattled around inside her. "Did you ever think to ask me first?"

"No."

The quick response had her sputtering. "That's really your answer?"

"I called you *lovely* in my interview with the *Insider*, which I think we can agree was a bit of a stretch since you looked ready to punch me the first time we met in person."

"Oh, you picked up on that?" *Good to know.*

"Let's get down to it." He leaned in again. Didn't break eye contact. "We're talking about a business arrangement."

"Who is?"

"You will pose as my girlfriend for an appropriate length of time, short though because the timing is important here. Long enough for us to sell that we've been dating. Then you'll act as my fiancée and—"

"Wait." That ringing in her ears turned into a loud clanging sound.

He stared at her. "I haven't finished explaining the plan."

When his PR team said he'd needed to create a diversion, it made sense in an abstract sort of way. But they could not have meant her. He—they—didn't even know her. And no way did they mean an engagement.

She suspected they'd talked about him finding a life outside the office. She tried to direct him there. "I'm sure there are women in town who would want to date you. It's tough out there and my brother isn't exactly highlighting your good side. But you have money and you're…you know…"

He studied her now, like how he might study something on the bottom of his shoe. "I have no idea what you're trying to say."

"Well, your face is…fine." As in perfect and compelling. Way too kissable.

His eyes widened. *"Fine?"*

Because space seemed like a good idea she stepped away from the desk. Tried to draw enough air into her lungs and head to be able to breathe again. "Don't rich people travel in packs? I'm sure you can hang out at your country club or polo club, or wherever it is you go for fun, and find a nice woman who—"

"I am not hard up for a date." He sounded stunned at the idea.

"Well, there." She almost clapped but decided that was too much. "Good for you."

"I am, however, on the wrong side of your brother's ill-advised rant." He made a face that suggested he thought she should be picking up on his point a bit faster. "I explained this to you at the hotel."

"You said you needed good news to balance out the bad." That made sense, which only made her wariness tick up even higher. "So, hire someone to pretend date you if you don't want an actual girlfriend."

"It needs to be you. You provide a reason for your brother's specific attack." When she tried to stop him, he kept right on talking. Rolled right over her. "We put on a very public show. We get people to see us as a couple, get engaged—not for real, of course—and we neutralize some of the damage your brother has done."

"A fake fiancée." She said the words nice and slow, thinking he'd stop her because he had to be kidding.

Never mind that she could barely stand him. Sure, she'd

spun wild daydreams about him. Even imagined what he might look like without that serious suit and the fancy office, but come on.

"Exactly." The phone on his desk rang. He hit a button and the sound cut off. "You've spent a significant part of your life protecting your baby brother and I suspect you will continue to do so now, even though it's misguided."

That hit a bit too close to the comments Vanessa had made last night. "Misguided? I'm confused. Are you arguing for this fake engagement thing or not?"

"People will see us together, which will telegraph the message that I am not the man your brother says I am. You wouldn't date me otherwise. It will be a business arrangement that will benefit you greatly, and it will keep me from going after him for the money." He shrugged. "And, since time is a factor, I went ahead and started the rumors. As you know."

"Because that made sense to you?"

"Because your brother is in serious legal trouble and I can help him. I can also provide some guidance for the future and take the pressure off you. In many ways."

For the first time she noticed his hands. Those long fingers. The strength. The way he rubbed his palms together as if that in-control voice didn't quite match whatever was happening inside him.

But none of that calmed her wariness. Not when every word he uttered carried a note of a threat. "What does that mean?"

"You were recently fired."

Her stomach dropped, and not in a good way. Forget his deep, soothing voice and the sexy confidence that thrummed off him. If he made one wrong comment about her losing her job she would lunge across the desk and strangle him with that blue tie. "Laid off."

"We both know that's not true." Derrick didn't stop talking long enough to let her break in. "It would appear I'm not the only one who has an image to salvage. While you're doing that, I will pay your bills."

That sounded like…well, not good. "No."

"Consider this an acting role of sorts. One for which you should be paid." He picked up the folder in front of him and slid it toward her. "Here."

"What's that?"

"A contract."

The guy was prepared. She had to give him that. "You think I'm going to say yes then sign something?"

"Why wouldn't you?"

"Love, honor, decency." She probably should have thrown in a few more words but her brain refused to reboot. It had been misfiring ever since he'd smiled that first time.

"I'm not sure what any of those have to do with this arrangement." He nodded at the folder. "Take a look. Everyone benefits."

"Mostly you."

"I don't deny I get something out of this, but so do you. More important, so does Noah."

That sounded good but she doubted Derrick would deal fairly with Noah at this point. She couldn't believe the charges against her brother. But the idea that Derrick would waste time going after Noah if he was innocent didn't make much sense, either.

As soon as the doubts crept into her head about her brother, she tried to push them out again. *Be loyal.* "Noah denies the charges."

"He's lying." Derrick didn't even flinch as he talked. Never broke eye contact. Didn't give away any sign that he doubted what he said.

Something about his coolness made her insides shake. "Why should I believe you over my brother?"

"Deep down, you know I'm right."

"I don't think—"

"Yes, it would be better if you didn't, but I'm betting you will study this proposal from every angle." Derrick put his hand on the folder. "You can have until tomorrow morning."

She had to grab on to the chair next to her for balance. The room had started spinning and with each word he said rocked her harder. "For what?"

"To give me your response. As I said, time is of the essence. I am currently holding off the prosecutor but he needs an answer about your brother."

"And he'll do what you say?"

"We went to college together."

"Of course you did." From her experience with the job search she knew powerful people stuck together. But the caress of Derrick's voice, the concern in his tone—it all had her taking another step back. "This bargain or offer or whatever it is…it's ridiculous. You know that, right? I need to know you know that."

But even as she said the words her mind starting working. He could help Noah. She could get her life in order. Derrick offered breathing room and support, and that tempted her even though she knew she couldn't trust him one inch.

"Your brother's actions leave me with little option, and he shows no signs of stopping even if he is arrested. Shareholder discontent is an issue. I also have a reputation in the community."

"One that would suffer if people found out you made an offer for a fake fiancée."

He hadn't been moving but still his body froze. "Is that a threat, Ellie?"

"I'm trying to understand why a man with your money and power would make this offer."

"That's my problem, not yours."

"If I'm going to be your fiancée then—"

He held up a hand. "In name only."

"No sex then?" *Where had that come from*?

His eyebrow lifted. "I am willing to negotiate that point. Very willing."

She could almost feel his fingertips brush over her. "Forget it."

"You have until tomorrow at ten to give me an answer." He broke eye contact and hit a button on his phone. "Not ten after, Ellie. Ten exactly."

It was a dismissal. She heard it, felt it and ignored it. "I wouldn't clear your calendar if I were you."

He didn't look up. "Ten."

Three

Derrick leaned back in his oversize desk chair and blew out a long, haggard breath as the door closed behind Ellie and she left his office. He'd expected anger and a hint of distrust. He would have worried if she'd said yes to his fake engagement offer and jumped in. Eagerness was not a bonus in this type of situation.

No, he'd been prepared for all that. The sucker punch of need that slammed in to his gut the second he saw her again? That one had been a surprise.

She'd walked in with her long brown hair tied up behind her head with those strands hanging down, all sexy and loose. She'd worn a thin black skirt and white shirt and all he could think about was stripping both off her. The tight body. Those legs. The way fire lit her hazel eyes as she argued.

It all worked for him.

His attraction to her had sparked the minute she'd opened her mouth. She was tough and smart, and not easy to throw off or to scare. She met every one of his verbal shots with one of her own.

The woman was hot, no question.

She didn't fit his usual type.

He thought about the women he'd dated over the past few years. All cool, reserved business types. He preferred competent over sparks and heat. Maybe that's why the last three were now some of this favorite business associates. Friends, even.

He didn't believe in the idea of grand love. That struck him as nonsense. He'd grown up in a family that yelled. His father pitted him and his two brothers against each other. At his urging, they'd been racing and competing since the cradle. Every mistake had been dissected and fed back to them in an endless loop by their unforgiving father and then by the press that followed the Jameson boys' every move.

Never mind that Derrick's grandfather was a disgraced congressman or that their father, Eldrick Jameson, a self-made man with three former wives and a new much-younger one, had made his initial millions, before he lost them, by not always playing fair. Derrick and his brothers were magazine and news favorites, and few in the press gave them favorable coverage no matter what they did.

No, Derrick didn't believe much in emotions. But he did believe in this company. He'd rebuilt it from the dust left over from his father's fires and while the old man ran through woman after woman. Derrick labored over every contract and every deal. Gave his life to it. And now he was getting screwed by the old man—again.

His father handed down his requirements for turning the business over, the main one being that Derrick clean up his reputation and resolve "the Noah problem" within ninety days. That meant dealing with Ellie since his PR team thought trying to deal with Noah directly could result in another video.

From the photos he'd seen of her before they met at the party, he'd expected pretty in a girl-next-door kind of way. Quiet. Not someone likely to light his fire. From what he knew about her job situation, he'd expected desperation and a willingness to deal.

He got none of that.

Jackson Richards opened the door and slid inside the office. He wore a stupid grin as he walked across the office and stopped in front of Derrick. “She’s not what I expected.”

Now there was an understatement. “Me, either. And did you call me *sir* earlier?” That was new and Derrick didn’t like it.

Jackson shrugged. “I thought it fit with the mood you were trying to create.”

“You can skip the overly deferential act. I have enough people around here who do that.”

“Are you engaged yet?” Jackson sounded amused at the idea.

Derrick was happy someone thought the nightmare situation was funny. “She’s difficult.”

“She sounds perfect for you.”

Jackson was one of the few people who could get away with the comment. They’d known each other for years and were about the same age, both in their midthirties. Eldrick had brought Jackson into the company, but Derrick liked him despite that. They’d been friends from the start. With Jackson, Derrick let the firm line between boss and employee blur.

But right now his mind was on the hot brunette with the impressive ass who’d just left his office. “She seems to think I should be able to find a real date.”

“Did you tell her about your father’s conditions for signing the business over to you and how you have something of an impossible deadline in which to meet them?”

The damn agreement. Leave it to Eldrick to make everything difficult. “You mean selling it to me? For a lot of money he can then spend on my new stepmother? Of course not.”

Jackson winced. “It might help your case.”

“I doubt Ellie would be sympathetic.”

“Not if you keep placing false rumors with the *Insider*.”

Jackson shook his head. "I warned you that could backfire. Women hate stuff like that, and with good reason."

"Speaking of which, is the photographer waiting outside?" That's why her tardiness mattered. Much later and she would have blown his plans.

"When Ellie figures out you staged this meeting to get a photo of her coming out of your office she's—"

"Going to yell." Derrick knew it. He even felt a twinge of guilt over it—one he could easily ignore. "But we know this is about more than a PR job. This is about saving the company and there's no way I'm letting her know I need her help for something that big. I'm not giving her that power over me."

"Very romantic."

"This is business. According to my father's stipulations, I have to get my brothers in line and in this office, clean up my image and stop Noah Gold's public hit job, all while single-handedly running a commercial real estate company."

After a lifetime of aiming his sons at each other, Derrick's father wanted them to be one big happy family, all working in the office and getting along. And if they didn't, Derrick would lose the business that meant everything to him. His father already had a buyer outside the family interested. A rich old friend with liquidity and the ability to move fast on the sale.

Just thinking about the requirements of his father's stupid business proposal touched off a new wave of fury in Derrick's gut. He literally could forfeit everything because of his father's stupid whims.

Derrick was about to launch into an angry rant about Eldrick when his office door pushed open. Ellie stepped inside again, looking a little flushed and not a bit worried or afraid of him.

He liked her attitude but the security lapse was a concern.

Then he thought about the photographer and wondered if the guy had moved too soon. "How did you get in here?"

"I walked."

He guessed he should have expected that answer from her. "You shouldn't be able to wander around the building without an escort."

She waved the concern away as she approached the desk and held out her hand. "You can worry about your over-the-top paranoid protocol later. Give me the agreement."

"What?"

She continued to hold out her hand. "If I'm going to consider this—"

"Are you?" That surprised him when almost nothing did.

"—I want to make sure you didn't add anything weird in here."

Whatever he planned to say left his head. He suddenly wanted to know what her definition of "weird" might be. "Like what?"

"With you?" She snorted. "Who knows? I don't trust you."

Jackson nodded as he grabbed the folder and gave it to her. "A very solid beginning for a relationship."

Her eyes narrowed as her gaze moved from Jackson to Derrick. "Your guy knows about this nonsense fake dating and engagement offer of yours?"

"Yes, and that document in your hand is nonnegotiable." Derrick knew from their combined thirty minutes together so far that she'd be whipping out the red pen and revising if he didn't put a stop to it now.

She shrugged at him as she opened the file and took a peek inside. "Whatever."

He fought back a sigh. "I'm serious, Ellie."

Her head shot up and she glared at him. "You're not going to win every argument."

"I think I am." He rarely lost and had no intention of starting now. "I'll see you at ten tomorrow."

She turned and headed for the door. "You'll get my answer when you get it."

She was gone before Derrick could respond.

Damn, he liked her. The fire and self-assurance were so sexy. She wasn't yet thirty but she'd grown up fast when she'd lost her parents. He understood what it was like to take on responsibility early. It was one of the reasons he thought they'd be able to handle this arrangement. She would get what she needed and he'd get his obstinate father off his back.

Jackson cleared his throat. "You're smiling."

Derrick refused to play this game. "She's…interesting."

"This engagement thing *is* fake, right?"

"Of course."

"Right." Jackson exhaled. "That explains the stupid look on your face whenever you see her."

Four

The DC Insider: *Visits to the prestigious Hay-Adams. Visits to his office. It appears Ms. Ellie Gold has not only snagged our Hottest Ticket in Town's attention but also has him spinning in circles. Well done, Ellie!*

He had to be kidding. That thought kept running through Ellie's mind as she paged through Derrick's ten—no, fourteen-page agreement while sitting on her couch the next morning.

The thing had tiny print, and rules, and footnotes to new rules and references to yet more rules. The list of restrictions seemed endless. She couldn't date anyone else. He had final approval over the people she saw on a friendly basis during the "term of their arrangement" and over any work plans she intended to pursue.

She had to act loving, whatever that meant. He hadn't used the word *obey* but it was implied in almost every line. And that wasn't even the most ridiculous part. He thought they'd live together. *Actually live together.*

She glanced around her small apartment, from one stack of empty boxes to another. She had savings but that would run out if she didn't find a new job and a cheaper place to live soon. That would be easier if her jackass of an ex-boss hadn't launched an offensive strike when she filed her internal complaint and fired her first, insisting she came on to him. As if that would ever happen.

The man's wife had left town to watch over a sick aunt and he'd had his hands all over her by the next day. Kicking him in the crotch had felt great, but being escorted out of the building hadn't.

His claims were nonsense. He had resources and family money…and a nasty reputation that people spoke about only in whispers and refused to confirm in public. She had documentation of the emails she'd sent after the incident and her complaint. No witnesses to what happened, unfortunately, but she guessed they'd be able to find a pattern of other women once they started digging.

Her lawyer was positive about her chances but cases cost money. She got that but employers weren't exactly lining up to hire a supposed human resources expert who had been fired for making a play for her boss. She could not let this go. Not when it was likely he would do this to someone else.

Thinking about Joe touched off that familiar spiraling sensation in her stomach. That mix of panic and worry. She liked to eat and have electricity. Which led her to the convoluted mess of an agreement on her lap.

Derrick's plan struck her as so odd. She had no idea if wealthy people usually did stuff like this, but she didn't.

She picked up her mug of now-cool tea and prepared to read through the agreement one more time. The doorbell stopped her in the middle of what looked like a never-ending sentence of legalese gobbledygook.

Grumbling, she put down the mug and stood. Slipping her feet into her fluffy pink slippers, she shuffled across the floor. That took about ten seconds since she lived in a studio.

When the doorbell rang again, she skipped her usual check in the mirror by the door. Anyone this impatient deserved to be greeted with the full hair-sliding-out-of-the-ponytail style she had going on.

She peeked through the peephole and froze. *Oh, no, no, no.*

He was here. Now. At her house.

"Open up, Ellie." Derrick's deep voice floated through the door.

She tried not to make a sound.

He sighed loud enough to shake the building. "I can see your shadow under the door."

"Fine." She performed the perfect eye roll as she undid the lock. "What?"

He started talking before she fully opened the door. "It's eleven."

"I own a clock." Though she guessed she looked as if she didn't own a brush. She could practically feel the tangles in her hair without touching it. Add in the shorts and oversize sweater that functioned as her pajamas and she was positive she made quite the picture.

"Are you sure?" His gaze wandered over her and stopped on her slippers. "Those are an unexpected choice."

"Imagine me kicking you with them." She stepped to the side and let him in. Why fight it? He was not exactly the type to scamper off.

He slipped past her, smelling all fresh and clean. Today's suit was navy blue and fit him, slid over every inch of him, perfectly.

He walked to the center of the room then turned around to face her. "You were supposed to be in my office at ten."

No doubt about it, he was much hotter when he didn't talk. "No, you commanded that I give you an answer to your absurd fake engagement suggestion by a stated time and I declined."

"Interesting."

Since that could refer to anything, she ignored it and focused on another annoying fact. “Hey, how did you know where I live?”

He shot her a look that suggested he found the question ridiculous. “Please.”

That was not even a little reassuring. “Did Jackson follow me?”

“Jackson is in the car.”

Okay… “Is that an answer?”

Derrick looked around the room, from the couch to the rows of bookcases lining the walls and holding her collection of romances and mysteries. He kept going, skipping over the kitchenette and falling on the unmade bed against the far wall.

He turned and stared at her again, his expression blank. “Yes or no, Ellie.”

She didn’t pretend to misunderstand. He was talking about the agreement. He needed a fake fiancée and, for whatever reason, thought she fit the description. “It’s not that simple.”

“It actually is.”

Of course he would think so. The entire agreement benefitted him. “We don’t know each other.”

He frowned. “You said that already. So?”

Such a guy. “Really? That’s your answer?”

“Again, for what feels like the tenth time, this is a business arrangement, not an actual romance.”

She joined him by the couch. “Now you sound ticked off.”

“I hate repetition.”

Poor baby. “Do you want a fiancée or not? Because I would be doing this for you, not me.”

“We both know that’s not true. You benefit. Your brother benefits.” Derrick shifted his weight and looked down. He stared at the magazines piled on her floor for a few seconds then pushed them to the side with his foot. “All you need to do is follow a few simple rules.”

She didn't bother to debate his idea of a "few" because that could take them all day. From his scowl she guessed he wanted to add another provision to the agreement to forbid her slight tendency toward clutter.

"You say that but everyone I know needs to believe it's real." She scooped up the agreement and flipped through the pages then began pointing. "Here, look at this."

He didn't bother to glance down. "I'm familiar with the contract."

"Then you know we're supposed to live together." Which sounded as absurd this time as when she'd read it earlier.

"My house is big." His gaze wandered again. This time over to the boxes she'd gathered in case she needed to move in a hurry. "But I prefer you not live out of boxes. Haven't you been in this apartment for seven months, like right before Noah started working for me?"

She snapped her fingers. "Derrick."

"Don't do that. Ever." He put his hand over hers and lowered it. "What do you want to say?"

The touch, so simple and innocent, shot through her. She felt it vibrate through every cell.

She pulled her hand from his and forced her breathing to slow. "We've barely spent an hour together."

"We'll have separate bedrooms."

As if that were the only problem. "But you expect me to act like a fiancée."

"Whatever that means, yes."

"It's a direct quote from paragraph twenty of this thing." She shook the agreement at him.

"I've never been engaged, but I figure we can work out the details as we go. You know, like do the usual things engaged people do."

She suddenly couldn't breathe. A big lump clogged her throat and she had no idea why. "Usual?"

"Shows of…affection."

He may as well have said poison. "You should hear yourself."

He exhaled as he stepped back. His hand swept through his hair and, for a brief moment, his thick wall of confidence slipped. He looked vulnerable and frustrated. She didn't think any of it was aimed at her. Not directly. This was more about the circumstances they'd gotten stuck in.

"We both need things, Ellie. You want to help your brother. You have some work issues that I can resolve for you."

"Are you going to give me a job?" She thought about her bills and her fears about losing her apartment. Growing up she never felt welcome or comfortable. Home hadn't been a sanctuary, but now it was. The idea she could lose that security left her shaken.

"Yes, as my fiancée."

With him that *did* sound like a full-time job. But pretending to have feelings might not be enough. They didn't run in the same circles. She didn't know anything about charity functions or season tickets to the Kennedy Center. "People aren't going to buy this."

He stepped closer again. This time his hands came up and his palms rubbed up and down her arms, gentle and warm. "We tell them we met while haggling about your brother. There was a spark and…boom."

"Did you just say *boom*?"

Instead of backing away, he leaned in. "The legal fees stop. Your brother gets some direction and guidance. Your bills get paid and my shareholders stop whining."

"You make it sound reasonable in a weird sort of way." She was practical and everything about this plan, including the very real problem of lying to her brother, was anything but.

"It is."

"My brother will go ballistic." And she feared that was an understatement.

"Trust me. We can sell this."

She didn't miss the fact his words sounded like a plea. She doubted he begged for anything. He probably didn't even ask others for help, but he was asking now.

The realization had her stomach tumbling. This close she could see the intensity in his gaze and feel the heat rolling off him.

"You can't fake a spark." Her voice sounded breathy even in her ears.

"Let's see if we need to."

He lowered his head as his hand slid into her hair. Fingers expertly massaged the back of her neck. His mouth lowered until it hovered over hers. For a second he hesitated, with his eyes searching her face, then his lips met hers. Mouth against mouth, he brushed over hers once. Twice. So enticing.

His scent wrapped around her and his fingers tightened on her. One second they stood a foot apart. The next he closed in. The caress turned to kissing, deep and alive with need. Energy arced between them. Every touch, every press of his lips, proved hot and inviting.

He pulled her tight against him and her common sense faltered. Heat burned through her as her arms slipped up to wrap around his neck. She'd just balanced against his body when he pulled back.

"Right." He cleared his throat as his chest rose and fell on harsh breaths. "There we go."

A haze covered her brain. *"There we go?"*

"Sure. That was fine." He set her away from him. Increased the distance between them to a few feet.

The man was an idiot.

"Fine?" She could barely feel her legs.

"Yes. I'm confident we can fake it." He started walking

around the room, almost pacing. "We'll start with dates. In public. Let people see us together." He nodded as he continued the one-sided conversation. "I'd say in a week we move you into my place and announce the engagement."

"That's too fast." She was impressed her brain even spit that sentence out. Right now she couldn't think at all. The kiss had blown out every rational thought and had her wanting to slide that tie right off him.

"Well, it looks as if you're ready to pack."

"I need to sit." She plunked down hard on the armrest of the couch and struggled not to run her fingertips over her lips.

"We'll have a party—"

"No." Good grief, he was already planning. That was enough to snap her out of it.

"Not a big, flashy Christmas party. Just the normal engagement party."

It took a few seconds but her common sense came back. Doubt rushed in right behind it.

"First, it's March. Second, I'm Jewish." That seemed important to throw in there even in a fake engagement, so she did. "And third… I fear your idea of normal."

"We invite the people who need to see us."

People who would later wonder what happened and why it all ended, but he seemed to ignore that part. Fine. It was his problem and they were his friends, so he could figure it out. But she did have one issue she could not ignore. "And what do I tell my brother to keep him from killing you?"

"That we sparked. Tell him a one-night stand turned into something more."

Derrick. Sex. She blocked the thoughts that rolled through her head. The kiss had been enough to unravel her. Anything more would be a huge mistake. "You want me to lie to him?"

"That's the point. We lie to him and the public to diffuse Noah's claims."

She couldn't blame Derrick for that requirement. Noah hadn't exactly been subtle in his attack on Derrick to date. But something about his self-assurance about this agreement and all these details started an alarm bell ringing in her head. "You have this all figured out, don't you?"

"I thought so."

She swung her foot, letting the pink slipper flip through the air. "What does that mean?"

"You're not what I expected."

She stilled. "Right back at ya."

"Lucky for us, I can adapt."

Yeah, lucky her. "You don't exactly strike me as a guy who enjoys surprises."

Some of the tension drained from his face as he stared at her. That sexy little smile of his returned. "Maybe I can change."

She hadn't known that to work with any guy ever. "Oh, come on."

He walked up to her and picked the agreement off her lap. "Sign."

"You know you can't date anyone else while we're pretending to like each other, right?" For some reason it was suddenly very important to her that he know if she did this, they did it together. They'd both suffer.

He made a face. "Does it say that?"

"It will when we write in a bunch of notes in the margin and both initial them." She tapped the agreement. "Basically, every ridiculous provision that applies to me will now apply to you."

He didn't hesitate. "Fine."

That was almost too easy. "That means you're stuck with me for… Wait, there's no end time on this agreement."

His eyebrow lifted. "I'm aware."

For about the hundredth time since she'd met him yesterday she got the sense she was being outmaneuvered. She hated the sensation. "You get two months of fake fiancée time."

"That might not be enough. Say at least three."

She reached down and picked a pen up off her coffee table. She clicked the end and handed it to him. "I'm sure you can adapt to two."

"It seems you think I'll be adapting a lot over the next few weeks." He sounded stunned by the idea.

"I'm happy you realize that. It will make our time together, limited though it may be, more tolerable."

His smile widened. "We'll see."

Five

The DC Insider: *We are hearing that our Hottest Ticket in Town wants to get serious with his new lady but the lady's disgruntled baby brother is having none of it. He's making some big claims, all of which Derrick Jameson denies with a shrug. But can this budding romance bloom with all these distractions?*

Ellie was starting to think her headache would never go away. It thumped in her ears and over her eyes. Even the back of her neck ached.

She'd had two employment interviews today and nothing. Well, not nothing. In the second, the interviewer wanted to talk about Derrick. He didn't specifically ask about her dating life but he bounced around the topic, honing in on her "influence" over Derrick and his decisions and questioning if that would be a conflict. Since she was trying for a generalist HR position—one unrelated to Derrick or his habit of buying up most of the property in the city—she couldn't imagine what Derrick had to do with her possible paycheck.

Being a fake fiancée had sounded easy, two months of playtime while they went to dinner and she didn't panic about the water bill, but it was starting to take over her life. In addition to thinking about him and that voice...and that face…she had other issues. She'd splurged on a muffin at the coffee place around the corner that morning and two people took her photo.

And then there was the *Insider.* Her teeth ground together at the idea of being in the *Insider*'s daily round-up section for two more months. Derrick needed to knock that off. She knew she should have insisted on a "no talking to gossip sites" clause in that stupid agreement. But she hadn't, so now she nursed a glass of wine as she propped her feet on her coffee table and tried to pretend she was stuck in a bad dream.

She'd managed to kick her heels off and find her pink slippers. She had no idea where she'd thrown her suit jacket. Since she couldn't afford new clothes or a big dry-cleaning bill right now, not when she was saving every penny just in case, that could be a problem. She'd just leaned her head against the couch cushion when she heard the rattling. She stared at the ceiling for a second, trying to place the sound.

Jingling. Keys.

The mix of sounds had her jackknifing and jumping to her feet. The wine went *everywhere.* Down her shirt. On her couch. A line ran over her hand as more dripped onto the carpet, destroying any chance of getting that security deposit she so desperately needed back.

The door opened and she spun around, ready to throw the glass. She stopped just in time.

The wind rushed out of her. "Noah?"

Her brother stood there with a face flushed red with fury and his hands balled into fists at his sides. He looked ready to launch. She stepped back without thinking and rammed her calf into the edge of the coffee table.

"What are you thinking?" He hovered in the doorway, with the open hallway to her neighbors in the three-story, converted apartment building right there.

That tone, deep and shaking, brought back memories

of the days before she'd found the right doctor for him. Once she'd understood that her parents had caused more trouble for him by not immediately seeking treatment and that the delay could lead to bigger issues later in life, she got Noah help.

But that didn't solve the problem completely. Even now, the more stressed, the more under fire he felt, the more skewed his boundaries became. The uncontrolled anger of the past when he would punch walls was gone, but the faint whisper of frustration remained.

Disregarding the way her shirt now stuck to her skin and the wet chilling her from the inside out, she inhaled and pitched her voice low. "Are you okay? It's not like you to barge in."

"I thought you might have someone in here and not let me open up," he said.

That struck her as the worst response ever. She set her now-empty glass on a months-old magazine and stared him down. "And you thought that entitled you to use the emergency key?"

"Do you really care that I came in without knocking?"

That was a typical Noah response. He flipped things around to make her feel like the unreasonable one. "It's a matter of privacy."

"I want an explanation." He stepped into the apartment, leaving the door hanging open behind him.

"You mean Derrick." At the use of the name, she could see Noah's jaw clench. His features hardened.

With the straight brown hair and dark brown eyes, Noah looked like their father. While Dad's perpetual good looks and boyish charm had helped to launch him in hundreds of get-rich-schemes over the years, including the one her parents were flying to when they died, Noah tended to be aloof and always assessing.

He came around to the same side of the couch as her.

"You're on a first-name basis with the guy who fired me and is trying to frame me?"

She wasn't sure how to broach this subject but she tried anyway… "Is it possible this thing between the two of you has gone off the tracks a bit?" When Noah's mouth dropped open, she hurried to finish the thought. "Maybe there was a miscommunication and then you—"

"He's brainwashed you." Noah sounded stunned at the idea.

She tried to ignore how insulting that was. Tried and couldn't. "What?"

"Is it the money?"

And he made it worse. "What are you talking about?"

"Look, I know you've had a tough time dating and stuff, but Derrick Jameson?" Noah asked. "People are asking me about you and Jameson in the comment sections of my videos. They're questioning *me* now."

So that was it. His precious videos. His crusade. Just once she wished someone would care about her. "That's what this is about? I'm messing up your revenge plans?"

"Having my sister sleep with my enemy is a problem, yes." Noah practically spat as he talked and stepped toward her.

Out of habit, she moved back. He wouldn't hurt her, but he sometimes still funneled his frustration into throwing things, and she did not want to be in the firing line. "You sound like you're twelve."

"He really does."

A now-familiar deep voice sounded from the doorway. Relief slammed into Ellie before she even looked over. It washed right through her, calming her down.

Derrick. He loomed there, wearing a dark suit and fierce frown. The glare did not waver away from Noah.

"You're here." Noah's shoulders fell as if a load of shock had replaced his anger. "In my sister's house."

"You always were very observant." Derrick stepped inside and closed the door behind him.

The soft thud snapped Ellie out of the haze enveloping her. That fast, she flipped from soothing mode to trying to wrestle control back. "Derrick, sarcasm is not helping here."

He looked at her then. His gaze traveled over her, hesitating on the stain plastering her silk blouse to her chest before bouncing up again. "Sorry."

The word sounded so sincere and heartfelt. As if he understood she was ten seconds away from shattering into a million pieces.

"You apologized to her?" Noah's full attention centered on Derrick. "What about me?"

"You stole from me and got caught." Derrick's voice stayed steady even as he shook his head. "If you needed money you could have asked for an advance on your salary." Derrick's eyes narrowed. "But I'm not sure any of this was about money."

Noah turned to face her again. "Do you hear him? His accusations?"

She did. Saw him, too. Watching Derrick was a revelation. If he carried around any guilt, he hid it well. If he had falsely blamed Noah...no, that didn't make sense. It had never made sense, but seeing Derrick now, in full de-escalation mode, made her brother's story even less believable.

She inhaled, trying to calm the last of her frayed nerves, and pointed toward the now wine-stained couch. "Maybe we could all sit down."

"Not with him." Noah pushed by Derrick. Shoved his shoulder into him and kept going. Didn't say anything until he reached the door. "Just wait until the next video."

As soon as Noah's hand hit the doorknob, Derrick spoke up. "Post whatever you want about me but keep your sister out of it."

Noah slowly turned around to face Derrick. "You think you get to order me around when I'm not working for you?"

"If you have a problem, you come for me." He pointed toward Ellie. "Not her. Not ever."

Noah's face went blank. "She's my sister."

"Then act like it."

Derrick forced himself not to follow Noah out the door. He wanted to have it out, make the kid understand he was playing in an adult world now.

Instead he stood there, staring at the door and trying to ease his temper. Something had happened before he'd walked down that hallway and heard the shouting. Ellie was drenched in wine. Hell, it beaded in her hair. But nothing, no furniture or glass, appeared to be broken.

She shook her head. "So much for thinking I was going to be able to enjoy two months of fake engagement bliss."

"Did I promise that?"

"Honestly, no. But I knew my brother would be a bigger problem than you thought." Ellie said the words on a heavy sigh.

Derrick looked at her again. "Your brother is—"

"Still my brother, so be careful with what words you use."

That seemed like the Ellie he'd experienced so far—tough and sure—but the tone sounded defeated. He hated that. "Right."

"He's upset." She lifted the wineglass from the coffee table and a magazine page stuck to it.

"Yeah, I picked up on that."

"He was diagnosed years ago with this disorder you've likely never heard of. Believe it or not, this is a thousand times better than he used to be." She held the glass in midair, peeling the paper off with a loud ripping sound. "His teen years were exhausting."

That was enough of that. Derrick stepped over to her and put his hand over hers. With one quick tug, he liberated the glass then carried it to her kitchen sink. "He's not a teen now, so don't make excuses for him."

"I'm explaining that this is not a matter of him being spoiled."

"Are you willing to concede that, maybe, you make it easy for him to not deal with his issues as an adult?" He stopped for a second with his hands wrapped around the edge of the counter.

Noah was nothing like Derrick's father, Eldrick, except that people rushed to forgive both of them. That innate ability to have people fall all over themselves trying to make things rights and ease any burden… Derrick didn't get it. No one had ever done that for him, which was probably a good thing.

"My point is that he doesn't always handle his anger and frustration the way others do."

Derrick turned around and watched her pick the soaked edge of her shirt up with two fingers and wave it around a little as if trying to dry it. Another button popped open under the strain of all that flapping. He couldn't imagine that move would dry her shirt, but it sure as hell was making him think about things other than this conversation.

From this angle he could see a sliver of skin and the outline of her bra, all lacy and, from the few peeks she'd given him, pink. This dating, no-touching, possible fake-engagement thing might be the death of him.

"Ellie, I have an office full of Noah types. I don't mind odd comments, social awkwardness or even controllable behavioral issues. But I do get pissed off when people steal from me."

She sat on the couch's armrest. "He insists you're lying."

"And I insist he is."

"So, we're at a stalemate."

"Are we?" He appreciated her loyalty to her brother, but she wore emotional blinders when it came to Noah.

He got it. He had brothers, too. Even though, thanks to their father, they didn't see each other much these days, he would do anything for them, including pushing them to take responsibility for their actions.

"If you had evidence..." With her head down, she picked at the couch's material.

"I'm not accustomed to having to prove myself. Most people take my word." Derrick heard his voice rising in volume and lowered it again. "It's one of those things I'm known for, which is why your brother's actions are doubly problematic."

"Any chance you could bend your rules and maybe..." She winced. "I don't know, review the evidence again? With me?"

It was a fair request but this sudden unexplained need to have her trust hit him. It wasn't rational. He hadn't earned it, but still. "We already have a deal, Ellie."

"I don't appreciate being made to choose."

She wasn't getting this. He pushed off from the counter and walked into the living room area. Stopped right in front of her so she had to look up to give him eye contact. "The point of the agreement is to defuse the issue with the public. Noah will either stop with the videos or he won't."

"And if he doesn't?"

The urge to reach out and brush his fingers over her cheek almost overwhelmed him. He shoved his hand into his pants pocket to prevent any touching.

It was bad enough he was there. That he had this odd need to see her, to make sure she hadn't changed her mind. He had a phone. He knew how to text. Hell, when he'd first thought about a fake engagement and how it would work, he'd assumed his assistant would be the one in contact with

Ellie. That his time with her would be for public view only and a complete farce. Yet, here he was. In her house. Talking family drama.

There was nothing disconnected about this arrangement that he could see.

"With us being together, Noah won't be able to hide from me. I'm confident I can get him to understand. I hired him, young and untested, because I saw something in him." He crossed his arms over his chest and scanned the room, not doing anything to hide his long look. "So…this."

"You're changing the topic." She stood as she talked.

The move put her so close. He could smell the shampoo clinging to her hair and the sharp scent of the wine.

"Obviously." His gaze drifted to her shirt. "Do you want to change?"

"I probably have to throw it away." She winced as she plucked at the material. "And I love this shirt."

He didn't become attached to clothes, so he had no idea how to respond to that. "Go ahead."

Without another word, she slipped into the bathroom, hesitating only long enough to grab a balled-up sweatshirt off the top of one of the boxes piled around the room.

He took the few minutes of alone time to study her apartment again. Tiny and cluttered but homey. There were things everywhere. Shoes piled under the window. A stack of magazines under the coffee table. A…was that a suit jacket on the floor? He scooped it up and draped it over the clean part of the couch. That took him to his next errand. Into the kitchen area to find something to clean up the wine on the cushion.

He was kneeling on the only clean and open part of the floor, doing a combination of dabbing and scrubbing on the stain. He was pretty sure it grew the more he worked on it.

Just as he decided it would be easier to buy her a new couch, she stepped into the room.

"Okay, I'm relatively dry…" Her laser gaze honed in on him right away. "You don't have to do that."

"I know."

"You probably have a team of humans who clean for you."

"Are we fighting again?" He hoped not because there was no way for him to win this battle. She clearly thought he was inept at anything but running a business, and since her brother was trying to ruin that, she might not even find him competent in that regard.

"No, but is there a reason you didn't tell me I had wine in my hair?"

This seemed like slightly safer ground. "I wasn't sure you cared."

She frowned at him. "You are an odd man."

That wasn't a topic he wanted to explore, so he stood with the wet rag still in his hand. "You have two choices."

"You're not planning on testing me on the agreement provisions, are you? I didn't memorize the thing."

Her mind really did bounce from topic to topic. Sometimes it took him a few minutes to catch up. He didn't want to admit that or how invigorating he found the entire verbal battle. "This evening we either can go to dinner or I can help you get packed."

"You make those sound like reasonable options."

She stood right in front of him now. Blame the pink slippers, but he towered over her. She wasn't petite or even short. She likely stood around five-seven. But compared to his six-one, he had the definite height advantage. "I can be reasonable."

"I haven't seen much evidence of that." Her voice took on a breathy quality.

He chalked it up to the room or dust or the boxes or something, because his breathing didn't sound right in his ears, either. "Well, I'm told the early days of fake dating can be rough. We'll both adjust."

"That almost sounded like a joke, but you're not wrong. There really should be a handbook."

"No kidding." He'd be studying that thing nonstop if it did exist.

"Dinner sounds fine, but I know there will be a reporter or photographer lurking somewhere, so what you're proposing is a setup with a side of food."

He sighed at her. "You're paranoid."

"Gee, I wonder why." She added an eye roll as if she didn't think he picked up on the sarcasm dripping from her voice. "And the packing thing…"

Any other time. Any other woman, he wouldn't ask. "Yes?"

The oversize gray college sweatshirt shouldn't even earn a second of thought from him. But on her, with her sexy mouth and those invigorating comebacks and her refusal to take any crap from him, he got reeled in. She talked and he wanted to know more. He'd studied her background in preparation for making their agreement, but now he wanted to hear the details straight from her, in her time.

"That suggests I'm moving in with you now, and I'm not," she said.

About that…he'd rethought that portion of the agreement. He didn't have much time to meet his father's conditions. His father demanded Derrick get this public fight with Noah wrapped up or he'd lose his chance at owning the company. Never mind that he'd brought it back from the brink of bankruptcy or that the Jameson coffers were now full due to Derrick's efforts. His father insisted, once again, that Derrick prove himself.

There were other conditions about bringing his brothers home and repairing the damage dear old dad had done to his sons' relationships. Derrick liked that part. Running the family business with his brothers and without his father's interference had always been his dream.

But the one issue Derrick had to handle first, the one he'd signed an agreement to fix, related to Ellie. She was the only one he could think about at the moment. That and her mouth and those big eyes.

"We should discuss the timing of your move," he said.

She exhaled long and loud and added another eye roll at the end. "Here we go."

Derrick decided to ignore the dramatics and go right to the heart of the issue. "You are out of work. Your brother clearly is not contained."

"You aren't exactly wooing me so far."

"I was *telling* you, not trying to convince you."

This time she made a clicking sound with her tongue. "Again with the blind obedience thing. So romantic."

He'd had girlfriends, dated other women, even managed to have sex now and then despite his overwhelming workload. None of that had prepared him for Ellie. He'd never met a woman less impressed with his wealth, position and power than her. It was endearing in some ways but it also messed with his usual way of winning an argument. "Should I call you lovely again?"

"Get to the point."

And now a third eye roll. Great.

He heard a noise and was pretty sure she was tapping her slipper against the floor. In his view, he was the one with the reason to want to move this along, but fine. "We should shift the engagement and—"

"Fake engagement."

"Those are words we only use with each other and when no one else is around."

Her eyes widened as she looked around the room. "Do you see someone else here?"

"I'm just saying." Her glare really could melt stone. He wasn't a fan, but he had to admit it was persuasive. "Fine. Anyway, we should get you settled in."

When he finally got all the words out, she stood there. Silence screamed through the room. Even the foot tapping stopped.

Then… "Wow."

He gave up. "Now what did I say?"

"It's the way you say things. Like, everything is an order."

Damn right. He realized too late he should have made that much more clear in the agreement. "I'm the boss."

"I don't work for you."

"Technically, you do." But he decided not to talk about the fact he was paying for her time, or was about to. She didn't seem to be in the mood to discuss that topic.

"You would be wise not to put this fake engagement in those terms right now."

Yeah, he gave up. "So, dinner?"

She shook her head. "Tomorrow, or maybe the day after. I need a bit of time."

Another zig when he expected a zag. He never thought she'd say no. "Ellie, come on."

"It's not a test." She rested a hand on his chest. "I haven't showered. If people are going to be taking my photograph every two seconds, I should have the opportunity to brush my hair."

He looked down at her fingers and the nails polished a soft pink. Felt the weight of her palm over his heart. "Is this a woman thing?"

"I don't even know what that means."

"Are you still upset about your brother?"

She hesitated then nodded. "Almost always."

"Listen—" Derrick put his hand over hers "—I'll talk to him."

"He'll kill you." And for once she didn't sound excited by the idea.

Still, it wasn't as if he hadn't dealt with trouble before.

Compared to the financial crew that wanted to dismantle the company when he became CEO over four years ago and all the fellow businessmen who mistook his youth for weakness, Noah was nothing more than a blip. A small nuisance. "Oh, please."

"I don't think any part of this charade will be as easy as you think it will."

He squeezed her hand. "Trust me."

Six

The DC Insider: *We are concerned, dear readers. It's been five days without a sighting of, or peep about, the most interesting romance in town. Did it already fizzle? There are some nasty whispers out there about the lady's last job. Goodness knows playboy Derrick Jameson has had some interesting things printed about him over the years but it's believed he's put those drinking and carousing days behind him. Maybe Ellie was too wild for her billionaire?*

Derrick sensed Jackson hovering by the door. He'd stepped inside the office but remained quiet. No surprise since Jackson had an uncanny ability to blend in. He overheard more than he should but wasn't the type to start rumors. His loyalty never wavered, which was only one reason Derrick considered Jackson his best friend.

After less than a minute of silence, Jackson cleared his throat. "Is everything okay?"

"With what?" Derrick didn't look up. It was the universal sign for "not now" but he knew Jackson would ignore it.

"Only you would answer that way." Jackson walked into the office. Sat in the chair across from Derrick without waiting for an invitation. "I meant with you…in general."

"I'm fine."

"Is that why you have a woman's shirt in a dry cleaning bag hanging on your office door?"

At the mention of the shirt, Derrick thought about the woman who owned it. Days had passed since they'd talked, and that was no accident. A bit of distance struck him as a smart move. Something about her had him spun around. He wanted her in his home. He'd visited her house for no obvious reason. He never did stuff like that.

"The shirt belongs to Ellie." Not that Derrick wanted to make a big deal about it.

"Yeah, I was hoping you didn't have a second fake fiancée wandering around here."

The comment got Derrick's attention. He settled in his chair as he looked at Jackson. "She had a fight with her brother and spilled wine."

Jackson's eyes narrowed. "Is she okay?"

"In what way?"

Jackson exhaled. "The human way, Derrick."

Derrick had no idea what that meant, but he did get Ellie. At least a little. She played the role of protector. She was the person who came in to clean up the mess, regardless if that meant she didn't have energy left to rescue herself.

"She's overly committed to babysitting her brother. She's been job hunting and I've gotten calls curious about the implications of our relationship. As if I'd get her hired to get the inside scoop on a company. And to top it all off, she's not that excited about moving in with me." The part about her brother should have been the most annoying part, but the last really ticked him off.

"I can't imagine why she doesn't have her bags packed. You're charming."

"It's a big house." Derrick wasn't sure why he needed to keep explaining that.

"Because that was my point." Jackson shook his head as he shifted in his chair. "Is that why you haven't been seeing her? Is she being punished for not jumping to obey your command?"

"What are you talking about?"

"It's as if you're hiding in your office to avoid her...and everything else."

"That's ridiculous." Derrick rubbed his thumb over the leather seam at the edge of the armrest. "I've been slammed with work and am still trying to unravel this Noah mess. It's almost as if he finished his work every day in about an hour and then spent the rest of the time working around our security and protocols and generally searching out every document and email ever sent around here."

"That's scary."

Derrick couldn't disagree with that assessment. "Understatement."

Boredom. That could be the explanation for why Noah had turned on him. Derrick originally assumed greed, but the more he learned about Ellie, inadvertently the more he learned about Noah. From what Derrick could tell, Ellie had eased Noah's way in the world. Maybe too much. It was all something a fake fiancé shouldn't worry about, yet he did. He told himself it was because Noah had stolen from him and he had to fix this, not because he cared.

"He's a genius, right?" Jackson asked.

Derrick was getting tired of hearing that excuse. He knew a lot of really bright people and none of them ever stole from him. "I guess you think that explains his behavior."

"Let's find a new topic. Have you seen the *Insider* today?" Jackson took his cell phone out of his jacket pocket and tapped the screen a few times.

"There shouldn't be anything worth reading about me since I didn't leak a story." Which made him realize he really had ignored Ellie and their arrangement. He should be two steps from putting a fake engagement announcement in the paper. Yet he couldn't pull that trigger, at least not until his brothers hit town and they were on their way.

The hesitancy wasn't based on fear. It was something else…a feeling he couldn't name. This flashing warning signal in his brain that told him to slow down and think things through.

He never expected to want her. This deal was supposed to exist on paper only. He should be able to leave her and not think about her. This whole thing where he wanted to drop by and see her, to call her and talk with her about nothing, made him desperate to create distance between them.

"That's the point. Someone did leak a story and it's not all that flattering to Ellie." Jackson turned his phone around and slid it across the desk toward Derrick.

"What?" Derrick glanced down, skimming the post. Then he read it again. One phrase stuck out: "nasty whispers out there about the lady's last job."

"Damn it."

"You're not the type to let details slip by you, so I'm guessing you knew about Ellie's job issue before you entered into your agreement?"

"Of course. It's all bullshit." He'd made it a point to investigate Ellie before offering her the agreement.

At first, he'd hoped to win her to his side with logic or even bribery, if needed. But the more he'd studied her photo and some bits and pieces of her history, the more the PR firm's offhanded comment about needing an old-fashioned, fake-relationship arrangement to make the Noah problem go away had sounded like the right answer.

And that's how he'd ended up in this mess, wanting her in his bed and at his breakfast table. Smelling her, touching her…tasting her.

"It still sucks for Ellie to have it out there, so public," Jackson said.

"I'll take care of Ellie."

* * *

"Did someone mention my name?" Ellie smiled at how the sound of her voice made two grown men freeze in their chairs. Just a handful of words and she had them spinning around and stopping. Now, that was power.

A few seconds later they both continued to stare at her. Jackson recovered first and returned the smile as he rose to his feet. Derrick's reaction was not as welcoming.

"How did you get in here?" Derrick practically barked the question.

Every single day she came up with more things she should have added to their ridiculous agreement. Today? A "no shouting" clause.

"I walked." And she did that again after closing the office door. In a few steps she joined the men by Derrick's desk.

"I'm serious. The protocol and security lapses are starting to annoy me."

Derrick's voice sounded low and growly. She refused to find that sexy. "So, I've been subjected to your nonannoyed personality to date?"

"Ellie." That's it. He said her name in a flat, monotone voice.

He truly was exhausting.

"A very nice woman showed me back. I told her my name and said we were dating—it's weird how much attention that attracted, by the way—and that I needed to talk to you about what was posted in the *Insider*." It had been the first time she talked to anyone about dating Derrick. The way the words had rolled out of her scared her. The lies should have caught in her throat, but no. "I think she took pity on me, probably because I said the part about us dating."

Derrick picked up his phone. "Who was it?"

"Why?"

"She should have called me first."

Truly exhausting. "Then I'm not telling you."

Derrick lowered the handset again. "The person works for me."

Every conversation with him turned into a debate. The few days apart hadn't done anything for his bossiness. She'd hoped he'd also magically turn less attractive. No luck there, either. "The person *helped* me. I'm not tattling on her."

"Tattling?"

She sighed, letting him know she was done with this topic, then glanced over at Jackson. "Did he really forget about dating me like the gossip post said?"

Jackson winced. "That's unclear at the moment."

"Trust me, ignoring you would be impossible," Derrick said.

"It's been days since we signed the agreement, then we had the canceled dinner plans because of your work emergency and then you went into hibernation mode. Even the *Insider* noticed, which is weird because I thought you were the one who fed them their intel."

She'd tried not to let the newest post bother her. Her ex-boss's accusations bordered on horrifying. They were the type to disqualify her for a human resources positions if they were true, which they were not. But no one would care about the veracity of his claims. It was his word versus hers, and now that her supposed relationship with Derrick fueled the town's gossip machine, those untrue accusations would grow even louder.

"Did you need something?" Derrick asked her.

She noticed he skipped right over her comment about the gossip post. She turned to Jackson for assistance. "Do you think he hears his tone when he talks?"

"I can only hope not." Jackson shook his head. "You should hear him when he actually yells."

She snorted. "No, thanks."

"Ellie!"

This time Jackson laughed. "There, that was close."

Yeah, it looked as if they fully had Derrick's attention now. He held the edge of his desk in a death grip.

Ellie took pity on him. From the exhaustion tugging at the corner of his eyes to the rumpled shirt to the loosened tie, he seemed to be working nearly round the clock after all. "I'm going to ignore the near shouting because I was purposely trying to prick your temper."

"Good Lord. Why?"

She hated to admit it but part of her was testing him. After a few tough years with Noah, running through their parents' life insurance and holding on to the family home only with the help of an aging aunt who lived with them to satisfy a well-meaning social worker, she needed to see if Derrick could control his temper. Then there was the issue of being ignored. "I texted you yesterday and you didn't text back."

Jackson cleared his throat. "So that we're clear, I really want to stay and listen to the rest of this and see how it turns out, but I sense you two need to hash this out without me."

Something in his tone, a mix of amusement and general fondness for Derrick, broke through, making Ellie smile. "Does that mean you'll make him tell you later?"

Jackson nodded. "Definitely."

With a final wink at her and a small nod in Derrick's direction, Jackson took off. He slipped out, closing the door behind him.

"I like him." She did a second glance when something about the door caught her eye. The shirt. The dry cleaning bag.

"I was working."

Derrick's comment dragged her attention to the conversation. She slipped into the seat Jackson had vacated. "Oh, you're answering my previous question now? No texting because you're a busy, busy man?"

"Yes."

"Just so you know, being ignored is frustrating even in a fake dating situation."

For a few seconds Derrick didn't say anything. His gaze searched her face then he leaned into his chair. "I'll do better."

"I'm impressed that's your response." Stunned was more like it. But at his words, she relaxed into the chair, letting her hand fall over the edge of the armrest.

"You strike me as the type who could bolt at any time, so I'm being careful."

Which lead her to another one of the reasons for her visit. "You should know my brother keeps calling me to complain about you. Fair warning, I think another video is coming."

"I'll try to talk to him."

She wanted to believe Derrick could get through to Noah before his behavior spiraled much more. He was fixated on Derrick. Part of her wondered if it was the shock of being fired. But she loved that Derrick promised to try and was holding firm to that vow. Her father used to promise a lot and never follow through. She sensed Derrick was not that kind of man.

"It's not easy to win him over." She hesitated, not sure who much more she should share. "I've tried."

"I get that, but let someone else carry the load for a change."

That sounded so good, so promising, that a wave of relief rolled through her. "We lived together for so long. Right up until he got a job with you and moved into his own studio. Even in college I commuted and went home to him each night."

"You raised him by yourself after you lost your parents?" He sounded horrified at the thought.

"A great-aunt lived with us, which made the court happy. Little did the judge know she chain-smoked, spent her days watching baseball and swearing at the television and was really eighty, even though she looked at least a decade younger." Just thinking about Aunt Lizzy made Ellie smile. "She died my senior year of college. By then I was old enough that the social worker didn't make a fuss."

"You haven't had it easy."

She didn't know anyone who did.

"We have this other thing we need to deal with." She bit her bottom lip as she tried to come up with the right words to describe what really happened. "Joe Cantor. The *Insider* brought up my work history. That can only mean people are whispering about it and making up details… Joe was my boss… He's been saying… I mean, it's not as if it actually happened."

Derrick reached his arm across his expansive desk. "Ellie? Breathe."

She did. "I did not come on to him."

Saying the words brought the frustration crashing down on her again. She had enough to deal with without Joe and his lies. But what she really wanted was to reach out, to grab on to the lifeline Derrick offered. Fighting that urge, she stayed still in the chair.

"Of course not."

"Yeah, that's…" Her brain caught up with the conversation and the air whooshed right out of her body. "Wait, you believe me?"

Derrick's chair squeaked when he got up. Footsteps thudded against the floor as he came around the desk to sit on the edge right in front of her. "Your former boss is a raving jackass."

"I could insert a general snide comment here about businessmen in DC." One that fit a lot of the men she'd met and worked both with and for in the two jobs she'd had since college, the first at a department store then the last one with Joe. But it didn't fit Derrick.

He folded his arms in front of him. "Please refrain."

"I'm stunned you're taking my side. I thought you rich sit-behind-a-desk dudes stuck together."

"And I'm ignoring that description." He continued to watch her. "But the firing was not news to me."

She wrapped her fingers around the edges of the armrests. The wood dug into her palms but she held on. "Technically, I was laid off."

"*Actually*, you were marched out of the office building by security."

She felt something inside her deflate. "Gossip really does run wild in this town."

"There's also rumor you kicked Joe during this argument?" There was no judgment in Derrick's tone. If anything, he sounded amused by the thought.

"Right between the legs." She sighed. "Yeah, that happened."

"Well, there you go."

"Excuse me?"

"Joe is said to enjoy the chase but he clearly doesn't like a woman escalating it to the point of kicking his..."

She laughed. "You can say it."

He smiled at her. Big and beautiful and warm. "Balls."

The amusement died down, leaving behind one unanswered question. "You know about how Joe acts but..."

"What?"

"Are you friends?"

"Hell, no." Derrick made a face that suggested he was appalled at the idea. "And since I hired four women in management positions away from his office years ago, before you were there, he's not my biggest fan."

"You did? I might need their names for my employment attorney. And maybe your testimony."

He nodded. "No problem."

Score one more for Derrick Jameson. He wasn't anything like she expected...well, in some ways, yes. The bossy, intimidating, totally hot part—yes. The kind of sweet side that peeked through now and then? Nope. She had not been prepared for that at all.

"You almost sound likable." More than almost, but that was enough to admit for now.

"Don't start that rumor." He gave her a conspiratorial wink. "Really, though, I'm surprised you lasted with him for more than a day. I can't imagine you taking his nonsense for five seconds without lecturing him to death."

"See, I think there was a compliment in there somewhere, so I'll just say thank you."

"You're welcome." He dropped his arms and let his hands rest on his lap. "And I'm sorry I ignored your text."

"I believe you." But that left one big question. "So, who planted the gossip in the *Insider*? It sounds like someone wants to discredit me."

"I don't know but I'll find out."

An edge had moved into his tone. Usually that sort of thing touched off her guard and her defenses rose. But not this time. She knew the temper wasn't directed at her. "Now you sound angry. Why?"

"Why?"

He sure did enjoy raising his voice. "It's a simple question."

"I don't want anyone messing with you."

"But this is…us…it's fake." She sputtered through the explanation.

"That doesn't mean I want people to spread false rumors about you. How much of a jackass do you think I am?"

"That's kind of sweet."

He frowned at her. "What is?"

"The protective thing. Well, so long as you don't go nuclear about it." She felt obliged to add that caveat since he tended to do things in a *big* way. The last thing she needed was him following her around threatening people.

"Let's say I know what it's like to be on the wrong end of gossip."

Her shoulders fell as some of the comfort that had seeped into her bones seeped right out again. "You're talking about Noah."

"I wasn't." Derrick stood, looming over her. "I don't want to fight with you tonight, and talking about your brother is a guaranteed way to get you fired up."

"What do you want?"

He inhaled deep enough to move his chest up and down. "This."

Then he reached for her. Those strong hands wrapped around her arms and pulled her out of the chair. The move was smooth and gentle; she was on her feet before she even knew what was happening.

He stopped right before kissing her, so she took over. Slipped her arms around his neck and pulled him in closer. He clearly took that as a yes because he regained control from there.

His mouth slid over hers in an explosive kiss that had her pushing up on her tiptoes. Heat washed over her and her muscles went lax. The soft sounds of their kisses mixed with a low grumble at the back of his throat.

This wasn't a test. This kiss lingered and heated. It seared through her, burned a trail right through the heart of her. Stole her breath and left her dizzy and more than a little achy.

When they finally broke apart, her brain had scrambled as her insides turned mushy. Seconds later, she still clung to him, half hanging off him. Those dark eyes searched her face, focused on her mouth, until she could barely breathe.

"Was that to make the engagement seem more real?" The question came out as a whisper. She regretted it a second later, sure that he would use it as an excuse to switch to the cool, in-control Derrick she'd met that first night.

He smiled at her. "Do you think there are cameras in here?"

"I meant were you trying to get me accustomed to kissing you."

"I kissed you because I wanted to kiss you." He skimmed his thumb over her lower lip. "For the record, fake engagement or not, I don't want you to kiss me unless you want to."

"We seem to be stepping into dangerous territory."

"Agreed." He pressed one last quick kiss on her mouth then stepped back. "Dinner?"

The sudden space between them had her emotionally flailing. She tried to act detached. Unaffected. "Okay, is *that* for the fake engagement?"

"You're going to make my head explode."

"Very sexy."

He cupped her cheek and his fingers slipped into her hair. "Yes, you are."

The simple touch, so light, felt so good…and so scary.

This was fake. This was about saving Noah and restoring Derrick's reputation. But still. "Derrick."

"Just dinner. For anything else I'll need a clear green light." He dropped his hand again.

"Wait, do you—"

"Since talking tends to get us in trouble, let's eat." He slipped around to his side of his desk and opened the top drawer. Out came his wallet and keys.

"This feels unsettled." Probably because she wanted to jump on top of him, wrap her legs around his waist and keep kissing him.

"That's my reaction every second since I met you." He headed toward the door, clearly expecting her to follow him.

She still was not a fan of the way he assumed she'd acquiesce like everyone else seemed to do for him. "Is that my shirt?"

"Well, it isn't mine." He took the hanger off the hook on the door and handed it to her. "Here you go."

She decided to ignore the sarcastic part of his response. "I've been looking for it."

"I had it cleaned."

The bag crinkled in her fingers. "For me?"

"I don't plan to wear it."

It sounded like they were back to the clipped sentences and defensive tone. She wondered if he was going to slip into that mode every time they kissed. "Are you being grumpy because I caught you doing a nice thing?"

"Don't get used to it."

She wasn't sure if he meant the grumpiness or the nice gesture. Right then, she didn't care.

Seven

The DC Insider: *What happens when a nice dinner turns into a near fistfight? We're not sure, either, but we think we came close to witnessing such an event. Rumors have been swirling about Ellie Gold's last job and her unceremonious firing, but Derrick Jameson set us straight. She's the innocent party, he insists. We would have asked more questions but he was busy taking his lady home for the evening—his home.*

Ellie Gold had him completely rattled. Just when Derrick thought he'd figured her out, she said something unexpected. He'd cleaned her shirt—a random, simple thing—and she'd cradled it in her hands as if it were an expensive diamond.

And that kiss.

Before that first one in her apartment about a week ago, he'd planned to keep things on a friendly, nonkissing level. But then his lips had met hers and his brain misfired. He hadn't been able to speak or to think. All he'd wanted to do was to hold on and keep going. He told himself it was because Noah had stolen from him and he had to fix this, not because he cared, but even he was having trouble buying that.

He didn't do overwhelmed. He didn't believe in rainbows or stars or whatever people claimed to see when they experienced a great kiss. He certainly didn't get all breathless and confused when a woman's lips touched his. Not usually, anyway. But with Ellie his body and brain went into free fall.

And it wasn't a onetime thing. The second kiss today nearly scrambled every bit of common sense he possessed. He had been two seconds away from pinning her to the wall and tunneling his hand up that slim skirt when he forced his body to pull back.

She messed him up. Took his balance and his control and ground them into nothing.

Now he watched her study the dinner menu. She even managed to make that look sexy. Her fingers slid along the edge. She lifted her chin as she scanned the page.

He was beginning to think he was losing it.

They sat at a small table near the window of a wildly popular French bistro near Logan Circle. It hadn't been hard to get a last-minute reservation because Derrick had a financial interest in the place. A chance he took on a chef he knew with some of the money he'd stockpiled over the years and it worked out. It also meant there was always room for him. He had to assume the position of the table, out in the open, was the overeager manager's way of capitalizing on his presence there tonight.

People noticed. Quite a few businessmen turned around when he entered the restaurant with Ellie on his arm. Some came over and said hello. One let his gaze linger a bit too long on Ellie's chest for Derrick's liking.

Bottom line—he didn't like being on display. "I feel exposed."

Ellie hummed as she continued to scan the food options. "You picked the game."

"What does that mean?"

"I'm assuming you chose this place, one of the hardest

restaurants to get a reservation at right now, to be seen." She peeked at him over the top of the menu. "I'm not even going to ask how you got us in on such short notice. I'll assume this is a case of you being ready at all times for a photo op."

He reached over and lowered her menu so he could meet her eyes without anything getting in the way. "This is dinner, not a photo op."

"That's a first."

"And I'm part owner of this place. The behind-the-scenes money guy."

Her mouth opened a few times before she actually spat out any words. "Well, of course you are."

"Sarcasm?"

"More like *is there any part of this town you don't own* awe." She folded her menu and set it on the space in front of her. "You seem to have an interest in everything."

She was joking but he decided to give her a real answer. "For the record, I am a minority owner in the family business. My father has the largest stake, and likes to hold that over me. I've tried to branch out with some other investments so I'm prepared."

She frowned. "For what?"

"His whims."

And that's exactly how Derrick saw it. His father played games. He liked to make his sons prove themselves over and over.

Derrick refused to be pushed aside or run off because he viewed the family business as his legacy. He'd worked there during college summers and all throughout business school. After that, he'd come on board full-time and worked his way up. Spent months in every department.

His father demanded perfection and when he didn't get it he'd resort to public humiliation. So, Derrick learned quickly not to make any mistakes. Four years ago his father offered more responsibility and Derrick grabbed at the chance. He'd expanded the family's commercial real estate and construction business and personal holdings.

Ellie watched him for a second then rested her hand on the table. "He's difficult."

"Understatement." Derrick noticed she didn't ask it as a question, so she must have heard at least some of the rumors about his notoriously demanding father. "He put me in charge of expansion, sure I'd fail. He questioned every decision, every strategy. Made it nearly impossible to move forward then yelled because we weren't moving forward."

He was going to say more but stopped. He never talked about family stuff with anyone except Jackson and his brothers. Battling for the business he dreamed of running since he was eighteen was a constant frustration for him. He thought he'd earned it, but no.

"But you eventually convinced him." She leaned in. "You're the big boss now. Right?"

"I'm in charge of the day-to-day operations, but there's no guarantee it's permanent. There are some…things I need to accomplish first." Derrick pivoted off that subject before he divulged something he didn't mean to divulge. "The only reason my father isn't here, picking every move apart, is because he's in love."

Derrick heard the snide edge to his voice but didn't bother trying to hide it. The idea of his father spending his days laughing and drinking after having spent so many years making his sons' lives a constant competition, pitting them against each other and punishing them for any perceived failure, rubbed Derrick raw.

Ellie blinked. "Excuse me?"

"Wife number four."

"Oh." Ellie's mouth dropped open. "Do we like her?"

"Thanks to Jackie, my father is testing out possible retirement far away on a beach in Tortola." He laughed. "So, yes."

"Your family is not dull."

No kidding. "And since you commented on my businesses, you should know I have no financial interest in the gas station across the street. I wish I did because I think my tank is almost empty."

"You'll probably buy that next week."

Since she sounded amused by his comments he played along, happy to move off a subject that kept him up at night worrying. Off the fear his father would show up and take it all away without warning. Derrick would survive, of course, but he wanted the family business and the family that went with it. "If I find some extra time at lunch to buy a multimillion-dollar venture, sure."

"Ellie."

Her smile disappeared as she looked up at their unwanted dinner guest. "Mr. Cantor."

Joe Cantor, Ellie's former boss, stood at the edge of the table. A guy known to have a wandering eye and a big mouth. He wasn't half the businessman he thought he was. The only thing that saved him was a mix of old family money and a forgiving wife. As far as Derrick was concerned, the wife could do a lot better than Joe—a man still trying to live off his former reputation as a big-man-on-campus almost two decades later.

Joe glanced at Derrick then focused on Ellie again. "I've been reading about the two of you."

Yeah, Derrick was done. "And I've been reading about you."

Joe's eyes narrowed. "What?"

"I thought you'd like to explain why Ellie was fired." Derrick didn't bother lowering his voice. He wanted people to know how little he thought about Joe's fake dismissal story. "Right here. To my face. In front of her. Let her finally tell her side."

Joe's smirk didn't waver. "Look, it's over. You two are together now."

"Clearly." Before tonight Derrick didn't think much of Joe. Now he thought even less. This intimidation tactic was a clear misstep. A smart guy wouldn't have tried it.

"Whatever happened between us—"

"Nothing." Ellie's eyebrow lifted as she stared Joe down. "Nothing happened between us. Ever."

Joe shook his head. "Ellie, it's okay. It's done."

"Not really." Derrick hated this guy now. "She's still waiting on your apology."

For the first time Joe's mouth fell into a flat line. "What?"

"I don't like when people make up stories about my woman."

Ellie made a humming noise. "*My woman*? Do we like that phrase?"

"Too much?" Derrick asked, seeing in Ellie's eyes that she was enjoying Joe's public takedown. Derrick looked at Joe again, who didn't appear as smug now. "Then ignore the word choice, but the result is the same. One more false word about her coming on to you—which we both know is complete bullshit—and you get to fight me."

Joe let out a pathetic strangled laugh and did a quick glance around. "Are you threatening me, Derrick?"

"I'm actually threatening your business. I thought that was obvious." He glanced at Ellie. "No?"

She put her hand over his. "I thought you were very clear."

"Thank you, dear." Derrick winked at Ellie then turned to Joe again. "Clean up the *misunderstanding* about her firing and then keep your mouth shut, and we're good. Maybe she'll even decide not to sue you."

She shrugged. "I can't promise that."

Joe glared at Derrick. "You can't be serious."

"We're done here." Derrick slid his hand out from under Ellie's and picked up his menu again. "You hungry? I am."

Joe closed in on Ellie. "Tell him the truth."

She didn't even flinch. "Your wife went out of town, you came on to me, I kicked you and then I got fired."

"That's not—"

"Illegal?" More than one table of restaurant patrons was watching now. The manager even made a move toward the table, but Derrick gave a small shake of his head to keep him back. He had this handled. "Yes, Joe. I think it is."

She shrugged. "My lawyer says it is."

Fury flashed in Joe's eyes. "You can't outlast me and you know it."

Ellie deserved better and this show. Even though they kept it respectable, Derrick knew the gossip would make the rounds. They'd proved their point. Now it was time for Joe to get the message and slink away. "For us, it's a date. For you? This is a chance to move without increasing your liability. I'd take it."

Joe gave them one last stare then turned and walked off. He was smart enough to not cause a bigger scene or to storm away. He slipped through the tables with a smile on his face as if they'd been having a nice dinner talk.

The second after he was gone the restaurant's noise level rose again. People seated nearby returned to eating and servers ran around getting food and drinks to the crowded tables.

When Derrick finally glanced across the table again he saw Ellie staring at him. A smile played on her lips. A sexy smile that jolted through him.

"That was thoroughly satisfying," she said.

"Now that's the sort of thing I like to hear from a date."

The rest of the dinner consisted of talking and some verbal sparring, but the fun kind. Ellie finished her meal in a satisfied haze. She enjoyed letting her guard down and ignoring all the stress for an hour.

After her parents died she'd juggled college and Noah.

She'd waded through their mess of an estate. All those failed ventures her father had started and driven into bankruptcy. All the debts that had to be paid and the questions people had looked to her to answer.

She'd handled all of it. Put her personal life on hold, limited dating to brief flings and friendships to a minimum. She'd worked hard, kept her head down and never expected anything from anyone. That's why her friendship with Vanessa meant so much.

Vanessa was the kind of best friend you could call in the middle of the night and she'd come running. She was smart and supportive. They could sit in silence for hours and watch movies. Gossip. Ellie was comfortable around Vanessa when Ellie wasn't all that comfortable with most people. Not on a deep level. Not enough to trust.

It's why Derrick's near automatic defense took Ellie by surprise. For the first time in ages, she had someone other than Vanessa looking out for *her.* Willing to stand up to someone else and protect her from the fallout. Willing to take care of her. It was a heady and humbling feeling.

That was the only explanation she had for why she stood in the middle of his kitchen at after nine that night instead of in her apartment. That and the fact she wanted to be there. Wanted to spend time with him. Wanted to know more about the man who fought so hard against his father.

She'd seen the stark ache in Derrick's eyes at dinner as he talked about the business. He tried to joke about finances, but she'd heard the roughness in his voice. She tried to imagine what it was like to be the oldest son of a man who enjoyed demeaning people, including his own children.

They'd walked in from the garage with the lights clicking on as they'd moved through the high-ceilinged, expertly-carved-moldings, man-this-is-expensive Georgetown house. Even in the dark she had seen rows of impeccably kept brick town houses as they'd driven through the tree-lined streets. The whole area dripped with wealth.

By the time they'd pulled off a narrow street and into Derrick's garage—a thing she didn't really think existed in this part of town outside of huge mansions—she'd confirmed she was way out of her league.

Now she looked around the pristine kitchen with the gray cabinets and swirling white-and-gray-marble countertops that looked like they should be on the cover of some fancy home magazine. Not a pot out of place. Not a glass in the sink.

For the fourth time since they'd left the restaurant, confusion crashed into her. She'd been riding this emotional roller coaster for most of her life but with Derrick the ride turned wild. She flipped between interest and frustration. One minute she wanted to kiss him. The next, punch him.

They were supposed to be in a business arrangement and nothing more. But those kisses and the way he touched her, looked at her…how her heart thundered in her ears when he smiled. How she wanted to peel away the layers and peek beneath to see the real man.

Her attraction to him in more than an objective "oh, he's good-looking" way was unexpected and kind of unwanted. It clouded everything. They were from different worlds and using each other. But the glimpses she'd seen weren't of a thoughtless playboy who liked to throw money around. He was deeper than that. Far too likeable. Very tempting.

She sat on the stool at the massive kitchen island then stood again. "I feel like we're inviting trouble being here alone."

"You're going to be moving in here soon." Derrick took off his suit jacket and loosened his tie. Next he reached for one of the big double doors to the refrigerator and brought out two bottles of water. "You should get used to the place."

"Not that soon."

He set the bottles next to her on the countertop. "I'm thinking within days."

"I'm saying within weeks." She tried to mentally slam the brakes on all of this. The move, the engagement, the agreement. If the attraction she felt for him was real, should she really mix in the parts that weren't? She really didn't know anymore.

Life whizzed by her so quickly since she'd met him. Her brain rushed to keep up, but when that failed, her emotions took over. Her wants and needs won out. She wanted him to touch her again. To give in and take something for herself for a change.

"You really do thrive on being difficult," he said.

She thought they were well matched on that score, but she didn't bother to argue since that would only prove his point. "Maybe, but I'm still grateful."

He put his hands on the counter on either side of her, trapping her there in a warm cocoon. "For what?"

Tension spun up inside her. She knew she could break out of his hold but the problem was she didn't want to. That's how little it took. He moved in, close enough for her to smell the soap on his skin, and her heartbeat took off in an all-out race. She wanted to run her fingers over the light stubble on his chin. Feel his mouth on hers.

She fought for breath as she pretended to stare at the white farmhouse sink behind him. "Look at this kitchen. My entire apartment would fit in here."

His gaze searched hers until she looked at him again. "For what, Ellie?"

"What you said to Joe. How you stuck up for me without making me prove my side of the story." She gave in to the need to touch him then. Let her fingers trail over his tie, follow it to the end and hang there. "For the nice dinner."

"I don't want your gratitude."

Her stomach took off on a frenzy of somersaults. "What do you want?"

"You."

The deep voice, having that laser-like focus trained on her, the combination pushed the fight out of her. She'd been running and making excuses and coming up with arguments. But there, staring up at him, seeing the intensity in those eyes, she gave in.

She tugged on his tie and brought him in even closer. The air between them burned with a new energy. His mouth met hers and the rest of the world blinked out.

Heat roared through her as his lips crossed hers. Firm kisses. The sweep of his tongue over hers. One minute she stood there and the next he lifted her onto the counter. Her tight skirt bunched high on her thighs as he pushed them apart to stand between them.

His hands roamed over her back then to her neck. Fingers slid through her hair. His touch managed to be soothing and demanding at the same time. Heat radiated off him as she unknotted his tie. And when his mouth moved to her cheek then to her ear, a shiver stole her balance. She fell hard against him as his tongue traced a line down her neck.

They both made hungry, growling sounds and she ached for more. Her heels closed around his thighs, tightening his body against hers.

"Ellie?"

"Yes. Green light." She caught his mouth again. The kiss seared through her, destroying her worries.

His hands skimmed around her body, over her breasts. She almost sighed in relief when she felt his fingers on her shirt buttons. The voice inside her head screamed for him to hurry, but a part of her wanted to savor every minute. Every lingering touch.

"Oh, damn. Sorry!"

The deep male voice rang out in the kitchen. Ellie heard

it but it took her another few seconds to realize what was happening.

Someone was there, in the house. As soon as that thought registered in her brain, she shoved against Derrick's chest. Their legs tangled together and his hand got caught in her shirt. When he stepped to the side, turned around and stood in front of her like a human shield, he almost ripped her silk blouse.

Derrick's shoulders went from stiff to relaxed as he looked at the intruder. "Spence?"

She didn't have the same reaction as she worked in double time to line up her shirt buttons and get them closed again.

The other man held up a hand but he didn't try to hide his smile. "I can leave."

"Of course not." Derrick glanced at her over his shoulder. His gaze bounced to her shirt and he nodded before stepping to the side and helping her from the counter. "Ellie Gold, this is one of my brothers, Spencer."

She grabbed for her skirt and tugged it down before she gave his brother an unexpected show. "Right."

Heat flamed in her cheeks. She could only imagine the force of her blush, but she pushed through and gave him eye contact. She should have done that first because she would have known the two men were related.

Spencer was a slightly stockier version of Derrick. They both towered over her and were blessed with that's-almost-unfair good looks. The Jameson family had a heck of an impressive gene pool. Their father might be a jerk but he churned out dark-haired hotties without trouble.

Spencer's smile reached his eyes, which made her think he did it more than his brother. That might also explain the lightness about him. Derrick walked around as if he carried the responsibility for the world on his shoulders. Spencer didn't give off that vibe.

"I'm Spence." He held out his hand. "The middle Jameson brother."

Derrick snorted as they shook hands. "The one with the shitty timing."

"I didn't know… See, Derrick never really brings… Okay then." Spence made a hissing sound. "I'll stand here and not talk."

His stumbling eased her discomfort at having been caught like a naughty teen on prom night. "What were you trying not to say?"

"He's pointing out that I'm not in the habit of bringing women to my house," Derrick said.

Spence nodded. "Yeah, that."

"Ellie is different." Derrick picked up one of the water bottles off the counter and offered it to her. "She's moving in."

Spence's eyes grew even wider. "Really?"

She waited for Derrick to explain about the agreement and Noah and all the trouble they were trying to fix. When Derrick didn't say anything, she glanced over at him. "And?"

He wrapped an arm around her shoulders. "We're still fighting over the date."

Her mind jumbled again. "Wait…"

"Ah, now I get it," Spence said.

That made one of them. She was still lost. "Want to explain it to me?"

Derrick moved then. He put down the water and reached for his suit jacket. His keys jangled in his hand a second later. "Let me run Ellie home then we'll catch up."

Spence frowned. "She's the one who should stay."

She wanted some air…and an explanation. "No, it's fine." She glanced at Derrick, sending him a we-need-to-talk glare. "You ready?"

If she knew her way around the house she would have

taken off without him. Instead she followed him along a hallway and a set of stairs to the bottom level of the grand three-story home.

Her head was pounding too hard for her to concentrate but as soon as they were in the garage with the door shut behind them, she spun around to confront Derrick. "Your brother doesn't know."

He had the nerve to stare at his keys and not her. "About what?"

She put her hand over his. "That this is a fake arrangement, Derrick."

"It didn't feel fake a second ago." He hit her with intense eye contact. The kind that made her breath catch in her throat.

"I refuse to regret that."

"I hope not since I'm planning on finishing it very soon." He blew out a long breath. "Look, if you can't tell your brother, I can't tell mine. That seemed fair to me."

He said it as if the logic made perfect sense. She didn't buy it. Jackson knew. She had every intention of telling Vanessa when they met for lunch tomorrow as planned. She had no idea how she held it in this long, except that Vanessa had gone away on a work trip for four days.

No way did Derrick's brother need to be kept in the dark about something this big. He should know he wasn't really about to get a sister-in-law. "I hate when you sound reasonable because it convinces me you're hiding something."

"I think our agreement makes it clear we both are."

It was hard to argue with that. "Okay, but when it comes to this agreement and what we both get out of it, we'll be honest with each other, right? We need each other, and I'm not talking about the kissing."

"I'm happy to talk about the kissing."

Her stomach did a little tumble. "I'm not kidding, Derrick."

"Trust me."

He made it sound so easy, but he had no idea. Her father used to say that, too. *We'll be fine, Ellie. This time the plan will work. You won't have to switch schools.* Then he broke the promises almost as quickly as he made them.

"You've been in charge and getting your way for too long." She'd thought that from the first minute she'd met him and she still believed that was true.

"I have a feeling that's about to change."

Sounds as if he was finally getting it. "Count on it."

Eight

The DC Insider: *There is a lot happening in the Jameson household these days. Middle brother and perennial black sheep, Spencer, has returned to the nest. Does that mean baby brother Carter is on his way? Bigger question: if the family is coming into town, do Derrick and Ellie have big news to share?*

Derrick couldn't fight off the very strong feeling he'd screwed things up tonight. He didn't regret kissing Ellie, touching her. Hell, he'd been five seconds away from slipping her underwear off and carrying her upstairs when Spence showed up.

Them in bed. Sex. All that was going to happen. When he'd first met her, he'd thought he could keep the attraction separate, but since it sparked both ways, why fight it? They could enjoy each other, help each other with their family issues and have a good time. Win, win.

The only problem, as usual, came from his father. Those damn requirements of his. The ones that stood between Derrick and the business he'd always wanted.

In Derrick's head it made sense to hide from Ellie the fact that he could lose the business. Why give her that much power over him? It also made sense to hide the fake engagement part from Spence and Carter, because they would never agree with his decision to make that choice.

But all the half-truths, the partial information, meant lying to the people around him. He'd never out-and-out deceived his brothers before. Sure, when they were younger, he'd downplayed their father's crappy actions and how poorly he'd treated their mom before she died. What kind of man went to his wife's deathbed and asked for a divorce so he could marry his mistress sooner?

This was different. He wasn't protecting them as much as trying to handle everything his own way without interference. He worried that made him the asshole this time.

"So." Spence made the word last for three syllables. "I think you left something out of our weekly phone call. We talked about Dad's stupid business agreement, but I don't remember you mentioning Ellie."

That call was a tradition Derrick would not let die. Their father had tried to drive the brothers apart by making them compete over everything from sports to his affection. Derrick refused to let the bond break. He hadn't always been a great brother. At times he'd outright failed at keeping the family running, but Carter and Spence mattered to him and losing them was not an option. Ever.

They were both welcome in his house anytime. He'd bought a five bedroom so they'd have a place to stay when they were in town. Carter rarely came in from the West Coast. Not since the huge falling-out with their father over the running of the family estate in Virginia—the Jameson property no Jameson currently lived in.

Spence had been bouncing around from place to place, but stopped in for a few days now and then. His timing kind of sucked this time because Ellie was moving in and the fake engagement was moving forward. Having Spence there and not telling him the whole story would only make that all the more awkward.

"Ellie was a surprise." Derrick turned the words over in his head and decided that might be the most truthful statement he'd ever made.

"Women are like that."

Derrick leaned against the sink, facing Spence. "Not for me. Not usually."

"So, let me get this straight." Spence balanced his palms on the counter behind him. "Right now you're dealing with Dad and the business. He's insisting you bring Carter and me home or he'll sell it out from under you."

That was the biggest of the moving parts. "About that—"

"Wait, I'm not done." Spence paused, as if he needed more drama here. "Some kid has launched a campaign to paint you as a…what, bad boss? And on top of that and all the work you're putting in you found time to date. And not just date, to seriously date for the first time in…ever, right?"

That about summed it up. "Yes."

"Anything else I should know? Like maybe you invented something or cured cancer while I was gone."

"Ellie is his sister." That much Derrick could tell. Maybe Spence would have some ideas on how to shut down Noah without ticking off Ellie, because Derrick hadn't come up with one yet.

"Now you've lost me."

"The guy who worked for me, the one who stole, but insists I fired him out of spite and that I'm completely incompetent. His name is Noah and he's Ellie's little brother."

Spence whistled. "You do like to make your life as shitty as possible, don't you?"

"He's how I met Ellie."

"And now you're going to be living together."

"Yes." Unless she killed him first, which Derrick thought was a strong possibility.

"You, who has only ever introduced me to the women you dated after you stopped dating them and once they've moved into friend mode."

"I'm a complex guy."

Spence shook his head. "I'm not sure that's the word I'd use."

"Ellie is…" Man, Derrick didn't even know what to say next. Hot, special. Annoying yet energizing. He didn't get her at all or understand her hold on him. All he knew was that she'd flipped his life upside down and had him scrambling, and that a part of him enjoyed the chaos. "Different."

Derrick thought he found a nice, safe description until Spence frowned at him. And stared…then kept staring. "What?"

Spence made a groaning sound. "You should work on that."

"What?"

"How you describe Ellie and your feelings for her. An orange car is different. Your girlfriend should warrant a better word." Spence glanced at the very spot where Ellie had been on that counter. "If you plan to make out with her in the kitchen again, that is."

Oh, that was definitely happening. Derrick didn't even have to think about that. Forget hands-off and common sense. The next time he'd lock the door and strip her clothes off. "I was doing fine."

"I think I arrived just in time."

That's not how Derrick saw the situation at all. "Two hours from now would have been better."

Spence stepped away from the counter and headed for the living area off the kitchen. "Well, since neither of us is having sex tonight, you may as well fill me in."

"On what?"

"Ellie. I want details." Spence sank into one of the

couches set up in front of the massive stone fireplace. "I can get them from you or I can ask her."

"Subtle."

"Start talking."

Breakfast with Vanessa went great, as usual, until Ellie mentioned Derrick and dating and the whole *big lie for good press* thing. Amazing how that brought all of the other conversations to a standstill. Even now, twenty minutes later as they walked to Ellie's apartment, Vanessa barely said anything.

Ellie was about to make a joke about how her timing of the news messed up any chance at getting more coffee when Vanessa finally piped up. "A fake engagement."

They turned the corner at the end of Ellie's block and headed toward her building. "I know it sounds ridiculous."

"You mean like we've stepped into some weird novel? Yeah."

"It's the best option for Noah."

Vanessa stopped stared at Ellie. The look on her face hinted at the confusion pinging around inside her.

"What about what's best for Ellie?" Vanessa asked.

That wasn't the reaction Ellie expected. Yelling, yes. Even a few well-placed "Are you out of your mind?" comments. But that? No. "What does that mean?"

"We need to talk about your propensity to look out for everyone but yourself." Vanessa sounded furious at the idea.

Cars whizzed by and Ellie could see the stoplight in the distance. She wanted to focus on all of that and drown out the voice inside her head that told her she was getting in deep with Derrick. That she would never be able to keep sex and her attraction separate from her growing feelings for him. That, most troubling of all, she was starting to like him and was desperate to spend time with him.

She focused on the practical instead. "I need a job, security and some relief from the ongoing Noah drama. Derrick provides that."

"At the risk of violating the Bechdel test and talking only about men, isn't Derrick the reason Noah is spinning right now?"

"I used to think so."

"And now?"

"As Derrick keeps reminding me, Noah is an adult. He's had therapy and needs to figure out how to control the frustration when it tries to overtake him. He won't be able to survive in the work world otherwise." Ellie hated to admit that.

After all these years of guiding him and handling the oppositional defiant disorder so that it didn't morph into something even more serious, she had to start to back away. Not completely. She'd always be there for him, but he needed to be in charge of his behavior and take responsibility for his actions. It was time to let him make mistakes like everyone else.

Even now he texted and called every day. He insisted he was about to break some new story about Derrick. Something awful that would make her see the man he really was. She begged him not to and so far he hadn't, but she sensed it was only a matter of time.

Vanessa exhaled and some of the concern seemed to leave her face. "Well, if Derrick convinced you to give Noah some space, then I might learn to like him, though I'm not promising."

Of course Vanessa liked the comment because she'd been suggesting the same thing for a while now.

"Derrick also went after Joe Cantor."

Vanessa smiled and started walking again. "I know. I read the *Insider*."

Ellie almost choked. "Good grief, why?"

"It's wildly entertaining. If I had known the business

world was so full of gossip and sex, I might have traded in some of my art history classes for economics."

They dodged a group of men loading boxes into a truck and jogged up the steps to the front of her building. Kept going past the mailboxes and the elevator that seemed to be stuck with an open door and not moving.

"Derrick keeps planting stories. And now someone else is." She could barely handle Derrick's PR campaign, though she had to admit he had eased off a bit. Photographers weren't lurking around capturing pictures of them every second, as she once feared. But the *Insider* still churned out tidbits about their dinners and her movement every time she stepped outside.

"Who else?"

"Joe, more than likely." And that was the bigger concern. Someone wanted to discredit her. Derrick had vowed to stop it. But what happened to her once he was done with their fake arrangement? She still had to work. To eat. To find a real job.

Her stomach tumbled and a wave of nausea battered her. She wanted to think it related to the very real fear of not being able to support herself in the future, but she sensed it had something to do with the idea of waking up one day and not seeing Derrick again. Of losing the talking and arguing and zap of attraction that struck her whenever she saw him.

"The men in your life are exhausting," Vanessa said.

They turned the corner and moved into the hallway leading to her apartment door. Ellie reached for her keys and nearly dropped them. "Tell me about it."

Vanessa stopped in midstep. "What's going on?"

Ellie's head shot up. Her front door was open and two boxes were piled right outside in the hall. Panic surged through her as she ran to the doorway. "Hey!"

She didn't go in. There really was no reason to since the

room, her studio, stood empty except for a few stray pieces of paper and what looked like a community of dust bunnies she'd missed living under her couch.

"Did you get evicted?" Vanessa asked, her gaze zooming from one end of the room to the other.

"No." At least she didn't think so.

Her mind flashed to the van outside. To the packed boxes. To the movers.

Derrick.

"Good afternoon." Jackson stepped out of her bathroom, carrying her robe.

Ellie wasn't sure what stunned her more, him being in her apartment or the sight of him holding a ball of pink fluff in his arms. "Jackson?"

"You know him?" Vanessa asked.

"He works for Derrick. They're friends…" Ellie didn't know how to describe their relationship. She knew Jackson was loyal to Derrick but there was a part of her that viewed him as an ally. Or she had until this. "It's complicated."

"Most things with Derrick are." Jackson put down the robe and shook Vanessa's hand.

Vanessa stared at their joined hands then at Jackson. Finally she shrugged. "What's happening?"

Jackson frowned. "Ellie is moving in to Derrick's place today."

He said the words slowly, as if he thought they were true at one time but now wasn't sure. Ellie blamed Derrick. He had that effect on her, as well. "I didn't agree to do that now."

"He said…" Jackson's frown deepened. "Wait, you guys didn't agree today was the day? Then where did he get the key he gave me?"

"Good question." If Ellie had to guess she'd bet he somehow convinced her landlord to turn one over. Or he bought the building and now *was* her landlord.

"I figured you weren't here and weren't packed up because Derrick told you I'd handle it."

Yep, this was definitely Derrick's fault. He ordered and manipulated. Looked like Jackson got stuck in his trap this time, too.

"I'm going to kill him." Ellie had threatened it before but this time she just might do it.

Jackson swore under his breath. "I'll take that as a no. Derrick did this all on his own."

Ellie shouldered part of the blame. A very small part. She'd let Derrick lure her in. He did nice things for her. He kissed like he'd been born to do it. All that stopped now. She needed some control and she would wrestle him for it, if needed. "I'll handle this."

"Are you sure?" Jackson looked as skeptical about her statement as he sounded.

"Yeah, really?" Vanessa gestured toward Jackson. "Listen to him."

She got it. Vanessa was fighting a bout of friendly concern. Jackson likely thought this was one step too far, even for Derrick. They were both right and she appreciated it, but she and Derrick had an agreement. She also thought they had an understanding and possibly something bigger that might lead to getting naked.

"If Derrick wants a showdown, we'll have one."

This time Vanessa looked skeptical. Also a bit worried. "Is this a good idea? Derrick isn't exactly a lightweight. I'm guessing he barges in and gets his way a lot."

Ellie couldn't deny that, but he wouldn't hurt her. His yell didn't even scare her that much. No, this was about Derrick Jameson understanding how far he could push her. And he'd gone too far. "He needs to learn."

Jackson hadn't moved. It was as if he were rooted to that spot on her floor. "True, but…"

"I'm looking forward to meeting Derrick," Vanessa said. "Sounds like the guy needs a good kick."

Vanessa wasn't wrong on that, either. Ellie vowed to be the one who administered the blow.

"You will soon enough." Ellie looked at Jackson. "I need your help."

"I almost hate to ask what for." But he smiled.

"You'll see."

Nine

The DC Insider: *Living together? Why, Derrick Jameson. You are a fast worker. And, Ellie? You're our hero. Tame that rowdy billionaire.*

Jackson didn't sound an alarm unless something was really wrong. So, when he called from Derrick's house, insisting there was a problem, Derrick got his butt over there and fast.

Driving up outside, everything looked normal. The usual cars on the street. Nothing odd in his driveway. It wasn't until he got out of the garage and reached the bottom of the stairs to the main living area that he heard the deafening thumping. He didn't know how he'd missed it earlier.

Music. Blaring music.

After marching upstairs, he turned the corner and stepped into the open kitchen and living room area…and stopped. Both the television and stereo were on, and at what sounded like full power. Magazines were strewed all over his usually clutter-free space. There were open boxes and balled-up piles of clothes. Books everywhere. He couldn't see an inch of his hardwood floor.

Ellie sat in the middle of it all, sprawled on his couch with her feet propped up on the coffee table. She wore a pink robe and matching slippers. Ate potato chips right out of the bag. Drank…was that red wine? One wrong move and his light gray couch, the one he'd owned for less than a year, wouldn't survive the alcohol bath.

It took a few seconds for her to stop her off-key singing and look up at him. "Hey, roomie."

So that's what this was. Payback. He had to give her credit because little surprised him and this did. He'd expected a series of nasty texts or an office visit. Not this.

To avoid yelling over the song he didn't recognize, he went to the stereo and turned it off. That left the talk show, which raged in a circus of screaming. He scanned the stacks of crap for his remote and didn't see it. Realizing he had no idea how to turn the television off without it, he gave in. "Any chance you could take care of that?"

She pretended not to hear. Put her hand behind her ear, leaned in and everything. Apparently full drama mode had been activated.

He tried again. "Turn. It. Off."

"Oh, sure." She reached under the chip bag and produced the remote. The noise clicked off a second later. "I'm recording this, anyway. Actually, I'm recording a lot of programs." She studied the remote and its buttons. "Did you know your DVR is empty? There's plenty of room for my stuff."

He inhaled, trying to hold on to the fleeting sense of control he'd had when he'd started the day. "I don't watch much TV."

"Then it's good I rented a whole bunch of movies. Your on-demand options are impressive."

He could hardly wait to see that bill. "Are you done?"

"Enjoying the house? Not even close." She continued to sit there with one leg crossed over the other, her pink slipper bouncing up and down.

The robe slipped, treating him to miles of toned thigh. When she didn't rush to close the material again, a new sensation hit him. She was making a point but she might also be making a play.

Now he needed to know what she had on under there and how long it would take him to peel it off her.

But he forced his mind to focus. He looked around again, wondering how long it had taken her to make this much mess and how many days it would take him to undo it. "I'm assuming this is your way of saying you don't appreciate the manner in which I moved you in here."

Even he had to admit he'd crossed a line, but he wasn't up for a debate about something he thought should be simple. Today, Spence had agreed to come into the office for a few hours, and Derrick knew Ellie had made plans to spend a few hours with Vanessa. It struck him as the perfect time to get the job done.

He'd taken care of it all, which meant delegating to Jackson. The bigger benefit—he thought—was shutting down Ellie's attempts to stall by complaining about packing.

The plan may have worked if he hadn't gotten tied up in a meeting that ran long. He'd planned to meet up with Ellie *before* she'd headed to her apartment. To warn her. That had failed.

"Derrick, this is better than any hotel." She wore one of those sickeningly sweet smiles that silently telegraphed her desire to push someone in front of a speeding bus. "I plan to stay right here. And I mean *right here*. In this spot. With my boxes stacked all around me as I collect more and more stuff. Now that I know the official address for your house I can have even more boxes delivered."

"Okay, I get it."

Her head fell to the side as she stared up at him. "Do you?"

He should be furious or at least frustrated. He was turned on. Like, ten-seconds-from-stripping-that-robe-off-her turned on.

What he should do is explain the reason for his actions then get back to work. End any temptation and not go near her.

All good thoughts…smart. But he didn't intend to do any of it. No, they were going to be naked and soon. Her legs wrapped around him. Her mouth on his. The wall, the couch, the floor. He didn't care where so long as they got there soon.

He walked over to her. Maneuvered through the piles and kicked aside more than one stray shoe. No question her entire closet now rested on his floor.

She didn't bother to move the chips or the pillows she had stacked on one side of her, so he picked the coffee table. Sliding some books aside, he sat across from her, right next to her legs.

Through it all, she watched him. Her expression bordered on a smile. A satisfied one. Clearly she enjoyed this moment and the statement she was making.

That seemed fair, because he was a reluctant fan, too. "I may have been a little heavy-handed in my approach to making your relocation happen."

She rolled her eyes. "Saying 'I'm sorry' would have been a shorter sentence."

He held in a smile. "True."

"Do you want to try it? I promise it won't hurt at all." Her voice dipped lower, grew sexier, as she finally put aside the chips and the magazine and folded her hands on her lap.

His mind went back to that robe. Her long, sexy legs were right next to him. He glanced over, taking in the bare skin and those muscles, all sleek and sexy. Suddenly he had only one question…

"What are you wearing under that?"

Amusement danced in her eyes as she reached for the belt and untied it. The slow reveal had his heart hammering in his chest. She must have sensed it because she took her time peeling the sides apart to reveal a pair of running shorts and a formfitting tank top. On her, the combination was just about the hottest thing ever.

His gaze traveled down her neck and over the slope of her shoulder. To her chest. Had she skipped the bra?

Damn...

She snapped her fingers. "That apology?"

Maybe it was the way she sat there, looking ready to do battle, but his usual hate-to-lose-at-anything armor fell. "I should have talked to you first."

Silence thumped between them after he ended the sentence. For a few seconds they sat there.

"That's it?" she asked.

"Yes."

She sighed at him. "Try again."

Apparently his defenses hadn't fallen far enough for her liking. "I was attempting to honor our agreement."

"For the record, you're getting farther away from an actual apology, not closer." She glared at him.

He was surprised she didn't have a headache from doing that. "You said—"

"Nope."

On anyone else the refusal to back down would piss him off. He liked to be in control, to come out on top of any argument. But he loved that she pushed him. She didn't try to impress him. She didn't need to try because she did it naturally, just by sitting there.

He conceded this point to her, expecting it to cost him something. For it to grate against his nerves. "I apologize for unilaterally making the decision. I should have conferred with you."

Once it was out there, he waited for a kick of frustration to nail him. He should be running to work. He didn't spend afternoons hanging around at home. Hell, he spent most nights at his desk. Until he'd met her, that was the only answer. Push forward, drive in more business. But now, today, he was perfectly content to sit and look at her, to wait to see what she would say next.

Lately his frustration with his father's demands, the needs of the company, his brothers and his own instincts were pulling him in too many directions. Ellie cleared away all the noise and stress and let him relax. It had been a long time since he'd felt comfortable in his own skin—then again, it wasn't really comfort he was feeling.

But he was holding back details. They'd agreed to be honest with each other, but he hadn't told her all of it. She didn't know that him being successful in calming Noah down was part of a bigger plan to win the business. That, in reality, he needed her. He hated needing anything but this time he did.

"That sounded more like a presentation to your bankers than a real apology, but I'll take it."

He finally let out that laugh he'd been holding inside. Leave it to her to judge his apology and sincerity and find both lacking.

He glanced around. "So, how exactly did you make all this happen in such a short amount of time?"

"I told your movers to leave the boxes here then I dumped the contents all over your living room."

Joe Cantor was an idiot to fire her. If he'd harnessed her drive and talent, his business would be doing much better today. Derrick would bet the Jameson water properties on it. "By yourself?"

"It was my idea but I asked Jackson to help."

The idea of Jackson and Ellie teaming up against him hit Derrick like a shot to the chest. He would stand almost no chance against their joint forces. But he did like that they seemed friendly, that Jackson was protective of her.

Still, he was the boss and there should be limits, at least in theory. "He's fired."

"We both know that's not true."

He peeked at her legs again. Followed the long line to her knee then to the line where that soft skin disappeared under the shadow of the robe.

He dragged his gaze away. Moving forward meant letting her into his life in a real way. Not telling her everything risked her wrath.

He was torn and frustrated. He was also on fire for her.

Without thinking he reached over and slipped his hand under her ankles. Picked up her feet and put them on his lap, slippers and all. "You must be exhausted."

The move knocked her off-balance, but only for a second. Her hands went to the cushions on either side of her to steady herself. "I'm still on a bit of an adrenaline high."

That made two of them and Derrick didn't see the rush dying any time soon. "Interesting."

His palm skimmed up her leg from her ankle. He massaged first one calf then the other, with his thumb tracing gentle circles over her skin.

Her fingers flexed against the couch material. "Derrick Jameson, are you flirting with me?"

"I'm trying."

Heat flared in her eyes. "That's dangerous."

He'd skated way past that point. For him there was no longer an *if.* It was all about *when.* And if she showed any sign of agreeing, he'd have their clothes off in record time. "No, dangerous is what I *want* to do to you."

She didn't move. "Tell me."

He said goodbye to the idea of getting any work done today. "Any chance you'd let me show you?"

Her gaze went to the floor then to the boxes leaning against the end of the couch. "There's not much room in here."

"My bedroom is pretty spacious." Not his most subtle

line, but it was out there now. "Unless you dumped boxes up there, as well."

"I was tempted, but now I'm happy I didn't."

His hand stilled on her calf. "Be sure, Ellie."

"The answer is yes, Derrick."

She didn't know how they made it upstairs without breaking something. The barriers she'd erected, the promises she'd made to herself about not getting involved and the need to ignore her attraction to him…it all floated away.

This was for her. For the first in a long time, she took something she needed and ignored all the sensible reasons to hold back. There, with him, she didn't want to be rational and careful. She wanted heat and passion. Touching and kissing.

She'd stripped his suit jacket off him before they'd gotten out of the living room. She'd had his tie unknotted and slipped off by the time they'd hit the bottom step of the staircase curving up to the second floor.

His footsteps thudded on the stairs as he walked backward, his hand curled around the banister.

He stopped when she dropped the robe. His chest rose and fell on heavy breaths as he stared at her. He didn't touch her, but his gaze traveled over her like a gentle caress.

Never breaking eye contact, he drew her closer, moving her to the step above him. Let his gaze dip to her stomach… to the tops of her legs. The anticipation burned through her. Labored breathing echoed in her ears, a mix of hers and his.

When he grabbed the back of her thighs and pulled her tight against him, her breath escaped her lungs with a hard punch. The next minute he lifted her off her feet. Without any thought from her brain, she wrapped her legs and arms around his firm body. Held him close.

Her fingers slipped into his hair. She loved the feel and smell of him. His strength. His determination.

She lowered her head and kissed him. Poured every ounce of need and want into it, and felt his arms tighten around her in response.

Boy, the man could kiss.

“Damn.” He whispered the word when he finally lifted his head. Then he started moving.

There was something breathtakingly sexy about having Derrick carry her up the stairs. About the way his fingers clenched and unclenched against the bare skin on her thighs. He didn’t break a sweat.

Their relationship had a ticking clock. For once, she didn’t hear it thumping in her head, threatening to steal him out of her life.

The house whirled until everything blurred. At the top of the stairs they passed a doorway, then another. She saw a bed and, in another room, what looked like a desk and a wall of bookcases.

None of it stopped him. Derrick kept walking until they got to the shadowed room at the end of the hall. He hit the light switch with his elbow. A soft light bathed the room in white.

She could see the deep blue walls and closed curtains. So soothing. A huge bed sat smack in the middle of the room with pillows stacked against the headboard. It dominated the space.

The furniture was sleek. Clean lines that hinted at a big price tag. Dark and mysterious…perfect for him.

“Are you sure?”

His question, asked in a deep, even voice, broke through her gawking. She looked at him again. Saw the warmth in his eyes, felt the need vibrating through him. There was only one answer. “Yes.”

His hold loosened and she slid down the front of him, felt every inch of his excitement. As soon as her feet hit the floor, her hands went to his chest and she started unbuttoning his shirt. Once she got it open and untucked, he captured her mouth in a kiss that made her knees buckle.

He caught her around the waist and held her with one hand while his other tunneled under her shirt. Then both of his hands were on her, caressing her breasts, learning her curves.

Tension ripped through her. The soft cotton of her shirt suddenly scratched against her. She wanted it up and off. As if she'd said the words out loud, he peeled the shirt up, lifting it off her, leaving her exposed to his gaze.

His thumbs rubbed over her as he cupped her. That intense gaze stayed locked on her breasts, on how they fit his hands. "Ellie…"

He barely touched her and her skin caught on fire. Every nerve ending snapped to life. Every instinct told her to hold him again.

He sat on the edge of the bed and she wanted to slip onto his lap, but he held her between his legs. Had her stand there as he spread his hand over her stomach…as he slid his fingertips under the band of shorts. With a tug, he had them skimming her body to the tops of her thighs. Wriggling her hips, she shimmied them the rest of the way off.

He stared at her white bikini bottoms. She knew they were see-through. She knew how much she wanted them off.

She climbed on him then. Straddled his lap and pressed her body against his. The way he inhaled, sharp almost as if on a gasp, empowered her. She loved the sound and his loss of control. When he fell onto the mattress, she went with him. They tumbled down and he shifted up on one elbow until he hovered over her.

He trailed his fingers over her stomach to the top of the bikini bottoms.

"You still have a lot of clothes on, big guy."

"I can be naked in two seconds." His palm flattened over the front of her underwear.

She could feel her body getting ready for him. Something inside her tightened and a tumbling started deep in her stomach. "Let's see."

For a second he didn't move. Then his eyebrow lifted. "Anything you want."

He sat up next to her and did a slow striptease, taking his time unbuttoning his dress shirt and sleeves before shucking it off. She couldn't really see anything but the firm muscles of his chest. She wanted to reach up and trail her fingers over that sexy dip between his collarbone and his shoulder. Over every pronounced angle.

"How does a man who spends all of his day at a desk look like you?"

"I don't spend *every* hour there." He winked at her then stood.

His hands went to his belt and that got her moving. She shifted to the side of the bed and dropped her legs over the side. Fit her hands over his and took over the task of undoing his belt. Slid the leather out of the loops and dropped it to the floor.

Next came the zipper. The ripping sound echoed through the room as she lowered it and pressed her palm against his bulge filling the space. Caressed him through his pants.

His fingers tightened against the side of her head. "Ellie, I'm not going to last very much longer."

"Good." She slid her legs beneath her and moved back. Lay against the mattress with her feet flat on the bed and her knees in the air.

He visibly swallowed. She watched him do it. Smiled when he nearly ripped his pants and boxer briefs getting them off. Then he was naked and so fit, so lean and sexy, as he crawled up the mattress to get to her.

That fast her heart flipped over. A revving sensation took off inside her. She slid her leg up the back of his, loving the burst of energy that flowed through her at the touch.

She wanted this. Him. That first time she'd seen him in person the air had left her lungs. Seeped out until she couldn't breathe. Every time since, her heartbeat did a little dance. His face, his body, even his grouchy personality combined in one intriguing package that she itched to open.

They had weeks left on the agreement and a need to make it look real. For whatever time they had left, she would. She'd put aside the worries and the ways it could go wrong and would dive in. And then she'd somehow walk away from him.

Right as he dipped his head to kiss her again he froze. "Damn."

She grabbed on to his upper arms. "What is it?"

The sound coming from him could only be described as a growl. "I bought condoms but I left them at work."

For some reason that made her laugh. "Did you think we were going to have sex on your desk?"

"It is a reoccurring fantasy of mine." He lifted up, just a fraction, and looked down her body. "But I can still touch you. Give you what you need."

Before she could say anything or even put a sentence together, his fingers slipped into her underwear. He skimmed his hand between her legs, over her. Gentle yet demanding. When one finger slid inside her, her breath caught in her throat.

His tongue swept over her nipple in a long lick that left her shaking. Sensations bombarded her from all directions. The mix of touching and tasting had her lower back lifting off the bed. When he did it again, all the air sucked out of her.

She felt light and dizzy and so ready for him. Her fingernails dug into his shoulders to hold him close. "Derrick, yes."

He pumped his finger inside her, bringing her body to

snapping attention. Every intelligent thought left her head, leaving only one lingering fact. "I have an IUD."

His head shot up. "What?"

"Birth control."

His mouth dropped open before he said anything. "I got tested."

Now it was her turn to be confused. "I don't…"

"I have a report for you to see. You know, just in case. Not sure why I forgot the condoms."

His finger stayed inside her during the surreal and very not sexy conversation. But it was practical and smart… and it pushed out thoughts of risk and most of her common sense.

She slipped her hand down his body, between them, and circled his length. Her palm slid against him from base to tip.

"Ellie, please be sure." He shook his head. "We can wait if you—"

His words cut off when she wrapped her fingers around him and squeezed. "Now, Derrick."

Light flashed in his eyes as he nodded. Then he was on his knees between her legs. Her body hummed as he peeled her underwear off. Pushing her legs apart, he settled between them. His tongue replaced his fingers and excitement surged inside her.

Her heels dug into the mattress and she twisted the comforter in her balled hands as his mouth worked its magic. When he hit the right spot, her thighs pressed against his shoulders. A moan trapped in her throat begged to escape.

She shifted and twisted as the pleasure threatened to overtake her. Still, he didn't stop his sensual caress. That tongue. Those fingers. Every part of him, from the heat of his mouth to the expert use of his hands, had her straining to hold back as her body bucked.

Right as she hovered on the edge, he got to his knees.

He was hard and ready and he didn't wait. She lost her breath as he pushed inside her, filling her. Her breath hiccupped as her inner muscles tightened around him. When he pulled out and pushed in again, she grabbed him and brought him closer.

He leaned over and his chest pressed against her. Heat pounded off his skin and a thin sheen of sweat appeared along his shoulders. She held on to him, traced a line of kisses up his throat.

Their bodies moved as he plunged in and out. The pressure built as she fought her release. She ached to make it last but Derrick's muscles began to shake. When he slipped his hand between their bodies and touched her again, her control broke.

The winding inside her shattered and her body let go. She rode out the pulses and pleasure, gasping as his head fell to her shoulder. She could hear the uptake in his breathing and feel the muscles across his back stiffen. She caressed and kissed him as he came. When his body finally stopped moving, he balanced against her. The weight made her feel warm and secure. Happy even.

After a few seconds he turned his head to the side and his breath blew across her neck. "That was pretty great."

Her fingers lingered in his damp hair. "It was the slippers. They're sexy."

She burst out laughing first, then he joined her. It took them almost a full minute to stop. But they didn't move for a lot longer. What scared her was she didn't want to. She was content to stay there forever.

Ten

The DC Insider: *It looks like we may need to find a new Hottest Ticket in Town. Derrick Jameson and Ellie Gold have been living it up. Dates and dinners. There's even a rumor that they'll be attending a charity event together next week. Does this mean Derrick plans to put a ring on it? We'll have to wait and see.*

Derrick knew he was in trouble the second he opened his office door. Both Spence and Jackson were in there. Spence looked at home in the big chair with his feet up on the desk. A bit too comfortable, but at least he was in the office, which was more than he'd been in months.

Spence made a show of looking at his watch. "You were gone for two hours."

Yeah, that was the last thing Derrick intended to talk about. "I had something I needed to do."

Truth was the sex had him reeling. He hadn't even used protection. That had never happened in his adult life. He'd never even been tempted to skip that step. With Ellie, he wanted it all. He ignored the risks.

The idea of a fake arrangement had backfired on him. He didn't want an on-paper-only relationship with Ellie. Then again, he didn't know *what* he wanted with her. Nothing made sense, including his choices, at the moment.

"How is Ellie adjusting to her new house?" Jackson asked.

Her house. Just the thought of that should have set off an explosion in Derrick's brain. He was not a guy to settle down. He rarely invited women to his house. That's what hotels were for.

He maintained a strict wall, keeping almost everyone but a select few out of his most personal space. But with Ellie the lines had blurred from the very start.

"She was less than impressed that I went ahead and scheduled the movers." Talk about an understatement.

"Women." Spence shook his head. "Man, you'd think they'd love having their stuff packed up without telling them first."

Derrick glared at Jackson. "You told him."

"It was too good not to share," Jackson said, not even bothering to deny it.

Spence leaned back with his arms folded behind his head. "Big brother, can I give you some advice?"

That wasn't what Derrick wanted right now. "Get up first."

Spence whistled. "You're grumpy for a guy who had sex. You did, right? I hate to think you look that disheveled just from talking."

"I was fine until I walked in here." That was pretty much all Derrick wanted to say on that topic, so he gestured for Spence to get up then took his seat.

"The advice?" Spence leaned on the edge of Derrick's desk.

"Right. From the guy who isn't dating anyone." Derrick held out a hand. "Please enlighten me."

"I talked with Ellie for fifteen minutes and I think you need to be careful."

That got Derrick's attention. "Of her?"

"Of losing her, dumb-ass. Don't mess this up."

Not bad brotherly advice. "I'm trying not to."

Spence shook his head. "Try harder."

* * *

The day had been this whirlwind of emotions. As soon as Derrick left the house to go back to work—because *of course he did*—panic set in. She worried about what would happen when he came home and what they'd say to each other tonight. The whole thing was now awkward and weird.

Planning the rest of the day after surprise sex was not easy. So, Ellie relied on the same thing she always did—Vanessa. She moved around Derrick's chef-caliber kitchen right now, cutting vegetables and making a salad.

Vanessa was there, just in case. Kind of like a shield against bumbling conversation. How Derrick would feel about guests in his house was a different question, one Ellie hadn't thought about until right now as she heard footsteps on the stairs. Well, if he didn't like it, that would teach him to move her in without talking to her first.

Ellie plastered on a smile as soon as she saw him. "You're home."

His gaze hesitated on her face before skipping to the counter and the stack of cutting boards and knives sitting there. "You're cooking?"

"Don't sound so surprised." Sure, it was fair, but still.

Vanessa popped her head around the corner. "Also, don't panic. I'm helping."

Derrick gave Vanessa a small wave as he stopped beside Ellie. "You can't cook?"

She snorted. "Can you?"

"I can grill. Men grill."

Vanessa winced. "Oh, boy."

"Typical," Ellie said at the same time. "Well, if you're done impressing us with your testosterone… Derrick, this is Vanessa, my best friend." She rushed to add one caveat. "The one person other than Jackson who knows this—us—isn't real."

His expression went blank. "It's not?"

"The contract thing." For some reason it hurt to say the words this time.

It's not as if they had some sort of miracle sex. It was great and her body still hummed, but she didn't think sex solved everything. Though she had to admit, something did change. Inside her, deep inside.

Together they were sexy and comfortable…they worked. The churning, that ramped-up feeling of being excited to see him and to hear his voice, didn't strike her as fake. She'd never experienced it before and it made her a little twitchy now because she hadn't had enough time to analyze it, but she knew it amounted to more than a practical agreement between friends.

She had such a short time to savor this feeling. She'd been the one who insisted on limiting the time of the agreement to two months. He had wanted more months and now she did, too.

Derrick still didn't show any reaction. His affect had gone flat and stayed there. "You told her."

She rewound the comment in her head, looking for any judgment, but didn't hear it. That didn't mean it wasn't there. "Is that a problem?"

For a second he just stood there, not talking. Then a lightness stole over him and he glanced at Vanessa. "You don't have a habit of gossiping or talking to the *Insider*, do you?"

The hint of amusement calmed Ellie. Her neck muscles unclenched as she relaxed again.

"Any secret Ellie tells me stays with me," Vanessa said.

"Happy to hear it." Derrick stopped in front of the lasagna pan and put his finger out as if he intended to poke it. "So, what's this—?"

"Stop." Ellie slapped his hand away. "You have to wait."

He smiled at her. "Should I order takeout to be safe?"

That look… His walls fell and he stopped being the commanding-man-in-charge-of-everything to be a man. This was at-home Derrick and she had no defense against this sexy side of him. This was the Derrick who had landed her in his bed—and would put her back there. This Derrick was dangerous.

But that didn't mean that she was ready to let him off the hook for his behavior earlier. Her arms still ached from the quick move she and Vanessa had made of most of her stuff to one of the extra bedrooms upstairs.

Oh, no. He'd be paying for that one for a while. "Tough talk from a guy who made a big mistake today."

Vanessa turned around, spoon in hand. "Yeah, you owe me for carrying all those books around."

"Technically, that's Ellie's fault since I hired movers. She sent them away," Derrick said.

Vanessa shook the long spoon at him. "I heard you were Mr. Bossy Pants."

Derrick groaned as he made his way around the counter and took a seat on one of the bar stools. "Oh, good. Now I get to fight two of you."

The byplay made Ellie smile. She hadn't been raised with banter in the kitchen. Her entire childhood had raged like a house on fire. There was always some new crisis and not enough money to handle it.

There were no settled moments of her parents joking with each other, or very few of them. Stealing a few now with Derrick had a warmth settling deep inside her. She'd always wanted this—a home and security. Someone who made her hot but also made her want to snuggle on the couch.

"Are we wrong?" she asked, wanting the moment to continue for just a bit longer.

"No." He rested his hands on the counter. "Today I was an overbearing jackass."

Ellie almost dropped the glass she'd picked up. "Whoa?"

Vanessa looked from Derrick to Ellie. "What?"

"What you heard was progress."

"I can learn." He shrugged as he stole a mushroom off the salad and popped it in his mouth.

Ellie wanted to believe that. She was desperate to believe that and she wasn't even sure why. "But can you set the table?"

He winked at her. "I'm on it."

She watched him meander around the kitchen. He rolled up his shirtsleeves and dug in. Grabbed the plates and silverware. Even hummed while he did it, which Ellie found oddly endearing.

And the man could move. Those long, determined strides. The long legs and that flat stomach. She'd seen him without his clothes and with them on, and she was a fan of both.

She glanced at the table. "Three? Isn't Spence coming home?"

"He's having dinner with Jackson. There was some thought tonight might be loud around here." Derrick shot her a sexy little smile. "From all the yelling, which Spence thinks I deserve."

"I like him."

"Yeah, I figured you would." Derrick finished with the table and walked back to the counter.

Ellie expected him to stand there or look at his watch, or even try to fit in a half hour of work before dinner. Instead he draped an arm loosely over her shoulder and brought her in close to his side.

Vanessa did a double take but didn't say anything.

"So, what else can I do?" he asked.

As far as Ellie was concerned, he was doing it.

Hours later dinner was over and the dishes were done and put away. Vanessa hung around, telling stories about the men they'd dated and some of their stranger travel adventures. To Derrick's credit, he listened and asked questions. He genuinely seemed to enjoy the night even though Ellie guessed he'd rather be tied to his desk working.

Now it was almost midnight. Vanessa had gone and Spence had come home. After a bit of small talk, he'd settled into the bedroom he always used when he was in town. Ellie started the night in Derrick's bedroom because it would have been weird for them to sleep separately if they were really dating.

Some of her clothes, the ones she and Vanessa managed to collect before dinner, hung in Derrick's oversize closet. The thing was as big as two rooms with shelves and racks and drawers and a chair.

A chair.

When the house went quiet, she'd snuck to the bedroom she intended to sleep in even though she wanted to stay with him, wanted to forget that Spence slept nearby and that stupid agreement. She craved his touch. Needed him to hold her, kiss her, roll around in that big bed with her.

She wasn't really the casual sex type. She needed a connection, a relationship. She didn't have a lot of experience but all of it included condoms.

So much had happened over the last few months. She couldn't even process it all. Her nerves were frazzled. A list of pros and cons kept cycling through her head.

With Derrick everything was different. More intense. Less clear. She'd bent her personal rules until they broke. Instead of feeling guilty or thinking she'd messed up, a wave of sadness hit her. A sense of loss at not being with him now. Of not being able to hold him, to touch him tonight, like she'd thought about all day.

She thought back to the first time he'd proposed this fake arrangement. The whole thing had confused and annoyed her, but something in his eyes and voice had compelled her.

She'd agreed to an arrangement she'd never go for under any other circumstance.

Sure, there was the Noah piece. The part about her needing money and some bit of security. All that was real, but the truth was she'd signed that agreement because she'd *wanted* to. Because, for once, she took something she wanted—Derrick.

For the first time in her life she operated without a road map. She let emotion guide her. She saw the risks and accepted them, even knowing that the likelihood was this would end in pain and heartache. There really was no other way for a relationship built on fake facts to finish.

She was so lost in thought she almost missed the soft knock on the door. When it sounded the second time, she scooted out of bed, careful to make sure her shorts and T-shirt were in place when she opened the door in case the visitor was Spence.

Derrick stood there in what looked like lounge pants and a gray T-shirt that fit him like a second skin. That fast, her temperature spiked and her insides started to whirl.

She gripped the side of the door. "Are you okay?"

They'd worked out this plan about getting up early and keeping her bed made and door shut. Derrick had talked about using the excuse of her stacking her stuff in here until she could go through it all. She was accustomed to living with boxes, so having them around now didn't bother her.

"I wanted to check on you." Derrick shifted his weight from foot to foot.

The move struck her as uncharacteristic and a bit vulnerable. "I don't—"

"May I come in?"

Good grief, it was his house. She stepped back. "Of course."

He walked in and caught her up in his arms. His mouth covered hers in a kiss that had her forgetting about boxes and clothes and just about everything else. She grabbed his shoulders, dug in and held him close as pleasure pulsed through her. When he lifted his head a few seconds later, she felt breathless and weak. Her resolve had melted along with her resistance.

"I've wanted to do that since I got home from work," he said in a whisper against her lips.

Tonight had been incredibly special. She'd laughed until she couldn't breathe. She'd built memories. Discovered a warmth she'd never known growing up because everything had been so uncertain between her father's and Noah's moods.

She trusted and loved Vanessa. She was an integral part of Ellie's life. Derrick was supposed to be temporary, but her feelings for him, how she thought about him during the day, were anything but fake. They'd started this ruse by barely talking and now she texted him every day. Sometimes she made up silly things to ask, just to see his response. And he always responded.

"We are inviting trouble." She said it more to convince herself than him.

"I know." Derrick rested his forehead against hers. "I guess I can't convince you to join me in my bedroom?"

He could, so easily. That was the problem. "We should..."

"Right." He gave her arms a gentle squeeze then dropped his hands.

She felt the loss to her bones. It settled in and had her trembling. But she couldn't go overboard with her feelings. "Derrick."

"I'll let you get some sleep." He kissed her on the forehead, quick and simple.

Then he was gone and it was all she could do to keep from calling him back.

Eleven

The DC Insider: *We're hearing there are a few snags in the Derrick and Ellie forever plan. Her baby brother refuses to stay quiet. Her past continues to be a problem. And is our Hottest Ticket in Town having second thoughts about a serious relationship?*

Two days later Derrick sent Noah a message from Ellie's phone, asking him to meet her at her old apartment. This was the last day before she turned the keys over. Noah didn't know that, but Derrick did. He hoped that excused him sneaking her phone while she'd gone upstairs to shower this morning after their coffee together.

They'd done that for the past two days. No more sex, despite his attempts to make it happen. But she was holding back and having Spence hanging around turned out to be a bit of a mood killer. So did the calls from their father. All of a sudden he had work questions again, and that made Derrick nervous.

Through it all, she wandered around in her pajamas each morning. If that's how people acted when they lived together in a real relationship, Derrick kind of got it. There was something energizing about spending those fifteen minutes with her in the morning before he took off.

She didn't have to get up when he did or to fumble her

way downstairs like she had this morning when she'd looked half-asleep and almost missed the bottom step. The coffee time didn't have to happen to prolong the ploy for Spence because he was still asleep at that time of the morning. That meant she did it for him, and that thrilled Derrick more than he wanted it to.

The door opened behind him and Noah stormed inside. He took a few steps then stopped. "Where is my sister?"

He sounded more concerned than angry, which may have saved him from the full-scale ass-kicking Derrick wanted to unleash. But they still had issues, and Derrick had promised Ellie he'd put those to bed, so he tried one more time. "We need to talk."

"Her stuff is gone from her apartment." Noah still frowned as he turned around in a circle in the middle of the room. "Her couch and her—"

"Noah, stop." He seemed locked in some sort of shock. "I called you here."

"But she's—"

"Living with me."

That got Noah's attention. He stopped moving and stared at Derrick. "You can't be serious."

"I am."

That familiar red flush of anger spread over Noah's face. "Nothing is off-limits with you."

The comment hit harder than Derrick expected. He felt the shot right to his gut. When it came to Ellie, he had crossed a bunch of lines, most Noah didn't even know about, but Derrick couldn't pretend he hadn't backed her into a corner and used her love for her brother against her.

He had to deal with that. Take it apart and assess it because now that he did, it seemed like an Eldrick Jameson move. Something his father would do to ensure he got his way. Derrick didn't like that comparison one bit.

"There aren't any cameras or videos in here. You don't

need to pretend we had a confrontation at work. You can drop the bullshit." Derrick had to accept his part in a lot of sins where the Gold family was concerned, but not that one.

"I didn't steal anything."

"Noah, come on." Derrick didn't know how the guy could stand there and lie. How he could actually frown, curl his shoulders in and look like the injured party.

Derrick had taken a chance on him. They met when a friend from high school, now a college professor, called Derrick about a kid he found sneaking around the computer labs at George Washington University. The kid—Noah—had created a student ID and had been using university resources to play games and check out the internal supposedly confidential workings of the school.

Noah hadn't had the experience or the college requirements for the job he'd held at Derrick's company. But like the professor, Derrick had seen something in Noah. A need to prove himself. The brilliance waiting to be tapped. He'd given him a chance and brought him on. Thought of him as a mentee of sorts…then he'd stolen from the company and tried to turn Derrick's life upside down.

Noah shook his head. "You don't get it."

Something in his words and that tone got to Derrick. The sentence he was about to say died in his head. Now he wanted to know what was happening in Noah's head. "Explain it to me."

Noah went to the window and looked out. "I found out about you."

Other than the agreement with Ellie and his father's stipulations, Derrick didn't have much to hide. There were things he wished people didn't know, but he never had that luxury. "Noah, I hate to break this to you but my life is not exactly a big secret. I've had the press on me since I was in elementary school."

Thanks to his family, starting with his politician grandfather, the family got in the news and stayed there. Derrick started dating and the cameras were there to capture his young bachelor days. When they broke up, the girl's family sold a story about him to the tabloids.

The only time he ever got behind the wheel after drinking, the dumbest thing he'd ever done, the press had shown up then, too. He'd learned a harsh lesson that time, and many others.

His mistakes played out in public. His father excused them before the cameras and berated him behind the scenes. That's how it worked in the Jameson household.

"Did you cheat then, too?" Noah asked as he turned around to face Derrick.

Derrick's mind went blank. "What?"

"Abby."

There was an Abby who worked for him. She had a history with the Jameson men, but not him. He searched his mind for another woman with that name. Any woman named anything close. "Abby who?"

"My sister is going to find out who you really are." Noah nodded. All traces of uncertainty had disappeared. "She will. The people at the *Insider* will."

"Have you been talking with them, Noah?" If he'd planted that story about Ellie and her former job, his blood relationship to her would not save him. Derrick would move in and set him straight.

Noah shrugged. "What if I have?"

It took every ounce of willpower Derrick possessed to tamp down on his anger. "Do not ruin your sister's reputation."

"Me?"

Derrick tried reason one more time. "You stole from me and I caught you. You're trying to blow this up into something else and hurt Ellie, and I'm not sure why."

"Did you lead Abby on, too? Make her promises and then dump her?"

"What are you talking about?"

"I know what it's like to be one of your chosen few then get kicked aside." Noah was yelling now, but there was an underlying thread, an edge that suggested he'd been hurt.

The words crashed through Derrick. "Is that what this is really about? Because that did not happen."

"I'm leaving." Noah headed for the door.

Everything was so unsettled, maybe even worse than before they'd talked. Derrick wasn't sure what to say because nothing Noah mentioned made any sense to him. "You've got to stop, Noah. I don't want to hurt you and I certainly don't want Ellie hurt."

"This is your fault." Noah shook his head then slipped into the hallway, but not before taking one final shot. "You'll see."

It had been three days since they'd had sex. Every night they'd pretend to go into his bedroom together then she'd sneak out. Inevitably, about fifteen minutes later there would be a knock on the door. Derrick saying good-night. Derrick kissing her. Last night, Derrick tunneling his hands up her shirt and touching her, which she'd absolutely encouraged.

But when he showed an interest in more, she pulled back. She had to until she could get her thoughts in order. Being there, the domesticity, it all felt real. The first time together had been all consuming. She wanted to act like she could handle a no-strings fake relationship and walk away, but she wasn't sure.

She waited for those before-bed visits. Yearned for them with a fierceness that scared her. Last night she sat on her bed, staring at the doorknob, willing it to turn. It took him a full eighteen minutes to show up. She'd spent every one of those extra seconds counting down, trying to drown out the doubts welling inside her and making her jumpy.

That sort of unsettled sensation couldn't be normal. It had her reassessing, even as she knew she'd give in. Because she wanted to give in. She wanted more from him, for them…and that was the problem.

Now, they were out in public. All dressed up, with him in a tux that looked like he'd been born to wear. The black coat with his nearly black hair…she'd actually made a small *pfffing* sound when he'd come out of the bedroom. No one should look that good. Ever.

When Derrick mentioned a charity gala a few days ago, she'd told him she planned to be sick that day. Gala sounded like an opportunity for more cameras and she was about done with that part of their arrangement. He responded by threatening to drag her to it in her gym shorts, which left her no choice but to borrow a fancy dress from Vanessa. Thank goodness for those money-raising gallery events Vanessa hosted all the time.

The gown was beautiful in a princess sort of way. It had a fitted sleeveless top covered with beads and a long, flowing, light blue skirt in a fabric soft enough to beat out those expensive sheets Derrick had at the house. Vanessa was taller, so Ellie had on three-inch heels she was pretty sure would snap her ankle in two if she stepped the wrong way.

Vanessa also wore a smaller bra size, so the top of the dress, while stunning and sparkly, was also slowly strangling Ellie. She put her hand on her stomach and tried to figure out how to permanently suck it in. "I think I'm going to pop."

Derrick looked over at her. His gaze slipped to her hand, which had moved to her chest. "I have no idea what to say to that."

"The bodice on this is a bit tight." It was choking her.

But why be dramatic about it? "It has to be to hold everything in, but wow."

His gaze shifted to the tops of her breasts, which were spilling out more than they probably should be. "Well, we wouldn't want anything sliding out."

"It's Vanessa's fault. My boobs are bigger." She touched them as if she needed to emphasize the point.

"Okay, yeah. I'm purposely not going to talk about your best friend's body."

Ellie couldn't help but smile at that. He looked on the defensive and a little haunted by the idea. "Good call."

"I'm not a total dumb-ass." He took a sip of his champagne as he glanced at the dance floor.

A few couples moved around, looking stiff and out of place. Between this event and the one where she'd met Derrick, Ellie had come up with a theory. Many DC business people didn't exactly thrive in social situations.

Derrick looked perfectly suited to the room. Just as he looked great behind his desk and adorable in the morning in his lounge pants as he sipped his coffee in the kitchen. She'd never met anyone who "fit" into any situation like he did before.

"You are such a guy." The comment slipped out before she could think it through.

Derrick being Derrick, he did not let it slide by him. "I'm going to regret this but…what?"

"You look like *that*." She waved a hand over him, up and down as she took in every perfect inch. "You probably get up looking like that."

He followed her gaze. "I don't generally wear the tux to bed."

"Well, you should. You look ridiculously hot." When his eyebrow lifted and his attention switched from half scanning the room to full force on her, she snorted. "Oh, please. Don't look surprised. You own a mirror. I'm sure there will be a thousand photos of us all over the internet tomorrow and you can see for yourself."

She hoped her too-tight dress photographed okay. It would suck to stand next to him, looking all Hottest Ticket in Town, and her coming off as someone who snuck her way into the photo.

He put his mostly full glass on the tray held by a passing server. "If that's what it takes to get you in my bedroom, I will wear the tux all the time at home. Honestly, the going-to-bed-alone thing sucks."

She thought so, too. She also knew it was over. With him looking at her like that and her willpower gone, it was inevitable.

"Shh. There are ears everywhere." No one stared at them after his comment. Well, no one other than the ones already staring. Derrick did attract attention. "And cameras."

"Don't blame me this time. The charity hired them."

His hand brushed against hers. She didn't realize what was happening until his warm fingers slid through hers. Hand holding. It was so innocent and sweet…she almost jumped him right there.

"What about the photographer who followed me home from the coffee place today?" The guy had stepped right in front of her. One second sooner and she would have thrown her coffee at him on instinct. "I had barely brushed my hair."

He lifted their joined hands and kissed the back of hers. "You look beautiful."

She was pretty sure she saw a camera bulb flash but she tried to ignore it. "I didn't then."

"I bet you did."

They stood in a room full of people and he made her feel like the only other person in the room. He had that gift. For a man who commanded his way through life, issuing orders, he didn't seem to get that just being there, looking like that, was enough to get people's attention.

A sudden case of nerves shot through her. She was out of her comfort zone and out with him, a man she'd started to dream about. People watched. Others whispered. Tomorrow every movement would be analyzed and dissected online.

It overwhelmed her, stole her breath. She rushed to find a non-Derrick thing to talk about. "My father would have loved this."

"He enjoyed parties?"

They still held hands and when she didn't answer right away, Derrick gave her fingers a gentle squeeze. That only confused her more. "Do you really not know?"

His smile lit up his face. "This cryptic thing you do is oddly endearing but it does confuse the hell out of me sometimes."

She refused to be sucked in by that sexy look. Talking about a harsh reality suddenly seemed easier than dealing with her growing and confusing feelings for Derrick. "My dad. He was *that* guy. The one who always had this big plan to make money. He met a man with a great idea here. He had a lead on something big there."

"Did anything ever pan out?" Derrick asked.

"No." She tried to remember a clear success and couldn't come up with one. "My entire childhood is filled with memories of him spending the last dollar on this dream or using the money for the electric bill to invest in some weird scheme."

She knew that sounded harsh. Maybe it was too much, but all she had was her perspective and the reality of moving around and never feeling secure.

"What about your mom?"

"She enabled it. I mean, she tried to talk to him. So much time was spent on dad's needs that I think maybe Noah's issues got overlooked." The pieces came together in her head. She'd tried for so long to keep it all separate but it did connect. Because of how her parents lived their lives, Ellie got stuck in a parental role that made her more sarcastic and less trusting. "I would hear her…"

Maybe that was enough of that. Ellie tried to concentrate on the music and the laughter floating through the room. To escape reality for a second.

"What?" he asked.

Derrick's gentle tone coaxed her on. "Crying."

"Ellie, I'm sorry." He slid his arm around her and pulled her closer.

"He always thought there was something better out there, you know. That if he could put the deals together the right way, he'd hit it big." No one could deliver the line like her dad. He had believed, or he'd sounded like he did. "He never understood that we didn't care about that. They died going to one last big event."

For a few seconds Derrick didn't say anything. He kept that reassuring hand on her lower back and they swayed to the music. People moved around them. A few stopped to say hello but didn't linger. They must have projected the couple-in-love vibe because most people just seemed to smile at them.

"It's possible he thought it was his job. You know, to make the family financially secure." Derrick made the comment without looking at her. He focused on a table of businessmen instead.

She saw Joe Cantor in the group. That explained Derrick's sudden interest. Since she didn't want another scene, she responded when she might otherwise have let it slip past her. "But he did the opposite."

Derrick glanced at her then. "That, I get."

"The rich boy understands being poor?" She tried to keep her voice light. Tried and failed. She regretted lashing out as soon as she did it. "Sorry. I didn't mean to take that shot."

"It's okay." He nodded toward the couples milling near them. "Dance?"

"Derrick." She reached for his hand and managed to snag it.

"We should dance, Ellie." With that, he pulled her into his arms and maneuvered them to the edge of the dance floor. After a few minutes the stiffness in his shoulders eased and the distance between them closed. Her body rested against his. The scent of his shampoo filled her senses.

She forgot about their conversation and the people watching them. The public ruse fell away until it was just the two of them—a man and a woman swaying on the dance floor. Holding each other, wrapped around each other.

She looked up and stared at his chin, those lips. "Derrick..."

"Keep that up and we're going to need to leave early." His voice sounded rough and lower than usual.

Feminine power surged through her. "Good."

The dance did it. He'd respected her boundaries and would keep doing so, but the dance brought her walls crashing down. He felt it as soon as it happened. Saw it in her eyes as she looked up at him.

He made a mental note to dance with her more often.

But that would come later. After all that touching he couldn't get them home fast enough. After the meal and the silent auction, both of which felt as if they lasted five lifetimes, he suggested they go. They'd said their goodbyes and scrambled for the door. He didn't think anyone noticed. The diced-up feeling came from inside him. He tried to hide it. They had that damn agreement to uphold, after all.

He stepped into the kitchen and dropped his tux jacket over the couch. His plan was to linger for a second, enough not to be rude, then head upstairs.

He got as far as the couch before Ellie started talking. "Have you forgiven me?"

He glanced over his shoulder, not really focusing on her

during his quick look. Call it self-preservation. "What are you talking about?"

"I was a jerk tonight."

He hadn't expected that. Debating whether he should let it drop, he turned around to face her. "That's quite an admission."

"Derrick, I'm serious."

She stood there in a dress that showed off her curves and lit her face. It had taken all of his strength to resist her tonight. When she'd first come downstairs in that, he'd wanted to skip the public event that would help shore up their arrangement and drag her right up to bed. The temptation still punched at him.

He remembered her shot about being poor. She clearly thought that was the only problem that could happen to a family. "My family isn't a good subject for me."

He didn't know where that came from or why he said it. Well, he knew *why* but not *why now.*

"They're part of you. Your dad, your upbringing. It's all a piece of who you are."

She didn't know but that was the absolute worst thing she could have said. "I sure as hell hope not."

Her head shot back. "I don't get it."

How did he explain? Did he even want to? Every slight and every fault piled up over the years. He knew he had it easy compared to others. This wasn't a race but he hadn't exactly had a smooth time, either.

Some of that had changed with his father's new wife, Jackie. Or so people said. Derrick didn't spend much time with his father since he'd been the one to suggest his father think about retiring. He and Jackie had been living on an island, racing through money ever since.

"You guessed before that my dad was difficult. He's a... I can't even think of a nice way to put it. An ass?" His father wasn't a great man. He hurt women. A lot of women. He treated them like property. He'd ruined their mother's life. He acted as if his employees and friends were expendable. He saw his sons as disappointing playthings to bring out for photo ops but little else. "He ran through women, never quite finishing with one before moving on to the other. He sucked with money."

"Your family is…well, aren't you all millionaires, or billionaires or whatever comes after that?" Ellie took a quick look around the house as she spoke.

Derrick got it. He lived a certain way. Not over-the-top or even equal to a lot of other business people in town with his level of success, but he didn't suffer many hardships. But that was all thanks to his hard work, not his father's.

"Both of our fathers had issues with money."

Her eyes widened. "Really?"

"Mine spent money faster than he made it. He was always more impressed with the public version of the family and work than what was happening in private."

She took a few steps and ended up in front of him. "What does that mean?"

"He asked my mother for a divorce while she was dying in a hospital bed." Derrick didn't reach out for Ellie even though he wanted to. The idea of saying those words and touching anyone seemed wrong.

Her mouth twisted in a sour expression. "Who does that?"

"Exactly." She got it. She understood Dad wasn't just the handsome face that appeared in the news now and then. "He spent money and pretended he had an endless supply of it. Meanwhile, he failed to reinvest in the company, retain good employees or expand when times changed."

She reached out first. Her palm flattened against his chest. "But you did. You rebuilt everything."

Derrick exhaled, liking the feel of her skin against his,

even through his shirt. He folded his hand over hers. "Me and the people who work for me."

The start of a smile kicked up the corner of her mouth. "You're not going to take credit?"

Not out loud. Not ever. "I've spent my entire life trying not to be him, Ellie. I keep my head down and work. I don't get involved with people."

"Wait, that's not true." Her fingers curled into the material of his shirt as if she were willing him to listen to her. "You and Jackson are close. I sense you're close to your brothers."

"True."

Her second hand slipped to his waist to rest on the top edge of his pants. "You're a good man."

Derrick tried not to think about her fingers or how good they felt on him. "Am I? Your brother hates me and I forced you into a fake relationship."

She threw her hands out to the sides. "Do I look like I don't want to be here?"

The words slammed into him. He wanted her there. Agreement or no, he wanted her in his house, in his bed. In his life. To hell with the emotional consequences. "Then why are we sleeping in separate beds?"

Those hands slipped up his chest to his tie. It loosened a second later. "That's over."

Twelve

The DC Insider: *Dear readers...why are hot millionaire businessmen so hard to read?*

Derrick's hands shook as he lowered the zipper of her dress. Ellie couldn't think of a more satisfying reaction. Couldn't believe how right it felt to be in this bedroom with him. His bedroom.

His fingers brushed over her skin and his hot breath blew against her hair. She held on to the front of the gown, trying to catch it before the whole thing whooshed to the floor. If it were hers she wouldn't care, but it wasn't and that meant being extra careful.

"You're not wearing a bra." Derrick's voice carried a note of awe as he trailed his palm over her back.

Her breath caught and she fought to hold her voice steady. "The dress held everything in."

More like sucked it in and made her skin roll in places she preferred not to have rolls. None of that took away from the specialness of it all. She'd never dreamed about being a princess. She'd let her father do the unrealistic dreaming in the family.

Even with her practical streak, the memory of standing there on Derrick's arm, feeling his strong hand in hers as they'd danced under the lights with her dress swirling around her ran through her mind. She wanted to store away every moment and hold on to how freeing every moment had been.

"Any chance Vanessa has ten or fifteen more like this for you to borrow?" With the zipper the whole way down, Derrick's fingers lingered at the small dip of her lower back. He traced a pattern there.

Her entire body shivered in reaction. Every muscle shook as waves of pleasure ran through her.

She cleared her throat, trying to sound somewhat coherent. "Do we have more fancy events to attend?"

He kissed her bare shoulder. The move relaxed her, lured her in. Then he bit with only the barest of pressure, licked the wound and kissed the spot again. Her pulse took off on a wild race. She could feel it thump in her neck and under his mouth.

That mouth, so perfect, knew just where to nip and how to drive her wild.

He started to trail the kisses up the side of her neck. "I thought you could model them here, in private. With me as your only, but very eager, audience."

He was about to get *so* lucky.

"Aren't you naughty?" She asked the question as she turned in his arms. Seeing his face, running her finger over the stubble on his chin, set off a flurry of activity in her stomach.

On purpose, she let the top of the dress fall to her waist. Only the flare of her hips kept it up at all, and that balance was tenuous at best. She didn't cover herself. Didn't have to. He'd seen every inch of her. Toured his hands and mouth all over her. And when he saw her breasts now, all he could do was stare.

She couldn't imagine a better reaction. His pleasure became her pleasure.

Her feminine power exploded.

"I want to be a bad boy but I'm afraid of tearing the dress."

"Good call." She wiggled her hips and the material fell. She caught it before it hit the floor and handed it to him. "Here."

For a second he stood there with the dress draped over his arm. "Damn."

He wasn't looking at her face. No, his gaze traveled up and down her legs. To her thigh-high stockings with the lacy tops and the matching nude-colored underwear. She'd worn the combination for him.

"You like?" she asked, even though she knew from his expression he did.

"So that you're clear, I like you pretty much any way you'll let me have you." He used his finger to trace the lace pattern on the top of her thigh. "But damn."

Perfect reaction.

He'd stripped his tie off and shrugged out of his jacket. She went to work on his shirt. It took her about two seconds to get those small white buttons undone and to pull back the edges to reveal that firm, tanned chest. "Let's get this off you."

"I can do it." But he didn't make any move to help.

"I'll take care of you." She stripped the shirt off then sat on the edge of the bed.

She skipped the talking and asking and went right to the button at the top of his pants. His breathing kicked up as she lowered the zipper then pushed his dress pants to his knees. The boxer briefs went next.

When she took his length into her hand, his fingers slipped through her hair and held her close. The noise he made when she took him in her mouth, half moan, half yell for joy, sounded like music. It would stay in her head for a long time.

"Ellie." His voice dipped even lower than normal and held an extra-rough edge.

She licked her tongue over his tip then peeked up at him. "I didn't think you'd mind."

"I'm trying to figure out how I've stayed away from you for the past five nights."

"Sheer willpower on both our parts." Wasted time, as far as she was concerned. She wanted this. Wanted him. "To prove we could."

To continue the farce that this was fake and meant nothing…that was over. In reality, what they shared had started to mean everything.

She was falling for him. The words rolled through her head without a signal from her brain. They should have scared her and had her ducking for the toilet. She'd refrained from any real involvement up until now. Found excuses with other boyfriends to cut things off. With Derrick she wanted more, not less.

She understood him. They were good together. He made her rethink some of the views she held and things she took for granted. Made her assess Noah from a fresh perspective. And she smoothed out Derrick's rough parts. Had him thinking about something other than work every second of every day.

This—what they shared—may have started off as nothing, but it was something now. At least to her. The only fear, and it was a very real fear, was that this newfound reality only ran one way.

The room spun around her. He'd pulled her up and flopped onto the mattress, taking her with him. It was not the most dignified sprawl, but she landed on top of him—exactly where she wanted to be.

She scrambled to her knees and shimmied out of her underwear then took care of getting his pants and briefs the rest of the way off. He was left wearing socks and she had the thigh-highs on. That seemed like a pretty great combination to her.

She dipped her head to kiss him and he caught her face and held her steady. Cupped her cheeks in his palms and ran a thumb over her bottom lip. "I brought the condoms home."

The practical words shot through her. It took her a second to process what he was saying, but the choice was smart and made sense. They hadn't talked the "us" part of them through yet. That first time they'd had sex had been a risk. They could get it right now.

She looked around the bedroom. "Where?"

He pointed at the nightstand next to him. "Drawer."

That was the only word he could seem to get out, which only made him sexier. As she reached, he took advantage of her unguarded position and brought his mouth to her breast. Licked all around her nipple before sucking her.

She tried to slouch on the top of his thighs, but he held her firm. His fingers traveled down her stomach and kept going lower. Between that hot mouth and those searching fingers, she lost all sense of time and what she wanted to do next. She got lost in a swirl of energy. It thrummed through her. The tension ratcheted up as her body got nearer to the edge.

"Ellie."

She looked at his determined expression and wet lips. "Yeah?"

"Ride me."

Yes. She thought it rather than said it. Without a word, she moved over his body. Straddled those impressive hips and pressed her hands to the rippled muscles of his stomach. "Have you been a good boy?"

"Very." His finger slipped inside her.

Her muscles strained as her head fell forward. Her hair slid off her shoulders and hung down. She could feel him curl a strand around his finger.

Heat radiated off their bodies. She tore open the packet and took out the condom. It should only have taken a second to roll it over his length, but she drew it out. Squeezed him as she covered him, inch by inch. By the time she was done, he squirmed on the bed. His fingers dug into her hips as he tried to draw her closer.

Then she lifted her body up and slid over him. Every cell screamed for her to finish it, but she didn't rush this part, either. She enveloped him. Measured each second before going lower. Waited until his back lifted off the bed and his eyes glazed with need.

She could feel him pulse inside her. After all those nights of limiting themselves, their bodies craved the completion now. She ached for it. When she lifted and returned to him again, her body started to shake. She was so close.

Tiny sounds escaped her throat. She hit a steady rhythm but she couldn't hold on. Her control shattered and the orgasm tore through her, surprising her with its intensity. She could hear Derrick saying her name and feel him lift his body to meet hers. Then she couldn't think about anything except how good he felt and how much she wanted this to last.

Derrick snuck down to the kitchen about a half hour later than usual the next morning. He wanted to get Ellie a cup of coffee and serve it to her in bed. The longer he could keep her there, the happier he would be.

He hit the bottom step and knew he'd miscalculated the time. Spence was already sitting at the bar, scrolling through his cell and drinking from a mug.

He didn't lift his head as he spoke. "You're tiptoeing around your own house. That's not sad or anything."

Derrick jerked at the unexpected sound but tried to hide it. Good thing he'd put pants on or Spence would have had quite the morning show. "You're up early."

"It's about time you two slept together." Spence just kept scrolling. "All that pretending was driving me nuts. I don't know how you stood it for all those nights."

Derrick froze. "Excuse me?"

"Oh, please." Spence put his cell to the side and smiled at his brother over the top of the mug. "My door is between your bedroom and the one she goes to...and you sneak off to each night."

So much for being stealthy. Derrick should have asked her to stay in his room and forget all the subterfuge. After last night, after the hangover from the personal information he'd shared with her, he was ticked off he hadn't ended the fake part of their relationship sooner.

Screw the agreement, he wanted to actually date her. He had no idea if she could make it work, but he really wanted to try.

But that didn't mean he wanted his brother knowing all about his sex life. "That's not—"

"I could never figure out why you didn't get right into bed with her." Spence shook his head as he made a tsking sound. "She's hot. You have to be smart enough to see that."

"Careful where you go with this." The brothers didn't touch each other's dates. Not ever. That was an unspoken rule. But the real problem for Derrick was that he wasn't in top form for sparring thanks to the lack of sleep, which he did not regret one bit.

"I have eyes. I hear the way you two talk to each other." Spence's smile was far too wide and snarky for this hour. "All tinged with unspent energy."

Tinged? Yeah, way too early. "You can stop talking now."

Spence had the nerve to shrug. "I'm reporting on what I've witnessed."

"You were spying on me?" For some reason that struck Derrick as ridiculous as he leaned against the sink.

Spence hadn't asked a lot of personal questions when he'd checked in by phone over the past few months. He wasn't the type to be up in someone else's business.

"I'm trying to figure out what's happening with you." Spence drained his mug. "I promised Carter I would find out and report back."

The alarm chimed and the front door downstairs opened and closed. Only a few people knew the code and had a key. Three of them were in the house right now and one was driving cross-country to get here for what appeared to be a brotherly interrogation. That left one other option.

Jackson stepped into the room. He carried a brown bag imprinted with the name of the nearby bagel chain.

This informal breakfast looked prearranged to Derrick. Jackson didn't just stop in with snacks. His smirk didn't make his surprise appearance any less annoying.

"What's going on?" Jackson asked the room in general as he unloaded the contents of the bag onto the counter.

"I'm digging into my brother's odd relationship to figure out why it's odd," Spence said.

Jackson hesitated for a second before reaching in and pulling out a tub of cream cheese. "Aren't we all?"

"He's got it bad for her."

Derrick put his mug down and took a step toward the staircase, making sure they didn't have nosy company hovering around upstairs. "Keep your voices low."

"Are you sure it's not that you're making this complicated?" Spence shook his head. "Because, I gotta tell you. From where I'm sitting, you seem to be messing this up."

Jackson opened two drawers before he found a knife for the cream cheese. Derrick was pretty sure it was a steak knife, but it worked.

"He's not wrong about the 'messing up' part," Jackson noted.

"You like her. A lot." Jackson pointed to the bagels and

kept pointing until Spence picked up a specific one. "You're kind of stupid with how much you like her."

Jackson took care of slathering the spread on one side of the bagel then handed it to Spence before giving Derrick a quick glance. "Notice he's refraining from using the bigger L-word."

"I don't want to send him running." This time Spence focused on Derrick, too. "But, really, you've got it bad for her. You're living together. So what's the holdup? Why all the weirdness?"

Derrick didn't bother answering because they really weren't talking to him. This show was for the two of them and they really seemed to be enjoying it.

Jackson shrugged. "Don't look at me. I'm waiting for an answer, too."

"Well, you both think on it while I jump in the shower." Spence shoved a large piece of bagel into his mouth and took off for the stairs.

Derrick waited until the thumping on the steps faded and Spence disappeared upstairs before saying anything. "You didn't exactly help me there."

"You need to tell him the truth." Jackson dropped the uneaten half of the bagel on the counter. "Carter is on the way. You need to tell them both. They came back to town because you asked them to. They are trying to help you, even though neither wants back in the business as your dad is insisting."

Despite the annoying display of friends-gone-wild this morning, the advice was good. Derrick knew he had to come clean. He hated lying to his brothers, anyway. But he wasn't sure what to tell them now. The thing with Ellie had started off fake. Now it felt anything but. How the hell did he describe that state?

"I will. When they're together. There's no need to tell

this tale more than once." And maybe he would know the right words to say when that day came.

"And Ellie? Are you going to tell her all of it?"

"One problem at a time." Derrick leaned over and picked up the uneaten bagel half. "Until I find the right opportunity, I'll continue to fumble my way through all of this."

"I told you this would be fun to watch."

Suddenly, Derrick wasn't that hungry. "Did you?"

"Maybe I just thought it."

"I could fire you."

Jackson laughed. "But you won't."

Thirteen

The DC Insider: *Word on the street is Ellie Gold is working miracles with Derrick Jameson. Is he getting soft? There are no signs of that in business, of course, but she has him jumping to her commands in private. So maybe those nasty rumors we're hearing aren't true?*

Two days later Ellie was still in a good mood. She even managed to ignore the guy taking her photo as she walked into the coffee shop a few blocks from Derrick's house.

They had hit a bit of a bump at the charity event but they'd ridden through it. She wanted that to mean something. They could talk about work and their arrangement and even their families. Right from the beginning they'd vowed not to lie to each other.

Despite all that, she couldn't think of a way to broach what, a few weeks ago when they'd first met, would have been unthinkable—talking about them. She knew it was easier to ignore the elephant standing in not only the room but also right on top of them than to deal with him. "Going along as is" meant dating and living together and getting to know each other.

For her, something deeper and meaningful had grown out of that. Derrick was so much harder to read.

And he wasn't the only one. She entered the coffee shop and slipped through the long line of people waiting to order. Noah sat at a table across the room, head down and not talking to or looking at anyone. He wore a baseball cap pulled low, like every other twenty-year-old in DC, and studied his phone.

Derrick told her he'd talked with Noah but hadn't been able to break through. Seeing her brother spin and knowing he would be in very big trouble without Derrick's interference was the kind of thing that kept her up at night.

She made it the whole way to the table without him looking up. Nothing new there. Eye contact was not one of his strengths.

She pulled out a chair and sat across from him. "Why did you want to meet here?"

She'd given him her new house address. The temporary one with Derrick. Suggested he come over and they talk in private. Noah had said no to all of it.

He kept tapping buttons on his phone, only sparing a glance or two in her direction. "To avoid Derrick."

"Are you afraid of him now?" When she didn't get an immediate answer, she put a hand over the screen and lowered the phone to the table. "Well?"

"Let's say I know he'll do almost anything to get his way."

"You might want to lay off the videos because you now talk in shortcuts. It's annoying."

"Then how about this." Noah leaned forward, his elbows on the table. "He's cheating on you."

The word bounced through her. A wave of nausea followed right behind it. "What?"

"There's a woman at work."

The accusation didn't make sense. "No way."

"I'm serious, Ellie."

If Derrick had a girlfriend, then why wasn't she visiting his house? Why wasn't he using this other woman as his fake girlfriend?

How could he sleep with her but be with someone else?

Ellie couldn't imagine any woman going along with that type of ruse and all the lies. Not if she cared about Derrick and vice versa. It was too dangerous and so disrespectful. Which brought her full circle. Derrick had a lot of flaws. She could spend an hour listing them, but being crappy to women wasn't one of them. Not that she'd seen.

Too many people would have to be quiet. She'd overheard the whispers at his office and none of them were about another woman. Someone at the *Insider* would know the truth and report it.

As soon as she reasoned it out, the choking sensation in her throat eased. So did the need to pound things.

She inhaled, trying to stay focused. If she let her mind wander, she'd be on the phone or in Derrick's office demanding an explanation and she didn't want to do that. He'd been accused of enough. "You're saying you know this because you worked there?"

"I never met her. This Abby. Apparently something happened with her months ago."

That barely sounded like a thing. A bit more of her anxiety disappeared. "Noah, you're talking about rumors and not facts."

Noah spun an empty coffee cup around between his palms. The edges clicked against the table. "I'm trying to make you see that he's not worth it."

"Why?"

He closed his fist over the cup with enough force to collapse the sides with a loud crunch. "What?"

"Why is it so important to you that I think that?" That part never made sense to her. It was one thing if he thought he was falsely accused and wanted revenge. But he seemed so determined for her to think *everything* about Derrick was awful. That he wasn't only a bad boss or a mean one, but a terrible cheating human being, as well.

The whole thing struck her as overkill. Like hurt feelings and crushed emotions.

"I know what it's like to be taken in by him." Noah continued to stare at his smashed cup.

"He hired you without any experience. Gave you a job and a place to go."

Noah's head shot up. "He abandoned me as soon as he needed a scapegoat."

The conversation pinged around. Noah seemed to move from one perceived Derrick sin to another. All of them seemed to come from the same place—somewhere personal. For the first time she realized this was about way more than work or a paycheck.

She slid her hand across the table, not quite touching Noah's. "Meet with him. I'll be there and we'll talk this out."

"We've talked. He tried to convince me I was wrong when the two of us met at your apartment."

"Try again."

"Can't you just believe me?" His voice grew louder until a few people sitting nearby glanced over at them.

She refused to be derailed. "I know you're angry with him."

"Forget it." He pulled the brim of his hat down even further and stood. The legs of the chair screeched against the hard floor.

"Noah."

He finally gave her full eye contact. "I never thought you'd pick some random guy over me."

Her heart hurt. "That's not what this is."

He shrugged. "Feels like it."

Then he walked away.

Ellie was waiting for him when he got home tonight. Not upstairs in the kitchen or sitting on the couch. Not even on her laptop searching for jobs. She was actually standing at the top of the steps.

He knew that was a really bad sign.

He barely reached the second floor when she launched into her question. "Who is Abby?"

She didn't move when he got to her. No, she stood there, arms crossed, wearing what looked like a day-long-practiced frown.

He should work from home while they were in this relationship. That would stop ambushes like this from happening. "You talked with your brother."

"I tried to get through to him again."

When she didn't move, he put a hand on her arm and gently guided her into the kitchen with him. "I thought we agreed I'd handle it."

They didn't even get to the counter before she turned and faced him again. Stopped them both in their tracks. "By putting our names in the paper all the time? That's defusing his impact, but it's not stopping him for good."

The *Insider* again. The gossip column proved useful. Everyone seemed more interested in his love life than in a dispute with a former employee. No one was taking Noah seriously and he was losing viewers, which meant losing some of his power.

Derrick didn't know how people could stand to sign on and hear Noah rave about one guy all the time. That thing had to get old. It certainly had for Derrick.

So did fighting with Ellie. Usually the verbal battles invigorated him. Not the ones about Noah. Talking about him seemed to suck the life out of both of them.

He set his briefcase on the counter and brushed his fingers through her soft hair. "Any chance you could trust me?"

"I do."

It sure as hell didn't feel like it. "You're asking about Abby. You're meeting with Noah without telling me."

"And you're sounding more like my boss than…"

"What?"

"The man I'm sleeping with."

Okay, he liked that answer and since he intended to keep doing just that, he loosened his rule on talking about this subject. The Abby issue went back to his father and their family dysfunction, but there was no way to explain that without blowing his relationship with Spence apart. "Abby has nothing to do with me."

Ellie frowned at him. "Derrick, that's not an answer."

He tried again. "She works for me."

"Okay." Ellie's eyebrow lifted as if she expected more.

But to him that's exactly what Abby was—a great employee he'd fought not to lose. "That's it."

Ellie stepped away from him. She walked around the counter to sit on one of the stools. "You are making this unnecessarily difficult."

"I'm answering you."

"Did you sleep with her?" Ellie ticked off the questions on her fingers. "Are the two of you having an affair?"

"When the hell would I have time for that? I'm here with you or at work with Jackson. That's it. That's all I do."

"That answer." She shook her head. "Good grief, Derrick."

He had no idea what she wanted from him. This part of a real relationship…he wasn't a fan. People trusted him. The idea that, after a brief meeting with her brother, she no longer did, made Derrick want to rip down the walls of his house with his bare hands.

"I haven't been with anyone since I met you. I haven't even thought of anyone else since I met you." The idea of touching another woman made everything inside him rebel. "You are it for me."

The words had slipped out. He didn't mean to say them, not like that. Certainly not out loud. He was talking about her being it *for now*…right?

There were many facts stacked against them. He hadn't told her everything. They had a mess with her brother. He needed to come clean with his brothers. Hell, he wasn't even sure she liked him all that much. He could ask, but he dreaded the answer.

She was supposed to be temporary. His focus had to stay on the business and meeting his father's requirements and getting the work part of his life settled. The company meant everything to him. He'd poured so much into it. He couldn't lose focus or his father would swoop in.

That reality of his whole life being up in the air scared the hell out of him. He tried to manage everything around him and suddenly his usual skills failed him. Admitting that he might be on a road that was off his plan made him want to head to work. Do something to burn off the odd sensation running through him. This unsettled feeling he was losing control of every single part of his life.

"Right now. I mean, I feel that way right now." He had no idea why he'd added that except that he'd been trying to convince himself it was true.

Her smile fell. "Interesting qualification."

"I'm not sure what you want me to do here. I feel like there isn't a right answer." If there was, he sure as hell couldn't find it.

She sighed at him in that way that told him he was missing the mark by a mile. "Who is Abby? A real answer this time."

"She and Spence had a thing. It's complicated, and messy, and my dad screwed it all up. Honestly, it's not my story to tell. I mean, I will if you want me to, but we have a bigger issue."

"Noah." She nodded. "He delivered some envelope to the *Insider* about you cheating on me, or is about to. I think this might be your new PR issue."

"No one is going to care that a single businessman is sleeping around."

She snorted. "How comforting."

He sensed trying to explain would only make it worse, so he skipped ahead. "My point is I can fix it."

"What?"

His heart thundered in his chest. It echoed in his ears. This wasn't supposed to mean anything. They had talked about it and she had known it was coming. But taking the step proved bigger than he thought.

He forced his fingers to work. Clicking the locks, he opened the briefcase and dug around until he found the small box. The one he'd had since the day after their first date.

"This is the way we start taking control." He took the blue box out and skidded it across the marble countertop in her general direction. "Here."

She stared at it but didn't pick it up. "What are you—?"

"An engagement ring."

When she looked up at him again… That was not happiness he saw. Her teeth clenched.

"Did you hand me a box with a fake diamond ring in it?"

What the hell? "It's not fake."

"You're offended by my comment about the cost?"

The conversation was spinning away from him. He could see it, feel it. Hear the thread of anger in her voice. He ignored every warning sign and dived in. "I picked the ring out for you."

"You did?" She didn't sound even a little impressed.

"Of course. It has to look real."

She glared at him then took a turn glaring at the box. "And now you've handed it to me."

"Okay, wait a second." He rested his palms against the counter. "I don't get this. Are you upset about it being real or do you need it to be fake? Fill me in here."

She looked ten seconds away from kicking him. Derrick appreciated that there was a heavy kitchen island between them right now.

"You shoved an unopened box at me and said 'here.'" Her eyebrow lifted in challenge. "Yes?"

Okay, that sounded bad. Even he could admit that. "Uh, yeah."

"Derrick, you have to know there's a better way to do this." She waved a hand in the air. "Forget that. You should see your face. You clearly don't get it."

"Do I look confused? Because that's kind of where I am."

"Fine. I'll take this." She grabbed the box and opened it.

She made a noise that sounded like a gasp. Hesitated before picking it up. But she did pick it up. Slid it on her finger as if it didn't matter to her at all.

Yeah, this was not going well. "Wait."

"I have the ring. Next provision of our agreement satisfied. Congratulations." She slid off the bar stool and headed toward the stairs.

He didn't even realize they were done talking. "You're upset?"

"Yes, genius. I am."

"But this is what we agreed to."

She shrugged. "Then I guess we're good."

She sounded far from good. And if the kicking in his gut was any indication, he wasn't doing so great, either. "I don't understand what's happening."

"Your fake fiancée is going outside."

It was nighttime and she had a rock on her finger and a heap of attitude. "Why?"

"Because you're not there."

Ellie managed to ignore him for the rest of the night and all of the next morning. Maybe it was immature but she needed a Derrick break. He hadn't even let her walk away from him in peace. He'd texted her the second she stepped outside and said he was worried about her safety. She stayed on the front steps until she cooled off enough to go inside and walk right by him.

For the first time since she'd moved in, she missed morning coffee with him. She decided to have it with Vanessa instead. They sat in the same coffee shop where she'd had it out with her brother.

Vanessa stirred her second sugar packet into her coffee. "So, let me get this straight. He gave you a ring for a fake engagement you agreed to and now you're ticked off at him for giving it to you."

Ellie had to admit her anger sounded ridiculous when her friend put it that way. "Please don't make me sound like the unreasonable party in this."

Vanessa held up a hand in mock surrender. "I'm on your side. Always."

Silence fell over the table as Ellie tried to find the right words. She was furious and hurt. This dragging sadness exhausted her.

She hated that battered-from-the-inside gnawing sensation that overtook her when she thought about the ring and Derrick. She was not the crying type, but right now she wished she was.

She didn't even know what to say to Derrick because he wasn't wrong. She had agreed to the fake arrangement. It had just taken him longer to launch into this part than she'd expected. She'd hoped that meant something.

"It was the way he did it." And that was true. Even a fake arrangement deserved some sense of importance. He'd handed her a ring without even bothering to open the box.

Thinking about it, reliving the moment in her head, had fury bubbling up inside her again. Really, the man was clueless.

"You're angry because he didn't get on one knee and ask you?"

Ellie didn't like that question, either. "Maybe I'm not telling this story right."

"Hey, listen to me." Vanessa reached her hand across the table. "There is an obvious problem here."

"Derrick."

"Him, too. But I think the real issue is you're in love with him." Vanessa winced as she said the words.

"This is about the way he—"

Vanessa fell back in her chair. "Oh, my God. You didn't deny it."

She couldn't because she was. Vanessa said the words and they didn't sound wrong. The realization terrified Ellie. She'd tried to be smart and careful, but she'd fallen. It was stupid and dangerous and would likely break her heart, but it happened.

She thought the truth would hit with a jolt. Instead it settled in and snuggled around her. But she still wanted to throw up.

Rather than deal with any of that, she fell back on her anger. On Derrick's depressing choices. The least he could do was fall with her.

"You don't start a fake engagement by shoving a ring at someone." How could she not see that? Ellie thought for sure she would get an immediate agreement on that topic.

Vanessa nodded. "Okay."

"Stop smiling."

"I should because I'm worried about you." The amusement left her tone. "You changed the rules in this thing. You fell for him."

"I thought… I mean, we've slept together." When Ellie realized she'd yelled that bit of information, she immediately lowered her voice. "We've gone out on these dates. None of it feels fake."

"Maybe that's what the two of you need to talk—" Vanessa stopped herself midsentence then leaned in closer. "You're not confronting this because you're afraid the relationship didn't change for him."

Exactly. That was it. She should clear all this up. But what if the answer was something other than what she wanted it to be? "Maybe I should sell the ring and move to Alaska."

Vanessa's eyes bulged. "Wait, is that thing real?"

"He said it was." Ellie studied it for the fiftieth time. It was stunning. Big. But not too much. A solitaire surrounded by smaller diamonds, and a perfect fit. She didn't even want to know how he'd pulled that off.

"Damn. Go Derrick."

Anger or not, the ring made a statement. "Right?"

"I'm going to give you some advice."

Ellie didn't hide her groan. "About shoes? That's about all I can handle right now."

"You need to end this."

Her stomach went into free fall. "Did you miss the *in love with him* part?"

"That's my point. You guys need a do-over. Start fresh and honest."

"We've been honest with each other." With a few false starts, they had made a deal. They'd both known, going in, what this was and what it would mean: solving problems for both of them and little more.

Well, damn. Vanessa was right. She was the one who changed the deal.

"Since you're here and not with him, I think that's not true." Ellie started to talk and Vanessa talked over her. "You did storm out, right?"

"I do not storm."

She rolled her eyes. "I've seen you storm."

"He makes me want to throw things."

"Not the ring." Vanessa picked up Ellie's hand and gave

the ring a closer inspection. "You're keeping that if the knucklehead doesn't get his act together. I mean, come on."

"The problem is I want to keep it all—his friends, his house, his brother." The words ripped out of Ellie. It hurt to admit all of that.

"Oh, man. You have it bad."

Ellie was starting to realize that. "No kidding."

Fourteen

The DC Insider: *They're engaged! You know who they are and what we're talking about. We're hoping for a September wedding. You?*

"He didn't actually steal the money." Derrick said the comment more to himself than to any one person. He'd forgotten Jackson was sitting in the chair across from him, one leg crossed over the other, so he did have a captive audience.

He looked up. "Excuse me?"

Derrick wasn't sure how to explain how he'd come to that conclusion, but he tried, anyway. It was more of a feeling than any one specific grounded in fact. Still, he thought he'd stumbled over the right answer. "It was this thing Noah said. He talked about being my mentee."

From the beginning Derrick had assumed the situation with Noah was about money. That fact fit with what he knew about Ellie's precarious finances and now with what he knew about her unstable upbringing and the limited resources and attention given to Noah.

Noah hadn't been searching for easy money. He hadn't even tried to take the amount he'd managed to gather out of the account he'd created, which would have been easy. He'd moved the money the same way he'd moved around everything else in the company's system. Without one person noticing. And Derrick hired smart people. They knew what they were doing but their brains were no match for Noah's. He'd acted almost as if he were bored and looking for a better way to categorize things.

Derrick's tech people were still trying to figure out how the kid's mind worked so they could mimic it.

"You know you've been sitting for three hours without moving."

"So?"

"You worked late last night." Jackson nodded in the direction of Derrick's cell. "You haven't been texting with Ellie today like you usually do."

Derrick had no idea what that had to do with the information Jackson mentioned, except to question why he spent so much time tracking Derrick's movements. "I'm working."

"Are you sure you're not pouting?" Jackson dropped the file he was looking at on his lap. Closed the cover and focused on Derrick instead.

"Does that seem like something I'd do?"

Jackson snorted. "Not before Ellie."

Derrick didn't know how he felt about that answer, either. He knew she'd turned his life upside down. He'd lost control of his office and his home but he'd hoped no one else had picked up on that.

While they were spinning around topics without finding answers, he figured he might as well add one more fact. "We're engaged, by the way."

Jackson's foot fell to the floor. "What?"

Derrick returned to looking at the printouts in front of him. "I need you to send out that press release and leak the info to the *Insider*."

That was the game, after all. A fake engagement to clean up his reputation and defuse Noah. The idea had once made sense but Derrick had grown to hate the words. Now he wanted a shot at making it real.

"Back up." Jackson knocked his fist against the desktop. "When did this big event happen?"

"Yesterday." A day that now ranked as one of the most confusing days of Derrick's life.

He'd thought he was doing the right thing when he'd taken out the box. Settling the unsettled between them. Giving Noah another reason to calm down. Feeding the PR machine. But he'd forgotten that Ellie didn't always do and say what he expected. She worked in this other world that he didn't get.

Bottom line, he'd hurt her and she didn't seem ready to let him fix the damage. That might have been good since he had no idea *how* to fix it.

"And we aren't celebrating the big event?" Jackson asked.

There would be a party. That was the point. A public coming-out of sorts. But he had one problem with arranging it right now… "She hasn't talked to me since."

Jackson laughed. "That sounds like a good start to a marriage."

"A fake marriage." For some reason everyone kept forgetting that part. Sure, the ring was real. It seemed like a dick move to get her a fake one of those. Besides, he liked the idea of her wearing his ring. Of seeing it on her finger.

He was totally losing it. He no longer knew exactly what he wanted. His emotions bounced back and forth along with his priorities.

Jackson exhaled long and loud. "We're back to that. The damn agreement you two signed."

"Did we ever leave it?"

Jackson tapped his pen against his folder. The clicking sound thumped through the room. "Derrick, what did you do?"

Derrick wanted to dig in to his work. Buying properties, selling properties, building properties. He could assess a piece of land and pinpoint its future value, see what it could be once he was done with it.

Figuring out Ellie? He needed a team of experts for that mission. Maybe Jackson could be on it. "What do you mean?"

Jackson exhaled a second time. "How did you ask her?"

"You're coming up with a lot of questions." For some reason that made Derrick nervous. Very little made him nervous.

"Maybe answer one."

"I gave her the ring." There. Simple.

Jackson's pen stopped midtap. "Gave?"

Since Ellie had treated him to a similar response, Derrick decided to stall. His delivery of the ring had been off. He got that now. Interesting how everyone seemed to know the fake engagement rules better than he did.

"Can you only talk in questions now?" he asked, ignoring the irony of that.

"What do you think?"

Some days it was hard to like Jackson. "Very funny."

"When you say 'gave,' you mean you asked her..." Jackson made a face. "Please mean that."

"No."

"Ah, I see." Jackson coughed, clearly trying to hide a smile. "How did that romantic gesture go over?"

"I slept alone last night, so not well." Derrick had walked to her door. Before they'd started sleeping together, every night he'd knock and go in. Once they were together and not fighting the sex, where she slept hadn't been a question...until yesterday.

"Do you really not see the problem or what your contribution to the mess you're in now actually was?" Jackson asked.

Of course he did. *Now.* "No."

"Damn it. I'm going to lose that bet."

That stopped Derrick. "What bet?"

"The one I made with Spence."

"Want to fill me in?"

"You'll figure it out." Jackson stood and took out his cell. "If you don't, I'm out two hundred dollars, so please figure it out fast."

"I'm here as ordered." Noah sat at Derrick's dining room table. "I'm not sure why we couldn't meet at the coffee place again."

"Because I can't go outside without having my picture taken." Ellie had about reached the end of her patience on that subject. She glanced to where Derrick sat at the head of the table. "We're going to talk about that, by the way."

His gaze went to her ring then bounced to her face. "What did you expect would happen?"

He had an uncanny knack for saying the wrong thing at the wrong time. The man built an impressive enterprise that churned out money, yet he failed on a simple people skills level some days. She might lecture him about that, too.

Noah frowned at both of them. "What's happening? Why am I here?"

"We're clearing the air."

Noah started to get up as soon as Derrick stopped speaking. "No, thanks."

"Sit." Derrick issued the order. "We're also engaged."

He really would be the death of her. Ignoring Noah's stunned expression, she glared at Derrick. "Really? That's how you drop that information?"

"If you have a script you want me to follow, please let me know."

He was in fine Derrick form today. He shot back the one-liners faster than she could come up with them on her end.

Noah sat hard in the chair again. The thud seemed to

wake him out of his stupor. "What are you talking about? You can't marry him."

Through the haze of frustration winding around her, she could see him. She and Derrick might have an odd arrangement they worked out, but that didn't mean her brother was prepared for the roller coaster they'd all jumped on.

"Noah, let me explain." Though she had no idea what she could say.

"At least wait until you see this video." Noah slipped a thumb drive out of his jeans' pocket and dumped it on the table.

"What's on it?" Derrick asked.

Noah didn't even spare him a glance. "I bet you'd like to know."

"I can take it and watch it right now or you can save us some time and talk." Derrick snatched the drive and held it in the air.

"You and your father and a certain woman at work."

"This is old news." Derrick shook his head. "This is about Abby, right? I'm not sure where you're getting your information but Abby dated my brother. Not me."

Noah blinked a few times. "That's not what Joe—"

Ellie wasn't about to let Noah stop there. "Who?"

Noah shook his head. "Nothing."

"Joe Cantor? Is he the one who's been feeding you false intel, hoping you'd fall for it?" Derrick asked.

"Joe?" Ellie thought her head might explode.

The ramifications of what Noah admitted flowed through her brain. Joe had planted that story in the *Insider* about her work. He was trying to undermine Derrick and his relationship with Spence. And this poor Abby person was stuck in the middle. Sure, Derrick had made Joe look stupid, but the timing didn't seem right. And what kind of man would take that bait and go to all this trouble?

"You've been working with my former boss?" It sounded

awful when she said it out loud. "The one who kicked me out of the office and sent me home without a paycheck?"

"It's not like that." Noah shook his head. "Only in the last few weeks when you guys started dating."

"Let's run through this." Derrick's firm voice broke through the room. "The *Insider* is not running anything about me cheating, because I'm not and they don't want to be sued."

"How did you—"

"And..." Derrick talked right over Noah's explanation or whatever else he was going to say. "If you put up that video, you'll hurt Abby. Not me. She deserves better than that. Honestly, she's been screwed over by my family enough without adding yours."

Noah shook his head. "Don't try—"

"Why did you move the money? Was Joe involved in that?"

Derrick's question came out of nowhere. Ellie had no idea what he was talking about.

But Noah didn't look even a little confused. "It's about time you figured it out, but Joe's not involved."

Ellie rushed to keep up. "What are you two talking about?"

"Noah moved money out of a bunch of work accounts and moved it into a fake client account he designed. Hid it all but didn't actually take it. I just figured that out." Derrick's gaze switched from her to Noah again. "So, did you run out of time to make a withdrawal?"

"I was never going to take it. I just wanted to prove I could do it."

It was such a Noah thing to say that Ellie's heart melted. He refused to see the results of his choices. He acted and let everyone else clean up his mess. Whatever his issues, he had to learn a new way. "Oh, Noah."

"You brought me on at the office then put me in that

room." Noah ignored her and turned on Derrick. "I tried to talk with you about problems in your system, but you said I had to talk with my direct boss."

Derrick's eyes narrowed. "You were trying to get my attention."

"Don't flatter yourself." Noah returned to staring at the table.

That was it. Ellie knew Derrick was right. Something in Noah's reaction or Derrick's tone. In the middle of their fight and Noah's threats, Derrick had gotten to the bottom of the stealing question. He wasn't blaming. He was laying out facts. Because he was a good man. A man worth loving. The man she'd fallen for.

This time the realization didn't make her want to throw up. She wanted to tear up that ridiculous agreement so she'd never have to think about it again.

Derrick shifted in his chair, clearly trying to get Noah to look at him again. "I didn't mean to ignore you in the office."

Noah snorted. "Stop acting like I cared."

But he did. No matter what Noah was saying, he did. It all made sense now. So many people ignored Noah and passed him over. They didn't take the time to see what he could do. Derrick had taken an interest in him. Hired him without a load of experience or an advanced degree.

Derrick had taken a chance and Noah had taken that to mean something more than the usual employer/employee relationship. Derrick never could have seen this coming.

"I asked the prosecutor not to move ahead with the charges," Derrick said in a low voice.

The sound shot through her. The words…he'd kept his promise. Of course he did.

Derrick looked at her then. "For you and for him."

"You're not doing me any favors." But all of the anger

had left Noah's voice. His outburst died as soon as the words were out. "Ellie, listen to me. You can't marry him."

"It's happening," Derrick said.

Noah stood. "I'll be back when he's not here."

That comment struck her as silly. "It's his house."

"Leave the video," Derrick said.

"Because you say so?"

Derrick shook his head. "Because I'm asking you not to release it."

"Fine." Noah slammed the drive onto the table and walked out.

Derrick watched Noah go. Apparently storming out in a huff was a Gold family tradition. Ellie did it better, but Noah was pretty good at it. Even slammed the front door.

Ellie stood. Derrick half expected her to go upstairs and not talk again this evening like a repeat of last night. He fought to find the right words to say but nothing came to him.

She stopped next to his chair. Her hand slipped into his. When she gave his arm a gentle tug, he figured she wanted him to stand.

The change in her mood confused him. "Are you okay?"

Instead of answering him, she kissed him. Her arms slipped around his neck and she pulled his head to her. Then her mouth met his and speaking wasn't on his mind.

Her tongue licked out to caress his bottom lip. She had his brain misfiring and his pants growing tighter. It took all the strength he possessed to lift his head and stare at her, to drag his mouth away from hers. "You don't need to thank me this way."

He waited for her shoulders to stiffen, for her anger to rise.

She pressed a finger to his lips. Traced the outline before letting her finger trail down his throat to his chest.

"You told me once that I should only kiss you if I wanted to kiss you."

The sound of her deep voice was enough to touch off something inside him. He got hard and his resistance to her, what little he still had, melted. "That's still the rule."

"I want to kiss you."

It took a second for her words to register in his brain. She wanted him. Through the missteps and the battles, after sleeping alone, she still wanted him.

Still, they'd been through some hard days. "Be sure."

She pressed her hand against his chest, backing him up until his butt hit the wall. "I am. I choose you, Derrick. Not because of an arrangement or money or my brother. I want you because of you."

That's all it took. The last of his defenses fell. Every argument for why he should hold back and not let this mean anything vanished.

His body vetoed his brain. They could talk later. They needed this now.

His mouth met hers in a kiss meant to possess. He wanted her to know this was real. There was nothing fake about how much he wanted to touch her, to be inside her. His hands traveled over her as she unbuttoned his shirt. She reached the bottom few and tugged. Buttons ripped off and pinged against the floor.

It was a wild frenzy to disrobe. He wanted her naked but settled for shoving her skirt up to her waist and tugging her bikini underwear down. Their legs tangled and he leaned against the wall for balance. When that didn't get him what he wanted, he spun them around.

With her spine pressed against the wall, he lifted her legs to his hips and settled his body between them. Her ankles balanced against his ass as he held her with one hand and rushed to unzip with the other.

Chaos filled his mind. A wild energy pounded through

him. All he could think about was being inside her, of feeling her body wrap around his. At the last second, he slowed. His finger went to the very center of her. When he found her wet and ready, he slipped into fast forward again.

"I'm going to help your brother, Ellie," Derrick said between stinging kisses.

She put her palms against his cheeks and forced him to look at her. "Yes, but later."

"Much later."

Then he was inside her. He plunged in and stopped. Ignored the sexy little growling sounds she made and just enjoyed the tight grip of her body around his.

She pinched his shoulder. "Derrick, move."

This one time he was happy to obey.

Fifteen

The DC Insider: *The party is on! We admit we were worried Derrick Jameson blew it, but friends and family are gathering. There's word of a sparkly dress and champagne being brought in by the truckload. Let the marriage plans begin.*

Two more weeks of tentative peace passed. Ellie returned to Derrick's bedroom. He hadn't proposed in a better way, but he did spend some time each night touching her ring. His finger smoothed over it with a near reverence. He'd spin it around on her finger as he watched in awe.

She still didn't understand him. His mood stayed relatively steady but he worked too much and continued to say the odd stray comment that made her wonder how often he dealt with actual human beings other than her.

A month had passed since they'd first slept together. After a detour to help a friend, Carter was on the way, which meant she would know both brothers soon. Even Derrick's father was flying in with his relatively new wife.

The idea of that made Ellie's stomach flip over. That was a lot of Jamesons in one house. She hoped they didn't kill each other. Even she thought about punching Derrick's father. The man had made a big mess of his family then snuck away to let Derrick clean it all up. What kind of man was that?

Friends and relatives officially would start pouring into town in two days. The party, the sheer scope of it, made no sense to Ellie. A hundred people. She didn't know five people she'd want in her house. This family had business associates and relatives everywhere.

This was the kind of shindig you threw when you really planned to walk down the aisle. Family met family. Friends traded stories. The happy couple showed off photos of their time together so far. None of that fit their situation, yet Derrick insisted.

He still hadn't filled Spence in about the truth of their relationship. Ellie hadn't because she no longer saw any part of what they shared as fake.

Jackson and Derrick had been trapped in the library all morning. There was talk of moving the party to the Jameson's Virginia property and holding it outside under the most expensive tent she had ever seen in her life. The thing had actual doors and windows.

She'd never seen the farm in person, but from the photos she thought it looked like a school. The idea that Derrick grew up there without his mom and with a distant father made her ache for him. The loneliness had to have been unbearable. Her parents had made a lot of mistakes, but they'd been around. Broke and confusing, but present.

She grabbed a mug of tea and headed for the library to see what ridiculous plans the men had dreamed up while she'd dressed this morning. She'd been dragging all week. She'd only ever needed about six hours of sleep each night. She'd swear she could use twice that much right now.

The stress was working on her. There was no other explanation. It also messed with her stomach. Coffee made it grumble these days.

If she were honest, she'd have to admit she didn't feel

great. A terrible cold might be headed her way. When she'd mentioned that to Derrick last night he'd made her promise it would come after the party. As if she could control life like that.

She sipped on the herbal mixture of lemon and peppermint. The warm liquid poured through her on the chilly spring day. She'd thrown on one of Derrick's sweaters and it swamped her. She didn't care. The soft material made her think of a blanket.

The closer she got to the room, she expected the voices to grow louder. They didn't. The door was open an inch or two. She pushed it open a smidgen. Took the opportunity to watch them.

Even at home, Derrick stayed in command. He wore black pants and a simple white shirt. On him, the combination proved stunning. She was about to tell him that, maybe embarrass him a little in front of Jackson, which was always fun, when she heard the ominous sentence.

You have to stop lying to Ellie.

She pushed the door open the whole way. Immediately she was greeted by the stares of the two men and Jackson's mouth dropped open. Derrick didn't show any reaction at all but his watchful eyes followed her.

"Lying about what?" That was the only question that ran through her head so she asked it.

Lies. The word stuck in her throat. She turned it over and tried to make it fit with everything she knew about Derrick and the upcoming party. Nothing matched the urgency she'd heard in Jackson's tone.

She couldn't ignore the comment. She'd grown up with lies. She'd lived with so many over the years and knew how they could burn away all the other good things in life. They stole security. She'd lost her job over one.

But Derrick had promised not to lie to her. He'd said it

more than once. It was one of the underlying principles of their agreement.

Time ticked by and neither man answered her.

She stepped closer. For a second the room began to spin. The walls of books blurred and she would have stumbled but she fought for balance.

"Someone answer me," she said in a louder voice. She would yell if she had to.

Jackson looked at Derrick. "I should go."

"Don't move." She wasn't letting either of them off the hook because this was clearly big. "Someone start talking."

"There was another reason for our agreement." Derrick's deep voice broke through the otherwise quiet room.

"The fake engagement." The words scraped against her throat.

"What started out as that, yes."

She ignored the comment. Pretended his words didn't echo what she'd wanted for the past few weeks—a real chance with him.

Her head started to pound. The drumming sensation started at the base of her neck. After a few more steps, it moved up to her nape. Her footsteps faltered. At first she thought her shoe had snagged the carpet, but no. Her balance was off. The room tilted on her.

"Explain." She somehow got the word out.

"My father said he would sell the business out from under me unless I met certain stipulations."

Eldrick Jameson. She should have known he was at the bottom of this. That bit of information fit everything Derrick had ever told her about his father. The man was pure trouble. He caused trouble, incited it.

But none of that explained Jackson's comment.

"What does that have to do with me?" She could no longer stand there. She set the mug down, ignoring her shaking hand.

“Are you okay?” Jackson asked, the concern obvious in his voice.

“Finish it, Derrick.” Because she knew there was more. This all related to her. All that talk at the beginning of their relationship about how they were helping each other. Yes, she’d let herself get sucked in because he’d wanted to. But the reasoning rang hollow now.

“Each brother has an obligation they have to meet or we lose everything. My obligation was multipart. I had to lure my brothers back to the business and I had to clean up my image.”

That didn’t sound so bad. It was close to what she knew with a few holes filled in. “Okay.”

“I told you I needed your brother to stop. I didn’t tell you my continued ownership of the business depended on it. Depended on you.”

“The deal was pretty lopsided,” Jackson said.

“I needed you more than you needed me. Without you, I lost everything.” Derrick hesitated for a few seconds. “For me this wasn’t about helping Noah. It was about keeping control of the business.”

“That’s pretty ruthless.” The room started to blur along the edge. She looked at him through this strange haze.

She had no idea what was happening. It was as if her body was shutting down, abandoning her. But she refused to give in. She wanted all of this information out between them. No more secrets.

“I never pretended to be anything but ruthless,” Derrick said.

That wasn’t true. She’d thought so at first, but that was part of his perfectly crafted image. The real man was much more complex. Decent.

“Why not tell me the truth?” That part didn’t make sense to her.

Derrick never left his place by the fireplace. He held on

to the mantel as if it were the one thing holding him up. "I didn't know you and didn't want you to have the upper hand against me."

"Weeks ago. But now?" She shook her head and almost dropped to her knees.

Jackson got up from his chair and Derrick took a step forward. She waved them both back. "Why, Derrick?"

"I didn't want what we had to stop."

The sex. He liked the sex and was willing to tell her half-truths and use her to keep getting it. "Maybe you are ruthless."

She saw Derrick rush forward and heard Jackson yell. Everything moved in slow motion as the air whooshed around her. Before she could call out, the pain closed over her and the room went dark.

Pregnant. Not just pregnant but a high-risk pregnancy.

Derrick sat beside Ellie's hospital bed and turned the doctor's words over in his head. He'd been pummeled with information since they'd arrived in the emergency room. Now she was settled in a private room and the facts still didn't make sense.

Spence and Jackson had stood next to him, taking it all in. Derrick had barely heard a thing. All he could think about was the ambulance ride. The first responders yelling, talking to the hospital. The noise as they'd driven at high speed. The beep of the machine next to him.

It had been a flurry of activity. Everyone rushed and ran. The stretcher. The blood from where her head had hit the floor before he could catch her. He'd thrown up twice while he'd waited for the doctor to come out and deliver some news.

And the news…pregnancy.

Now he had to tell her because this was not the ideal situation. Forget the state of their engagement. He would fix that as soon as she let him. He knew what he wanted now. Watching her fall, thinking he'd lost her, shifted his whole world into focus.

He'd told her he'd kept part of the truth about the agreement from her because he hadn't wanted their time together to end. What he hadn't said was that he loved her. He was couldn't-think-straight in love with her.

That losing her made him double over.

That he would forfeit the business if it meant she would stay with him.

His thumb slipped over the engagement ring on her finger and he thought back to the silly way he'd given it to her. So dismissive, ignoring her feelings. Jackson had unloaded, letting him know every way he'd messed up.

Derrick knew it was Jackson's way of handling his fear. Derrick's was to bury his brain in work and he couldn't do that now.

"Derrick?"

At the sound of her rough voice, he looked at her. Her eyes were open and filled with fear.

"Hey." He brushed her hair off her cheek. "You're okay."

"What happened?"

The worst. His nightmare. "You fainted."

But he'd thought it was something else. He'd never dreamed the answer would be pregnancy. He could handle that, or he would learn how to. But watching her drop…he never wanted to see that again.

"I did?" She tried to sit up.

He gently pushed her down. She'd be in the hospital for a few days. They had decisions to make. There were tests to run and precautions to take.

"My head is killing me." She lifted a hand and the tubes attached to her arm went with her.

"You're on an IV." He glanced at the bag hanging on the hook by his head. "You have some meds."

"What's wrong?"

He took a deep breath. "Well, here's some news. You can get pregnant with an IUD."

Her eyes widened. "What?"

"It's rare but it happens." He slipped his fingers through hers. "You're about five weeks along."

What little color was in her face drained away. Then her hand went to her stomach in a protective gesture that tugged at his heart.

"The first time we slept together," she said.

"Yeah." He didn't want her to be in danger but it was hard to want to call that night back. It had started them down this road.

She swallowed a few times before talking again. "Tell me all of it."

She deserved to know, so he didn't hide behind calls for her to wait or for rest.

"It means this is a risky pregnancy. Taking the IUD out now can be a problem. Leaving it in can, too." He swallowed before saying the part that made his voice break. "There's an increased chance of miscarrying and a lot of precautions we'll need to take if you decide you want to go through with the pregnancy."

Tears filled her eyes. "I understand."

So brave. No surprise there.

He leaned over and placed a sweet kiss on her forehead. "I will support whatever you want to do."

"You don't have to… I told you about the birth control, but…" This time the tears rolled down her cheeks.

"We created this baby together. Both of us."

She nodded but didn't say anything.

The quiet tears tore at him. "I will be with you no matter what."

She closed her eyes and nodded. The tears still fell harder. "I need to sleep."

"Okay." He had no idea if that was normal for her condition or if she was shutting off. He didn't want to ask. "I'll be right here."

"You do love her."

Derrick looked up an hour later to find Noah and Spence standing in the hospital room doorway.

"He wanted to see his sister," Spence said.

"Of course."

Derrick was more grateful for Jackson and Spence than ever. They stayed calm while he nearly lost it. He'd cradled Ellie, making sure she was breathing. They'd made the calls.

Noah came into the room then. He walked over to Ellie's bedside and stared at her. "She's really pregnant?"

Derrick couldn't believe it, either. "Yes, but it's risky."

Noah nodded without looking up. "Spence told me."

Spence. Interesting. Derrick hoped that meant they'd bonded. Noah needed guidance.

"Thanks."

The word came out soft. Derrick almost missed it.

"I'm not going to let anything happen to her, Noah." Derrick thought about what Noah had said about a mentee. "If you let me, I'll make it up to both of you."

"I shouldn't have moved the money."

"No."

"We can worry about that later," Spence said.

Noah nodded again as he stepped away from the bed. "I want to get her some flowers."

"I know the place for that." Spence gestured for Noah to follow then winked at Derrick.

He watched them go and thought about all that had happened. All the miscommunication and missed cues. He'd hidden behind his desk for so long, so focused on the business and not the people he cared about. But no more. He would do better. For her, he would try.

Sixteen

The DC Insider: *An ambulance. A family fight. These Jamesons know how to keep things interesting. But the fairy tale is back on! Congratulations to Derrick Jameson and Ellie Gold on their upcoming wedding... and the little surprise they've been keeping. We're hoping for a girl.*

Ellie was finally able to leave the hospital three days later. Not that anyone let her even take a step on her own. She'd tried to get off the couch for a drink of water this morning and men had come from every direction.

Derrick had turned away the engagement party guests. He'd explained that Ellie was sick. She didn't know much else because every time she opened her mouth Derrick tried to feed her or give her a pill.

The guy loved playing nurse. She let it happen because she worried about what would happen when he stopped. The game should be over. Everyone knew everything now. Noah had been by every day. He seemed connected to Spence's side and had made a tentative peace with Derrick.

She must have *really* been sick.

She heard male voices and Derrick's telling people to get out. His tone, frustrated and gruffer than usual, made her tense. She'd been waiting for bad news since she got home. Not that she needed to invite more.

Derrick hadn't been overstating what they faced with this pregnancy. It carried all sorts of risks. Not as bad as it could have been because she hadn't been that far along when they'd discovered it, but the risks were still pretty high. So she'd opted for keeping the IUD. Now she spent every day doubting the choice and worrying she'd lose the baby. Derrick's baby.

After everything that happened, she still wanted to build something with him. But could she trust him? He'd kept most of his promises to her, but he still lied. At the very least, he held information back because it benefitted him. She couldn't figure out a way to process that.

"Hey." That's all Derrick said as he walked into the room.

Just as he had since she'd come home, he seemed subdued and a bit on edge. Her insides churned and she half wondered if that rubbed off on him.

She tapped the couch cushion next to her. "Can you come sit with me for a second?"

He hesitated then nodded. "Everything okay?"

He'd asked her that so many times that she now dreaded the question. "Is it, Derrick?"

"What does that mean?"

The question had been right there, on her tongue. She'd bit it back for days. Didn't want to invite trouble. But she had to know. "Do you want me to leave?"

He made an odd face. "What?"

"This relationship was fake and now that—"

He swore under his breath. The sound of the harsh words made her jump. She wasn't afraid but he did let them fly. She started to get up, but he held her hands and pulled her closer to his side.

"Never."

The word didn't make any sense. "What?"

His chest visibly rose as he inhaled a deep breath. "Ellie, how can you not get this? I love you."

She didn't realize she was shaking her head until he touched her hair. "What?"

"I fell in love with you. Nothing about this or how I feel about you is fake."

Her mind refused to believe and that made his words that much sharper. "You don't mean that."

This was about guilt and the baby. He'd been moping around, not going to work. The pressure…she got it. It crushed her, too.

"We can figure something…" She didn't even know what to say. She'd practiced and now the words wouldn't come.

He slid off the couch and went to one knee. "Ellie Gold."

She froze. "What's happening?"

"Go ahead." Spence called out the encouragement from the top of the stairs. Jackson stood with him and Vanessa. Noah was there. And was Spence holding up a phone?

Jackson pointed at the cell's screen. "Carter didn't want to miss this. He's still ticked off that Derrick didn't tell the whole truth, either."

"You mention that now?" Derrick swore again. "You're all pains in the—"

"Keep going," Vanessa called out.

"Fine." But Derrick didn't sound fine. His voice was sharp and he was fidgeting. Something he rarely did. Then he looked at her and the scowl disappeared. A softness moved into his eyes. "Hi."

"Hi." She had no idea what else to say.

"I think I loved you from the first time I met you." He laughed then. "You were so unimpressed with me and who I was. So beautiful and not interested in anything I had to say. It was a potent combination."

The room started spinning again. This didn't have anything to do with her pregnancy or fainting. It was the punch of happiness—hope—that seared through her. It left her breathless.

"I should have told you everything from the start, but I didn't want you to find a new place to live." Derrick laughed as he bent to kiss her hand. "Hell, it took forever to get you to agree to share a bed with me."

He reached out a hand and fit it over her stomach. "Not that long, I guess."

"Derrick..." She didn't know what she wanted to say except his name.

"What I should have said when I gave you this ring." He held it up.

They'd taken it off her in the hospital and she hadn't dared ask for it. She felt naked and half-sick without it. Relief nearly swamped her at seeing it again.

He turned it over in his fingers. "I picked this because it reminded me of you. Bold, sparkly, beautiful. Different in every perfect way."

Her defenses, already shaky, collapsed. Seeing him kneeling there, usually so strong but now so vulnerable, won her over. He'd messed up but they could fix this. They could learn to communicate better, to share. Together, they'd unlearn some of the damaging interpersonal skills passed down from their parents. They would do better.

She reached out and cupped his cheek. "Yes."

He shook his head but this time he was smiling. "No, I'm asking this time."

She bit back a laugh because he seemed so determined.

"Ellie Gold, I love you more than anything. I loved you before I knew about the pregnancy and I'll love you forever, if you let me."

"Yes." The word rushed out of her. She was laughing and crying and nodding. One big weepy mess.

"Marry me."

This time she fell against his chest and felt his strong arms wrap around her. He whispered something into her hair. She could hear her name and the cheers from their family and friends who were sharing the moment. She loved all of it, all of them; mostly she loved Derrick.

She pulled back and stared up at him. Derrick, the strong and determined man who liked to boss her around and argue for no good reason. With him she felt the intoxicating mix of comfort and heat. She loved him and wanted him. She knew he would help protect their baby and they'd save each other if they lost it.

"I love you." Her voice was soft but mighty.

"About time you said that." He rested his forehead against hers. "I'm going to need to hear it a lot."

"You know, if this is a real engagement—"

"It is." He practically barked the response at her.

"You should know that I plan to be a bossy fiancée and an even bossier wife." And that was an understatement.

Once she checked with the doctor about what she could do and couldn't, she'd try to return to the work she loved. She'd also control his schedule a bit better than he did. No more all-nighters in the office or dinners at ten. She was going to get his life in line.

"Wait, what?" But he didn't sound even a little worried about the idea.

"We'll start with your work hours." She glanced over his head at Jackson. "They are decreasing."

He nodded. "Yes, ma'am."

Derrick cleared his throat. "We'll talk."

"I'll win." She looked around and realized she already had.

"I can hardly wait to negotiate our new agreement."

She heard groans that matched the one she was holding back. "You're not going to believe what provisions I add."

He kissed her then. Long and lingering. When he lifted

his head, all the stress he'd carried on his face for the past few days was gone. "You can have everything you want."

Her heart swelled. "You're going to be a great husband."

Carter would arrive tomorrow, after what had turned out to be a ten-day trip across the country. Only his baby brother would draw out something like that.

"What are you laughing about?" Spence asked.

Derrick looked up to see Spence staring at him. He stood at the kitchen sink, nursing his morning coffee. Ellie wasn't up yet, which Derrick assumed would become a new thing now that she was pregnant.

They had a wedding and a baby ahead of them. His father was coming for the rescheduled engagement party in a few weeks. All of the things Derrick never thought he'd have, a family of his own and the stability of friends and family around him, were happening.

"Life is pretty good," he said in response to his brother's question.

"For you." Spence shook his head. "You've met Dad's conditions. Noah is quiet, your PR image is pristine, and Carter and I are both here, at least for the short-term. For as long as you need us, actually."

"Thanks."

"Yeah, well. Apparently, I'm up next. Dad has some stipulations Carter and I need before we can settle the business and get him out for good."

"You don't have to—"

Spence made a strange noise. "I do."

Derrick didn't want to subject his brothers to their father's stipulations, to have them run around trying to meet his conditions. He was willing to stop the nonsense. The business used to mean everything but his priorities had shifted. He knew he'd survive without the office now.

"This isn't up for debate, Derrick." Spence stared at him. "Got it? No more secrets or arguing."

That loyalty meant more to Derrick than he ever thought possible. "Yes."

"And the business is yours." Spence smiled over his mug. "Just do a good job once Dad steps fully out so I can keep collecting the checks for my minority interest."

Derrick lifted his mug in a fake toast. "Happy to."

"And we'll be here for you and for Ellie." He made a groaning sound. "Even for Noah."

Noah was one more thing Derrick needed to deal with. But not today. For the next week, Ellie was his only priority. He was stepping aside and letting Jackson do what Jackson did best—run things.

He had a party to plan and a wedding to set. There were about a billion doctor's appointments they needed to go to. A bunch of specialists. He vowed that Ellie would not go through any of it alone.

"I appreciate that." Derrick let his mind wander to the one place he didn't want to go. "With this pregnancy—"

"She needs you. We'll take up the slack and do Dad's bidding."

Derrick had no idea how to thank Spence for that. He tried anyway. "I truly appreciate that."

Spence put down the mug and moved to the other side of the kitchen island, across from Derrick. "Stop doing that."

"What?"

"Being grateful." He snorted. "It's annoying."

"Only you would think so."

"We're going to get through this. She's going to be fine—so is the baby."

Derrick needed to hear the words. They might be empty, but he could tell Spence believed them. That was enough for now. "I believe I remember something about a bet?"

"Hell, no. You weren't in on it."

Derrick held out his hand. "Two hundred or I tell Ellie."

"Unbelievable." Spence slipped his wallet out of his pocket. "You only get this if I have a chance to win it back."

That sounded ominous but Derrick took the cash anyway. "How?"

"Give me the baby's due date so I have the inside scoop and can take a bunch of Carter's money."

"Sold." The sound of their laughter filled the kitchen.

For the first time ever, Derrick finally felt like he was home.

* * * * *

Look for Spence's story,
coming in summer 2018!